Right Click

Lisa Becker

6/14

Robyn,
I'm so glad that
Meadows brought
us together. You
inspire me with
your kind heart
and wonderful
sense of humor.
♡, Lisa

Thank you SJB, TMZ and AKS
for being my balcony people. XOXO!

CHAPTER 1: THE NEW NORMAL

From: Renee Greene – June 26, 2013 – 8:22 AM
To: Shelley Manning
Subject: Calling it quits?

I saw the weather report in Seattle. It's raining today…again…in
June! That makes three days straight, no? I'm sure you've already
hit all of the tourist spots by now. You ready to move back to LA?
Sunny and 75 today…as usual. Ashley and I (and Siobhan) will treat
you at Mel's.

From: Shelley Manning – June 26, 2013 – 8:33 AM
To: Renee Greene
Subject: Re: Calling it quits?

Stop gloating. It's an unattractive trait. And yes, I've hit all of the
hot spots already. I've visited the towering Space Needle many
times…but I've never left the house. Zing!

From: Renee Greene – June 26, 2013 – 8:42 AM
To: Shelley Manning
Subject: Re: Calling it quits?

Ha! Ha! You are a dirty, dirty girl. How is everything? I feel like I
haven't talked to you in ages. Not the superficial stuff, but really
talked. Work going okay or is it hard being a telecommuter?

From: Shelley Manning – June 26, 2013 – 8:55 AM
To: Renee Greene
Subject: Re: Calling it quits?

Actually, I LOVE working remotely. I'm so much more productive.
Who knew that I was wasting so much time hanging out at the water
cooler, so to speak? And Nick's friends have been great about
helping me get acclimated to my new surroundings.

In fact, I'm having dinner tonight with Nick's best friend's wife, Amber. She and her husband just moved back to Seattle from New York. She's an interior designer and has the most fantastic taste. Hoping she can help me feminize (is that even a word?) Nick's place, (well, now our place) a bit. While it's very modern and stylish, it's a bit manly for me.

From: Renee Greene – June 26, 2013 – 9:02 AM
To: Shelley Manning
Subject: Re: Calling it quits?

Really? You were getting distracted from work at the office? Shocking! Glad you've made a new friend there. Just don't go replacing me with a new bestie.

From: Shelley Manning – June 26, 2013 – 9:15 AM
To: Renee Greene
Subject: Re: Calling it quits?

No one could replace you, Sweetie. And yes, I was getting distracted from work at work. Now if I could only get you to stop emailing me every minute of the day with your incredulous-but-true life stories, man troubles and horrible pun-offs, then I would really be onto something. In fact, I might get a commendation from work. Can you say the same?

From: Renee Greene – June 26, 2013 – 9:17 AM
To: Shelley Manning
Subject: Re: Calling it quits?

What? You love my emails and you know it. And stop gloating. I've heard it's an unattractive trait.

From: Shelley Manning – June 26, 2013 – 9:18 AM
To: Renee Greene
Subject: Re: Calling it quits?

Indeed it is. Gotta go. Mwah! Mwah!

From: Renee Greene – June 26, 2013 – 9:20 AM
To: PBCupLover, Ashley Gordon, Mark Finlay, cassidy
Subject: Shelley update

Hi, all. I finally heard from Shelley today after a week. She's so hit
or miss lately! To answer all of your questions, she's doing well,
enjoying telecommuting and making friends. In fact, she has plans
with Nick's best friend's wife named Amber who just moved to town.

From: Ashley Gordon – June 26, 2013 – 11:30 AM
To: Renee Greene
Subject: Re: Shelley update

Glad to know she hasn't fallen off the face of the Earth and is
acclimating. And a new friend, huh? You okay with that? I
wouldn't worry too much. Amber is always on one of those lists of
names you never give your daughter because it sounds like a stripper,
right?

From: Renee Greene – June 26, 2013 – 11:33 AM
To: Ashley Gordon
Subject: Re: Shelley update

OMG! That was such a Shelley remark. I miss her so much, I think
I'm going to cry. And I must confess that I do fear we're going to
grow apart. For years we've been super close but I wonder if
geography was keeping us together.

From: cassidy – June 26, 2013 – 2:35 PM
To: Renee Greene
Subject: Re: Shelley update

oh i love the name amber. it brings love, healing, protection, power
and luck, all things that shelley could use in her new home. its a
good thing.

From: Ashley Gordon – June 26, 2013 – 3:32 PM
To: Renee Greene
Subject: Re: Shelley update

You have nothing to worry about. You two are kindred spirits. Come to think of it, maybe the spirits (i.e. booze) was what was keeping you together. Just kidding!

From: Renee Greene – June 26, 2013 – 3:40 PM
To: Ashley Gordon
Subject: Re: Shelley update

LOL! Boy, you're really coming up with the zingers today. Thanks for stepping it up on my behalf.

From: Ashley Gordon – June 26, 2013 – 3:48 PM
To: Renee Greene
Subject: Re: Shelley update

Sure thing! Got to run. I have a Mommy & Me class with Siobhan followed by dinner at the mall food court. Living the dream, as they say sarcastically.

From: Renee Greene – June 26, 2013 – 4:16 PM
To: PBCupLover
Subject: Fwd: Re: Shelley update

Ugh! I see this email from Cass and all I want to do is forward it to Shelley so I can hear some snarky remark about her. But I can't do that because then Shelley will know I was talking about "my replacement."

I can't send it to Ashley because (1) she's so busy with Siobhan these days and all of her new mommy friends and (2) she'll probably turn it all around and make it some comment about how she dislikes my hair.

So I have to send this to you. And you'll be all pragmatic about things and tell me (1) Shelley is not replacing me as her BFF and that it is important for her to develop friendships in Seattle otherwise she will be lonely and I will ultimately feel guilty for her misery and (2) Ashley needs to make friends that have kids so she can have a support network of people going through the same challenging transitions from corporate America and independence to full time parenthood and (3) Cassidy is a punctuationally-challenged loon but I just need to accept it.

Ugh! I do not like this one bit. But I suppose I just need to accept things for what they are.

From: PBCupLover – June 26, 2013 – 4:22 PM
To: Renee Greene
Subject: Re: Fwd: Re: Shelley update

Why don't you just save these things as some sort of therapeutic draft because you seem to have worked it out all by yourself.?

From: Renee Greene – June 26, 2013 – 4:24 PM
To: PBCupLover
Subject: Re: Fwd: Re: Shelley update

It wouldn't be as much fun if I couldn't share it all with you. That's what being a couple is all about, right?

From: PBCupLover – June 26, 2013 – 4:25 PM
To: Renee Greene
Subject: Re: Fwd: Re: Shelley update

Glad you are having fun, Babe.

From: Renee Greene – June 26, 2013 – 4:25 PM
To: PBCupLover
Subject: Re: Fwd: Re: Shelley update

Now you miss Shelley too, right?

From: PBCupLover – June 26, 2013 – 4:26 PM
To: Renee Greene
Subject: Re: Fwd: Re: Shelley update

It certainly was nice having her around to help deal with your daily crises.

From: Renee Greene – June 26, 2013 – 4:26 PM
To: PBCupLover
Subject: Re: Fwd: Re: Shelley update

:) See you at home soon. XO

From: Renee Greene – June 29, 2013 – 2:32 PM
To: Ashley Gordon
Subject: Am I hated?

Does your friend Ilana absolutely hate me?

From: Ashley Gordon – June 29, 2013 – 6:08 PM
To: Renee Greene
Subject: Re: Am I hated?

She doesn't hate you. She just feels really strongly about not squashing her son's creativity.

From: Renee Greene – June 29, 2013 – 6:10 PM
To: Ashley Gordon
Subject: Re: Am I hated?

Well, I think it's ridiculous not to teach your kid to color in the lines.

From: Ashley Gordon – June 29, 2013 – 6:12 PM
To: Renee Greene
Subject: Re: Am I hated?

She's just trying to have him grow up feeling free to express himself and not constrained by society.

From: Renee Greene – June 29, 2013 – 6:16 PM
To: Ashley Gordon
Subject: Re: Am I hated?

I'm all for freedom of expression, but that's just laziness. A kid who doesn't know *how* to color in the lines is just scribbling. A kid who knows *how* to color in the lines but *chooses* not to, well, he is making an artistic and creative statement.

From: Ashley Gordon – June 29, 2013 – 6:18 PM
To: Renee Greene
Subject: Re: Am I hated?

You could be right.

From: Renee Greene – June 29, 2013 – 6:18 PM
To: Ashley Gordon
Subject: Re: Am I hated?

Could be?

From: Ashley Gordon – June 29, 2013 – 6:19 PM
To: Renee Greene
Subject: Re: Am I hated?

Well, I'm not going to judge her. She's really smart and her son is already reading and he's only 4.

From: Renee Greene – June 29, 2013 – 6:21 PM
To: Ashley Gordon
Subject: Re: Am I hated?

Is she teaching him the alphabet, letter sounds and phonics or just letting him make things up on his own?

From: Ashley Gordon – June 29, 2013 – 6:24 PM
To: Renee Greene
Subject: Re: Am I hated?

Be serious! You're not a parent so you just don't know what style you want to have yet.

From: Renee Greene – June 29, 2013 – 6:26 PM
To: Ashley Gordon
Subject: Re: Am I hated?

My style is going to be normal parenting, not this new-age BS. That's for sure! Just don't judge me for doing this differently. And by differently, I mean normally.

From: Ashley Gordon – June 29, 2013 – 6:30 PM
To: Renee Greene
Subject: Re: Am I hated?

Ha! Ha! What, me judge anyone? I've got to put Siobhan down for the night. I'll call you later in the week.

CHAPTER 2: FIREWORKS

From: Renee Greene – July 3, 2013 – 10:02 AM
To: Shelley Manning
Subject: Par-Tay?

What are you guys doing for the Fourth? Neil from the office is having a block party and invited us. It's going to be a bunch of families, but with kids come juice boxes and cupcakes, so I'm in. Can't believe that it's a year until my wedding. Hurrah!

From: Shelley Manning – July 3, 2013 – 10:03 AM
To: Renee Greene
Subject: Re: Par-Tay?

Making some fireworks of my own.

From: Renee Greene – July 3, 2013 – 10:04 AM
To: Shelley Manning
Subject: Re: Par-Tay?

<eye roll!> I walked right into that one, didn't I?

From: Shelley Manning – July 3, 2013 – 10:06 AM
To: Renee Greene
Subject: Re: Par-Tay?

Ha! We're going to dinner and then will watch fireworks from Nick's friend's loft balcony, which overlooks Puget Sound. Have fun, Sweetie. Gotta run. Mwah! Mwah!

From: Renee Greene – July 3, 2013 – 10:07 AM
To: Shelley Manning
Subject: Re: Par-Tay?

Sounds beautiful. Enjoy!

From: cassidy – July 4, 2013 – 9:08 AM
To: <undisclosed recipients>
Subject: Fwd: Meow 4th Mix

precocious, don't you think?

From: Shelley Manning – July 4, 2013 – 9:10 AM
To: Renee Greene
Subject: Fwd: Fwd: Meow 4th Mix

Precocious? I'm going to blow a fuse!

From: Renee Greene – July 4, 2013 – 9:11 AM
To: Shelley Manning
Subject: Re: Fwd: Fwd: Meow 4th Mix

I'm fairly certain she meant precious.

From: Shelley Manning – July 4, 2013 – 9:12 AM
To: Renee Greene
Subject: Re: Fwd: Fwd: Meow 4th Mix

Oh. In that case, I'm still going to blow a fuse! Have fun today.

From: Renee Greene – July 5, 2013 – 11:01 AM
To: Shelley Manning
Subject: Fireworks?

Just doing a quick check-in. So, how was last night? I'm assuming fireworks after the fireworks?

From: Shelley Manning – July 5, 2013 – 12:31 PM
To: Renee Greene
Subject: Re: Fireworks?

Damn straight. How was the Fourth in suburbia?

From: Renee Greene – July 5, 2013 – 12:32 PM
To: Shelley Manning
Subject: Re: Fireworks?

We won't be invited back next year, that's for sure. Granted we'll be getting married that day next year. But you know what I mean.

From: Shelley Manning – July 5, 2013 – 12:33 PM
To: Renee Greene
Subject: Re: Fireworks?

What happened?

From: Renee Greene – July 5, 2013 – 12:34 PM
To: Shelley Manning
Subject: Re: Fireworks?

Neil's wife now officially HATES Ethan.

From: Shelley Manning – July 5, 2013 – 12:36 PM
To: Renee Greene
Subject: Re: Fireworks?

How could anyone hate Ethan? Unless she is a Michigan alum or Wolverines football fan, he pretty much charms everyone.

From: Renee Greene – July 5, 2013 – 12:42 PM
To: Shelley Manning
Subject: Re: Fireworks?

He is pretty charming, isn't he? But I digress. All of these kids were running around and playing. Neil's wife brought out some water balloons that they were lobbing at each other. One hit the ground near Ethan and splashed him. Then it happened again.

Finally after the third splash, Ethan told the kids if they get him wet again, they'd better watch out. Needless to say, they made a direct hit and it all went downhill from there.

From: Shelley Manning – July 5, 2013 – 12:44 PM
To: Renee Greene
Subject: Re: Fireworks?

I can see that.

From: Renee Greene – July 5, 2013 – 12:51 PM
To: Shelley Manning
Subject: Re: Fireworks?

Oh, it was far worse than you could, or I could have, imagined. By the end of the day, every child there – including Ethan – was soaking wet from head to toe.

He grabbed two "super soaker" squirt guns and started attacking right away. At one point, a kid ran up to him and said, "Mister, I want to be on your team." Ethan responded, "Kid, I don't need anyone on my team," before squirting him with both guns.

From: Shelley Manning – July 5, 2013 – 12:53 PM
To: Renee Greene
Subject: Re: Fireworks?

Hilarious. That sounds like a scene out of a movie.

From: Renee Greene – July 5, 2013 – 12:57 PM
To: Shelley Manning
Subject: Re: Fireworks?

There was another "movie moment" where Ethan is running down the street with a super soaker in each arm. There's a five second delay and then you see every kid in the neighborhood chasing after him. I wish I had been recording it, because it was almost too outlandish to be believed. However, it's ALL true.

From: Shelley Manning – July 5, 2013 – 1:02 PM
To: Renee Greene
Subject: Re: Fireworks?

Why would anyone be mad about that? I would think the parents would be thrilled someone else was keeping their brats occupied.

From: Renee Greene – July 5, 2013 – 1:07 PM
To: Shelley Manning
Subject: Re: Fireworks?

I think that was initially the case. I managed to broker a truce and all was well. But then Neil's wife brought out the hose and helped the kids spray Ethan. Then she proclaimed they were all done.

Ethan took that as an act of war and said he wouldn't stop until *she* was soaked. At some point things turned ugly and hoses and big buckets of water came out.

I finally grabbed the hose from his hand and said "enough!" He was like a crazy man. I grabbed his face and forced him to look in my eyes repeating "Enough! Enough!" until he calmed down. Neil's wife was livid!

From: Shelley Manning – July 5, 2013 – 1:10 PM
To: Renee Greene
Subject: Re: Fireworks?

Why should she be angry? She got it all started again. Serves her right.

From: Renee Greene – July 5, 2013 – 1:12 PM
To: Shelley Manning
Subject: Re: Fireworks?

That's what Ethan said. But I tried explaining that she was our host and we needed to be gracious.

From: Shelley Manning – July 5, 2013 – 1:15 PM
To: Renee Greene
Subject: Re: Fireworks?

Screw gracious. If a bunch of bratty kids dumped water on me - and ruined my hair <gasp!> – I would be pissed, too.

From: Renee Greene – July 5, 2013 – 1:18 PM
To: Shelley Manning
Subject: Re: Fireworks?

I think Ethan's hair was okay but his ego was a bit bruised. So anyway, I assume we won't be invited back next year.

From: Shelley Manning – July 5, 2013 – 1:22 PM
To: Renee Greene
Subject: Re: Fireworks?

I would think not. Wish I had been there to see it. Well, Sweetie, your quick "checking in" email has turned into – as usual – quite the long conversation. Gotta run. Mwah! Mwah!

From: Ashley Gordon – July 12, 2013 – 10:02 AM
To: Renee Greene, Shelley Manning
Subject: Barf!

ARG! I'm so frustrated. Siobhan has been barfing all day. I've already bathed her twice and changed her clothes 4 times and it's only 10 am.

From: Shelley Manning – July 12, 2013 – 10:10 AM
To: Ashley Gordon, Renee Greene
Subject: Re: Barf!

It will get easier. Before you know it, she'll be barfing in the toilet like a big girl.

From: Renee Greene – July 12, 2013 – 10:25 AM
To: Shelley Manning, Ashley Gordon
Subject: Re: Barf!

Not necessarily. Funny story. When I was about 7 years old, my parents put new carpeting in our den and bought new beige fabric couches with light blue and pink pillows. (How 80's!)

I was home sick from school and resting on the couch watching "My Little Pony" videos when I felt like I was going to hurl. You guys KNOW how I cannot stand to do it, so I was panicked. I called up to my mom, "I'm going to throw up." She yelled "Run to the bathroom! Run to the bathroom!" I did run to the bathroom, and while I ran there, I threw up all over the new couches and carpet. Oops!

From: Shelley Manning – July 12, 2013 – 10:29 AM
To: Ashley Gordon, Renee Greene
Subject: Re: Barf!

Are those the same beige couches you had in our apartment in college?

From: Renee Greene – July 12, 2013 – 10:30 AM
To: Shelley Manning, Ashley Gordon
Subject: Re: Barf!

They are indeed the same.

From: Shelley Manning – July 12, 2013 – 10:31 AM
To: Ashley Gordon, Renee Greene
Subject: Re: Barf!

Then I've thrown up on those couches, too.

From: Renee Greene – July 12, 2013 – 10:31 AM
To: Shelley Manning, Ashley Gordon
Subject: Re: Barf!

LOL! So does that make you feel better, Ash?

From: Ashley Gordon – July 12, 2013 – 11:12 AM
To: Renee Greene, Shelley Manning
Subject: Re: Barf!

No. Just shows me all of the additional body fluid grossness I have to look forward to.

From: Renee Greene – July 12, 2013 – 11:14 AM
To: Shelley Manning, Ashley Gordon
Subject: Re: Barf!

Hang in there!

From: Shelley Manning – July 12, 2013 – 11:16 AM
To: Renee Greene, Ashley Gordon
Subject: Re: Barf!

I've had some mighty fine times with the grossness of bodily fluids. It's not all that bad.

From: Renee Greene – July 12, 2013 – 11:19 AM
To: Shelley Manning
Subject: Re: Barf!

Have you no sympathy, woman?

From: Shelley Manning – July 12, 2013 – 11:19 AM
To: Renee Greene
Subject: Re: Barf!

You can't tell because this is email, but I'm giving you the finger right now.

From: Renee Greene – July 12, 2013 – 11:20 AM
To: Shelley Manning
Subject: Re: Barf!

Ew! Who knows where that finger has been.

From: Shelley Manning – July 12, 2013 – 11:21 AM
To: Renee Greene
Subject: Re: Barf!

The list is long...but distinguished. Mwah! Mwah!

From: Renee Greene – July 17, 2013 – 10:23 AM
To: cassidy, Mark Finlay
Subject: Dinner tomorrow

Hello there, friends. Just confirming that we are still on for dinner Saturday night. Shall I make a reservation somewhere?

From: Mark Finlay – July 17, 2013 – 11:22 AM
To: cassidy, Renee Greene
Subject: Re: Dinner tomorrow

Cass is working mornings for a few more weeks and then switches to nights. Her call time is 5:00 a.m. Could we do an early dinner somewhere?

From: cassidy – July 17, 2013 – 11:27 AM
To: Renee Greene, Mark Finlay
Subject: Re: Dinner tomorrow

im pretty tired. could we make it an early causal night?

From: Renee Greene – July 17, 2013 – 12:01 PM
To: cassidy, Mark Finlay
Subject: Re: Dinner tomorrow

Yes! Let's be like old people and hit up an early bird special. I'll figure out a place and text you the details. Can't wait to hear all about the movie making, Cassidy. Talk soon!

From: Renee Greene – July 26, 2013 – 8:05 AM
To: Ashley Gordon
Subject: Still on?

Hey there. Are we still on for lunch tomorrow at Mel's? Hope so. My sweet angel must miss her Auntie Renee terribly.

From: Ashley Gordon – July 26, 2013 – 9:22 AM
To: Renee Greene
Subject: Re: Still on?

Yes, we are still on. I'll meet you there at noon. I'll be easy to spot. I'll be the frazzled woman with spit up on her clothes toting around a 9 month-old and all of her gear.

From: Renee Greene – July 26, 2013 – 9:24 AM
To: Ashley Gordon
Subject: Re: Still on?

Save a little room in that ginormous diaper bag of yours. I have a present for her.

From: Ashley Gordon – July 26, 2013 – 9:27 AM
To: Renee Greene
Subject: Re: Still on?

That's nice of you, but you don't need to keep buying her things. She's getting spoiled rotten.

From: Renee Greene – July 26, 2013 – 9:29 AM
To: Ashley Gordon
Subject: Re: Still on?

Speaking of getting spoiled rotten, I'm going to get a pedicure after lunch. Care to join me?

From: Ashley Gordon – July 26, 2013 – 9:32 AM
To: Renee Greene
Subject: Re: Still on?

Wish I could. Oh, how I wish I could. I haven't had a pedicure in months. Sadly, I don't think Siobhan will be welcome at Tip Toes nail salon.

From: Renee Greene – July 26, 2013 – 9:34 AM
To: Ashley Gordon
Subject: Re: Still on?

Well, if you ask me, her little piggy toes make that all worthwhile. See you tomorrow.

CHAPTER 3: MAJOR CONUNDRUM

From: Renee Greene – July 27, 2013 – 2:32 PM
To: PBCupLover, Shelley Manning, Ashley Gordon
Subject: Major conundrum

Fuck! Okay, so if I'm starting off this email with the mother of all curse words, you KNOW it's gotta be bad. Fuck! Fuck! Fuck! Triple bad. Like "the worst thing in the world" bad.

I was at the nail salon getting a long overdue pedicure. Ethan can attest, they were like bear claws down there. And no, my gnarly toenails are NOT the worst part of this email.

I was reading an US Weekly from three weeks ago - again not the worst part of this email, but perhaps a close second - and there's a picture of Cassidy kissing Marcus Wright on the set of his new movie. It's not a harmless peck on the cheek kiss either. It's a full-on, making out kiss. The caption says, "Marcus Wright sneaking a kiss with a mystery lady on the set of King's Final." Fuck!

From: PBCupLover – July 27, 2013 – 2:34 PM
To: Renee Greene, Shelley Manning, Ashley Gordon
Subject: Re: Major conundrum

Oy! This is bad. Very bad.

From: Ashley Gordon – July 27, 2013 – 3:22 PM
To: PBCupLover, Shelley Manning, Renee Greene
Subject: Re: Major conundrum

Holy moly!

From: Shelley Manning – July 27, 2013 – 4:01 PM
To: PBCupLover, Ashley Gordon, Renee Greene
Subject: Re: Major conundrum

Let's not get ahead of ourselves here, folks. This happened three weeks ago. Maybe Finlay already knows about it and they're working through it.

From: Ashley Gordon – July 27, 2013 – 4:05 PM
To: PBCupLover, Shelley Manning, Renee Greene
Subject: Re: Major conundrum

Do you really think Mark could look past infidelity? I know I couldn't. I would never be able to look at Greg the same way again. Would you be able to forgive Nick?

From: Shelley Manning – July 27, 2013 – 4:11 PM
To: PBCupLover, Ashley Gordon, Renee Greene
Subject: Re: Major conundrum

We're talking about Mark, not Nick. Nick would never stray. Believe me, he's one satisfied man. Anyway, first off, if he has seen this, they aren't married yet so he may be willing to forgive her this transgression. For all we know, it is only one kiss. Second, maybe there's an innocent explanation.

From: Renee Greene – July 27, 2013 – 4:17 PM
To: PBCupLover, Shelley Manning, Ashley Gordon
Subject: Re: Major conundrum

I'm certain Mark has NOT seen this. If he ever opened a trashy, tabloid celebrity magazine, I'd be shocked. And I'm confident Cassidy hasn't confessed all, because we just had dinner with them last week and everything seemed fine.

He would definitely tell me if he knew she had cheated on him. There's no way he could forgive her. He's such a straight arrow and is so particular about things. And believe me, there is no innocent explanation for this embrace and lip lock. Fuck! What the hell am I supposed to do now?

From: PBCupLover – July 27, 2013 – 4:22 PM
To: Renee Greene, Shelley Manning, Ashley Gordon
Subject: Re: Major conundrum

You need to tell him. He can't marry this woman if she's being unfaithful to him. He needs to know.

From: Ashley Gordon – July 27, 2013 – 4:24 PM
To: PBCupLover, Shelley Manning, Renee Greene
Subject: Re: Major conundrum

Ethan's right. Poor Mark. He's going to be devastated. I'm so glad you are the one that's going to tell him. I don't think I could do it.

From: Renee Greene – July 27, 2013 – 4:25 PM
To: PBCupLover, Shelley Manning, Ashley Gordon
Subject: Re: Major conundrum

Wait. Why am I going to be the one to tell him?

From: Ashley Gordon – July 27, 2013 – 4:28 PM
To: PBCupLover, Shelley Manning, Renee Greene
Subject: Re: Major conundrum

You are the one who found the photo. You are closest to him. It'll be best coming from you.

From: Shelley Manning – July 27, 2013 – 5:02 PM
To: PBCupLover, Ashley Gordon, Renee Greene
Subject: Re: Major conundrum

Even if Finlay got screwed over big time because she screwed someone else, I'm not sure we want to get involved.

From: Shelley Manning – July 27, 2013 – 5:03 PM
To: PBCupLover, Ashley Gordon, Renee Greene
Subject: Re: Major conundrum

Oh hell, you're all right. Disregard my last email. He needs to know. Okay, I'll tell him, although I can't guarantee I'll be as gentle as you will, Renee.

From: Ashley Gordon – July 27, 2013 – 5:10 PM
To: Renee Greene
Subject: Re: Major conundrum

Don't let Shelley tell him. The guy's going to be heartbroken enough.

From: Renee Greene – July 27, 2013 – 5:11 PM
To: Ashley Gordon
Subject: Re: Major conundrum

You think he's heartbroken over Shelley?

From: Ashley Gordon – July 27, 2013 – 5:14 PM
To: Renee Greene
Subject: Re: Major conundrum

Renee! Give it a rest already. Shelley is with Nick. Mark loves Cassidy - at least right now he does. There is nothing going on between Mark and Shelley, nor will there ever be.

From: Renee Greene – July 27, 2013 – 5:17 PM
To: Ashley Gordon
Subject: Re: Major conundrum

You're right. You're right. On both counts. Shelley and Mark together is just a crazy pipe dream of mine. And I can't let her break the news. I need to do it.

From: PBCupLover – July 27, 2013 – 5:23 PM
To: Renee Greene, Shelley Manning, Ashley Gordon
Subject: Re: Major conundrum

Babe, you need to tell him. I'll do it with you. See if he's free
tomorrow and we'll go together.

From: Renee Greene – July 27, 2013 – 5:26 PM
To: PBCupLover, Shelley Manning, Ashley Gordon
Subject: Re: Major conundrum

Thank you! I don't think I can bear the thought of telling him alone.
I'll email him now.

From: Shelley Manning – July 27, 2013 – 5:32 PM
To: Renee Greene
Subject: Re: Major conundrum

Don't forget to email me all of the juicy details after.

From: Renee Greene – July 27, 2013 – 5:34 PM
To: Shelley Manning
Subject: Re: Major conundrum

Shelley! You wicked, wicked girl.

From: Renee Greene – July 27, 2013 – 5:45 PM
To: Mark Finlay
Subject: Re: Major conundrum

Hey, Mark. Wanted to see if you were free tomorrow night? Can we
grab a drink or dinner or something?

From: Mark Finlay – July 27, 2013 – 5:52 PM
To: Renee Greene
Subject: Re: Major conundrum

Cass is busy on set this week but I could meet up. Where did you have in mind?

From: Renee Greene – July 27, 2013 – 5:59 PM
To: Mark Finlay
Subject: Re: Major conundrum

Actually, why don't I swing by your place with some takeout? I'm going to be near Bamboo Garden. I'll get your usual. How about seven?

From: Mark Finlay – July 27, 2013 – 6:02 PM
To: Renee Greene
Subject: Re: Major conundrum

Bamboo Garden. My favorite. You know me so well. Sounds perfect. See you then.

From: Renee Greene – July 27, 2013 – 6:04 PM
To: PBCupLover
Subject: Re: Major conundrum

Okay, we're set to take Bamboo Garden over to Mark's tomorrow around seven. I think Gift-Wrapped Chicken might help ease the pain.

From: PBCupLover – July 27, 2013 – 6:10 PM
To: Renee Greene
Subject: Re: Major conundrum

While I'm sure it's not the "gift" he's looking for, it is the best thing for him.

From: Renee Greene – July 27, 2013 – 6:11 PM
To: PBCupLover
Subject: Re: Major conundrum

Yeah, I'm afraid it will be the gift that keeps on giving…and not in a good way.

From: PBCupLover – July 27, 2013 – 6:13 PM
To: Renee Greene
Subject: Re: Major conundrum

Hold strong. I'll see you home later tonight.

From: Shelley Manning – July 29, 2013 – 8:52 AM
To: Renee Greene
Cc: Ashley Gordon
Subject: Finlay's Folly

Well…

From: Renee Greene – July 29, 2013 – 9:37 AM
To: Shelley Manning
Cc: Ashley Gordon
Subject: Re: Finlay's Folly

It was AWFUL! Ethan was going to go with me but of course got stuck at work. His stupid boss William said he needed his help on something. Of course I'm sure it was something totally non-work related, like checking out new cell phones or looking at pictures of hot chicks on his Facebook page.

Anyway, I started off making small talk and then told him I had something hard to tell him. His first response was, "Is everything okay with Ethan?" Little did he know! I told him that there was something he needed to know and that this was really hard for me to share.

Then, I pulled out the magazine. He sort of stared at it for a while. After a few blinks, he threw it across the room then ran to the bathroom and threw up in the toilet. From there it was just a jumble of tears and rants.

I didn't even know what to do or say, so I just let him let it all out. After about 30 minutes he asked me to leave. Thankfully Ethan was home by the time I got there and was a shoulder for *me* to cry on.

From: Shelley Manning – July 29, 2013 – 10:12 AM
To: Renee Greene
Cc: Ashley Gordon
Subject: Re: Finlay's Folly

Oh, Sweetie. I'm sure that was hard on you and even harder on Finlay. And as much as I feel badly for him to be cheated on, I must say, "Death to Finnady!" So glad to have that whack job out of our lives. Good riddance, I say. Good riddance!

From: Ashley Gordon – July 29, 2013 – 11:04 AM
To: Shelley Manning
Cc: Renee Greene
Subject: Re: Finlay's Folly

I agree with Shelley. Shocking, I know. But I think we are all better off without her, especially Mark. He deserves better.

From: Renee Greene – July 29, 2013 – 11:08 AM
To: Ashley Gordon
Cc: Shelley Manning
Subject: Re: Finlay's Folly

It was just so hard to see him so hurt. I wish I could take it all back. Damn toes!

From: Shelley Manning – July 29, 2013 – 11:17 AM
To: Renee Greene
Cc: Ashley Gordon
Subject: Re: Finlay's Folly

Damn toes?

From: Renee Greene – July 29, 2013 – 11:19 AM
To: Ashley Gordon
Cc: Shelley Manning
Subject: Re: Finlay's Folly

If I hadn't gotten that pedicure because of my unladylike, hoof-like digits, I never would have seen that photo and never would have had to break Mark's heart.

From: Shelley Manning – July 29, 2013 – 11:24 AM
To: Renee Greene
Cc: Ashley Gordon
Subject: Re: Finlay's Folly

You didn't break his heart, Sweetie. That whore did. Better for him to find out now than after he married her.

From: Ashley Gordon – July 29, 2013 – 11:32 AM
To: Shelley Manning
Cc: Renee Greene
Subject: Re: Finlay's Folly

Once again, I agree with Shelley.

From: Renee Greene – July 29, 2013 – 11:40 AM
To: Ashley Gordon
Cc: Shelley Manning
Subject: Re: Finlay's Folly

Not sure what is worse. Having our dear friend heartbroken, or seeing you two agreeing with each other so much.

From: Shelley Manning – July 29, 2013 – 11:45 AM
To: Renee Greene
Cc: Ashley Gordon
Subject: Re: Finlay's Folly

It's definitely worse that we are agreeing with each other. The apocalypse might be near.

From: Ashley Gordon – July 29, 2013 – 11:51 AM
To: Shelley Manning
Cc: Renee Greene
Subject: Re: Finlay's Folly

I'd like to think that Nick has helped Shelley mellow out a bit.

From: Shelley Manning – July 29, 2013 – 11:53 AM
To: Ashley Gordon
Cc: Renee Greene
Subject: Re: Finlay's Folly

If anything, he's brought out the even wilder side of me.

From: Renee Greene – July 29, 2013 – 11:59 AM
To: Shelley Manning
Cc: Ashley Gordon
Subject: Re: Finlay's Folly

Okay, okay. That's enough, Shelley. We don't need to hear about your and Nick's exploits. Oh, who am I kidding? Ashley doesn't want to hear about your and Nick's exploits. But I really, REALLY do.

And we'll all be together in a few weeks for Shelley to share too much and Ashley to cringe. YIPPEE!

From: Ashley Gordon – July 29, 2013 – 12:05 PM
To: Renee Greene
Cc: Shelley Manning
Subject: Re: Finlay's Folly

And now I agree with Renee. Maybe it's just me. Maybe Siobhan has made me more agreeable. Keep me posted and let me know if there's anything we can do for Mark.

From: Renee Greene – July 29, 2013 – 12:07 PM
To: Ashley Gordon
Cc: Shelley Manning
Subject: Re: Finlay's Folly

Will do!

From: Shelley Manning – July 29, 2013 – 12:16 PM
To: Renee Greene
Subject: Re: Finlay's Folly

She thinks Siobhan has made her more agreeable? Maybe more delusional, but definitely not more agreeable. I can't say, do or purchase anything right.

I sent her a darling baby doll that I found at a boutique in Belltown, which is definitely the trendy part of Seattle. She responded with a "thank you but in the future, please refrain from buying Siobhan gifts that perpetuate gender stereotypes."

From: Renee Greene – July 29, 2013 – 12:22 PM
To: Shelley Manning
Subject: Re: Finlay's Folly

Good to know. Even though it's months away, I'm already thinking through ideas for her first birthday and thought of buying her a play kitchen. Don't want to get scolded for making Siobhan think she has to perform in the kitchen. Also, THANK YOU, THANK YOU for remembering to remove Ashley's email address from your reply. I really didn't have the energy to deal with another friendship crisis.

From: Shelley Manning – July 29, 2013 – 12:26 PM
To: Renee Greene
Subject: Re: Finlay's Folly

Of course you are thinking through a gift months in advance. You're such a thoughtful girl and great gift giver.

Most of the world's famous chefs are men, aren't they? And yes, I believe I've learned my lesson and now check everything before I hit "send."

From: Renee Greene – July 29, 2013 – 12:31 PM
To: Shelley Manning
Subject: Re: Finlay's Folly

You're right (and before you say, as usual, let me add), as usual. I will get her the kitchen and let her know I hope she aspires to be like the world's famous (male) chefs.

From: Shelley Manning – July 29, 2013 – 12:37 PM
To: Renee Greene
Subject: Re: Finlay's Folly

Well, I'm going to get her a drum set or maybe an accordion. I've read that learning to play a musical instrument can help kids improve their math skills. I'll be sure to put that in the card. The fact that it's noisy and quite possibly a large annoyance for Ashley is just an added bonus. Consider it friendly payback.

From: Renee Greene – July 29, 2013 – 12:41 PM
To: Shelley Manning
Subject: Re: Finlay's Folly

I love it! And I love you! MISS YOU TONS! Can't wait to see you!!!

From: Shelley Manning – July 29, 2013 – 12:43 PM
To: Renee Greene
Subject: Re: Finlay's Folly

Of course you do, Sweetie. Mwah! Mwah!

From: Shelley Manning – July 29, 2013 – 12:37 PM
To: Mark Finlay
Subject: Crappy

Tough break, Finlay. You deserve better. A lot better. Hang in there.

From: Mark Finlay – July 29, 2013 – 12:38 PM
To: Shelley Manning
Subject: Re: Crappy

Thanks, Shelley. I know you never liked her.

From: Shelley Manning – July 29, 2013 – 12:40 PM
To: Mark Finlay
Subject: Re: Crappy

No, never did. But I know you did and I just want you to be happy. Sorry she turned out to be as bad as I thought.

CHAPTER 4: SEATTLE BOUND

From: Renee Greene – August 2, 2013 – 9:54 PM
To: Ashley Gordon
Cc: Shelley Manning
Subject: Land of Oz

I am so excited we are headed to the Emerald City, my pretties.

From: Ashley Gordon – August 3, 2013 – 1:12 AM
To: Renee Greene
Cc: Shelley Manning
Subject: Re: Land of Oz

Sounds great. So looking forward to this getaway. I feel like I haven't had any fun in a long time.

Even if it means hanging out with Shelley, it should be fun. (Just kidding!)

From: Shelley Manning – August 3, 2013 – 9:02 AM
To: Renee Greene
Subject: Fwd: Re: Land of Oz

And just who is Ashley in this Oz-themed scenario? The one without a brain or a heart? Or are you suggesting she has a broom?

From: Renee Greene – August 3, 2013 – 9:04 AM
To: Shelley Manning
Subject: Re: Fwd: Re: Land of Oz

Oh, you're the wicked one, for sure!

From: Shelley Manning – August 3, 2013 – 9:08 AM
To: Renee Greene
Subject: Re: Fwd: Re: Land of Oz

I wish you were the one with courage and would just tell her to stop her futile attempts at put-down humor. It just comes across as sad.

From: Renee Greene – August 3, 2013 – 9:12 AM
To: Shelley Manning
Subject: Re: Fwd: Re: Land of Oz

Behave now. I'm used to her and her ways. As much as it sometimes becomes a bitter pill to swallow, she's a dear, dear friend and she's going through a rough time right now. She needs our support.

From: Shelley Manning – August 3, 2013 – 9:16 AM
To: Renee Greene
Subject: Re: Fwd: Re: Land of Oz

Who am I? Her Auntie Em? I'll be supportive when monkeys fly. So, what's the scoop on your flight?

From: Renee Greene – August 3, 2013 – 9:20 AM
To: Shelley Manning
Subject: Re: Fwd: Re: Land of Oz

Ha-larious! We are on Alaska Airlines and get in at 8:02. I can hardly stand it. I'm so excited to see you. My pre-flight jitters are being replaced with sheer giddiness at the prospect of hanging out with you.

From: Shelley Manning – August 3, 2013 – 9:28 AM
To: Renee Greene
Subject: Re: Fwd: Re: Land of Oz

I do have that effect on people and not just those who don't like to fly. Okay, I will pick you up curbside. Text me when you land and I'll hop in the car. At that time of day, it won't take more than 15 minutes for me to get to the airport from our place. I'm assuming you are checking bags, no?

From: Renee Greene – August 3, 2013 – 9:33 AM
To: Shelley Manning
Subject: Re: Fwd: Re: Land of Oz

Of course I'm checking a bag. I need a lot of stuff including multiple products for my hair. That Seattle weather is so unpredictable and I don't know what kind of anti-frizz or straightening help will be needed. Here's hoping both the weather and my hair cooperate!

From: Shelley Manning – August 3, 2013 – 9:37 AM
To: Renee Greene
Subject: Re: Fwd: Re: Land of Oz

Traveling with Ashley, that's a smart idea. Let's hope she cooperates too. Okay, Sweetie. Gotta run. Mwah! Mwah!

CHAPTER 5: FALL OUT

From: Renee Greene – August 5, 2013 – 9:00 AM
To: Mark Finlay
Subject: Checking in

Are you okay?

From: Mark Finlay – August 5, 2013 – 10:32 AM
To: Renee Greene
Subject: Re: Checking in

No.

From: Renee Greene – August 5, 2013 – 10:34 AM
To: Mark Finlay
Subject: Re: Checking in

Are you mad at me? Do you want to talk?

From: Mark Finlay – August 5, 2013 – 10:35 AM
To: Renee Greene
Subject: Re: Checking in

No.

From: Renee Greene – August 5, 2013 – 10:36 AM
To: Mark Finlay
Subject: Re: Checking in

Are you sure?

From: Mark Finlay – August 5, 2013 – 10:37 AM
To: Renee Greene
Subject: Re: Checking in

No.

From: Renee Greene – August 5, 2013 – 10:38 AM
To: Mark Finlay
Subject: Re: Checking in

Really?

From: Mark Finlay – August 5, 2013 – 10:41 AM
To: Renee Greene
Subject: Re: Checking in

I'm not mad at you, Renee. You're a good friend and did the right thing. I'm just not ready to talk right now. I hope you understand.

From: Renee Greene – August 5, 2013 – 10:42 AM
To: Mark Finlay
Subject: Re: Checking in

Okay. Just know that I'm totally here for you.

From: Mark Finlay – August 5, 2013 – 10:43 AM
To: Renee Greene
Subject: Re: Checking in

I know.

From: Renee Greene – August 5, 2013 – 10:43 AM
To: Mark Finlay
Subject: Re: Checking in

Now leave me alone, right? ;)

From: Mark Finlay – August 5, 2013 – 10:44 AM
To: Renee Greene
Subject: Re: Checking in

I'll call you soon. Just give me some time.

From: cassidy – August 6, 2013 – 1:02 AM
To: Mark Finlay
Subject: im sorry!

im sorry. so so sorry. can we talk, please. i dont want to loose you over this. dont throw what we have away.

From: Renee Greene – August 6, 2013 – 9:10 AM
To: Shelley Manning
Subject: Finlay update

He's miserable. And I'm miserable. And not just because I haven't spoken to you in so long. Too busy with your new beau or Amber to email or call? At least I get to see you soon.

From: Shelley Manning – August 6, 2013 – 9:11 AM
To: Renee Greene
Subject: Re: Finlay update

So, you think Finlay's mad at you?

From: Renee Greene – August 6, 2013 – 9:12 AM
To: Shelley Manning
Subject: Re: Finlay update

Of course I do! He says no but we've barely spoken these past 10 days.

From: Shelley Manning – August 6, 2013 – 9:15 AM
To: Renee Greene
Subject: Re: Finlay update

Renee, you've got to give the guy a break. He just found out that his fiancé cheated on him….and in a really public way.

From: Renee Greene – August 6, 2013 – 9:18 AM
To: Shelley Manning
Subject: Re: Finlay update

I know. But why, WHY, did I have to be the one to see that photo in US Weekly? Why, WHY, did I have to be the one to tell him that Cassidy was caught kissing another man on set? Why? WHY?

From: Shelley Manning – August 6, 2013 – 9:19 AM
To: Renee Greene
Subject: Re: Finlay update

That'll teach you to get a pedicure.

From: Renee Greene – August 6, 2013 – 9:21 AM
To: Shelley Manning
Subject: Re: Finlay update

It really will. Every time I look at my toes, I feel pangs of guilt.

From: Shelley Manning – August 6, 2013 – 9:23 AM
To: Renee Greene
Subject: Re: Finlay update

Seriously, Renee, it's not your fault. Isn't it better for him to find out now that Cassidy is a lying, cheating whore rather than when they are married?

From: Renee Greene – August 6, 2013 – 9:24 AM
To: Shelley Manning
Subject: Re: Finlay update

Whoa! Have a strong feeling about this?

From: Shelley Manning – August 6, 2013 – 9:26 AM
To: Renee Greene
Subject: Re: Finlay update

Absolutely! You mess with the bull and you get the horns. Right? Just bad timing though.

From: Renee Greene – August 6, 2013 – 9:29 AM
To: Shelley Manning
Subject: Re: Finlay update

That's an understatement. A few months before his wedding and my best friend finds out - from me, no less - that he's being cuckolded.

From: Shelley Manning – August 6, 2013 – 9:31 AM
To: Renee Greene
Subject: Re: Finlay update

Oh Renee, why do you have to make everything sound so dirty?

From: Renee Greene – August 6, 2013 – 9:34 AM
To: Shelley Manning
Subject: Re: Finlay update

I thought you would like that. But seriously, I just feel awful for Mark and don't know what I can do to make things better. And I know this has forever altered our friendship. He'll never look at me the same way again.

From: Shelley Manning – August 6, 2013 – 9:42 AM
To: Renee Greene
Subject: Re: Finlay update

Sweetie, this is probably the worst thing that has ever happened to him. I know what you are thinking, "Oh, thanks a lot, Shelley. As if I didn't already feel awful enough..."

This isn't about you! It's like he's dealing with a death right now. The death of the woman he loved and thought he knew. He's grieving for the life he thought he was going to have and all of the plans he had made in his head. So give him some time and space. When he's ready for your sympathy, he'll let you know.

From: Renee Greene – August 6, 2013 – 9:43 AM
To: Shelley Manning
Subject: Re: Finlay update

You're right.

From: Shelley Manning – August 6, 2013 – 9:44 AM
To: Renee Greene
Subject: Re: Finlay update

As usual. What about the ring? Did he take the ring back?

From: Renee Greene – August 6, 2013 – 9:45 AM
To: Shelley Manning
Subject: Re: Finlay update

Oh, that's a good question. I didn't even ask about that. I sure hope so.

From: Shelley Manning – August 6, 2013 – 9:45 AM
To: Renee Greene
Subject: Re: Finlay update

Me too!

From: Renee Greene – August 6, 2013 – 9:47 AM
To: Shelley Manning
Subject: Re: Finlay update

Not only is it a gorgeous, expensive ring, but he spent countless hours researching all about diamonds to pick the perfect one.

From: Shelley Manning – August 6, 2013 – 9:48 AM
To: Renee Greene
Subject: Re: Finlay update

Of course he did. How Finlay of him.

From: Renee Greene – August 6, 2013 – 9:52 AM
To: Shelley Manning
Subject: Re: Finlay update

Hey now. The boy likes to be thorough and I think it's lovely that he spent so much time and consideration finding the perfect ring to symbolize their love for each other.

From: Shelley Manning – August 6, 2013 – 9:54 AM
To: Renee Greene
Subject: Re: Finlay update

Perfect until she turned out to be a lying sack of shit.

From: Renee Greene – August 6, 2013 – 9:55 AM
To: Shelley Manning
Subject: Re: Finlay update

Mother bear protects her cubs, doesn't she?

From: Shelley Manning – August 6, 2013 – 10:00 AM
To: Renee Greene
Subject: Re: Finlay update

You bet, Sweetie. I didn't like that twit from day one with her fake Southern charm and toned triceps. You don't want to fuck with my friend unless you want to endure my wrath.

From: Renee Greene – August 6, 2013 – 10:02 AM
To: Shelley Manning
Subject: Re: Finlay update

I'll find out and keep you posted. What else is new with you? I miss talking with you.

From: Shelley Manning – August 6, 2013 – 10:06 AM
To: Renee Greene
Subject: Re: Finlay update

Everything's fine. Wish I could talk more but I've got to run. I'll see you soon and we'll have plenty of time to catch up. Mwah! Mwah!

From: Renee Greene – August 8, 2013 – 11:02 AM
To: Shelley Manning
Subject: Celebrity Madness

I know how you HATE celebrities, so prepare yourselves for another wild but true story from the annals of Renee Greene's surreal life. Our client Halloturn just signed a deal with Natalie Franklin, the R&B singer, to be a spokesperson for their diabetes medication.

It's well known she has type 2 diabetes. Her "people" just sent over her "green room" requirements for an upcoming appearance we are booking for her on the Today Show to talk about diabetes management and childhood obesity.

Read on for true, unedited, unembellished excerpts from her green room needs. "4. Gel pens: one blue, two black, one red 12. Six bottles of Evian chilled and six bottles at room temperature 19. 2 "squeezy" bottles clear honey (not organic) 23. NO WHITE FLOWERS! There shall be NO WHITE FLOWERS!"

She's crazy, no?

From: Shelley Manning – August 8, 2013 – 11:38 AM
To: Renee Greene
Subject: Re: Celebrity Madness

NuttyNat (what I will be calling her now) is not only crazy but stupid. Evian? I NEVER drink Evian. Do you know what Evian spells backwards?

From: Renee Greene – August 8, 2013 – 11:40 AM
To: Shelley Manning
Subject: Re: Celebrity Madness

OMG! I'm busting a gut right now. Naive! Naive! That is SO funny.

From: Shelley Manning – August 8, 2013 – 11:46 AM
To: Renee Greene
Subject: Re: Celebrity Madness

Yep. Naive. I feel like a sucker anytime I pop one open. I'm sure there is some guy in Kenosha kicking up his heels as he fills them up with tap water, slaps on a high-end looking label and racks up the dough. I'm surprised that with your marketing prowess, you never noticed that before.

From: Renee Greene – August 8, 2013 – 11:47 AM
To: Shelley Manning
Subject: Re: Celebrity Madness

Now I'm feeling naive.

From: Shelley Manning – August 8, 2013 – 11:48 AM
To: Renee Greene
Subject: Re: Celebrity Madness

HA-LARIOUS! And what's with the white flowers?

From: Renee Greene – August 8, 2013 – 11:49 AM
To: Shelley Manning
Subject: Re: Celebrity Madness

No idea. But you can bet I'm going to find out.

From: Renee Greene – August 8, 2013 – 1:32 PM
To: Shelley Manning
Subject: White Flowers Mystery Solved!

So, I found out why NO WHITE FLOWERS! is in all caps on her list. They remind her of Whitney Houston, her childhood hero.

From: Shelley Manning – August 8, 2013 – 1:35 PM
To: Renee Greene
Subject: Re: White Flowers Mystery Solved!

NuttyNat be crazy indeed. See you tomorrow, Sweetie. Mwah!
Mwah!

CHAPTER 6: INSECURITIES

From: Renee Greene – August 11, 2013 – 11:08 AM
To: Shelley Manning
Cc: Ashley Gordon
Subject: YES!

It was great seeing you after way too long. I'm so glad we got the chance to catch up: meaning gossip, get manicures and eat cupcakes. Just reminds me how very much I miss you, my friend. You know how special you are to me and I would never want to let our friendship change because of some measly miles. I love you! As you would say, MWAH! MWAH!

From: Ashley Gordon – August 11, 2013 – 11:09 AM
To: Renee Greene
Cc: Shelley Manning
Subject: Re: YES!

Ditto from me.

From: Ashley Gordon – August 11, 2013 – 11:10 AM
To: Renee Greene
Subject: Fwd: Re: YES!

And well (and quickly) written my friend as we sit next to each other at the airport to return home. HA! HA!

From: Renee Greene – August 11, 2013 – 11:11 AM
To: Ashley Gordon
Subject: Re: Fwd: Re: YES!

Enough of this email business. I'm sitting right next to you.

From: Ashley Gordon – August 11, 2013 – 11:11 AM
To: Renee Greene
Subject: Re: Fwd: Re: YES!

;)

From: Shelley Manning – August 12, 2013 – 12:04 PM
To: Renee Greene
Cc: Ashley Gordon
Subject: Re: YES!

It was wonderful to see you guys, too. And I miss you, too. Off to grab lunch with Amber. Talk soon. Mwah! Mwah all around!

From: Ashley Gordon – August 12, 2013 – 5:34 PM
To: Renee Greene
Subject: Catty Comment Warning

Okay, did you notice how much Shelley was talking about Amber this weekend? I mean, who is she in love with more - Nick or her? Even her email back to you, after you basically poured your heart out, had to include Amber. It's been bugging me since we got back. Just saying.

From: Renee Greene – August 12, 2013 – 6:02 PM
To: Ashley Gordon
Subject: Re: Catty Comment Warning

Well, if I'm being perfectly honest, it would be tough not to notice the love fest Shelley feels with Amber. I mean I get it. She's really glamorous and beautiful and charming and all. And she's one of only a few people Shelley knows in Seattle. But it was a bit unsettling for me. Reconfirmed to me how I've been feeling - like she's replacing me as her best friend.

From: Ashley Gordon – August 12, 2013 – 6:04 PM
To: Renee Greene
Subject: Re: Catty Comment Warning

Are you crying?

From: Renee Greene – August 12, 2013 – 6:05 PM
To: Ashley Gordon
Subject: Re: Catty Comment Warning

How did you know?

From: Ashley Gordon – August 12, 2013 – 6:09 PM
To: Renee Greene
Subject: Re: Catty Comment Warning

Lucky guess. Really, I don't think she could replace you at all. She's just trying to fit into a new place. Now wipe away your tears and get back to whatever you were doing.

From: Renee Greene – August 12, 2013 – 6:10 PM
To: Ashley Gordon
Subject: Re: Catty Comment Warning

Just watching Sports Center with Ethan. And by "watching Sports Center" I mean checking my emails and playing Words with Friends. I'll call you later.

From: Renee Greene – August 12, 2013 – 7:32 PM
To: Shelley Manning
Subject: Burger recipe

Hey, Shelley. Hope you have recovered from our fun-filled weekend. I totally forgot to ask: Can I get Nick's recipe for the burgers? They were amazing. What's his secret?

From: Renee Greene – August 13, 2013 – 9:05 AM
To: Shelley Manning
Subject: Fwd: Burger recipe

Not sure if you got my original message.

From: Renee Greene – August 14, 2013 – 8:57 AM
To: Shelley Manning
Subject: Fwd: Burger recipe

<crickets!>

From: Shelley Manning – August 14, 2013 – 6:02 PM
To: Renee Greene
Subject: Re: Burger recipe

The secret ingredient is love.

From: Renee Greene – August 14, 2013 – 6:04 PM
To: Shelley Manning
Subject: Re: Burger recipe

So sentimental for you.

From: Shelley Manning – August 14, 2013 – 7:32 PM
To: Renee Greene
Subject: Re: Burger recipe

Oh, and it's also 2 tablespoons of his semen warmed up in my mouth.

From: Renee Greene – August 14, 2013 – 7:35 PM
To: Shelley Manning
Subject: Re: Burger recipe

Shelley Manning! Even for you, that was too much. Much much too much.

From: Shelley Manning – August 14, 2013 – 9:38 PM
To: Renee Greene
Subject: Re: Burger recipe

You're right. That was too much. You'll be pleased to know that I did NOT write that. I left my email open and my account was hijacked by Nick.

From: Renee Greene – August 14, 2013 – 9:40 PM
To: Shelley Manning
Subject: Re: Burger recipe

Oh my! Nick wrote that?

From: Shelley Manning – August 14, 2013 – 9:41 PM
To: Renee Greene
Subject: Re: Burger recipe

Yes. I'm a lucky girl, aren't I?

From: Renee Greene – August 14, 2013 – 9:41 PM
To: Shelley Manning
Subject: Re: Burger recipe

Indeed!

From: Shelley Manning – August 14, 2013 – 9:52 PM
To: Renee Greene
Subject: Re: Burger recipe

Hi, Renee. It's me, Nick. I've been told that if I don't apologize to you, I will not get to see Shelley naked again for the foreseeable future. So I formally apologize to you if I had offended your sense of decency and decorum.

From: Renee Greene – August 14, 2013 – 9:54 PM
To: Shelley Manning
Subject: Re: Burger recipe

You're forgiven.

From: Shelley Manning – August 14, 2013 – 9:55 PM
To: Renee Greene
Subject: Re: Burger recipe

And that's that.

From: Renee Greene – August 14, 2013 – 9:56 PM
To: Shelley Manning
Subject: Re: Burger recipe

Well, you certainly know how to keep him behaving, don't you?

From: Renee Greene – August 14, 2013 – 9:57 PM
To: Shelley Manning
Subject: Re: Burger recipe

Damn right. Mwah! Mwah!

CHAPTER 7: ASSISTANCE

From: Renee Greene – August 19, 2013 – 10:31 AM
To: PBCupLover, Ashley Gordon, Mark Finlay, Shelley Manning
Subject: Movin' on up!

Guess who is movin' on up the ol' corporate ladder? Me! I have been informed that I get to hire my own assistant. We've gotten so busy that I apparently need someone to schedule meetings, do research, help me with new business proposals, etc. I'm big time now.

From: Ashley Gordon – August 19, 2013 – 11:32 AM
To: Renee Greene
Subject: Re: Movin' on up!

Oooh. Fun. I've always wanted to hire an assistant. I'm sure you'll be a great boss.

From: Renee Greene – August 19, 2013 – 11:36 AM
To: Ashley Gordon
Subject: Re: Movin' on up!

Me, too. Not that I think I'm going to be a great boss, but that I've always wanted an assistant. But more I think about it, I do think I'll be a good boss - fair, supportive, fun.

From: Ashley Gordon – August 19, 2013 – 12:22 PM
To: Renee Greene
Subject: Re: Movin' on up!

Just remember that you're the boss, not a friend or a colleague. Being fair and supportive is great, but you've also got to set expectations and be firm.

From: Renee Greene – August 19, 2013 – 12:23 PM
To: Ashley Gordon
Subject: Re: Movin' on up!

Hmmm. Maybe I'm not up for this after all.

From: Ashley Gordon – August 19, 2013 – 12:26 PM
To: Renee Greene
Subject: Re: Movin' on up!

You'll be fine. Just remember to wear something professional – not that purple sweater you seem to favor – when you do the interviews, to set the right tone.

From: Renee Greene – August 19, 2013 – 12:27 PM
To: Ashley Gordon
Subject: Re: Movin' on up!

Thanks for the suggestion.

From: Renee Greene – August 19, 2013 – 12:28 PM
To: Shelley Manning
Subject: Fwd: Re: Movin' on up!

See below for an exchange between me and Ashley. Don't say it!

From: PBCupLover – August 19, 2013 – 1:25 PM
To: Renee Greene
Subject: Re: Movin' on up!

Don't let the power go to your head.

From: Renee Greene – August 19, 2013 – 1:28 PM
To: PBCupLover
Subject: Re: Movin' on up!

Well, after dating/being engaged to you this long and acting as your personal assistant, it's nice to know there is someone to help *me*.

From: PBCupLover – August 19, 2013 – 1:30 PM
To: Renee Greene
Subject: Re: Movin' on up!

What do you mean, *my assistant*?

From: Renee Greene – August 19, 2013 – 1:33 PM
To: PBCupLover
Subject: Re: Movin' on up!

Who schedules everything for you and keeps track of all of your stuff? That would be me. Let's just say the hours are long and the pay is lousy. I hope to be a better boss to my assistant.

From: PBCupLover – August 19, 2013 – 1:34 PM
To: Renee Greene
Subject: Re: Movin' on up!

Ouch! I'll show you who's boss tonight.

From: Renee Greene – August 19, 2013 – 1:35 PM
To: PBCupLover
Subject: Re: Movin' on up!

Sounds intriguing. Can't wait. XOXO

From: Renee Greene – August 21, 2013 – 11:32 AM
To: Shelley Manning
Subject: Boston Babe

I just interviewed a great candidate to be my assistant. She's got a year of experience at another PR firm, wants to learn and move up the corporate ladder and went to school in Boston, which as we know is my favorite American city. The only problem is that she's super hot – tall, leggy but thankfully not blonde. If I don't hire her, is that discrimination?

From: Shelley Manning – August 21, 2013 – 12:45 PM
To: Renee Greene
Subject: Re: Boston Babe

Now that you've put it in writing, yes that is discrimination.

From: Renee Greene – August 21, 2013 – 12:50 PM
To: Shelley Manning
Subject: Re: Boston Babe

Damn! I think you're right. Darn electronic footprint! Oh well, I was going to hire her anyway. She's the best person for the job, even if she's gorgeous and young. And her name is Skye.

From: Shelley Manning – August 21, 2013 – 12:53 PM
To: Renee Greene
Subject: Re: Boston Babe

Of course her name is Skye. I will now refer to her as Skinny Skye. Will she have access to your email account?

From: Renee Greene – August 21, 2013 – 12:57 PM
To: Shelley Manning
Subject: Re: Boston Babe

No, that will still be password protected – thankfully. So we can talk about our insane jealousy of her without fear of discovery or reprisal. So feel free to tell me something completely unfit for the workplace. I'm all ears!

From: Shelley Manning – August 21, 2013 – 12:58 PM
To: Renee Greene
Subject: Re: Boston Babe

Excellent. Wish I could dazzle you with inappropriate stories of sexual adventures but I've gotta run. Mwah! Mwah!

From: Renee Greene – August 22, 2013 – 3:34 PM
To: Shelley Manning
Subject: Re: Boston Babe

Skinny Skye is on board. She starts next Monday.

CHAPTER 8: LIFE GOES ON

From: Mark Finlay – August 25, 2013 – 2:03 AM
To: Renee Greene
Subject: Hey

Hey, Renee. I didn't want to call in the middle of the night but I wanted to say hey.

From: Renee Greene – August 25, 2013 – 8:59 AM
To: Mark Finlay
Subject: Re: Hey

You're not answering your phone. I miss you, too. I'm sorry. So so sorry. Sorry for what you are going through and sorry for being the one to find out and tell you.

From: Mark Finlay – August 25, 2013 – 10:54 AM
To: Renee Greene
Subject: Re: Hey

There's no reason to be sorry. You did me a huge favor. I just wish I had known earlier.

From: Renee Greene – August 25, 2013 – 10:55 AM
To: Mark Finlay
Subject: Re: Hey

Was there something to know about earlier?

From: Mark Finlay – August 25, 2013 – 12:36 PM
To: Renee Greene
Subject: Re: Hey

No. She said this was the first time but I don't know if I can trust what she says. I just mean that I wish she had cheated on me sooner so that I wouldn't have wasted so much time with her. God, writing that sounds so strange. Who wishes they could be cheated on sooner?

From: Renee Greene – August 25, 2013 – 12:40 PM
To: Mark Finlay
Subject: Re: Hey

Give yourself a break. I know what you mean. Did she offer any kind of explanation? Was she contrite? Does she want you back? Would you consider forgiving her? Am I asking too many questions? Should I butt out?

From: Mark Finlay – August 25, 2013 – 12:50 PM
To: Renee Greene
Subject: Re: Hey

I would expect nothing less than lots of questions and probing from you. I'm actually okay talking about it now…with you. But I don't want Shelley and Ashley knowing all of this. I know that's going to be hard for you. You tell them everything even though you say you don't. Can you at least keep this to yourself?

From: Renee Greene – August 25, 2013 – 12:54 PM
To: Mark Finlay
Subject: Re: Hey

Yes, absolutely. I won't tell a soul. Not even Ethan. And you only need to tell me what you want to tell me. Don't feel pressured to say anything you don't want to.

From: Mark Finlay – August 25, 2013 – 1:16 PM
To: Renee Greene
Subject: Re: Hey

I know how curious you are and I've been keeping this all bottled up for weeks now. I'm already feeling good letting my fingers roll over the keyboard to get this all out. I confronted her when she got home from work the night you showed me the magazine photo. I said, "What the fuck is this?" I know, me swearing is very unusual, but honestly, I've never been this angry before. She didn't try to deny it. How could she? It was right there on page 36 for the world to see.

From: Renee Greene – August 25, 2013 – 1:19 PM
To: Mark Finlay
Subject: Re: Hey

Right there for me to see. <sigh!>

From: Mark Finlay – August 25, 2013 – 1:26 PM
To: Renee Greene
Subject: Re: Hey

She said it just sort of happened and that she didn't plan it and hadn't been wanting for it to. But it did. I asked if he kissed her, she kissed him or they kissed each other. At least she had the decency to tell me the truth – that they kissed each other. She told me how sorry she was and that she didn't tell me about it because she still loves me and didn't want it to jeopardize our future. She said she wanted us to get past this and asked what she could do.

From: Renee Greene – August 25, 2013 – 1:29 PM
To: Mark Finlay
Subject: Re: Hey

And…is there anything she can do?

From: Mark Finlay – August 25, 2013 – 1:34 PM
To: Renee Greene
Subject: Re: Hey

I don't think so. Looking back now, I realize she was wrong for me. I think I so badly wanted what you and Ethan had that I was willing to compromise on things that were important to me. I was fooling myself into thinking that her flaws didn't drive me crazy. Her infidelity just gave me the impetus I needed to be real with myself.

From: Renee Greene – August 25, 2013 – 1:38 PM
To: Mark Finlay
Subject: Re: Hey

Well, I'm sorry that it took something so painful and public to give you the clarity to see things for what they are.

From: Mark Finlay – August 25, 2013 – 1:41 PM
To: Renee Greene
Subject: Re: Hey

You mean to see things that all of you have been seeing for a long time now.

From: Renee Greene – August 25, 2013 – 1:47 PM
To: Mark Finlay
Subject: Re: Hey

It's no secret that we weren't fans of Cassidy. If I had a cupcake for every one of Shelley's eye rolls, I would weigh a lot more than I do now. But it really shouldn't matter what we think.

It is about you and your happiness. And if you were happy – which of course now we've established that you weren't – but if you were happy, we would want you two to be together. All we've ever wanted is for you to find happiness.

From: Mark Finlay – August 25, 2013 – 1:50 PM
To: Renee Greene
Subject: Re: Hey

I know. And I appreciate you all for it. I just need time to process this all. Let's plan on dinner next week, okay?

From: Renee Greene – August 25, 2013 – 1:51 PM
To: Mark Finlay
Subject: Re: Hey

Absolutely. I'll give you a call.

From: cassidy – August 27, 2013 – 2:45 AM
To: Mark Finlay
Subject: cmon!

mark please stop ignoring me. how can i make things up to you? what can i do?

From: Renee Greene – September 4, 2013 – 10:12 AM
To: Shelley Manning
Subject: NuttyNat Nonsense

You were right. NuttyNat is stupid!

From: Shelley Manning – September 4, 2013 – 10:14 AM
To: Renee Greene
Subject: Re: NuttyNat Nonsense

Oh no, what happened?

From: Renee Greene – September 4, 2013 – 10:22 AM
To: Shelley Manning
Subject: Re: NuttyNat Nonsense

We went to "The Today Show." Because of 9/11, everyone has to sign in to security, show ID, give a blood sample, etc. It's strict. We go to check-in and the security guard asks her to sign in with her name and address. This is what transpires.

> Security Guard: Ma'am, I need you to sign in with your name and address please.

> Diva: I don't know.

> Security Guard: You don't know where you live?

> Diva: No. I have people for that.

Then she snapped her fingers and one of her six (six!) entourage members came forward and filled in the missing address.

From: Shelley Manning – September 4, 2013 – 10:28 AM
To: Renee Greene
Subject: Re: NuttyNat Nonsense

Another reason I HATE celebrities. I read once that the more keys you have, the less important you are. And vice versa. Donald Trump doesn't carry any keys because he has people to do everything for him. Whereas his building janitor has keys for every room in the building. Seems to me, Donny is the one mired in filth and shit which makes him low man on my totem pole of import.

From: Renee Greene – September 4, 2013 – 10:30 AM
To: Shelley Manning
Subject: Re: NuttyNat Nonsense

I love it! I miss these conversations. When can we talk?

From: Ashley Gordon – September 9, 2013 – 9:32 AM
To: Renee Greene
Subject: My apologies

Sorry I snapped at you when you called this morning. It's just that Greg and I were arguing when the phone rang because Siobhan....oh, I just can't say it.

From: Renee Greene – September 9, 2013 – 9:34 AM
To: Ashley Gordon
Subject: Re: My apologies

Oh, come on. What did my sweet angel do?

From: Ashley Gordon – September 9, 2013 – 9:36 AM
To: Renee Greene
Subject: Re: My apologies

She's no sweet angel. That's for sure. She...I am shuddering just thinking about it...she removed her diaper this morning and proceeded to fingerpaint all over the mattress and wall with her own feces.

From: Renee Greene – September 9, 2013 – 9:37 AM
To: Ashley Gordon
Subject: Re: My apologies

LOL! So she's a Poop Picasso.

From: Ashley Gordon – September 9, 2013 – 9:38 AM
To: Renee Greene
Subject: Re: My apologies

It's not funny!

From: Renee Greene – September 9, 2013 – 9:39 AM
To: Ashley Gordon
Subject: Re: My apologies

Oh, was her work rather shitty? HA! HA! HA! I really can't stop laughing.

From: Ashley Gordon – September 9, 2013 – 9:46 AM
To: Renee Greene
Subject: Re: My apologies

You and Greg. He just found it to be hilarious, too. And why would he be bothered? He gets to have a hearty laugh and then go to work. I'm the one who had to put on a surgical mask and gloves and clean it all up. Do you know how hard it is to get feces off of a wall?

Even with Greg working at a paint company and knowing that we have the highest quality paint to withstand stains and dirt, it's still not easy getting it all off.

And the mattress. I could go on about the mattress. I just had to throw it out. There's no way to clean it. It's not like I can put it in the washing machine. No, this is decidedly not funny.

From: Renee Greene – September 9, 2013 – 9:49 AM
To: Ashley Gordon
Subject: Re: My apologies

You're right. It doesn't sound funny or fun. I'm sorry. I'd offer to help but I'm swamped at work right now.

From: Ashley Gordon – September 9, 2013 – 9:51 AM
To: Renee Greene
Subject: Re: My apologies

That's just what Greg said. No, I did it. Everything's clean but now I need to run to the baby store and buy a new mattress. I'll call you later.

From: Renee Greene – September 9, 2013 – 9:52 AM
To: PBCupLover
Subject: Fwd: Re: My apologies

See below. I can't stop laughing.

From: PBCupLover – September 9, 2013 – 9:53 AM
To: Renee Greene
Subject: Re: Fwd: Re: My apologies

That sounds awful. I can't believe you don't have more sympathy for her.

From: Renee Greene – September 9, 2013 – 9:54 AM
To: PBCupLover
Subject: Re: Fwd: Re: My apologies

You're laughing too, aren't you?

From: PBCupLover – September 9, 2013 – 9:56 AM
To: Renee Greene
Subject: Re: Fwd: Re: My apologies

YES! I fell out of my chair in hysterics. While I do feel sorry for Ashley, just the thought of her wiping smeared shit off her walls is comic gold...or brown. Makes my crappy day look pretty good.

From: Renee Greene – September 9, 2013 – 9:58 AM
To: PBCupLover
Subject: Re: Fwd: Re: My apologies

Why is your day crappy? (And good pun!)

From: PBCupLover – September 9, 2013 – 10:00 AM
To: Renee Greene
Subject: Re: Fwd: Re: My apologies

Just the normal crap with William and the Board of Directors. I've got to go. I'll see you at home tonight.

CHAPTER 9: MAKE IT STOP!

From: Mark Finlay – September 13, 2013 – 11:30 AM
To: Renee Greene
Subject: Make it stop!

I don't know what to do. Cass keeps calling and emailing me. Every time I think about responding, I can feel the bile rising up in my chest. I just want to make it stop.

From: Renee Greene – September 13, 2013 – 11:31 AM
To: Mark Finlay
Subject: Re: Make it stop!

If you really want to make it stop, sick Shelley on her. She'll set her straight. ;)

From: Mark Finlay – September 13, 2013 – 11:32 AM
To: Renee Greene
Subject: Re: Make it stop!

That's actually not a bad idea.

From: Renee Greene – September 13, 2013 – 11:32 AM
To: Mark Finlay
Subject: Re: Make it stop!

I was just joking.

From: Mark Finlay – September 13, 2013 – 11:34 AM
To: Renee Greene
Subject: Re: Make it stop!

I'm half joking, too. I'm sure she knows all of the details already.
Even though you promised not to say anything, I'm sure you told her
anyway.

From: Renee Greene – September 13, 2013 – 11:38 AM
To: Mark Finlay
Subject: Re: Make it stop!

Hey now. Not all of the women in your life are liars. I have not told
her anything you did not want me to. Actually, I've barely spoken to
her lately. She just seems so busy in her new life. But that's neither
here nor there right now.

From: Mark Finlay – September 13, 2013 – 11:40 AM
To: Renee Greene
Subject: Re: Make it stop!

I didn't mean to imply that you were ANYTHING like Cass. I just
know how you girls like to gossip.

From: Renee Greene – September 13, 2013 – 11:43 AM
To: Mark Finlay
Subject: Re: Make it stop!

Gossip is one thing Mark. But you and your happiness is something
totally different. Seriously, you want me to ask Shelley to tell
Cassidy to leave you alone?

From: Mark Finlay – September 13, 2013 – 11:43 AM
To: Renee Greene
Subject: Re: Make it stop!

Okay.

From: Renee Greene – September 13, 2013 – 11:47 AM
To: Mark Finlay
Subject: Re: Make it stop!

Okay. I've been meaning to ask - and apologies if I'm overstepping my bounds here - did you get the ring back?

From: Mark Finlay – September 13, 2013 – 11:51 AM
To: Renee Greene
Subject: Re: Make it stop!

Damn! I hadn't even thought about that.

From: Renee Greene – September 13, 2013 – 11:52 AM
To: Mark Finlay
Subject: Re: Make it stop!

Well, I think you should ask for it back. Why should she get to keep it?

From: Mark Finlay – September 13, 2013 – 11:55 AM
To: Renee Greene
Subject: Re: Make it stop!

Honestly, I don't want it. What am I going to do with it? It's not like I could give it to someone else. It's not like I'm ever going to meet someone else.

From: Renee Greene – September 13, 2013 – 12:01 PM
To: Mark Finlay
Subject: Re: Make it stop!

Oy! You sound like me in my pre-Ethan days. "I'm never going to meet anyone…no one is ever going to love me…whine…whine." (That was supposed to make you laugh!)

I know it's only been a few months, but you will meet someone else. But let's not get ahead of ourselves. You spent a lot of time and money on that ring and I don't think she deserves to keep it.

From: Mark Finlay – September 13, 2013 – 12:03 PM
To: Renee Greene
Subject: Re: Make it stop!

This is all too much. I don't want to think about any of this stuff or make any rash decisions right now. I need to think through all of the options and ramifications.

From: Renee Greene – September 13, 2013 – 12:04 PM
To: Mark Finlay
Subject: Re: Make it stop!

Okay, friend. I'll call you tomorrow.

From: Renee Greene – September 13, 2013 – 12:10 PM
To: Shelley Manning
Subject: Your talents needed

Hold onto your hat. Your unique and special talent of telling it like it is, not holding back and laying it all on the line is now needed. Mark is giving you the green light to – wait for it – tell Cassidy (or should I say cassidy) to leave him alone.

From: Shelley Manning – September 13, 2013 – 8:32 PM
To: Renee Greene
Subject: Re: Your talents needed

Finally Finlay is understanding the value that I can bring to our friendship. Glad he's wised up and is ready to give that bitch what she deserves – a message from this bitch. Don't you worry. I will take care of it.

From: Renee Greene – September 13, 2013 – 8:35 PM
To: Shelley Manning
Subject: Re: Your talents needed

I'm confident your brand of justice will be just what is needed to remedy this situation. Please don't forget to bcc me.

From: Shelley Manning – September 13, 2013 – 9:15 PM
To: Renee Greene
Subject: Re: Your talents needed

Okay. Will fire off an appropriately-worded email tomorrow morning. Prepare to be dazzled with my rhetoric.

From: Renee Greene – September 13, 2013 – 9:18 PM
To: Shelley Manning
Subject: Re: Your talents needed

I'm just impressed you used the word "rhetoric" appropriately.

From: Shelley Manning – September 13, 2013 – 9:20 PM
To: Renee Greene
Subject: Re: Your talents needed

Watch it. Once I'm on a roll, it will be just as easy for me to fire off a rhetoric-filled email to you, too. Mwah! Mwah!

From: Shelley Manning – September 14, 2013 – 8:49 AM
To: cassidy
Bcc: Renee Greene
Subject: Back off bitch!

Cassidy: Consider this your official cease and desist letter. In other words, back the fuck off. Mark doesn't want to see you, hear from you or think about you anymore. But he wants his ring back. You have three days to return it to Renee's office in Century City between the hours of 9 am and 5 pm. Don't make me ask you twice.

From there, you can take your lying, cat-loving, lower-case-letter-typing, skinny ass out of our sight. None of us ever want to see or hear from you again and that includes forwards of stupid cat videos. That's all.

From: Mark Finlay – September 15, 2013 – 1:13 PM
To: Renee Greene
Subject: Re: Make it stop!

I've given it some more thought and I don't want the ring back. Let her keep it. I hope every time she looks at it, she feels like crap. I just want all of this to be over so I can move on.

From: Renee Greene – September 15, 2013 – 1:15 PM
To: Mark Finlay
Subject: Re: Make it stop!

Uh oh! Too late. She actually returned it to my office today.

From: Mark Finlay – September 15, 2013 – 1:16 PM
To: Renee Greene
Subject: Re: Make it stop!

What? She gave you back the ring? How? Why?

From: Renee Greene – September 15, 2013 – 1:18 PM
To: Mark Finlay
Subject: Re: Make it stop!

Yeah. Shelley sent her the "kiss off" email and told her to return the ring pronto to me so you wouldn't have to see her.

From: Mark Finlay – September 15, 2013 – 1:19 PM
To: Renee Greene
Subject: Re: Make it stop!

What?!? Shelley sent her an email?

From: Renee Greene – September 15, 2013 – 1:20 PM
To: Mark Finlay
Subject: Re: Make it stop!

You told me that you wanted Shelley to handle telling her to leave you alone.

From: Mark Finlay – September 15, 2013 – 1:22 PM
To: Renee Greene
Subject: Re: Make it stop!

I told you I didn't want to think about it right now. Shit! What did Shelley say? How did Cass respond?

From: Renee Greene – September 15, 2013 – 1:23 PM
To: Mark Finlay
Subject: Fwd: Back off bitch!

Cassidy: Consider this your official cease and desist letter. In other words, back the fuck off. Mark doesn't want to see you, hear from you or think about you anymore. But he wants his ring back. You have three days to return it to Renee's office in Century City between the hours of 9 am and 5 pm. Don't make me ask you twice.
From there, you can take your lying, cat-loving, lower-case-letter-typing, skinny ass out of our sight. None of us ever want to see or hear from you again and that includes forwards of stupid cat videos. That's all.

From: Mark Finlay – September 15, 2013 – 1:26 PM
To: Renee Greene
Subject: Re: Make it stop!

Shit! Cass must be so despondent right now.

From: Renee Greene – September 15, 2013 – 1:28 PM
To: Mark Finlay
Subject: Re: Make it stop!

Who cares about her?!? Oh, no. You still care about her.

From: Mark Finlay – September 15, 2013 – 1:32 PM
To: Renee Greene
Subject: Re: Make it stop!

Well, I was going to marry her and have children with her and grow old with her.

From: Renee Greene – September 15, 2013 – 1:34 PM
To: Mark Finlay
Subject: Re: Make it stop!

Yeah, and she tossed it all out the window for a stupid fling with a movie star. That should tell you everything you need to know.

From: Mark Finlay – September 15, 2013 – 1:35 PM
To: Renee Greene
Subject: Re: Make it stop!

I can't just turn off my feelings.

From: Renee Greene – September 15, 2013 – 1:40 PM
To: Mark Finlay
Subject: Re: Make it stop!

I'm not suggesting you turn them off, Mark. But I am suggesting that you put your feelings ahead of hers this time. She certainly put hers ahead of yours. She totally betrayed you and doesn't deserve the wonderful person you are.

From: Mark Finlay – September 15, 2013 – 1:41 PM
To: Renee Greene
Subject: Re: Make it stop!

I just can't deal with this right now.

From: Renee Greene – September 15, 2013 – 1:42 PM
To: Mark Finlay
Subject: Re: Make it stop!

Meet me tonight for dinner or a drink or something. Let's talk about this.

From: Mark Finlay – September 15, 2013 – 1:43 PM
To: Renee Greene
Subject: Re: Make it stop!

I just need some space. I'll call you in a few days.

From: Renee Greene – September 15, 2013 – 2:02 PM
To: Shelley Manning
Subject: Rings and regrets

FYI...I told Mark that you got the ring back from Cassidy and he's having regrets about sicking you on her. He's pretty upset and thinking that Cassidy is upset. Just be warned that he may reach out to you to talk about it. I may reach out to you, too. Are you around tonight to talk?

From: cassidy – September 15, 2013 – 3:52 PM
To: Mark Finlay
Subject: i still love you

i got your message loud & clear. at least i got shellys message loud and clear. i wont bother you again. for what its worth, i really am sorry i hurt you. please don't tell shelly i emailed you again for the last time.

From: Mark Finlay – September 15, 2013 – 3:54 PM
To: cassidy
Subject: Re: i still love you

I didn't ask her to email you. And I didn't want you to have to return the ring.

From: cassidy – September 15, 2013 – 3:55 PM
To: Mark Finlay
Subject: Re: i still love you

maybe i can come by this week to pick up the rest of my stuff and we can talk.

From: Mark Finlay – September 15, 2013 – 3:56 PM
To: cassidy
Subject: Re: i still love you

Okay. I'll call you later.

From: cassidy – September 16, 2013 – 10:32 AM
To: Mark Finlay
Subject: wonderful

last night was wonderful. want to get dinner at bamboo garden tonight?

From: Mark Finlay – September 16, 2013 – 10:34 AM
To: Renee Greene
Subject: Fwd: wonderful

I screwed up. Cassidy and I hooked up last night.

From: Renee Greene – September 16, 2013 – 12:32 PM
To: Mark Finlay
Subject: Re: Fwd: wonderful

What!?!? You didn't screw "up" you "screwed" her!

How the hell did that happen?

From: Mark Finlay – September 16, 2013 – 1:13 PM
To: Renee Greene
Subject: Re: Fwd: wonderful

She came by to pick up some of her stuff from my place. And before
I knew it, we were…you know.

From: Renee Greene – September 16, 2013 – 1:15 PM
To: Mark Finlay
Subject: Re: Fwd: wonderful

Oh, Mark. I do know how easy it is to fall back into old patterns.

From: Mark Finlay – September 16, 2013 – 1:21 PM
To: Renee Greene
Subject: Re: Fwd: wonderful

While we were together, all of the old feelings came back to me and I
missed her. I missed holding her and the sound of her laugh. It felt
like the way things were...before. But when we finished and were
just lying there in bed, all I could think about was whether she laid in
his arms afterward.

From: Renee Greene – September 16, 2013 – 1:24 PM
To: Mark Finlay
Subject: Re: Fwd: wonderful

Ugh! That's the worst. But do you want to get back together with
her? I thought you decided you weren't right for each other.

From: Mark Finlay – September 16, 2013 – 1:29 PM
To: Renee Greene
Subject: Re: Fwd: wonderful

I don't know. It's all so confusing. On one hand, I don't know how I can trust her. There's a part of me that hates her for what she did to me...to us. But there's a part of me that still loves her.

From: Renee Greene – September 16, 2013 – 1:34 PM
To: Mark Finlay
Subject: Re: Fwd: wonderful

I hope you don't take this the wrong way, but you're a guy and when it comes to beautiful blondes, guys tend to think with something other than their brains. Is it possible that you are mistaking love for attraction?

From: Mark Finlay – September 16, 2013 – 1:37 PM
To: Renee Greene
Subject: Re: Fwd: wonderful

It's more than just sex. I truly believe that part of me still loves her. I don't know how to turn that off.

From: Renee Greene – September 16, 2013 – 1:39 PM
To: Mark Finlay
Subject: Re: Fwd: wonderful

Do you want my advice or are you just venting/using me as a sounding board?

From: Mark Finlay – September 16, 2013 – 1:40 PM
To: Renee Greene
Subject: Re: Fwd: wonderful

That's a strange question.

From: Renee Greene – September 16, 2013 – 1:45 PM
To: Mark Finlay
Subject: Re: Fwd: wonderful

Ethan and I have had this argument many times. Apparently, I bring
home all sorts of problems and talk about them. He tries to find a
solution when all I really want is for him to listen to me. He says it's
a woman thing. Not that I'm comparing you to a woman. But I just
want to make sure I understand what you want from me.

From: Mark Finlay – September 16, 2013 – 1:46 PM
To: Renee Greene
Subject: Re: Fwd: wonderful

I want your advice.

From: Renee Greene – September 16, 2013 – 1:51 PM
To: Mark Finlay
Subject: Re: Fwd: wonderful

First thing, you need to not see her anymore. Tell her that you made
a mistake and that you don't want to get back together. Second, if
she has any more stuff at your place, you give it to me and I'll get it
to her. Third, you need to grieve. I don't mean to sound harsh, but it
is over. Once you grieve, you'll be ready to move on.

From: Mark Finlay – September 16, 2013 – 1:56 PM
To: Renee Greene
Subject: Re: Fwd: wonderful

You're right. All of this is right. I will email her now. She still has a
few things at my place. I'll give them to you and tell her.

From: Renee Greene – September 16, 2013 – 1:58 PM
To: Mark Finlay
Subject: Re: Fwd: wonderful

I know this is hard, Mark. It's the worst. But it's got to be done. It's the only way.

From: Mark Finlay – September 16, 2013 – 2:00 PM
To: cassidy
Bcc: Renee Greene
Subject: Re: wonderful

Last night was a mistake.

From: cassidy – September 16, 2013 – 5:02 PM
To: Mark Finlay
Bcc: Renee Greene
Subject: Re: wonderful

i dont understand. i thought we were getting back together.

From: Mark Finlay – September 16, 2013 – 5:13 PM
To: cassidy
Bcc: Renee Greene
Subject: Re: wonderful

I'm sorry if I led you to believe we could pick up where we once had been. I don't think I should see you anymore.

From: cassidy – September 16, 2013 – 5:15 PM
To: Mark Finlay
Bcc: Renee Greene
Subject: Re: wonderful

dont say that. we are so good together. you cant deny it.

From: Renee Greene – September 16, 2013 – 5:15 PM
To: Mark Finlay
Subject: Re: wonderful

Stay strong!

From: Mark Finlay – September 16, 2013 – 5:22 PM
To: cassidy
Bcc: Renee Greene
Subject: Re: wonderful

We were good together. But that was the past. We don't have a future. I'm giving the last of your stuff to Renee. You can call her to arrange to get it. Please don't call or email me anymore. I'm sorry that it has to be this way, but it's for the best. Take care of yourself, Cass.

From: cassidy – September 16, 2013 – 5:24 PM
To: Mark Finlay
Bcc: Renee Greene
Subject: Re: wonderful

maybe you just need a bit of time. i will call you next week.

From: Renee Greene – September 16, 2013 – 5:25 PM
To: Mark Finlay
Subject: Re: wonderful

Stay strong! You're doing great!

From: Mark Finlay – September 16, 2013 – 5:27 PM
To: cassidy
Bcc: Renee Greene
Subject: Re: wonderful

I don't need any time. I just need to move on with my life. And I can't do that if you're still around.

From: cassidy – September 16, 2013 – 5:28 PM
To: Mark Finlay
Bcc: Renee Greene
Subject: Re: wonderful

dont give up on me.

From: Mark Finlay – September 16, 2013 – 5:29 PM
To: cassidy
Bcc: Renee Greene
Subject: Re: wonderful

You gave up on us!

From: cassidy – September 16, 2013 – 5:30 PM
To: Mark Finlay
Bcc: Renee Greene
Subject: Re: wonderful

im sorry. is this about what your friends will think?

From: Mark Finlay – September 16, 2013 – 5:35 PM
To: cassidy
Bcc: Renee Greene
Subject: Re: wonderful

This has nothing to do with what my friends or anyone else will think. This has to do with whether I can look at myself in the mirror and not feel like a fool and look at you and not feel complete betrayal.

From: cassidy – September 16, 2013 – 5:39 PM
To: Mark Finlay
Bcc: Renee Greene
Subject: Re: wonderful

im sorry. i messed up. it will never happen again. why cant you forgive me?

From: Mark Finlay – September 16, 2013 – 5:42 PM
To: cassidy
Bcc: Renee Greene
Subject: Re: wonderful

I just can't. Goodbye, Cass.

From: Renee Greene – September 16, 2013 – 5:45 PM
To: Mark Finlay
Subject: Re: wonderful

I know how hard that must have been. We are all here for you. Let us know what we can do for you.

From: Mark Finlay – September 16, 2013 – 5:46 PM
To: Renee Greene
Subject: Re: wonderful

Thanks. I'll call you later this week.

From: cassidy – September 16, 2013 – 8:02 PM
To: Renee Greene
Subject: your help

renee, i know you probably dont want to talk to me or help me but im asking for it anyway. i think mark wants to get back together with me but is worried about what you and shelley will think. i know i hurt him and im sorry for that. it wont happen again. can you talk to him for me. maybe you can convince him to give me another chance.

From: Renee Greene – September 16, 2013 – 9:04 PM
To: Shelley Manning
Subject: Fwd: your help

Ay yay yay! See below. So Mark and Cassidy hooked up last night. She went there to get some stuff and before he knew it, they fell back into old patterns and back into bed. He thinks he still loves her but knows he can't trust her or be with her.

He bcc'd me on his "it's over" emails while I secretly gave him encouragement to break it off with her for good. Now she's emailing me asking for *my* help to get them back together. As I said, ay yay yay!

From: Shelley Manning – September 17, 2013 – 8:22 AM
To: Renee Greene
Subject: Re: Fwd: your help

I thought I told her to leave us all alone! Well, you're right. She can't be trusted and he has to stay broken up with her. I know Finlay's a nice guy and probably doesn't want to hurt her even though she doesn't deserve any mercy.

But I'm kind of surprised that he would shift the blame onto us; that the reason he won't take her back is because of what *we* would think. He needs to grow a pair and tell her the reason he won't take her back is because she's a lying, cheating whore.

From: Renee Greene – September 17, 2013 – 9:12 AM
To: Shelley Manning
Subject: Re: Fwd: your help

Get this. He never said that to her. In fact, she suggested that we were the ones holding him back from getting back together with her.

From: Shelley Manning – September 17, 2013 – 10:31 AM
To: Renee Greene
Subject: Re: Fwd: your help

That conniving bitch. She's trying to manipulate you into being her advocate.

From: Renee Greene – September 17, 2013 – 10:37 AM
To: Shelley Manning
Subject: Re: Fwd: your help

I was so caught up in the awkwardness of her asking for my help when I'm helping Mark, I didn't even see that. She's a lot smarter than I had given her credit for. If Mark hadn't copied me on those emails, I might have believed that was true. I see how hard he's aching and wants to get to a happy place.

From: Shelley Manning – September 17, 2013 – 10:41 AM
To: Renee Greene
Subject: Re: Fwd: your help

Well he's not getting back together with her if I have anything to say about it. The little respect I have for Finlay would be gone if he went back to that tramp.

From: Renee Greene – September 17, 2013 – 10:44 AM
To: Shelley Manning
Subject: Re: Fwd: your help

I must say I would be disappointed too if he got back together with her. He deserves to be with someone who loves him and cherishes him.

From: Shelley Manning – September 17, 2013 – 10:47 AM
To: Renee Greene
Subject: Re: Fwd: your help

He deserves someone who doesn't fuck someone behind his back and then gets caught on camera for the world to see. How humiliating.

From: Renee Greene – September 17, 2013 – 10:49 AM
To: Shelley Manning
Subject: Re: Fwd: your help

Agreed! Now I just need to think of a response to her.

From: Shelley Manning – September 17, 2013 – 10:50 AM
To: Renee Greene
Subject: Re: Fwd: your help

I'll gladly handle it.

From: Renee Greene – September 17, 2013 – 10:51 AM
To: Shelley Manning
Subject: Re: Fwd: your help

No! I will respond. I just need some time to craft the right message.

From: Shelley Manning – September 17, 2013 – 10:52 AM
To: Renee Greene
Subject: Re: Fwd: your help

Don't forget to bcc me!

From: Renee Greene – September 17, 2013 – 10:53 AM
To: Shelley Manning
Subject: Re: Fwd: your help

Oh, you know I won't.

From: Shelley Manning – September 17, 2013 – 10:54 AM
To: Renee Greene
Subject: Re: Fwd: your help

You won't bcc me or you won't forget?

From: Renee Greene – September 17, 2013 – 10:54 AM
To: Shelley Manning
Subject: Re: Fwd: your help

I won't forget!

From: Shelley Manning – September 17, 2013 – 10:54 AM
To: Renee Greene
Subject: Re: Fwd: your help

Good girl. Mwah! Mwah!

From: Renee Greene – September 17, 2013 – 12:43 PM
To: cassidy
Bcc: Shelley Manning
Subject: Re: your help

Cassidy: I can appreciate that you still care for Mark and want a chance to make amends. But I can't help you.

I don't like you. I don't like how you betrayed the trust of my dear, dear friend and broke his heart. And I don't like how you tried to manipulate me into helping you by making it sound like I was the reason he didn't want to get back together with you. (Mark bcc'd me on his email exchange with you. So I know what you said and I know what he said.)

I will have the rest of your stuff tomorrow and will leave it at the front desk of my office. You remember how to get here. It's where you returned the engagement ring Mark spent hours researching/shopping for so he could make sure to get just the right one because that's the kind of thoughtful, generous and loving man he is. The kind of man you don't deserve.

Please don't make this harder or more awkward. If you really care for Mark, leave him alone so he can move on and find happiness.

From: Shelley Manning – September 17, 2013 – 12:50 PM
To: Renee Greene
Cc: cassidy
Subject: Re: your help

Couldn't have said it better myself, unless I threw in a few expletives and profanity-laden insults to that lying bitch.

From: Renee Greene – September 17, 2013 – 12:52 PM
To: Shelley Manning
Subject: Re: your help

You realize that once again you didn't remove Cassidy from a cc on an email.

From: Shelley Manning – September 17, 2013 – 12:55 PM
To: Renee Greene
Subject: Re: your help

Oh yes, I realize that. I did that on purpose. I wanted to let her know that I'm well aware of everything going on.

From: Renee Greene – September 17, 2013 – 12:56 PM
To: Shelley Manning
Subject: Re: your help

Putting the fear of God in her, huh?

From: Shelley Manning – September 17, 2013 – 12:56 PM
To: Renee Greene
Subject: Re: your help

You know that's right.

From: Renee Greene – September 17, 2013 – 12:57 PM
To: Shelley Manning
Subject: Re: your help

And always causing trouble.

From: Shelley Manning – September 17, 2013 – 12:57 PM
To: Renee Greene
Subject: Re: your help

You know that's right, too. Mwah! Mwah!

From: cassidy – September 17, 2013 – 3:34 PM
To: Renee Greene
Cc: Shelley Manning
Subject: Re: your help

ill come by tomorrow afternoon.

CHAPTER 10: WEDDING PLANNING

From: PBCupLover – September 21, 2013 – 2:13 PM
To: Renee Greene
Subject: What the hell?

Why did a UPS truck just unload 4 enormous shipping boxes from Zappos? This stuff barely fits in the apartment. I know you love shoes, but this is ridiculous!

From: Renee Greene – September 21, 2013 – 2:17 PM
To: PBCupLover
Subject: Re: What the hell?

Wow! That was fast. I thought they wouldn't arrive until Monday. Just doing some shoe shopping for the wedding. I'm just running the last of my Saturday errands. Be home soon. XO

From: PBCupLover – September 21, 2013 – 2:19 PM
To: Renee Greene
Subject: Re: What the hell?

You bought all of these shoes - there must be 20 pairs of them - for the wedding? Planning some award-show-style wardrobe changes throughout the night? Don't answer that! It's like the ring is on the finger and all common sense is out the window.

From: Renee Greene – September 21, 2013 – 2:26 PM
To: PBCupLover
Subject: Re: What the hell?

Calm down! There are only 18 pairs of shoes in those four boxes. Now before you get your boxers in a twist, I'm just kidding. Well, I'm not kidding about the number of shoes. There really are 18 pairs. But I am kidding about keeping them all. You're a guy so you don't "get" shoes. It's hard to find the perfect pair of heels that aren't too high or too low, that are the right color and style, and you can wear all night long.

So I ordered every pair online that looked like even a remote possibility. I need to try them on and pick the one that's the perfect glass slipper for my fairy tale. Then I just return the rest. Free shipping and free returns. So stop hyperventilating. I know what I'm doing.

From: PBCupLover – September 21, 2013 – 2:29 PM
To: Renee Greene
Subject: Re: What the hell?

All right then. Carry on.

From: Renee Greene – September 21, 2013 – 2:31 PM
To: PBCupLover
Subject: Re: What the hell?

That's all. No apology for jumping to conclusions and overreacting?

From: PBCupLover – September 21, 2013 – 2:35 PM
To: Renee Greene
Subject: Re: What the hell?

Considering all of the deposits I've been putting down these past few weeks for a photographer, videographer, florist, caterer, venue, etc., I figured it wasn't that big of a leap to think you were spending more…again.

From: Renee Greene – September 21, 2013 – 2:39 PM
To: PBCupLover
Subject: Re: What the hell?

You're the one who didn't want to let my parents pay for the wedding. They generously offered to foot the bill for everything. YOU declined, remember?

From: PBCupLover – September 21, 2013 – 2:41 PM
To: Renee Greene
Subject: Re: What the hell?

If your parents are paying, then I may not get what I want. And I have specific interests here.

From: Renee Greene – September 21, 2013 – 2:44 PM
To: PBCupLover
Subject: Re: What the hell?

Specific interests, my ass. Everytime I try to talk with you about these things, you say, "Whatever you want." The only thing you've taken an interest in is the food and the cake. Figures! I've heard of Bridezilla before, but Groomzilla?

From: PBCupLover – September 21, 2013 – 2:45 PM
To: Renee Greene
Subject: Re: What the hell?

I can't tell if you are really mad at me.

From: Renee Greene – September 21, 2013 – 2:46 PM
To: PBCupLover
Subject: Re: What the hell?

Of course not. I'm literally shaking my head and laughing as I wait in the line at the drycleaners.

From: PBCupLover – September 21, 2013 – 2:48 PM
To: Renee Greene
Subject: Re: What the hell?

Good. I just want this to be a great day for us and that means letting you have everything you want and letting me have a peanut butter cup groom's cake.

From: Renee Greene – September 21, 2013 – 2:52 PM
To: PBCupLover
Subject: Re: What the hell?

I know that, Babe. I want this to be a great day for us too. And I am being cost conscious. It's lucky for you that I am a consumate PR professional with experience planning major events and great contacts within the industry for discounts galore. We don't need to hire a wedding planner. We've got one in me.

From: PBCupLover – September 21, 2013 – 2:56 PM
To: Renee Greene
Subject: Re: What the hell?

I'm thrilled to save the money on a wedding planner and appreciate your efforts to save us some dough. But I don't want this stressing you out. No use saving on a wedding planner only to need a mediator, therapist or masseuse later.

From: Renee Greene – September 21, 2013 – 2:59 PM
To: PBCupLover
Subject: Re: What the hell?

Ha! Ha! I can pretty much guarantee a mediator and therapist won't be needed. But a massage sounds mighty nice. Be home soon so you can rub my aching shoulders.

From: PBCupLover – September 21, 2013 – 3:01 PM
To: Renee Greene
Subject: Re: What the hell?

I'd be happy to help but I think you're going to be too busy trying on shoes.

From: Renee Greene – September 21, 2013 – 3:03 PM
To: PBCupLover
Subject: Re: What the hell?

I totally forgot about all of those beautiful shoes. Squee! See you soon!

From: Renee Greene – September 26, 2013 – 1:12 PM
To: Mark Finlay
Subject: I'm here

Hi there. Just wanted to let you know that I'm here if you need anything or want to talk.

From: Mark Finlay – September 26, 2013 – 1:18 PM
To: Renee Greene
Subject: Re: I'm here

I know and thanks. I just don't get it. I don't lie and pretend to be into a girl just to get her into bed. I call back and pay attention. Yet I'm single…for the minute I'm not single, I get cheated on.

From: Renee Greene – September 26, 2013 – 1:20 PM
To: Mark Finlay
Subject: Re: I'm here

You're right. It's totally not fair. You're one of the good guys and you deserve far better.

From: Mark Finlay – September 26, 2013 – 1:22 PM
To: Renee Greene
Subject: Re: I'm here

I'm just going to focus on work. At least there I know that my efforts pay off.

From: Renee Greene – September 26, 2013 – 1:26 PM
To: Mark Finlay
Subject: Re: I'm here

Don't give up on love, Mark. I know you're hurting right now. Really, really hurting. But I promise you that it's out there. Things will get set right. I just know it.

From: Mark Finlay – September 26, 2013 – 1:28 PM
To: Renee Greene
Subject: Re: I'm here

Thanks, Renee. Let's grab some lunch next week. Okay?

From: Renee Greene – September 26, 2013 – 1:29 PM
To: Mark Finlay
Subject: Re: I'm here

Absolutely! Hang in there!

CHAPTER 11: CHANGES

From: Renee Greene – October 3, 2013 – 11:02 AM
To: PBCupLover, Shelley Manning, Mark Finlay, Ashley Gordon
Subject: QUIT MY JOB!

Holy shit! I just quit my job. I am literally shaking and freaking out. Why is no one picking up their phones? Someone, anyone, call me. Please!!!

From: PBCupLover – October 3, 2013 – 11:14 AM
To: Renee Greene
Subject: Re: QUIT MY JOB!

I just tried your cell but there's no answer. You're probably on the phone with Shelley. Call me at the office. Don't panic. Everything is going to be fine.

From: Renee Greene – October 3, 2013 – 11:17 AM
To: PBCupLover
Subject: Re: QUIT MY JOB!

Why is your frickin' voice mail picking up again? Where are you?

From: PBCupLover – October 3, 2013 – 11:19 AM
To: Renee Greene
Subject: Re: QUIT MY JOB!

I just got on a conference call that I can't get off of. I will be at least 40 more minutes. Are you okay? What happened?

From: Renee Greene – October 3, 2013 – 11:32 AM
To: PBCupLover
Subject: Re: QUIT MY JOB!

Neil called me into his office and told me that we just won a new global assignment and I was being assigned as the lead for the U.S. The client is Monsanto. You know, the company I believe to be greedy bastards who are poisoning the food supply with their genetically modified seeds?

I explained to him – calmly and rationally, of course – that I just couldn't in good conscience work on this account. I have a huge objection to what they do and what I think are the terrible effects their products are having on our food, the environment etc. He – calmly and rationally, of course – told me this was the single biggest account the agency has ever won and that it's not a choice. I was being assigned to this account.

I said, "Is this because of Ethan's behavior at your July 4th party?" He said no, but I'm not so sure. ;) I once again – calmly and rationally, yada yada yada – explained that I couldn't be effective on their behalf. He – VERY bluntly and rudely – said, "Renee! Either roll with it or get rolled over!" So, I walked out.

From: PBCupLover – October 3, 2013 – 11:35 AM
To: Renee Greene
Subject: Re: QUIT MY JOB!

It's going to be okay. You can only shoot an arrow by pulling it backward. This is just going to launch you into something even better.

From: Renee Greene – October 3, 2013 – 11:36 AM
To: PBCupLover
Subject: Re: QUIT MY JOB!

OMG! Could you be any more perfect...or annoying?

From: PBCupLover – October 3, 2013 – 11:37 AM
To: Renee Greene
Subject: Re: QUIT MY JOB!

Perfect? Why, thank you! Annoying? WTF!

From: Renee Greene – October 3, 2013 – 11:42 AM
To: PBCupLover
Subject: Re: QUIT MY JOB!

You just always have these perfect expressions for every occasion when all I really want is to feel sorry for myself and have you feel sorry for me, too.

From: PBCupLover – October 3, 2013 – 11:45 AM
To: Renee Greene
Subject: Re: QUIT MY JOB!

Well, I don't feel sorry for you. You can let this get you down or you can pick yourself up and get motivated to move ahead.

From: Renee Greene – October 3, 2013 – 11:46 AM
To: PBCupLover
Subject: Re: QUIT MY JOB!

Again, could you be any more perfect...or annoying?

From: PBCupLover – October 3, 2013 – 11:49 AM
To: Renee Greene
Subject: Re: QUIT MY JOB!

Fine. You're right. This is the worst thing that could ever have happened to you. Your life is a mess. I don't know how you will be able to get yourself out of bed each morning. Maybe we should just stay in bed all day tomorrow...together.

From: Renee Greene – October 3, 2013 – 11:51 AM
To: PBCupLover
Subject: Re: QUIT MY JOB!

Leave it to you to find a way to turn this around and make it about having sex.

From: PBCupLover – October 3, 2013 – 11:53 AM
To: Renee Greene
Subject: Re: QUIT MY JOB!

What can I say? I have been told I couldn't be any more perfect.

From: Renee Greene – October 3, 2013 – 11:54 AM
To: PBCupLover
Subject: Re: QUIT MY JOB!

I wasn't suggesting that comment was an example of you being perfect.

From: PBCupLover – October 3, 2013 – 11:55 AM
To: Renee Greene
Subject: Re: QUIT MY JOB!

Trying to cheer you up with a day in bed certainly doesn't qualify as annoying, does it?

From: Renee Greene – October 3, 2013 – 11:56 AM
To: PBCupLover
Subject: Re: QUIT MY JOB!

Nah. I'm just teasing.

From: PBCupLover – October 3, 2013 – 11:58 AM
To: Renee Greene
Subject: Re: QUIT MY JOB!

Aha. You must be feeling better. I was going to bring a can of frosting home, but looks as though you don't need that.

From: Renee Greene – October 3, 2013 – 12:00 PM
To: PBCupLover
Subject: Re: QUIT MY JOB!

That truly would be the perfect – and not in the least bit annoying – thing you could do.

From: PBCupLover – October 3, 2013 – 12:00 PM
To: Renee Greene
Subject: Re: QUIT MY JOB!

Consider it done.

From: Renee Greene – October 3, 2013 – 12:01 PM
To: PBCupLover
Subject: Re: QUIT MY JOB!

But did I make a huge mistake?

From: PBCupLover – October 3, 2013 – 12:14 PM
To: Renee Greene
Subject: Re: QUIT MY JOB!

When I was in business school, there was this snooty girl who had done her undergrad at Yale. She walked around like she was better than everyone because she went to an Ivy League college. Big deal!

We had this crotchety old statistics professor who would go off on tangents a lot. (Kind of like you, my love.) One day he started ranting about morals and ethics. He explained that you might be asked to do things in your career that are ethical but against your personal morals. At some point, if you can't reconcile the two, you just need to walk away, like you did (for which I'm so proud of you!).

This girl raised her hand and asked (I am just shaking my head again thinking about it), "do you mean like go into another room?" We all just whipped our heads around looking at her like we couldn't believe what a dipshit she was. She had never heard that expression before. Dr. Lowell just snapped at her. "No! I mean you quit!" What an idiot.

At least you not only have the right morals but the street smarts and savvy to know you'll be okay.

From: Renee Greene – October 3, 2013 – 12:15 PM
To: PBCupLover
Subject: Re: QUIT MY JOB!

At this moment, I'm not so sure.

From: PBCupLover – October 3, 2013 – 12:19 PM
To: Renee Greene
Subject: Re: QUIT MY JOB!

I am! See you at home later where we'll talk all of this through. In the meantime, I'm proud of you, Babe, for standing up for your convictions. I love you.

From: Skye@skyesloane.com – October 3, 2013 – 12:31 PM
To: Renee Greene
Subject: I'm with you!

I just tried calling your cell phone, but you didn't pick up. I imagine you are talking with your fiancé right now. Anyway, I wanted you to know that I think what you did is just amazing. Quitting your job because of this is incredibly noble. So much so, that I just quit, too.

I don't know if you have a plan of where you're going to go next, but I'm sure you do. You're so organized and on top of things. Just know, I want to go with you. So call me.

From: Renee Greene – October 3, 2013 – 3:32 PM
To: PBCupLover, Shelley Manning, Mark Finlay, Ashley Gordon
Subject: Re: QUIT MY JOB!

Sorry all. I know I told you all to call me and then I didn't answer my phone.
I initially panicked and felt like I needed to talk, but then panicked and realized I needed some time to sort all of this out. What the hell was I thinking quitting my job before having another job...and in this shitty economy?

And not only that, but now I have another person to worry about. Skinny Skye pulled a "Jerry Maguire" and walked out after what I did in solidarity with me. She doesn't have a job lined up either but was certain that I knew what the hell I was doing. What the hell am I doing?!?

From: Ashley Gordon – October 3, 2013 – 3:54 PM
To: PBCupLover, Shelley Manning, Mark Finlay, Renee Greene
Subject: Re: QUIT MY JOB!

You're not picking up. Hope you are doing okay. Call me when you get this message. I'm here. Or come over if you want to. Just do me a favor and DON'T ring the doorbell. I don't know if Siobhan will be napping and I don't want to risk waking her up. She's been teething and if I can get her down, then I want to let her sleep.

From: Renee Greene – October 3, 2013 – 3:59 PM
To: Shelley Manning
Subject: HR Question

I'm freaking out! I gather you're busy because you haven't emailed me or called me back. I could really use your help. Can you see what legal rights I have with regard to my job?

From: CarrHR@carr.agency.com – October 3, 2013 – 4:02 PM
To: Renee Greene
Subject: Exit materials

Renee: I'm emailing to let you know that pursuant to your dismissal from The Carr Agency, a packet of exit materials is being mailed to the home address we have on file for you. In addition, you will receive a check for your last days worked and your severance pay - two weeks for each year of service to the agency. Please don't hesitate to contact me with any questions.

From: Karen Corley – October 3, 2013 – 4:11 PM
To: Renee Greene
Subject: On your side

Renee: I'm now emailing you from my personal account because I didn't want there to be a record of this email on the agency's servers. I'm SO sorry to hear that you have left. You were truly my favorite account person. You were always so respectful and appreciative of the job we have in HR. We all know why you quit and support you in your decision to stand up for what you believe in.

But if you quit, you don't get severance pay. So I coded your exit as a dismissal so you're now eligible for both severance and unemployment benefits. Knowing you, you won't be unemployed for long, so you probably won't even need to file.

But I figured the extra months of severance you've earned would help ease the financial burden until you figure something out.

Please don't share this email with anyone at the agency, or I'll get fired and will wish I had a severance package of my own. Wishing you the absolute best of luck!

Best, Karen

From: Renee Greene – October 3, 2013 – 4:18 PM
To: Karen Corley
Subject: Re: On your side

Karen: You are a rock star. Thank you! Thank you! First, thank you for saying such nice things about me. I truly did (or should I still say do) appreciate all of your efforts in making sure everyone in the office is doing the right thing and getting all they deserve.

And more importantly, thank you for looking out for me. While being "dismissed" – which is a total euphemism for being sacked – is not something I ever wanted on my permanent record (that sounds so elementary school), it never occurred to me why that was so much better than quitting.

I'm so grateful to you for continuing to look out for me. Wishing you the best as well!

From: Renee Greene – October 3, 2013 – 4:31 PM
To: PBCupLover
Subject: Fwd: On your side

So, turns out that while I thought I quit, I was officially sacked. Turns out that if HR codes it as a "dismissal" instead of a resignation, I get severance and am eligible for unemployment if needed. But my severance is more than 4 months pay.

From: PBCupLover – October 3, 2013 – 4:56 PM
To: Renee Greene
Subject: Re: Fwd: On your side

It's like that Seinfeld episode where George gets six months severance and decides to have "The Summer of George." Just don't squander it like he did. Now you have the financial cushion to start your own agency. We'll talk about it tonight.

From: Renee Greene – October 3, 2013 – 5:02 PM
To: Skye@skyesloane.com
Subject: Re: I'm with you!

Wow! I'm just speechless. Sorry now that I didn't give a Jerry Maguire-style, inspiring, compelling and erratic speech upon my departure. I'm so flattered by this, Skye. I'm also just horrified to say that I don't have a plan in place. I was blindsided by Neil and made a rash decision without thinking through the next steps. I'm sorry. So so sorry. I'm sure if you call Neil, he'll give you your job back. Just chalk it up to youthful idealism. He loves that stuff.

From: Skye@skyesloane.com – October 3, 2013 – 5:08 PM
To: Renee Greene
Subject: Re: I'm with you!

I'll be okay. My cousin owns a temp agency and I'm sure I can just get some work until you find a job at an agency. In fact, I'm sure he can get you some work too. When you do get an agency job, please keep me in mind. I would love to work with you.

From: Renee Greene – October 3, 2013 – 5:10 PM
To: Skye@skyesloane.com
Subject: Re: I'm with you!

Thanks, Skye. I'll be in touch. Good luck to you.

From: Renee Greene – October 3, 2013 – 5:12 PM
To: PBCupLover
Subject: Fwd: Re: I'm with you!

Oh, great. Skinny Skye's cousin owns a temp agency and she thinks he can find me some work. My problems are solved.

From: PBCupLover – October 3, 2013 – 5:14 PM
To: Renee Greene
Subject: Re: Fwd: Re: I'm with you!

Calm down, Babe. I'll be home soon and we'll figure this all out.

From: Shelley Manning – October 6, 2013 – 9:34 AM
To: Renee Greene
Subject: Re: HR Question

Sorry it's taken me so long to get back to you, Sweetie. I'm sure you've already got a plan all figured out. But I checked into things like you asked.

Under California's Labor Code, without an employment contract, you are considered an "at-will" employee. This means, with a few exceptions that you don't meet, that the employer may terminate the employment relationship at any time, with or without cause.

Even if you sued, you probably wouldn't win. Your case is classified as a dismissal according to the agency paperwork, but any testimony will contradict that and prove you quit in protest over an assignment.

From: Renee Greene – October 6, 2013 – 9:37 AM
To: Shelley Manning
Subject: Re: HR Question

Thanks for looking into it. The next stage in my seven stages of grief looks like depression. Watch out!

From: Shelley Manning – October 6, 2013 – 9:39 AM
To: Renee Greene
Subject: Re: HR Question

No need to be depressed! Just gloss over that and move onto stage 5 – "the upward turn." You'll enjoy it much more.

From: Renee Greene – October 6, 2013 – 9:42 AM
To: Shelley Manning
Subject: Re: HR Question

Since when do you know the stages of grief? What have you been mourning? Moving away from me – your best friend? The loss of your virginity? A missed sale on Kate Spade bags?

From: Shelley Manning – October 6, 2013 – 9:48 AM
To: Renee Greene
Subject: Re: HR Question

Ha-larious, Sweetie! I don't miss you that much (j/k), I certainly don't miss my lack of sexual experience, and I prefer Michael Kors. But seriously, you would be surprised what you pick up when you are involved in recruiting/HR. But I see the "upward turn" in your near future. You've certainly still got your sense of humor.

From: Renee Greene – October 6, 2013 – 9:51 AM
To: Shelley Manning
Subject: Re: HR Question

A sense of humor and penchant for frosting will only take me so far in the PR world. I may need to stay depressed for a little while.

From: Shelley Manning – October 6, 2013 – 9:52 AM
To: Renee Greene
Subject: Re: HR Question

Alright. Mourn away. Just don't wallow for too long.

From: Renee Greene – October 7, 2013 – 1:32 AM
To: Ashley Gordon
Subject: Are you up?

I figured you would be up right now, likely doing a feeding or something.

From: Ashley Gordon – October 7, 2013 – 1:38 AM
To: Renee Greene
Subject: Re: Are you up?

Good guess. Sorry to hear about your job troubles. That really
stinks. If you want to see how the other half live, just come hang out
here tomorrow. One day at home with Siobhan and you'll be
motivated to get a new job. It's a very long day with her when it's
just the two of you. I love her, but I think I need more adult
conversation. I'm thinking of going back to work.

From: Renee Greene – October 7, 2013 – 1:41 AM
To: Ashley Gordon
Subject: Re: Are you up?

Really? I know it's been tough adjusting to this new lifestyle, but I
thought you wanted to be home to raise her.

From: Ashley Gordon – October 7, 2013 – 1:43 AM
To: Renee Greene
Subject: Re: Are you up?

I do want to be with her during these formative years, but at the same
time, I need more.

From: Renee Greene – October 7, 2013 – 1:46 AM
To: Ashley Gordon
Subject: Re: Are you up?

Is there some way to find an outlet for yourself that doesn't involve
going back to work? You were always complaining about how
stressful it was and that nobody worked as hard as you did or
appreciated your contributions.

From: Ashley Gordon – October 7, 2013 – 1:48 AM
To: Renee Greene
Subject: Re: Are you up?

Well, motherhood is certainly stressful, I'm working hard and not feeling all that appreciated. At least I would get paid.

From: Renee Greene – October 7, 2013 – 1:52 AM
To: Ashley Gordon
Subject: Re: Are you up?

It's probably hard to see it now, but I'm sure that Siobhan is going to love that you were home with her, teaching her, caring for her, etc. And I know Greg is appreciative of all you do for the family.

From: Ashley Gordon – October 7, 2013 – 1:54 AM
To: Renee Greene
Subject: Re: Are you up?

Don't tell Shelley (or Greg) but I'm still taking the meds the doctor prescribed after Siobhan was born.

From: Renee Greene – October 7, 2013 – 1:59 AM
To: Ashley Gordon
Subject: Re: Are you up?

There's nothing wrong with needing some help dealing with all of the massive changes going on in your life and body. You don't need to keep secrets from Greg. From Shelley, I understand. But not Greg. He's your husband. He should know if things are hard for you. And I'm not convinced that going back to work is the solution. I think you need to fully embrace motherhood.

From: Ashley Gordon – October 7, 2013 – 2:02 AM
To: Renee Greene
Subject: Re: Are you up?

I fully embrace motherhood daily…actually several times a day with the breastfeeding.

From: Renee Greene – October 7, 2013 – 2:08 AM
To: Ashley Gordon
Subject: Re: Are you up?

Ha. That was funny. What I mean is that you need to accept that this is your life now. No more complaining. No more whining. No more wishing it was different. I don't mean to get all "tough love" on you, but that's what you need. THIS IS YOUR LIFE.

And honestly, Ashley, you are damn lucky to have it. You know I love you, but you've got to snap out of this funk and realize how good you have things. You have a husband that loves and adores you. You have a beautiful, healthy baby that is cute as a button and sweet as pie. You don't *have* to work and endure the stress of the corporate world. You *GET* to stay home and mold a young mind, bond with your child, etc.

From: Ashley Gordon – October 7, 2013 – 2:11 AM
To: Renee Greene
Subject: Re: Are you up?

If we're talking "tough love" here then you're the one who should stop complaining and whining. All you've done for the past few days is host a pity party of one over a lost job.

From: Renee Greene – October 7, 2013 – 2:15 AM
To: Ashley Gordon
Subject: Re: Are you up?

You're kidding me, right? I'm not allowed a few days to feel sorry for myself to have been forced out of a job that I loved and that I was really good at. You're comparing that to you not dealing with the fact that there is a little girl who needs you and loves you?

From: Ashley Gordon – October 7, 2013 – 2:17 AM
To: Renee Greene
Subject: Re: Are you up?

Well, that little girl needs to be burped now. So I need to go.

From: Renee Greene – October 8, 2013 – 10:08 AM
To: Ashley Gordon
Subject: I'm sorry

I know I left you a voicemail, but I wanted to say again that I'm sorry. I was out of line yesterday. Between the stress and the sleeplessness, I said some things I shouldn't have. Forgive me. Let's talk.

From: Ashley Gordon – October 8, 2013 – 11:21 AM
To: Renee Greene
Subject: Re: I'm sorry

I'm sorry too. I'll call you later.

From: Renee Greene – October 9, 2013 – 9:27 AM
To: Shelley Manning
Subject: Can we talk here?

I'm doing my best Joan Rivers impersonation. Can we talk here? Ashley and I got in a huge fight the other day and I'm just feeling...lost.

From: Renee Greene – October 11, 2013 – 9:48 AM
To: Shelley Manning
Subject: Where's the love?

I'm freaking out and you haven't emailed me back in two days. Are you there? Or are you too busy hanging out with Amber to support your best friend in her time of need?

From: Shelley Manning – October 12, 2013 – 9:02 AM
To: Renee Greene
Subject: Re: Where's the love?

It's only nine in the morning and I've already received 3 missed calls and 2 emails from you. I'm going to need more coffee.

From: Renee Greene – October 12, 2013 – 9:09 AM
To: Shelley Manning
Subject: Re: Where's the love?

Maybe you and Amber could go grab a cup, since you seem to be so fond of spending time with her these days.

From: Shelley Manning – October 12, 2013 – 9:13 AM
To: Renee Greene
Subject: Re: Where's the love?

Relax, will ya? Jeez. I don't email or call for two days and suddenly I'm on your shit list.

From: Renee Greene – October 12, 2013 – 9:17 AM
To: Shelley Manning
Subject: Re: Where's the love?

As you would say, "damn straight." I'm totally lost and need you and you can't be bothered to call me back. I suppose Amber is your new best friend now and you're too busy with her to care what happens to me.

From: Shelley Manning – October 12, 2013 – 9:20 AM
To: Renee Greene
Subject: Re: Where's the love?

Give me a break, Renee. Can we continue this conversation another time...say never?!?!

From: Renee Greene – October 14, 2013 – 10:13 AM
To: Shelley Manning
Subject: Re: Where's the love?

Hey. I thought I would be the first to reach out. I know how hard it is for you to apologize, so I'm being the bigger person here by saying that I forgive you.

From: Shelley Manning – October 14, 2013 – 10:15 AM
To: Renee Greene
Subject: Re: Where's the love?

Forgive me? Forget you! If anyone should be apologizing, it's you!

From: Renee Greene – October 14, 2013 – 10:19 AM
To: Shelley Manning
Subject: Re: Where's the love?

Are you serious? I've already lost my job (and my identity for that matter) and you're making me feel bad for being upset that I'm losing you, too?

From: Shelley Manning – October 14, 2013 – 10:23 AM
To: Renee Greene
Subject: Re: Where's the love?

You're not losing me! I am here for you and I always have and always will be. But honestly, Sweetie, I cannot continue to bear the weight of your world on my remarkably supple shoulders.

From: Renee Greene – October 14, 2013 – 10:27 AM
To: Shelley Manning
Subject: Re: Where's the love?

I'm not asking you to be my world. I just would hope that when I need you, you're there for me and not off gallivanting with your new buddy Amber. And lately, I don't feel like you've been there for me.

From: Shelley Manning – October 14, 2013 – 10:35 AM
To: Renee Greene
Subject: Re: Where's the love?

You're the most together person I know. You don't need me. You can manage on your own. If anyone's life is a struggle right now, it's me. Do you think it was easy to pick up and move thousands of miles away (for a man, no less!) to a place where I knew no one, have no workplace, no friends, no support?

I need to focus on building a life here and I need your support for once. I need you to stop making me feel guilty for trying to be happy here. I need you to stop feeling so insecure about a new friend I've made. And I need the time to move on a bit. I want to be there for you, but if I'm always solving your problems, I won't solve my own and move on.

From: Shelley Manning – October 14, 2013 – 2:43 PM
To: Renee Greene
Subject: Re: Where's the love?

Radio silence! Don't you have anything to say?

From: Renee Greene – October 14, 2013 – 3:02 PM
To: Shelley Manning
Subject: Re: Where's the love?

I'm so sorry, Shel. You've never mentioned that anything has been difficult. I just assumed you were fine.

From: Shelley Manning – October 14, 2013 – 3:12 PM
To: Renee Greene
Subject: Re: Where's the love?

Well, I'm not. It's been really hard and hearing you bitch and moan all of the time over shit that is so easily resolved, just doesn't help matters.

From: Renee Greene – October 14, 2013 – 3:14 PM
To: Shelley Manning
Subject: Re: Where's the love?

Why haven't you said anything to me about this before?

From: Shelley Manning – October 14, 2013 – 3:16 PM
To: Renee Greene
Subject: Re: Where's the love?

Not everyone wears their heart (and every emotion they have) on their sleeve.

From: Renee Greene – October 14, 2013 – 3:18 PM
To: Shelley Manning
Subject: Re: Where's the love?

Oh, Shel! I've been an awful and selfish friend. I'm sorry. So, so sorry. What can I do for you?

From: Shelley Manning – October 14, 2013 – 3:21 PM
To: Renee Greene
Subject: Re: Where's the love?

You're not awful and you're not selfish. Just be understanding when I don't call you back right away with the perfect advice for your crisis de jour.

From: Renee Greene – October 14, 2013 – 3:22 PM
To: Shelley Manning
Subject: Re: Where's the love?

I can do that. What else?

From: Shelley Manning – October 14, 2013 – 3:23 PM
To: Renee Greene
Subject: Re: Where's the love?

That's it. Just cut me some slack, okay?

From: Renee Greene – October 14, 2013 – 3:23 PM
To: Shelley Manning
Subject: Re: Where's the love?

I will. Again, I'm so sorry.

From: Shelley Manning – October 14, 2013 – 3:24 PM
To: Renee Greene
Subject: Re: Where's the love?

Okay. Stop apologizing.

From: Renee Greene – October 14, 2013 – 3:25 PM
To: Shelley Manning
Subject: Re: Where's the love?

Is Nick aware that all is not blissful on your end?

From: Shelley Manning – October 14, 2013 – 3:28 PM
To: Renee Greene
Subject: Re: Where's the love?

He is. Even though I'm not a complainer, he can sense when days are rough. He's being supportive about things and introducing me to friends, encouraging me to get out more and meet people, etc.

From: Renee Greene – October 14, 2013 – 3:29 PM
To: Shelley Manning
Subject: Re: Where's the love?

That's good!

From: Shelley Manning – October 14, 2013 – 3:32 PM
To: Renee Greene
Subject: Re: Where's the love?

Listen, I have to run. I'm taking a yoga class and it starts in 30. But I will call you when I'm back and we can talk through your identity crisis.

From: Renee Greene – October 14, 2013 – 3:33 PM
To: Shelley Manning
Subject: Re: Where's the love?

Yoga?

From: Shelley Manning – October 14, 2013 – 3:36 PM
To: Renee Greene
Subject: Re: Where's the love?

Yeah, yeah. I know. I've always mocked those pretzels for their bendable poses. But I'm finding it relaxing and it seems to be a good way to make some new friends up here.

From: Renee Greene – October 14, 2013 – 3:38 PM
To: Shelley Manning
Subject: Re: Where's the love?

Okay, Gumby. But no need to call – unless you just want to chat or talk about you. I'm going to address this on my own.

From: Shelley Manning – October 14, 2013 – 3:40 PM
To: Renee Greene
Subject: Re: Where's the love?

Gumby?!? If that wasn't so damn funny, I would be offended. Gumby it is.

From: Renee Greene – October 14, 2013 – 3:41 PM
To: Shelley Manning
Subject: Re: Where's the love?

Enjoy!

From: Shelley Manning – October 14, 2013 – 3:31 PM
To: Renee Greene
Subject: Re: Where's the love?

Talk soon, sweetie. Mwah! Mwah!

From: Shelley Manning – October 16, 2013 – 4:25 PM
To: Renee Greene
Subject: Smooth like velvet!

Sweetie, my sincerest thanks. You didn't need to do that. But I'm oh-so-glad that you did. Might need to hit yoga a few extra times to work off the calories, but that taste of home was well worth it.

From: Renee Greene – October 16, 2013 – 4:31 PM
To: Shelley Manning
Subject: Re: Smooth like velvet!

I'm so glad the cupcakes – my effort to "smooth" things over – arrived safely to you. I figured if you are missing home and I can't fly up to see you, then red velvet goodness would be the next best thing.

From: Shelley Manning – October 16, 2013 – 4:34 PM
To: Renee Greene
Subject: Re: Smooth like velvet!

It is a close second, for sure. Thanks again! How are you doing today? Feeling better?

From: Renee Greene – October 16, 2013 – 4:42 PM
To: Shelley Manning
Subject: Re: Smooth like velvet!

I've decided to embrace the identity crisis. So for Ethan's work Halloween party, that's what I'm going as – an identity crisis. I'm going to wear nametags with 50 different names all over my body.

From: Shelley Manning – October 16, 2013 – 4:44 PM
To: Renee Greene
Subject: Re: Smooth like velvet!

Ha-larious! Gotta run. Hitting the yoga studio again. Will try calling you later.

From: Renee Greene – October 16, 2013 – 4:45 PM
To: Shelley Manning
Subject: Re: Smooth like velvet!

Okay, Gumby. Bend away. ;)

From: Renee Greene – October 20, 2013 – 11:31 AM
To: Shelley Manning
Subject: Gumby a go-go or Gumby a no-no?

How is yoga going?

From: Shelley Manning – October 20, 2013 – 11:34 AM
To: Renee Greene
Subject: Re: Gumby a go-go or Gumby a no-no?

While I'm grateful for this morning's class which reminded me to take care of myself and BREATHE, I seem to forget that lesson soon after leaving the mat.

From: Renee Greene – October 20, 2013 – 11:37 AM
To: Shelley Manning
Subject: Re: Gumby a go-go or Gumby a no-no?

Things are better when they are allowed to breathe. Have a glass of red wine and prove me right.

From: Shelley Manning – October 20, 2013 – 11:38 AM
To: Renee Greene
Subject: Re: Gumby a go-go or Gumby a no-no?

Namaste!

From: Renee Greene – October 20, 2013 – 11:38 AM
To: Shelley Manning
Subject: Re: Gumby a go-go or Gumby a no-no?

What does that even mean?

From: Shelley Manning – October 20, 2013 – 11:39 AM
To: Renee Greene
Subject: Re: Gumby a go-go or Gumby a no-no?

I bow to the spirit within you.

From: Renee Greene – October 20, 2013 – 11:43 AM
To: Shelley Manning
Subject: Re: Gumby a go-go or Gumby a no-no?

Aha! Well, I appreciate that you are bowing down to me like the goddess I am. (Boy, that's something you would say!) And knowing you, you'll be bowing down to some "spirits" soon.

From: Shelley Manning – October 20, 2013 – 11:44 AM
To: Renee Greene
Subject: Re: Gumby a go-go or Gumby a no-no?

Indeed!

From: Shelley Manning – October 22, 2013 – 9:04 AM
To: PBCupLover
Subject: Tell the truth

I'm sure Renee has filled you in on all of our recent "discussions." She's now being super chipper and overly concerned about me and my life. Tell the truth, how is she doing?

From: PBCupLover – October 22, 2013 – 10:31 AM
To: Shelley Manning
Subject: Re: Tell the truth

Honestly, not great. She really defined herself with that job for a long time and now she's not really sure who she is. She could use some cheering up, for sure. I know you've got a lot on your plate and are focusing on yourself – as you should be. But if you've got the chance, check in with her. I know she'll appreciate it.

From: Shelley Manning – October 22, 2013 – 10:33 AM
To: PBCupLover
Subject: Re: Tell the truth

I know just what to do!

From: Shelley Manning – October 25, 2013 – 11:32 AM
To: Renee Greene
Subject: Chocolates!

Hey there. Just wanted to see if you got the chocolates we sent to cheer you up?

From: Renee Greene – October 25, 2013 – 11:34 AM
To: Shelley Manning
Subject: Re: Chocolates!

Yes, they arrived an hour ago but there's a bite taken out of each one.

From: Shelley Manning – October 25, 2013 – 11:36 AM
To: Renee Greene
Subject: Re: Chocolates!

I took a bite out of each one because I couldn't wait to share. Ha! Ha!

From: Renee Greene – October 25, 2013 – 11:38 AM
To: Shelley Manning
Subject: Re: Chocolates!

They are delicious. I've eaten half the box already.

From: Shelley Manning – October 25, 2013 – 11:41 AM
To: Renee Greene
Subject: Re: Chocolates!

Slow down! I know this has been a bit of a shock for you and a challenge, but you'll get through this. Chocolate is not the answer.

From: Renee Greene – October 25, 2013 – 11:43 AM
To: Shelley Manning
Subject: Re: Chocolates!

If it's not the answer, then why did you send them?

From: Shelley Manning – October 25, 2013 – 11:45 AM
To: Renee Greene
Subject: Re: Chocolates!

Okay smart ass, chocolate is the answer. But half a box before noon is not the answer.

From: Renee Greene – October 25, 2013 – 11:46 AM
To: Shelley Manning
Subject: Re: Chocolates!

Better to be a smart ass than a dumb ass.

From: Shelley Manning – October 25, 2013 – 11:48 AM
To: Renee Greene
Subject: Re: Chocolates!

This seems to be beyond your normal malaise. What's up?

From: Renee Greene – October 25, 2013 – 11:51 AM
To: Shelley Manning
Subject: Re: Chocolates!

I don't want to say. It was so nice of you to send the candy and I don't want you to feel bad.

From: Shelley Manning – October 25, 2013 – 11:54 AM
To: Renee Greene
Subject: Re: Chocolates!

I won't feel bad. Clearly all of this time off of work is turning your brain to mush. I don't have remorse or regrets, remember? So...

From: Renee Greene – October 25, 2013 – 11:56 AM
To: Shelley Manning
Subject: Re: Chocolates!

The only other time I've ever been fired is when I worked at the candy store when I was in high school. Eating the chocolates is just reminding me of being a failure.

From: Shelley Manning – October 25, 2013 – 11:58 AM
To: Renee Greene
Subject: Re: Chocolates!

First of all, you are not a failure. Second, take that piece of chocolate out of your mouth.

From: Renee Greene – October 25, 2013 – 11:59 AM
To: Shelley Manning
Subject: Re: Chocolates!

How did you know I was eating a piece of candy?

From: Shelley Manning – October 25, 2013 – 12:00 PM
To: Renee Greene
Subject: Re: Chocolates!

Because I am your best friend and I know you.

From: Renee Greene – October 25, 2013 – 12:00 PM
To: Shelley Manning
Subject: Re: Chocolates!

Okay. I spit it out.

From: Shelley Manning – October 25, 2013 – 12:01 PM
To: Renee Greene
Subject: Re: Chocolates!

No, you didn't.

From: Renee Greene – October 25, 2013 – 12:02 PM
To: Shelley Manning
Subject: Re: Chocolates!

Okay. I really did this time.

From: Shelley Manning – October 25, 2013 – 12:02 PM
To: Renee Greene
Subject: Re: Chocolates!

Good girl. Now tell me what happened with the candy store.

From: Renee Greene – October 25, 2013 – 12:09 PM
To: Shelley Manning
Subject: Re: Chocolates!

I had only been working there a few weeks. The owner was this heavy set, elderly Scandinavian woman named Wally. (Yes, *her* name was Wally.) I was in the front of the store and she was in the back room doing paperwork.

I went back to ask her a question and found her lying on the floor on her back. I panicked, started to freak out a bit and leaned over shaking her to see if she was conscious. She woke up startled and said she was just taking a nap.

I looked around the room and saw a chair and a couch, so I wondered why she was lying on the floor to sleep. She said she didn't think I was mature enough to handle the job and that she needed to let me go.

From: Shelley Manning – October 25, 2013 – 12:11 PM
To: Renee Greene
Subject: Re: Chocolates!

So she was sleeping on the floor instead of on the couch?

From: Renee Greene – October 25, 2013 – 12:13 PM
To: Shelley Manning
Subject: Re: Chocolates!

Exactly! I don't think it was a stretch for me to think that she was ill.

From: Shelley Manning – October 25, 2013 – 12:15 PM
To: Renee Greene
Subject: Re: Chocolates!

Sweetie, if I saw an old, fat lady lying on the ground, I would have thought the same thing, too. But I seem to recall you worked there for two summers, no?

From: Renee Greene – October 25, 2013 – 12:17 PM
To: Shelley Manning
Subject: Re: Chocolates!

She hired me back a few weeks later.

From: Shelley Manning – October 25, 2013 – 12:21 PM
To: Renee Greene
Subject: Re: Chocolates!

So the lesson isn't that you once got let go for "being a failure" as you call it. Rather, you were hired back because she realized she needed you.

From: Renee Greene – October 25, 2013 – 12:22 PM
To: Shelley Manning
Subject: Re: Chocolates!

I guess.

From: Shelley Manning – October 25, 2013 – 12:25 PM
To: Renee Greene
Subject: Re: Chocolates!

What do you mean, "I guess?" This is just further evidence that you were and still are an amazing, hard working, fantastic asset. So get that piece of chocolate out of your damn mouth.

From: Renee Greene – October 25, 2013 – 12:26 PM
To: Shelley Manning
Subject: Re: Chocolates!

How did you do that?

From: Shelley Manning – October 25, 2013 – 12:28 PM
To: Renee Greene
Subject: Re: Chocolates!

Stop questioning my abilities…and yours too. Would it cheer you up to hear that I was once fired from a job?

From: Renee Greene – October 25, 2013 – 12:30 PM
To: Shelley Manning
Subject: Re: Chocolates!

Really? Where was this?

From: Shelley Manning – October 25, 2013 – 12:32 PM
To: Renee Greene
Subject: Re: Chocolates!

I was doing an internship in the HR department at Coke in Atlanta.

From: Renee Greene – October 25, 2013 – 12:34 PM
To: Shelley Manning
Subject: Re: Chocolates!

You never told me you got fired from your internship at Coke. I thought it just ended because summer was over. Despite being unaware of this, my mind is already reeling at the possibilities. I could use a good laugh. Do tell.

From: Shelley Manning – October 25, 2013 – 12:41 PM
To: Renee Greene
Subject: Re: Chocolates!

No, I was asked to leave. It was 2001 and I was between my junior and senior years of college. My boss in the sales department was this rather bland looking middle aged man named Booker. He liked to go fishing and listen to cool jazz and country music. He was always going on and on about his equally bland-looking wife and their equally bland-looking children. He was BOR-ING! So much so, I called him...you guessed it...Boring Booker. (I wasn't as clever at nicknames as I am now).

One day he sneezed and I said, "You are sooooo good looking." (You know, from Seinfeld.) Well, Booker took this as a sign that I was interested in him. As if! He didn't make a move on me, thankfully. I must give him props for that. I am hard to resist. He just told his wife all about his desires who then told him that I had to go.

HR was called in and basically told me that I was too sexy for my boss to resist and in order to help him preserve his marriage, I was being fired. The injustice and sheer ridiculousness of it is what led me into HR, which eventually morphed into recruiting.

From: Renee Greene – October 25, 2013 – 12:45 PM
To: Shelley Manning
Subject: Re: Chocolates!

You got fired for being hot! That's just making me more depressed.
And honestly, I was thinking it would be more of a Monica
Lewinsky/Blue Dress-type story.

From: Shelley Manning – October 25, 2013 – 12:48 PM
To: Renee Greene
Subject: Re: Chocolates!

Sorry to disappoint. And I've always been hot, Sweetie, so no need
to be depressed about it now. I want you to put the chocolates away,
go take a shower ('cause I know you haven't done that yet today!)
and buck up. You hear me?

From: Renee Greene – October 25, 2013 – 12:50 PM
To: Shelley Manning
Subject: Re: Chocolates!

Yes, ma'am. Thanks, Shel. Love you!

CHAPTER 12: BIRTHDAY LOVE

From: Renee Greene – October 31, 2013 – 1:34 PM
To: Ashley Gordon
Subject: HAPPY BIRTHDAY SWEET ANGEL

Please give my sweet angel Siobhan a big hug and kiss from Auntie Renee and wish her the happiest of birthdays for me. Can't wait to see her to celebrate.

From: Ashley Gordon – October 31, 2013 – 3:45 PM
To: Renee Greene
Subject: Re: HAPPY BIRTHDAY SWEET ANGEL

Thanks, Renee. I can't believe she's already a year old.

From: Renee Greene – October 31, 2013 – 3:47 PM
To: Ashley Gordon
Subject: Re: HAPPY BIRTHDAY SWEET ANGEL

I know. Crazy, right? Has it just flown by?

From: Ashley Gordon – October 31, 2013 – 3:49 PM
To: Renee Greene
Subject: Re: HAPPY BIRTHDAY SWEET ANGEL

The days drag on, but the months have flown by.

From: Renee Greene – October 31, 2013 – 3:51 PM
To: Ashley Gordon
Subject: Re: HAPPY BIRTHDAY SWEET ANGEL

Hmm. That's interesting, but after babysitting her for a weekend, I can totally see that. We'll see you soon for her party.

From: Shelley Manning – October 31, 2013 – 7:02 PM
To: Ashley Gordon
Subject: Happy birthday to Siobhan

Hi, Ashley. Hope Siobhan has a great first birthday. Sorry Nick and I can't be there to help her celebrate. But hopefully you got the gift I sent.

From: Ashley Gordon – October 31, 2013 – 7:04 PM
To: Shelley Manning
Subject: Re: Happy birthday to Siobhan

Yes, we got the musical hand bells. She hasn't stopped ringing them.

From: Shelley Manning – October 31, 2013 – 7:06 PM
To: Ashley Gordon
Subject: Re: Happy birthday to Siobhan

Fantastic. She's already using and enjoying them. Give her a Mwah! Mwah! from me.

From: Shelley Manning – October 31, 2013 – 7:08 PM
To: Renee Greene
Subject: Fwd: Re: Happy birthday to Siobhan

I figured Ashley would "ring my bell" when she got them. Halarious!

From: Renee Greene – October 31, 2013 – 7:10 PM
To: Shelley Manning
Subject: Re: Fwd: Re: Happy birthday to Siobhan

You are wicked. What are you going to do next year to enliven Siobhan and madden Ashley?

From: Shelley Manning – October 31, 2013 – 7:13 PM
To: Renee Greene
Subject: Re: Fwd: Re: Happy birthday to Siobhan

Oh, I've got a whole list of passive/aggressive gifts that kids will love and parents will hate. Just wait until she's old enough for glitter! That shit gets everywhere.

From: Renee Greene – October 31, 2013 – 7:15 PM
To: Shelley Manning
Subject: Re: Fwd: Re: Happy birthday to Siobhan

You know she'll make some sort of "stripper" comment when you give Siobhan glitter.

From: Shelley Manning – October 31, 2013 – 7:16 PM
To: Renee Greene
Subject: Re: Fwd: Re: Happy birthday to Siobhan

Well, then that's just a nice bonus. Mwah! Mwah!

CHAPTER 13: LAUGHTER: THE BEST MEDICINE

From: Renee Greene – November 3, 2013 – 11:24 AM
To: Shelley Manning
Subject: Checking in

How are you?

From: Shelley Manning – November 3, 2013 – 11:25 AM
To: Renee Greene
Subject: Re: Checking in

I'm fine, Sweetie. What's up?

From: Renee Greene – November 3, 2013 – 11:26 AM
To: Shelley Manning
Subject: Re: Checking in

Nothing. I was just emailing to check in and see how you were doing.

From: Shelley Manning – November 3, 2013 – 11:27 AM
To: Renee Greene
Subject: Re: Checking in

I'm fine. Is that really all?

From: Renee Greene – November 3, 2013 – 11:31 AM
To: Shelley Manning
Subject: Re: Checking in

Yep. No interesting stories to tell. No crises to be solved. Just emailing because I was thinking of you and wanted to see how you were doing. This is all about you. Enjoy it. It likely won't last long.
;)

From: Shelley Manning – November 3, 2013 – 11:35 AM
To: Renee Greene
Subject: Re: Checking in

Thanks, Sweetie. Things are good. It's been a good week. I made some new friends – girlfriends – at the yoga studio. You'd like them. They are fun and don't take themselves too seriously. Only problem is that they've never had a mojito before. Looks like I'll be introducing them to the finer things in life this weekend.

From: Renee Greene – November 3, 2013 – 11:36 AM
To: Shelley Manning
Subject: Re: Checking in

More like corrupting them, I would say.

From: Shelley Manning – November 3, 2013 – 11:36 AM
To: Renee Greene
Subject: Re: Checking in

You say tomato, I say tomato.

From: Renee Greene – November 3, 2013 – 11:37 AM
To: Shelley Manning
Subject: Re: Checking in

That doesn't really translate well to email, does it?

From: Shelley Manning – November 3, 2013 – 11:37 AM
To: Renee Greene
Subject: Re: Checking in

No, but you get the gist.

From: Renee Greene – November 3, 2013 – 11:38 AM
To: Shelley Manning
Subject: Re: Checking in

I do and I miss you.

From: Shelley Manning – November 3, 2013 – 11:38 AM
To: Renee Greene
Subject: Re: Checking in

I can't really blame you. I'm pretty amazing.

From: Renee Greene – November 3, 2013 – 11:39 AM
To: Shelley Manning
Subject: Re: Checking in

LOL! You are. And comments like that just make me miss you more.

From: Shelley Manning – November 3, 2013 – 11:41 AM
To: Renee Greene
Subject: Re: Checking in

Again, I can't really blame you. However, I also can't really chat right now. I'm due in for a meeting. I'll call you later. Mwah! Mwah!

From: Shelley Manning – November 3, 2013 – 11:43 AM
To: PBCupLover
Subject: Do something!

Renee just emailed me to check in and see how I was doing. There's clearly something wrong with our girl. I suggest you do something…and toot sweet. Got it?

From: PBCupLover – November 3, 2013 – 11:45 AM
To: Shelley Manning
Subject: Re: Do something!

Got it. Thanks, Shelley.

From: PBCupLover – November 7, 2013 – 10:45 AM
To: Renee Greene
Subject: Lunch today?

Hey, babe. Thought you might want to come meet me for lunch today. I have a window of time between meetings and we could go somewhere nice and enjoy. Hop in the shower and come over.

From: Renee Greene – November 7, 2013 – 10:48 AM
To: PBCupLover
Subject: Re: Lunch today?

I just ate an entire cobbler.

From: PBCupLover – November 7, 2013 – 10:49 AM
To: Renee Greene
Subject: Re: Lunch today?

You ate a man who makes shoes?

From: Renee Greene – November 7, 2013 – 10:51 AM
To: PBCupLover
Subject: Re: Lunch today?

Yes. He was a bit leathery but still tasted good.

From: PBCupLover – November 7, 2013 – 10:53 AM
To: Renee Greene
Subject: Re: Lunch today?

At least you are keeping a sense of humor about things. Okay, let's plan on hanging out tonight when I get home. I love you.

From: PBCupLover – November 10, 2013 – 9:02 AM
To: Renee Greene
Subject: Pun fun, hun?

Okay, clearly you are still depressed about this whole job thing. But you need to get out of bed and figure out a plan. What better way to make that happen than with some pun fun, right hun?

From: Renee Greene – November 10, 2013 – 9:03 AM
To: PBCupLover
Subject: Re: Pun fun, hun?

UGH! I'm not ready to laugh.

From: PBCupLover – November 10, 2013 – 9:04 AM
To: Renee Greene
Subject: Re: Pun fun, hun?

Well, be prepared to. I've enlisted our favorite pun players to cheer you up.

From: PBCupLover – November 10, 2013 – 9:07 AM
To: Ashley Gordon, Mark Finlay, Shelley Manning
Subject: Pun fun for my hun

Renee needs our help. Bust out your best job loss related puns. Best one, with Renee as judge, wins a mojito at Flint's. Shelley, if you win, I owe you one on your next visit. Ready…go!

From: Ashley Gordon – November 10, 2013 – 10:02 AM
To: Renee Greene
Cc: Mark Finlay, Shelley Manning, PBCupLover
Subject: Fwd: Pun fun for my hun

The doctor got fired because he lacked "patience."

From: Mark Finlay – November 10, 2013 – 10:43 AM
To: Ashley Gordon
Cc: Shelley Manning, PBCupLover, Renee Greene
Subject: Re: Fwd: Pun fun for my hun

The orange juice factory worker got fired because he couldn't concentrate.

From: Shelley Manning – November 10, 2013 – 11:32 AM
To: Mark Finlay
Cc: Ashley Gordon, PBCupLover, Renee Greene
Subject: Re: Fwd: Pun fun for my hun

The frozen food factory worker got fresh and then got canned.

From: PBCupLover – November 10, 2013 – 11:35 AM
To: Shelley Manning
Cc: Ashley Gordon, Mark Finlay, Renee Greene
Subject: Re: Fwd: Pun fun for my hun

The butcher got fired because he backed into a meat grinder and got a little behind in his work.

From: Mark Finlay – November 10, 2013 – 11:41 AM
To: PBCupLover
Cc: Ashley Gordon, Shelley Manning, Renee Greene
Subject: Re: Fwd: Pun fun for my hun

The dairy worker got fired for getting in the whey.

From: Ashley Gordon – November 10, 2013 – 11:48 AM
To: Mark Finlay
Cc: PBCupLover, Shelley Manning, Renee Greene
Subject: Re: Fwd: Pun fun for my hun

The optician got fired for making a spectacle of himself.

From: Shelley Manning – November 10, 2013 – 11:53 AM
To: Ashley Gordon
Cc: Mark Finlay, PBCupLover, Renee Greene
Subject: Re: Fwd: Pun fun for my hun

The chef wanted to add some spice to his life but didn't have the thyme.

From: Ashley Gordon – November 10, 2013 – 11:59 AM
To: Shelley Manning
Cc: Mark Finlay, PBCupLover, Renee Greene
Subject: Re: Fwd: Pun fun for my hun

The tailor wasn't suited for the job.

From: PBCupLover – November 10, 2013 – 12:02 PM
To: Ashley Gordon
Cc: Mark Finlay, Shelley Manning, Renee Greene
Subject: Re: Fwd: Pun fun for my hun

The coffee shop worker got bored of the same old grind.

From: Mark Finlay – November 10, 2013 – 12:06 PM
To: PBCupLover
Cc: Ashley Gordon, Shelley Manning, Renee Greene
Subject: Re: Fwd: Pun fun for my hun

The muffler factory worker got fired for always being exhausted.

From: Shelley Manning – November 10, 2013 – 12:31 PM
To: Mark Finlay
Cc: Ashley Gordon, PBCupLover, Renee Greene
Subject: Re: Fwd: Pun fun for my hun

The masseuse got fired because he rubbed people the wrong way.

From: Renee Greene – November 10, 2013 – 12:33 PM
To: Shelley Manning
Subject: Re: Fwd: Pun fun for my hun

Why am I not surprised that all of your puns have sexual undertones?

From: Shelley Manning – November 10, 2013 – 12:36 PM
To: Renee Greene
Subject: Re: Fwd: Pun fun for my hun

Because I know what makes you laugh and I want to win. Love me some mojitos…and beating Finlay.

From: Renee Greene – November 10, 2013 – 12:38 PM
To: Shelley Manning
Subject: Re: Fwd: Pun fun for my hun

So far, you are in the lead. But I have a feeling there is more to come.

From: Shelley Manning – November 10, 2013 – 12:39 PM
To: Renee Greene
Subject: Re: Fwd: Pun fun for my hun

Now who's messages have sexual undertones?

From: Renee Greene – November 10, 2013 – 12:39 PM
To: Shelley Manning
Subject: Re: Fwd: Pun fun for my hun

LOL!

From: PBCupLover – November 10, 2013 – 1:12 PM
To: Shelley Manning
Cc: Ashley Gordon, Mark Finlay, Renee Greene
Subject: Re: Fwd: Pun fun for my hun

The deli worker got fired because no matter how he sliced it, he couldn't cut the mustard.

From: Ashley Gordon – November 10, 2013 – 1:49 PM
To: PBCupLover
Cc: Mark Finlay, Shelley Manning, Renee Greene
Subject: Re: Fwd: Pun fun for my hun

The plumber got fired because the work was too draining.

From: Mark Finlay – November 10, 2013 – 2:01 PM
To: Ashley Gordon
Cc: PBCupLover Shelley Manning, Renee Greene
Subject: Re: Fwd: Pun fun for my hun

The lumberjack got axed because he couldn't hack it.

From: Ashley Gordon – November 10, 2013 – 2:18 PM
To: Mark Finlay
Cc: PBCupLover, Shelley Manning, Renee Greene
Subject: Re: Fwd: Pun fun for my hun

The shoe factory worker didn't fit in.

From: PBCupLover – November 10, 2013 – 3:39 PM
To: Ashley Gordon
Cc: Mark Finlay, Shelley Manning, Renee Greene
Subject: Re: Fwd: Pun fun for my hun

The fisherman couldn't live on his net income.

From: Mark Finlay – November 10, 2013 – 3:41 PM
To: PBCupLover
Cc: Ashley Gordon, Shelley Manning, Renee Greene
Subject: Re: Fwd: Pun fun for my hun

The musician got fired because he wasn't noteworthy.

From: Ashley Gordon – November 10, 2013 – 4:02 PM
To: Mark Finlay
Cc: PBCupLover, Shelley Manning, Renee Greene
Subject: Re: Fwd: Pun fun for my hun

The gym club worker wasn't fit for the job.

From: Shelley Manning – November 10, 2013 – 4:07 PM
To: Ashley Gordon
Cc: PBCupLover, Mark Finlay, Renee Greene
Subject: Re: Fwd: Pun fun for my hun

The historian got fired because there's no future in being a fucking historian!

From: Renee Greene – November 10, 2013 – 4:10 PM
To: Shelley Manning
Cc: PBCupLover, Mark Finlay, Ashley Gordon
Subject: Re: Fwd: Pun fun for my hun

Okay. Okay. Enough. I'm laughing so hard my side is starting to hurt.

From: PBCupLover – November 10, 2013 – 4:13 PM
To: Renee Greene
Cc: Ashley Gordon, Shelley Manning, Mark Finlay
Subject: Re: Fwd: Pun fun for my hun

Well done, everyone. Alright, Babe. Time for you to select a winner.

From: Renee Greene – November 10, 2013 – 4:19 PM
To: PBCupLover
Cc: Ashley Gordon, Shelley Manning, Mark Finlay
Subject: Re: Fwd: Pun fun for my hun

It's a tough call. They are all so funny in their own way. But if I have to choose one, I pick…Lumberjack.

From: PBCupLover – November 10, 2013 – 4:20 PM
To: Renee Greene
Cc: Ashley Gordon, Shelley Manning, Mark Finlay
Subject: Re: Fwd: Pun fun for my hun

Congrats, Mark. I owe you one mojito.

From: Mark Finlay – November 10, 2013 – 4:22 PM
To: PBCupLover
Cc: Ashley Gordon, Shelley Manning, Renee Greene
Subject: Re: Fwd: Pun fun for my hun

Really? I won! I never win anything. I'm stunned. Thanks.

From: Shelley Manning – November 10, 2013 – 5:03 PM
To: Renee Greene
Subject: Re: Fwd: Pun fun for my hun

Finlay? Really? That lumberjack shit was the funniest? I think this was rigged.

From: Renee Greene – November 10, 2013 – 5:05 PM
To: Shelley Manning
Subject: Re: Fwd: Pun fun for my hun

Don't be a poor sport. Your masseuse was a close second.

From: Shelley Manning – November 10, 2013 – 5:07 PM
To: Renee Greene
Subject: Re: Fwd: Pun fun for my hun

If I had offered you with a real massage, would that have tipped the scales in my favor?

From: Renee Greene – November 10, 2013 – 5:09 PM
To: Shelley Manning
Subject: Re: Fwd: Pun fun for my hun

Yes, that would have. Too bad you didn't think of bribery to begin with.

From: Shelley Manning – November 10, 2013 – 5:09 PM
To: Renee Greene
Subject: Re: Fwd: Pun fun for my hun

Next time.

From: Renee Greene – November 10, 2013 – 5:14 PM
To: Shelley Manning
Subject: Re: Fwd: Pun fun for my hun

Okay, the scales are now tipping from my lack of energy/movement (aside from lifting a spoon of frosting or a chocolate into my mouth) never mind the chocolate and frosting themselves. It's time to do something.

From: Shelley Manning – November 10, 2013 – 5:17 PM
To: Renee Greene
Subject: Re: Fwd: Pun fun for my hun

Yes! Been wanting to hear that for a long time. Get that fire going in your belly, get out there and kick some ass.

From: Renee Greene – November 10, 2013 – 5:18 PM
To: Shelley Manning
Subject: Re: Fwd: Pun fun for my hun

Thanks, Shel. Love you!

From: Renee Greene – November 10, 2013 – 6:02 PM
To: PBCupLover, Ashley Gordon, Shelley Manning, Mark Finlay
Subject: Thank you, thank you!

Thank you all! I'm so lucky to have an amazing fiancé to orchestrate all of this nonsense and a group of hilarious friends to feed the frenzy. There's nothing like having a group of close friends who can support you when things get tough, laugh with you when things get ridiculous, console you when you're down, and cajole you into doing things that they can see are good for you, but you are reluctant to embrace. I love you all.

From: Renee Greene – November 13, 2013 – 10:01 AM
To: Mark Finlay
Subject: HAPPY BIRTHDAY

HAPPY BIRTHDAY! Hope you are having a great day! If you don't already have plans, want to grab some dinner tonight?

From: Mark Finlay – November 13, 2013 – 2:04 PM
To: Renee Greene
Subject: Re: HAPPY BIRTHDAY

Thanks for the email, call, text and cookies. You're such a
thoughtful and caring friend. I'm just hanging out on my own
tonight. Not feeling like doing anything special. But I appreciate the
offer to take me out.

From: Renee Greene – November 13, 2013 – 2:10 PM
To: Mark Finlay
Subject: Re: HAPPY BIRTHDAY

This is going to be a GREAT year for you. I can just feel it. Big
hugs, my friend.

CHAPTER 14: GETTING CLOSE

From: Renee Greene – November 17, 2013 – 9:32 PM
To: Shelley Manning
Subject: Mock me!

I think I'm going to join a gym. Perhaps you've inspired me with your yoga efforts. It's possible. I'm hopeful this will help cure my depression. And maybe it's because I've eaten so much frosting, I can't button my pants. Regardless of my motives, feel free to mock me!

From: Shelley Manning – November 18, 2013 – 9:21 AM
To: Renee Greene
Subject: Re: Mock me!

Why would I mock you? I think that's a great idea. Go for it! Just don't tell Ashley.

From: Renee Greene – November 18, 2013 – 9:32 AM
To: Shelley Manning
Subject: Re: Mock me!

I just figured you would have something funny to say that would have me laughing so hard my stomach would feel as though I'm doing crunches and therefore getting a solid ab workout and then I wouldn't have to stuff myself into yoga pants after all.

From: Shelley Manning – November 18, 2013 – 9:34 AM
To: Renee Greene
Subject: Re: Mock me!

So you're basically asking me to do all of the work so you don't have to work out?

From: Renee Greene – November 18, 2013 – 9:36 AM
To: Shelley Manning
Subject: Re: Mock me!

Something like that. I suppose I just miss you tons. I know you've got stuff going on. Just call me later when you have time.

From: Renee Greene – November 24, 2013 – 7:43 PM
To: Shelley Manning
Subject: Ready for my "Close" up

Just tried you again. Sorry I missed you. In case you try to call back, just know we are 15 minutes out from seeing Glenn Close reprise her Broadway turn as Norma Desmond in Sunset Blvd. Ethan got tickets to cheer me up. As noted in my email subject line, I'm ready for my "Close" up. HA! HA!

From: Shelley Manning – November 24, 2013 – 7:45 PM
To: Renee Greene
Subject: Re: Ready for my "Close" up

I don't get the joke. :(

From: Renee Greene – November 24, 2013 – 10:16 PM
To: Shelley Manning
Subject: Re: Ready for my "Close" up

You never saw the 1950's movie classic, Sunset Blvd.? It's about this aging movie star who has dementia and is being arrested for murder. She thinks that all of the camera crews covering her arrest are really a film crew reviving her career.

She slinks down the staircase and utters the line, "I'm ready for my close up, Mr. Demille" into one of the news crew cameras. Since Glenn is playing the lead role, I was ready for my "Close" up. Get it now? Are you around tomorrow? Can we talk then? I miss you.

From: Shelley Manning – November 24, 2013 – 10:22 PM
To: Renee Greene
Subject: Re: Ready for my "Close" up

Aha! Quite clever. Shouldn't have doubted you. Enjoy the show!

From: Renee Greene – November 25, 2013 – 10:16 AM
To: Shelley Manning
Subject: Re: Ready for my "Close" up

Just tried you again. Do you ever have your ringer on or are you avoiding me? ;) Glenn had laryngitis. Can you believe it? We had to see her understudy. She was great, but not really what I was hoping for. Think we can talk by phone today?

From: Shelley Manning – November 25, 2013 – 10:22 AM
To: Renee Greene
Subject: Re: Ready for my "Close" up

So she wasn't Glenn Close but Glenn Adjacent?

From: Renee Greene – November 25, 2013 – 10:26 AM
To: Shelley Manning
Subject: Re: Ready for my "Close" up

Are you kidding me? You did not just think of that? Tell me that Nick thought of that? I did not think that you had that in you!

From: Shelley Manning – November 25, 2013 – 10:31 AM
To: Renee Greene
Subject: Re: Ready for my "Close" up

You didn't think I had Nick in me or that clever joke in me?

From: Renee Greene – November 25, 2013 – 10:35 AM
To: Shelley Manning
Subject: Re: Ready for my "Close" up

That smutty comeback is all you, you jezebel. But I did not expect that clever play on words. No offense.

From: Shelley Manning – November 25, 2013 – 10:40 AM
To: Renee Greene
Subject: Re: Ready for my "Close" up

No offense taken. And regarding who thought of it, "close" but no cigar. It was Amber. We're sitting at brunch right now and then have a day planned of shopping, pedicures, etc. I don't want to be rude by typing on my phone. Don't make this more than it is! I know how you think! Mwah! Mwah!

From: Renee Greene – November 25, 2013 – 10:41 AM
To: Shelley Manning
Subject: Re: Ready for my "Close" up

Okay. Have fun!

From: Renee Greene – November 25, 2013 – 10:42 AM
To: Ashley Gordon
Subject: Fwd: Re: Ready for my "Close" up

Amber Alert!

From: Ashley Gordon – November 25, 2013 – 12:02 PM
To: Renee Greene
Subject: Re: Fwd: Re: Ready for my "Close" up

As someone with a young child, don't joke about Amber Alerts. Admonishments aside, why am I just getting copied into the clever banter now? That was some seriously funny stuff. Listen to Shelley. (Can't believe I just wrote that!) She's not replacing you.

As discussed - on numerous occasions - she needs a local friend. A "female" friend. We all know that she has had plenty of male companions but now that she's with someone she needs to meet some other women she gets along with. Let her have her fun and stop overthinking it.

From: Renee Greene – November 25, 2013 – 12:08 PM
To: Ashley Gordon
Subject: Re: Fwd: Re: Ready for my "Close" up

You're right. She's right. Okay, I need to stop focusing on this stuff and start focusing on finding a job. My goal is to have full employment by the new year.

From: Ashley Gordon – November 25, 2013 – 12:12 PM
To: Renee Greene
Subject: Re: Fwd: Re: Ready for my "Close" up

I think that's a great goal, Renee. Just keep in mind that the holiday period is a tough time to try and get hired. Between office closures and vacations, it might take a bit longer. Just being realistic.

From: Renee Greene – November 25, 2013 – 12:14 PM
To: Ashley Gordon
Subject: Re: Fwd: Re: Ready for my "Close" up

That's a good point. I'm going to be optimistic and ambitious. It's the hopeful me.

From: Ashley Gordon – November 25, 2013 – 12:15 PM
To: Renee Greene
Subject: Re: Fwd: Re: Ready for my "Close" up

Well, then I hope it works out for you.

From: Shelley Manning – November 27, 2013 – 9:54 AM
To: Renee Greene
Subject: Let's get physical?

Totally forgot to ask you earlier...so how's the workout queen doing?
Did you go through with it?

From: Renee Greene – November 27, 2013 – 10:08 AM
To: Shelley Manning
Subject: Re: Let's get physical

So good to hear from you. I've missed you! I did indeed join a gym.
I've been every day for a week. I've also been eating leftover
Halloween candy every day, so I'm likely at a zero or negative
balance here. Or would that be a positive balance, since I'm not
losing weight? I'm just talking out loud to myself.

From: Shelley Manning – November 27, 2013 – 10:10 AM
To: Renee Greene
Subject: Re: Let's get physical

So what kind of workouts are you doing? Cross fit? Zumba? Pole
dancing?

From: Renee Greene – November 27, 2013 – 10:11 AM
To: Shelley Manning
Subject: Re: Let's get physical

Pole dancing?

From: Shelley Manning – November 27, 2013 – 10:16 AM
To: Renee Greene
Subject: Re: Let's get physical

Yes, that is a legitimate form of exercise. It's only skanky when
you're covered in glitter (as opposed to glistened sweat) and letting
strange men jam dollar bills in your g-string.

From: Renee Greene – November 27, 2013 – 10:17 AM
To: Shelley Manning
Subject: Re: Let's get physical

No, I am NOT doing pole dancing.

From: Shelley Manning – November 27, 2013 – 10:18 AM
To: Renee Greene
Subject: Re: Let's get physical

I think you should try it. Ethan might enjoy.

From: Renee Greene – November 27, 2013 – 10:18 AM
To: Shelley Manning
Subject: Re: Let's get physical

Never you mind what Ethan would enjoy.

From: Shelley Manning – November 27, 2013 – 10:19 AM
To: Renee Greene
Subject: Re: Let's get physical

So, what are you doing?

From: Renee Greene – November 27, 2013 – 10:19 AM
To: Shelley Manning
Subject: Re: Let's get physical

Promise not to laugh?

From: Shelley Manning – November 27, 2013 – 10:26 AM
To: Renee Greene
Subject: Re: Let's get physical

I know we've not seen each other in a while, but surely you haven't forgotten my personality. I cannot and will not promise not to laugh and what I anticipate to be a hilarious story uttered from your lips/typed from your fingertips. So spill!

From: Renee Greene – November 27, 2013 – 10:26 AM
To: Shelley Manning
Subject: Re: Let's get physical

I joined Curves.

From: Shelley Manning – November 27, 2013 – 10:27 AM
To: Renee Greene
Subject: Re: Let's get physical

Curves? The gym for old ladies?

From: Renee Greene – November 27, 2013 – 10:28 AM
To: Shelley Manning
Subject: Re: Let's get physical

It's not for old ladies. It's for women. And I am a woman.

From: Shelley Manning – November 27, 2013 – 10:28 AM
To: Renee Greene
Subject: Re: Let's get physical

Okay. So you joined Curves.

From: Renee Greene – November 27, 2013 – 10:29 AM
To: Shelley Manning
Subject: Re: Let's get physical

You're laughing, aren't you?

From: Shelley Manning – November 27, 2013 – 10:29 AM
To: Renee Greene
Subject: Re: Let's get physical

Why would you think that?

From: Renee Greene – November 27, 2013 – 10:30 AM
To: Shelley Manning
Subject: Re: Let's get physical

Because I know you. You're laughing. Stop laughing.

From: Shelley Manning – November 27, 2013 – 10:30 AM
To: Renee Greene
Subject: Re: Let's get physical

I am not laughing (anymore). Go on.

From: Renee Greene – November 27, 2013 – 10:35 AM
To: Shelley Manning
Subject: Re: Let's get physical

So I joined Curves (I'll pause and allow you one more minor chuckle). And it's great for me. First, it's only about a half hour workout, which is about as much as my body and attention span can handle.

Second, I can do the entire workout without sweating buckets or feeling like I'm going to vomit afterward. Yet I still feel as though I'm getting a workout.

Finally, and this is truly the best part. Despite the extra 10 pounds saddled on my thighs and belly, I am the YOUNGEST, THINNEST and HOTTEST woman there.

From: Shelley Manning – November 27, 2013 – 10:37 AM
To: Renee Greene
Subject: Re: Let's get physical

So in other words, you are the "Skinny Skye" of Curves.

From: Renee Greene – November 27, 2013 – 10:39 AM
To: Shelley Manning
Subject: Re: Let's get physical

I hadn't thought of it that way, but I suppose you are right.

From: Shelley Manning – November 27, 2013 – 10:43 AM
To: Renee Greene
Subject: Re: Let's get physical

Damn straight I am! Just think of it. Those old hags are grumbling and moaning when you walk in. Cursing you and your slim physique. They're saying, "She must be a supermodel" and they're right.

From: Renee Greene – November 27, 2013 – 10:49 AM
To: Shelley Manning
Subject: Re: Let's get physical

Well, if my ego wasn't completely inflated before, it sure is now. Thank you for that little boost. Everyone can use a pick me up like that one day or another. I could just kiss you.

From: Shelley Manning – November 27, 2013 – 10:51 AM
To: Renee Greene
Subject: Re: Let's get physical

Get in line! I've got to go. Happy Thanksgiving! Mwah! Mwah!

CHAPTER 15: NEW OPPORTUNITIES

From: Kevin.Huntley@alistracorp.com – December 3, 2013 – 9:04 AM
To: Renee Greene
Subject: Let's Talk About Alistra

Renee: I'm sorry it has taken me so long to reach out to you. We heard about your departure from the Carr Agency and the reasons behind it. I must say, I'm so impressed that you would be willing to quit a job because you don't feel as though you can - in good conscience - represent a company you don't believe in. Thankfully, you are a believer in safe sex, which hopefully has made it easier to promote our brand of prophylactics.

When we hired Carr, we really were hiring you. Your passion and experience is exactly what we were looking for in the person to lead our outsourced marketing efforts. We would like to continue working with you.

Our contract with Carr ends this month. If you have already taken a position at another agency, we'd like to come in and meet with you to discuss moving our business to your new employer. Give me a call when you get a chance and we can discuss further.

From: Renee Greene – December 3, 2013 – 9:10 AM
To: Kevin.Huntley@alistracorp.com
Subject: Re: Let's Talk About Alistra

Kevin: Thank you so much for getting in touch with me. I'm incredibly flattered that you have such faith and confidence in me. I will give you a call tomorrow and would love to discuss a working arrangement. Thanks again.

From: Renee Greene – December 3, 2013 – 9:13 AM
To: Mark Finlay, Shelley Manning, PBCupLover, Ashley Gordon
Subject: Fwd: Let's Talk About Alistra

Holy cow! See below. Alistra Corporation is going to leave Carr and come with me when I get hired at a new agency.

From: Mark Finlay – December 3, 2013 – 10:12 AM
To: Renee Greene, Shelley Manning, PBCupLover, Ashley Gordon
Subject: Re: Fwd: Let's Talk About Alistra

Forget the "new agency." It doesn't get better than this, Renee. Start your own business! You have the seed money to buy any equipment you need. You can work from home to start. You already have a client (!) and you can hire Skye.

From: Shelley Manning – December 3, 2013 – 10:38 AM
To: Mark Finlay, Renee Greene, PBCupLover, Ashley Gordon
Subject: Re: Fwd: Let's Talk About Alistra

Hate to admit it, but Finlay is right. It really doesn't get more obvious than this.

From: Renee Greene – December 3, 2013 – 10:40 AM
To: Mark Finlay, Shelley Manning, PBCupLover, Ashley Gordon
Subject: Re: Fwd: Let's Talk About Alistra

You think I could do it? Start my own firm?

From: Shelley Manning – December 3, 2013 – 10:42 AM
To: Mark Finlay, Renee Greene, PBCupLover, Ashley Gordon
Subject: Re: Fwd: Let's Talk About Alistra

Why not!? How hard could it be if an idiot like Neil was running an office?

From: Renee Greene – December 3, 2013 – 10:44 AM
To: Mark Finlay, Shelley Manning, PBCupLover, Ashley Gordon
Subject: Re: Fwd: Let's Talk About Alistra

The billables from Alistra would probably cover Skye's salary and subsidize mine.

From: PBCupLover – December 3, 2013 – 10:51 AM
To: Mark Finlay, Shelley Manning, Renee Greene, Ashley Gordon
Subject: Re: Fwd: Let's Talk About Alistra

Go for it!

From: Kevin.Huntley@alistracorp.com – December 5, 2013 – 10:34 AM
To: Renee Greene
Subject: Thank you

Kevin: Thank you again for your time on the phone yesterday. I realize this arrangement is not exactly what you had in mind, but I assure you, I will do my very best work on your behalf. We can officially start our 6-month contract on February 1. I'll send something over for you to review shortly.

From: Renee Greene – December 5, 2013 – 10:50 AM
To: Skye@skyesloane.com
Subject: Job offer

Great news, Skye. I'm in a position to offer you a position. I've decided to start my own agency and I would love to have you part of my team. We'll be working out of my spare bedroom and living room until we get a few clients on board and can afford office space. But we do have one account. I can offer you the same salary you were making at Carr plus all of the cupcakes that you can eat. You would start January 6.

From: Skye@skyesloane.com – December 5, 2013 – 1:32 PM
To: Renee Greene
Subject: Re: Job offer

That sounds great, Renee. I'm in. Thank you! And if we ever need any temps, I can hook us up. Have a great Christmas and New Years. So stoked to get started.

From: Renee Greene – December 5, 2013 – 1:36 PM
To: Skye@skyesloane.com
Subject: Re: Job offer

Glad you're stoked, Skye. Best to you over the holidays as well. I'll see you soon.

From: Renee Greene – December 10, 2013 – 10:56 AM
To: Mark Finlay, Shelley Manning, PBCupLover, Ashley Gordon
Subject: My baby

Super psyched about my new agency. Thank you all for your support. I never imagined I would take on such a challenge and so appreciate knowing you are all here with your special talents including Mark with his spreadsheet prowess, Ethan with his financial wizardry and Shelley with her HR knowledge. I love you guys. Now, I just need to give this baby a name. Any thoughts?

From: Ashley Gordon – December 10, 2013 – 11:08 AM
To: Mark Finlay, Shelley Manning, PBCupLover, Renee Greene
Subject: Re: My Baby

I just glanced at your email and thought at first you were pregnant. But I suppose starting your own company is going to be a bit painful like childbirth. I'm sure you'll be great. And now for my name suggestion…Supernova because your ideas are out of this world.

From: Mark Finlay – December 10, 2013 – 11:32 AM
To: Ashley Gordon, Shelley Manning, PBCupLover, Ashley Gordon
Subject: Re: My Baby

Glue PR because your ideas really stick.

From: Renee Greene – December 10, 2013 – 11:35 AM
To: Mark Finlay, Shelley Manning, PBCupLover, Ashley Gordon
Subject: Re: My Baby

Hey, now. I'm not looking for puns. I'm looking for real ideas.

From: PBCupLover – December 10, 2013 – 11:38 AM
To: Mark Finlay, Shelley Manning, Renee Greene, Ashley Gordon
Subject: Re: My Baby

You're not pregnant, are you? J/K What about Langer5 which is what my mom used to stich into my clothes when I went to sleepaway camp. My last name and the fact I was the 5th kid. It sounds very esoteric. I think it works.

From: Renee Greene – December 10, 2013 – 11:41 AM
To: Mark Finlay, Shelley Manning, PBCupLover, Ashley Gordon
Subject: Re: My Baby

All of your siblings are girls. You didn't wear their clothes, did you?

From: PBCupLover – December 10, 2013 – 11:42 AM
To: Mark Finlay, Shelley Manning, Renee Greene, Ashley Gordon
Subject: Re: My Baby

No! I did not wear girls' clothes...very often.

From: Renee Greene – December 10, 2013 – 11:45 AM
To: Mark Finlay, Shelley Manning, PBCupLover, Ashley Gordon
Subject: Re: My Baby

Ha! Ha! There is still so much more I need to learn about you. But no, Langer5 is out. Anyone else?

From: Ashley Gordon – December 10, 2013 – 12:02 PM
To: Mark Finlay, Shelley Manning, PBCupLover, Renee Greene
Subject: Re: My Baby

What about using your name? Perhaps Greene PR?

From: Renee Greene – December 10, 2013 – 12:13 PM
To: Mark Finlay, Shelley Manning, PBCupLover, Ashley Gordon
Subject: Re: My Baby

No. I always felt that was so self serving and egotistical. I really don't want my name on doors across the world as my agency grows into an international powerhouse. I may not be egotistical, but I can dream. I want people to realize they found a gem by hiring us. You know, give them an "aha" moment when they discover how much we can help them.

From: Shelley Manning – December 10, 2013 – 2:02 PM
To: Mark Finlay, Renee Greene, PBCupLover, Ashley Gordon
Subject: Re: My Baby

Eureka!

From: Renee Greene – December 10, 2013 – 2:04 PM
To: Mark Finlay, Shelley Manning, PBCupLover, Ashley Gordon
Subject: Re: My Baby

Eureka? That's brilliant.

From: Shelley Manning – December 10, 2013 – 2:05 PM
To: Mark Finlay, Renee Greene, PBCupLover, Ashley Gordon
Subject: Re: My Baby

I know.

From: Renee Greene – December 10, 2013 – 2:09 PM
To: Mark Finlay, Shelley Manning, PBCupLover, Ashley Gordon
Subject: Re: My Baby

Eureka PR it is. Now on to creating a logo, website, business cards and more all within a few weeks. Hurrah!

From: Renee Greene – December 12, 2013 – 3:54 PM
To: Shelley Manning
Subject: What up buttercup?

So any big plans this weekend?

From: Shelley Manning – December 12, 2013 – 3:58 PM
To: Renee Greene
Subject: Re: What up buttercup?

I'm just going to hang out on my own this weekend. Nick is in Singapore on business.

From: Renee Greene – December 12, 2013 – 3:59 PM
To: Shelley Manning
Subject: Re: What up buttercup?

What? Not hanging out with Amber?

From: Shelley Manning – December 12, 2013 – 4:01 PM
To: Renee Greene
Subject: Re: What up buttercup?

Do I detect a hint of sarcasm in your voice?

From: Renee Greene – December 12, 2013 – 4:04 PM
To: Shelley Manning
Subject: Re: What up buttercup?

Even over the computer, you do know me well. Seriously, though, not hanging with Amber this weekend at all?

From: Shelley Manning – December 12, 2013 – 4:06 PM
To: Renee Greene
Subject: Re: What up buttercup?

Nah. I need a break from her. She's a bit of a snob and I can only take her in doses.

From: Renee Greene – December 12, 2013 – 4:07 PM
To: Shelley Manning
Subject: Re: What up buttercup?

Do tell!

From: Shelley Manning – December 12, 2013 – 4:12 PM
To: Renee Greene
Subject: Re: What up buttercup?

Yeah, I figured you'd want the scoop, Sweetie. Last week she asked me to come to a high-end cooking supply store. She wanted to buy a $500 kitchen knife. She decided to buy the $200 one and said if it works really well, then she would upgrade to the $500 version. I asked why she would upgrade to a $500 knife if the $200 is working "really well." She just looked at me as if she didn't understand the question.

From: Renee Greene – December 12, 2013 – 4:13 PM
To: Shelley Manning
Subject: Re: What up buttercup?

Hmmm.

From: Shelley Manning – December 12, 2013 – 4:13 PM
To: Renee Greene
Subject: Re: What up buttercup?

Holding your tongue, I see.

From: Renee Greene – December 12, 2013 – 4:18 PM
To: Shelley Manning
Subject: Re: What up buttercup?

Honestly, I just don't know what to say. Sorry it's not the friendship you were hoping for. And I mean that in all sincerity. I just want you to be happy.

From: Shelley Manning – December 12, 2013 – 4:22 PM
To: Renee Greene
Subject: Re: What up buttercup?

We're still friends and will continue to be. It's just that the role of "best friend" is already taken…by you.

From: Renee Greene – December 12, 2013 – 4:23 PM
To: Shelley Manning
Subject: Re: What up buttercup?

Squee!

From: Shelley Manning – December 12, 2013 – 4:25 PM
To: Renee Greene
Subject: Re: What up buttercup?

What about you? Any big plans this weekend?

From: Renee Greene – December 12, 2013 – 4:31 PM
To: Shelley Manning
Subject: Re: What up buttercup?

Just plugging away on Eureka. I have a design session with a graphic designer friend from Carr who is helping me with a logo and website. He's hoping that Eureka will grow and that we'll need to hire him full time. I'm hoping that's the case, too.

From: Shelley Manning – December 12, 2013 – 4:34 PM
To: Renee Greene
Subject: Re: What up buttercup?

Good luck, Sweetie. I have no doubt everyone will soon "discover" – my play on Eureka! – that you are a force to be reckoned with. Mwah! Mwah!

CHAPTER 16: HOLIDAY CHEER

From: Renee Greene – December 16, 2013 – 10:04 AM
To: Mark Finlay
Subject: Checking In

Hey there. Just checking in to see how you are doing. If I haven't told you lately, I want you to know how much you are loved.

From: Mark Finlay – December 16, 2013 – 10:08 AM
To: Renee Greene
Subject: Re: Checking in

Thanks, Renee. It has been tough but you and Ethan have been great about keeping my spirits up.

From: Renee Greene – December 16, 2013 – 10:09 AM
To: Mark Finlay
Subject: Re: Checking in

Is there anything we can do for you?

From: Mark Finlay – December 16, 2013 – 10:13 AM
To: Renee Greene
Subject: Re: Checking in

No. I think I've gained about 10 pounds between all of the dinners and batches of your world-class chocolate chip cookies. I've got to get back into shape if I'm ever going to start dating again.

From: Renee Greene – December 16, 2013 – 10:16 AM
To: Mark Finlay
Subject: Re: Checking in

That's the first time I've heard you talk about that. Are you ready to start dating again?

From: Mark Finlay – December 16, 2013 – 10:20 AM
To: Renee Greene
Subject: Re: Checking in

I don't think so. But I'm hoping that I will at some point. I do want to meet someone and have a family. I'm still just feeling kind of bruised by all the stuff that went down with Cass.

From: Renee Greene – December 16, 2013 – 10:25 AM
To: Mark Finlay
Subject: Re: Checking in

I can understand that. We won't pressure you and ply you with food either. Just let us know what we can do for you. You're so very special to us and we just want you to be happy. Let's talk next week and figure out plans for dinner. Oh, there I go again. ;)

From: Renee Greene – December 24, 2013 – 4:13 PM
To: Shelley Manning
Subject: Ho! Ho! Ho!

Hey, Shel. Just wanted to wish you and Nick a very Merry Christmas. Ethan and I are doing the traditional Jewish Christmas celebration: Bamboo Garden take-out. The manager told me they pull in about $25,000 that one day. Crazy, huh? Anyway, I hope you guys have fun with Nick's family. I hope Santa can find you there. XO

From: Shelley Manning – December 24, 2013 – 4:19 PM
To: Renee Greene
Subject: Re: Ho! Ho! Ho!

Who you calling a ho?!? Yes, Nick and I are on our way to Portland for a quick visit with his folks. I'm not worried about Santa finding me. In fact, Nick and I decided to just be naughty this year and save Santa the trip. It was delicious fun.

From: Renee Greene – December 24, 2013 – 4:21 PM
To: Shelley Manning
Subject: Re: Ho! Ho! Ho!

And you wonder why I'm calling you a ho!

From: Shelley Manning – December 24, 2013 – 4:24 PM
To: Renee Greene
Subject: Re: Ho! Ho! Ho!

Ha-larious! Well, you do know which is my favorite reindeer. Vixen, of course.

From: Renee Greene – December 24, 2013 – 4:25 PM
To: Shelley Manning
Subject: Re: Ho! Ho! Ho!

Now that's hilarious!

From: Shelley Manning – December 24, 2013 – 4:26 PM
To: Renee Greene
Subject: Re: Ho! Ho! Ho!

I know. It's not fair that I get to be so awesome in so many ways.

From: Renee Greene – December 24, 2013 – 4:28 PM
To: Shelley Manning
Subject: Re: Ho! Ho! Ho!

True. What you lack in humility, you more than make up for in sheer awesomeness. Enjoy your trip.

From: Shelley Manning – December 24, 2013 – 4:29 PM
To: Renee Greene
Subject: Re: Ho! Ho! Ho!

Mwah! Mwah!

CHAPTER 17: CRAPPY NEW YEAR

From: PBCupLover – January 2, 2014 – 7:02 AM
To: Shelley Manning, Ashley Gordon, Mark Finlay
Subject: Crappy new year!

Hey, guys. Sorry for the impersonal nature of this email given what I have to share, but I know Renee hasn't reached out because she doesn't want to burden you. But I thought you should know ASAP. Her dad had a stroke last night and is on life support at Cedars. It's not looking good and they are waiting for her sister to fly in so they can make some decisions. They don't want cell phones used because it interferes with the equipment and disrupts other patients. So email is best. Visitation is limited so don't rush over thinking you'll be able to see her. I know she would welcome hearing from you. I'll keep you posted.

From: Shelley Manning – January 2, 2014 – 9:31 AM
To: Renee Greene
Subject: Fwd: Crappy new year!

OMG! Ethan filled us in. I'm SO SORRY, Sweetie. I'm here for you. What do you need? What can I do? And why didn't you call me last night?

From: Renee Greene – January 2, 2014 – 9:41 AM
To: Shelley Manning
Subject: Re: Fwd: Crappy new year!

Hey. Thanks for your note. To answer your questions: (1) I need my dad to wake up! (2) There's nothing you can do, although I appreciate your offer. And (3) I didn't call last night because it was 3:00 am and I didn't want to trouble you.

From: Shelley Manning – January 2, 2014 – 9:50 AM
To: Renee Greene
Subject: Re: Fwd: Crappy new year!

Trouble me?!? Are you kidding! This is precisely the time when you are supposed to call me, regardless of the time. You've called me at 2 in the morning because you're worried what to wear on a New Year's Eve, three weeks away. And you didn't think this warranted picking up the phone?!?

From: Renee Greene – January 2, 2014 – 9:53 AM
To: Shelley Manning
Subject: Re: Fwd: Crappy new year!

Perhaps I swung too far the other way on the pendulum?

From: Shelley Manning – January 2, 2014 – 9:54 AM
To: Renee Greene
Subject: Re: Fwd: Crappy new year!

You think?!?

From: Renee Greene – January 2, 2014 – 9:55 AM
To: Shelley Manning
Subject: Re: Fwd: Crappy new year!

Okay, okay. I'm sorry.

From: Shelley Manning – January 2, 2014 – 9:56 AM
To: Renee Greene
Subject: Re: Fwd: Crappy new year!

Do you want me to hop on a plane?

From: Renee Greene – January 2, 2014 – 10:01 AM
To: Shelley Manning
Subject: Re: Fwd: Crappy new year!

You're so sweet, but that's okay. My sister is on her way and then we need to see what the doctors say. I'm hopeful Dad will open his eyes any minute now and ask when his tee time is.

From: Shelley Manning – January 2, 2014 – 10:04 AM
To: Renee Greene
Subject: Re: Fwd: Crappy new year!

I hope for that, too. In the meantime, let me know if I can do anything. I know you have Ethan there, but I can fly down on a moment's notice.

From: Renee Greene – January 2, 2014 – 10:09 AM
To: Shelley Manning
Subject: Re: Fwd: Crappy new year!

Thanks, Shel. I'm so grateful for your friendship and support. And while I've always been certain that this sensitive, caring and – frankly – appropriate side of you existed, I could use a good laugh right about now.

From: Shelley Manning – January 2, 2014 – 10:15 AM
To: Renee Greene
Subject: Re: Fwd: Crappy new year!

That I can do! Prepare yourself for something completely and unabashedly inappropriate. Cinderella's Fairy Godmother comes along and tells poor Cindy that she will help her. She waves her wand and does all of her magical shit transforming Cindy into the literal Belle of the Ball.

However, it comes with a hitch. If she doesn't leave by midnight, her lady parts (I would have used a more primitive term, but I know how you don't like that) will turn into a pumpkin. Good so far, no?

From: Renee Greene – January 2, 2014 – 10:17 AM
To: Shelley Manning
Subject: Re: Fwd: Crappy new year!

Oh my. This may be more than I bargained for. But, please
continue.

From: Shelley Manning – January 2, 2014 – 10:21 AM
To: Renee Greene
Subject: Re: Fwd: Crappy new year!

Cindy hits the ball and has a great time. The clock strikes midnight
but there's no sign of her. The clock strikes 12:30 and still, no
Cindy. The clock gongs 1:00 and Cindy is still no where to be
found. This continues until 2:30 am when Cindy comes strolling in
with a VERY satisfied look on her face. Eager to hear the end?

From: Renee Greene – January 2, 2014 – 10:23 AM
To: Shelley Manning
Subject: Re: Fwd: Crappy new year!

Actually, I am quite eager and excited for the conclusion.

From: Shelley Manning – January 2, 2014 – 10:26 AM
To: Renee Greene
Subject: Re: Fwd: Crappy new year!

Excited because you think my email joke telling sucks or because I'm
doing such a great job building suspense that you can hardly sit still?

From: Renee Greene – January 2, 2014 – 10:27 AM
To: Shelley Manning
Subject: Re: Fwd: Crappy new year!

A little bit of both. Go on. What happens next?

From: Shelley Manning – January 2, 2014 – 10:32 AM
To: Renee Greene
Subject: Re: Fwd: Crappy new year!

Well, as I said, Cindy comes strolling in with a quite satisfied look on her face. The Fairy Godmother says, "My dear! I guess you met your Prince Charming?" Cindy replies, "No, but I bumped into Peter Peter Pumpkin Eater."

From: Renee Greene – January 2, 2014 – 10:33 AM
To: Shelley Manning
Subject: Re: Fwd: Crappy new year!

Oh no you didn't!

From: Shelley Manning – January 2, 2014 – 10:33 AM
To: Renee Greene
Subject: Re: Fwd: Crappy new year!

C'mon! That was damn funny.

From: Renee Greene – January 2, 2014 – 10:35 AM
To: Shelley Manning
Subject: Re: Fwd: Crappy new year!

Yes, that was indeed funny. Quite dirty but funny. I should have expected nothing less from you.

From: Shelley Manning – January 2, 2014 – 10:37 AM
To: Renee Greene
Subject: Re: Fwd: Crappy new year!

Now don't go telling that joke to Ethan and taking credit for it. I know how you operate.

From: Renee Greene – January 2, 2014 – 10:39 AM
To: Shelley Manning
Subject: Re: Fwd: Crappy new year!

Oh, I don't think I could tell that joke to Ethan or anyone else for that matter.

From: Shelley Manning – January 2, 2014 – 10:41 AM
To: Renee Greene
Subject: Re: Fwd: Crappy new year!

True. You don't have the timing and comic genius that I truly embody.

From: Renee Greene – January 2, 2014 – 10:43 AM
To: Shelley Manning
Subject: Re: Fwd: Crappy new year!

Thank goodness you have a bit of humility, too.

From: Shelley Manning – January 2, 2014 – 10:45 AM
To: Renee Greene
Subject: Re: Fwd: Crappy new year!

Indeed. Okay, Sweetie. You hang in there. Keep me posted and let me know if you need anything.

From: Renee Greene – January 2, 2014 – 10:47 AM
To: Shelley Manning
Subject: Re: Fwd: Crappy new year!

He's going to wake up. He has to. I didn't get to say goodbye. So he just has to.

From: Shelley Manning – January 2, 2014 – 10:48 AM
To: Renee Greene
Subject: Re: Fwd: Crappy new year!

Anytime. Anything. I'm here.

From: Renee Greene – January 2, 2014 – 10:49 AM
To: Shelley Manning
Subject: Re: Fwd: Crappy new year!

Thanks, Shel. I love you!

From: Shelley Manning – January 2, 2014 – 10:50 AM
To: Renee Greene
Subject: Re: Fwd: Crappy new year!

Go be with him, Sweetie. Ethan will keep us posted.

From: Mark Finlay – January 2, 2014 – 11:22 AM
To: Shelley Manning, Ashley Gordon, PBCupLover
Subject: Re: Crappy new year!

I'm on my way! I know I probably won't be able to sit with Renee and you, but I want to be there. Have you guys even eaten anything since yesterday?

From: PBCupLover – January 2, 2014 – 11:25 AM
To: Mark Finlay, Shelley Manning, Ashley Gordon
Subject: Re: Crappy new year!

Actually, we're starving. At least I am. Some lunch would be awesome.

From: Mark Finlay – January 2, 2014 – 11:28 AM
To: Shelley Manning, Ashley Gordon, PBCupLover
Subject: Re: Crappy new year!

I'll swing by Bamboo Garden on my way.

From: PBCupLover – January 2, 2014 – 11:30 AM
To: Mark Finlay, Shelley Manning, Ashley Gordon
Subject: Re: Crappy new year!

Thanks, Mark. You're the best.

From: Ashley Gordon – January 2, 2014 – 12:06 PM
To: Shelley Manning, Mark Finlay, PBCupLover
Subject: Re: Crappy new year!

Oh, no! Poor Herb. He's been like a second father to me. I want to be there, but the ICU is no place for a baby. When Greg gets home from work tonight, I will come over and I can bring dinner. Give Renee and her mom a big hug for me.

From: PBCupLover – January 2, 2014 – 12:08 PM
To: Mark Finlay, Shelley Manning, Ashley Gordon
Subject: Re: Crappy new year!

Thanks, Ashley. See you tonight.

From: Shelley Manning – January 4, 2014 – 9:23 AM
To: PBCupLover
Subject: Update please!

Ahem…

From: PBCupLover – January 4, 2014 – 9:28 AM
To: Shelley Manning,
Cc: Ashley Gordon, Mark Finlay
Subject: Re: Update please!

There's no change yet. Renee's sister is here and they are waiting for the doctor to come in and talk with them. I'll keep you posted. Thanks, Ashley and Mark, for coming over. It meant a lot to Renee to have you stop by.

From: Ashley Gordon – January 4, 2014 – 9:31 AM
To: PBCupLover
Cc: Shelley Manning, Mark Finlay
Subject: Re: Update please!

Now I have a babysitter on stand by. Just say the word and I'll be there.

From: Mark Finlay – January 4, 2014 – 10:32 AM
To: Ashley Gordon
Cc: PBCupLover, Shelley Manning
Subject: Re: Update please!

I feel so helpless. What can we do?

From: PBCupLover – January 4, 2014 – 10:40 AM
To: Mark Finlay
Cc: Shelley Manning, Ashley Gordon,
Subject: Re: Update please!

Just keep them all in your thoughts. I'll let you know as soon as I hear anything.

From: PBCupLover – January 4, 2014 – 5:32 PM
To: Shelley Manning, Ashley Gordon, Mark Finlay
Subject: Beyond sad

Okay, here's the latest. Looks like the neurons of the brainstem were destroyed by the stroke. He's basically brain dead. He had previously expressed his wishes that he not be kept alive in this type of state. So they are going to remove life support shortly. They expect that he will pass within a few minutes of the removal from the machines.

After that, I hope I can get Renee to go straight home and get some sleep – she's been up all night – before we head over to the funeral home to deal with the next steps. I'll keep you posted as we know more about services.

From: Ashley Gordon – January 4, 2014 – 5:45 PM
To: PBCupLover, Shelley Manning, Mark Finlay
Subject: Re: Beyond sad

<sigh!> I'll call you guys tomorrow. Give Renee a warm hug for me.

From: Shelley Manning – January 4, 2014 – 6:09 PM
To: PBCupLover
Subject: Re: Beyond sad

I'm booking a flight now. Don't worry about picking me up from the airport. I'll take a cab and I already have a key to your place (don't ask!) Give Renee all of my love and tell her I will be there as soon as possible.

From: PBCupLover – January 4, 2014 – 6:14 PM
To: Shelley Manning
Subject: Re: Beyond sad

Thanks, Shelley. She needs you. Just call me when you land.

From: Mark Finlay – January 4, 2014 – 6:22 PM
To: PBCupLover, Ashley Gordon, Shelley Manning
Subject: Re: Beyond sad

Oh, man! Tell Renee how sorry I am. Her dad was a great guy and will definitely be missed. I'm here for whatever you guys need. Just let me know.

From: PBCupLover – January 4, 2014 – 8:23 PM
To: Mark Finlay, Ashley Gordon, Shelley Manning
Subject: Re: Beyond sad

Thanks, everyone. As you can imagine, Renee is just heartbroken….and exhausted…and eating a lot of frosting tubs. She is really appreciative of all of your emails, calls, offers to help, etc.. She's just not up for talking right now. I'm sure you all can understand. They are finalizing details of the service now and I'll let you know the details tomorrow.

From: Renee Greene – January 5, 2014– 12:02 AM
To: Shelley Manning
Subject: Awake?

Are you awake? I didn't want to call this late? Plus Ethan is sleeping and he thinks I am too.

From: Shelley Manning – January 5, 2014 – 12:07 AM
To: Renee Greene
Subject: Re: Awake

I'm here, Sweetie. And I'm on the first flight out tomorrow morning. I'm sorry. So, so sorry. Your dad was probably my favorite of all my friends' parents. I know he was your hero.

From: Renee Greene – January 5, 2014 – 12:09 AM
To: Shelley Manning
Subject: Re: Awake

I'm lost, Shel. I'm completely lost.

From: Shelley Manning – January 5, 2014 – 12:11 AM
To: Renee Greene
Subject: Re: Awake

I can't imagine how your heart is hurting right now.

From: Renee Greene – January 5, 2014 – 12:17 AM
To: Shelley Manning
Subject: Re: Awake

I'm trying to write a eulogy and I'm blocked. I write stuff for a living
– news releases, bylined articles, marketing proposals, brochures,
advertising copy, public service announcements, radio copy, mat
columns, fact sheets, photo captions, media alerts, pitch letters,
letters to the editor, video news releases, etc. Yet I just can't seem to
do my dad justice.

From: Shelley Manning – January 5, 2014 – 12:22 AM
To: Renee Greene
Subject: Re: Awake

I know that writing is therapeutic for you, but I think you should try
and get some sleep. You're likely exhausted and maybe inspiration
will strike after you've gotten a bit of rest.

From: Renee Greene – January 5, 2014 – 12:41 AM
To: Shelley Manning
Subject: Re: Awake

I'm sitting here with a tear on one cheek and a smile on the other as I
think about him. How do you explain how important someone is
when they have taught you everything…everything you know and
everything that's important in life.

Sure, he taught me to walk and talk, ride a bike and factor equations in Algebra. But he taught me so much more like how to be a good and kind person, how to treat people with respect, how to act as a professional and how to have fun.

He totally got me and never made me apologize or compromise for being who I am. I don't think I ever told you this story. I was about 29 years old and my dad was golfing with a buddy and his buddy's friend. The friend was asking about me and my sister. When my dad explained that my sister was married and I was single, he offered to fix me up with is brother-in-law. He said he was a nice guy and very successful. "Your daughter will be very well taken care of." My dad responded, "My daughter doesn't need anyone to take care of her."

He totally understood me. I mean, really! How do you put that into words?!?

From: Shelley Manning – January 5, 2014 – 12:43 AM
To: Renee Greene
Subject: Re: Awake

You just did, Sweetie.

From: Renee Greene – January 5, 2014 – 12:49 AM
To: Shelley Manning
Subject: Re: Awake

I guess I did. I just don't think this is enough to explain how amazing and important he is...was. I'm heartbroken just typing about him in the past tense. How do I   Shelley: It's Ethan. Renee's a wreck. I just put her to bed. We'll see you tomorrow when you get here. Have a safe flight!

From: PBCupLover – January 5, 2014 – 11:31 AM
To: Mark Finlay, Ashley Gordon
Subject: Services

The funeral for Renee's dad will be on Wednesday at 10. We'll be sitting Shiva with her mom and sister until then, so feel free to come by her folks' place if you want to. See you guys soon and thanks again for all of the support.

From: Shelley Manning – January 5, 2014 – 2:35 PM
To: Mark Finlay
Subject: Need a lift

I need a lift to Herb's funeral. Renee and Ethan are going early. Pick me up at 9.

From: Mark Finlay – January 5, 2014 – 2:36 PM
To: Shelley Manning
Subject: Re: Need a lift

Please...

From: Shelley Manning – January 5, 2014 – 2:36 PM
To: Mark Finlay
Subject: Re: Need a lift

Oh, right. Please, Finlay.

From: Mark Finlay – January 5, 2014 – 2:38 PM
To: Shelley Manning
Subject: Re: Need a lift

Just giving you a hard time. Haven't been able to do that for a while since you moved to Seattle.

From: Shelley Manning – January 5, 2014 – 2:40 PM
To: Mark Finlay
Subject: Re: Need a lift

You giving me a hard time? More like the other way around.

From: Mark Finlay – January 5, 2014 – 2:41 PM
To: Shelley Manning
Subject: Re: Need a lift

I suppose so. I've missed that.

From: Shelley Manning – January 5, 2014 – 2:42 PM
To: Mark Finlay
Subject: Re: Need a lift

Me too. But if you tell anyone, I'll deny it.

From: Mark Finlay – January 5, 2014 – 2:43 PM
To: Shelley Manning
Subject: Re: Need a lift

You just put it in writing. I have irrefutable proof.

From: Shelley Manning – January 5, 2014 – 2:45 PM
To: Mark Finlay
Subject: Re: Need a lift

You know how easy it is to hack a phone these days?

From: Mark Finlay – January 5, 2014 – 2:46 PM
To: Shelley Manning
Subject: Re: Need a lift

I design cell phone games for a living, so yeah, I do.

From: Shelley Manning – January 5, 2014 – 2:49 PM
To: Mark Finlay
Subject: Re: Need a lift

Well then, there you go. How do you even know you aren't talking to Renee right now?

From: Mark Finlay – January 5, 2014 – 2:52 PM
To: Shelley Manning
Subject: Re: Need a lift

You're the only one who calls me Finlay. At least you're calling me that now instead of Finnidy.

From: Shelley Manning – January 5, 2014 – 2:53 PM
To: Mark Finlay
Subject: Re: Need a lift

You knew about that?

From: Mark Finlay – January 5, 2014 – 2:53 PM
To: Shelley Manning
Subject: Re: Need a lift

Yep.

From: Shelley Manning – January 5, 2014 – 2:54 PM
To: Mark Finlay
Subject: Re: Need a lift

You probably want an apology.

From: Mark Finlay – January 5, 2014 – 2:58 PM
To: Shelley Manning
Subject: Re: Need a lift

We are all currently in the mindset that life is fleeting and we should tell the important people in our lives how we really feel about them. After all, you never know if it's the last time we'll ever talk to them.

From: Shelley Manning – January 5, 2014 – 3:00 PM
To: Mark Finlay
Subject: Re: Need a lift

Do you promise to delete this email after you read it?

From: Mark Finlay – January 5, 2014 – 3:00 PM
To: Shelley Manning
Subject: Re: Need a lift

Sure.

From: Shelley Manning – January 5, 2014 – 3:01 PM
To: Mark Finlay
Subject: Re: Need a lift

Here goes. Finlay, you're not so bad. Now delete.

From: Mark Finlay – January 5, 2014 – 3:02 PM
To: Shelley Manning
Subject: Re: Need a lift

Thanks, Shelley. See you soon.

From: Mark Finlay – January 5, 2014 – 3:04 PM
To: Renee Greene
Subject: Fwd: Re: Need a lift

I'm giving Shelley a lift to your dad's service and figured you could use an emotional lift right about now. Read on.

From: Renee Greene – January 5, 2014 – 4:09 PM
To: Mark Finlay
Subject: Re: Fwd: Re: Need a lift

Thanks, Mark. That actually brought a brief smile to my face. I so appreciate everything. I'll see you soon.

From: Renee Greene – January 9, 2014 – 7:31 AM
To: Mark Finlay, Shelley Manning, Ashley Gordon
Subject: THANK YOU!

Thank you guys so very much for being there for me throughout this trying time. I'm so grateful for your friendship and support. You've always been with me through the good times and – what I thought at the time – bad times. But nothing can compare to this. I'm just gutted. Nothing can fill the void and probably never will.

But your friendship is certainly helping to ease this emptiness - not to mention the can of frosting that Mark brought. Extra gold star for you, my friend. I just want you to know how much you are all loved and appreciated.

From: Shelley Manning – January 9, 2014 – 8:45 AM
To: Renee Greene, Mark Finlay, Ashley Gordon
Subject: Re: THANK YOU!

Sweetie, it's nothing you wouldn't do for any of us. In fact, you would probably do more with that huge heart of yours. As for Finlay and his gift of frosting, stop being such a suck up!

From: Mark Finlay – January 9, 2014 – 10:02 AM
To: Renee Greene, Ashley Gordon, Shelley Manning
Subject: Re: THANK YOU!

There's this saying that your life is filled with balcony people and basement people. Balcony people bring you up and basement people pull you down. You're our penthouse, Renee. We're just repaying the favor.

From: Renee Greene – January 9, 2014 – 10:31 AM
To: Mark Finlay, Shelley Manning, Ashley Gordon
Subject: Re: THANK YOU!

Oh c'mon Shelley. I know you think Finlay is "not so bad." And Mark, that's beautiful. I will be stealing, uh, er, I mean borrowing that expression from you (without giving you credit).

From: Shelley Manning – January 9, 2014 – 10:34 AM
To: Renee Greene, Mark Finlay, Ashley Gordon
Subject: Re: THANK YOU!

Quotation marks mean a direct quote, eh grammar queen? That means Mark didn't delete a certain email message, which means someone's gonna be sorry.

From: Renee Greene – January 9, 2014 – 10:35 AM
To: Mark Finlay, Shelley Manning, Ashley Gordon
Subject: Re: THANK YOU!

He knew I needed some cheering up.

From: Mark Finlay – January 9, 2014 – 10:39 AM
To: Renee Greene, Shelley Manning, Ashley Gordon
Subject: Re: THANK YOU!

I deleted the message as instructed. You never said anything about not sharing with anyone first.

From: Ashley Gordon – January 9, 2014 – 10:41 AM
To: Renee Greene, Mark Finlay, Shelley Manning
Subject: Re: THANK YOU!

I'm clearly not in the loop on something and that's not acceptable.
Please explain.

From: Shelley Manning – January 9, 2014 – 10:43 AM
To: Renee Greene, Mark Finlay,
Subject: Fwd: Re: THANK YOU!

Don't you dare! This does not need to go any farther.

From: Renee Greene – January 9, 2014 – 10:48 AM
To: Shelley Manning, Mark Finlay, Ashley Gordon
Subject: Re: THANK YOU!

Shelley sent Mark an email and basically told him he's a good guy
but asked him to delete the message after reading it. He did, but not
before forwarding it to me. She's a softy!

From: Renee Greene – January 9, 2014 – 10:51 AM
To: Shelley Manning, Mark Finlay
Subject: Re: Fwd: Re: THANK YOU!

Oops. Didn't see your message in time. Oh well, it's all out in the
open now and we can all move on.

From: Ashley Gordon – January 9, 2014 – 10:54 AM
To: Renee Greene, Mark Finlay, Shelley Manning
Subject: Re: THANK YOU!

I would have done the same. A compliment from Shelley is a rare
and special thing. I would have probably printed it out and framed it.

From: Shelley Manning – January 9, 2014 – 10:57 AM
To: Renee Greene, Mark Finlay, Ashley Gordon
Subject: Re: THANK YOU!

Alright. Alright. Not sure how we got off on this tangent, but that's quite enough. How about them Yankees?

From: Renee Greene – January 9, 2014 – 10:59 AM
To: Shelley Manning, Mark Finlay, Ashley Gordon
Subject: Re: THANK YOU!

LOL! You guys always know how to make me smile. XOXO

From: Shelley Manning – January 10, 2014 – 8:45 AM
To: Renee Greene
Subject: Okay?

How you doing today, Sweetie?

From: Renee Greene – January 10, 2014 – 9:33 AM
To: Shelley Manning
Subject: Re: Okay?

I'm okay. There are bad days and worse days and today is only a bad one, so I'm thankful for that. I know it will get easier, but I'm not sure I want it to. Doesn't seem right that my pain should lessen. I don't want to stop missing him.

From: Shelley Manning – January 10, 2014 – 9:38 AM
To: Renee Greene
Subject: Re: Okay?

Herb would NEVER want you to forget him or stop missing him. But he would also NEVER want you to be miserable. You are truly his daughter.

From: Renee Greene – January 10, 2014 – 9:51 AM
To: Shelley Manning
Subject: Re: Okay?

I know. I remember a few years ago, my accountant, who is also my dad's accountant and golfing buddy, wanted to get a little "aggressive" with my tax return. I told him I just wanted to do the right thing.

He said, "You are your father's daughter." I thought at the time – and I still do – what a compliment! I know he will always live on through me.

But it's just sad to think I won't be able to get his advice about work or just hang out and have a pizza with him. He won't be able to walk me down the aisle or know his grandchildren. Even worse, they won't get to know him. It's just so very...sad. There really isn't any other way to say it. It's just sad.

From: Shelley Manning – January 10, 2014 – 9:55 AM
To: Renee Greene
Subject: Re: Okay?

Okay. Be sad. I give you permission to be really, really sad for a while longer. But then I will be giving you a swift kick in the ass to be less sad. Your agency officially starts on February 1 and he was surely so proud of you and what you accomplished.

From: Renee Greene – January 10, 2014 – 9:56 AM
To: Shelley Manning
Subject: Re: Okay?

Thanks, Shel.

From: Shelley Manning – January 10, 2014 – 9:57 AM
To: Renee Greene
Subject: Re: Okay?

Mwah! Mwah! And a big hug with it.

From: Shelley Manning – January 12, 2014 – 11:01 AM
To: PBCupLover
Subject: Reality check

How's she doing? Really?!

From: PBCupLover – January 12, 2014 – 11:04 AM
To: Shelley Manning
Subject: Re: Reality Check

She's hanging in there. She has good days and bad days. Scratch that. She has bad days and worse days. But she's managing.

From: Shelley Manning – January 12, 2014 – 11:06 AM
To: PBCupLover
Subject: Re: Reality Check

That's exactly how she described it. Bad and worse.

From: PBCupLover – January 12, 2014 – 11:11 AM
To: Shelley Manning
Subject: Re: Reality Check

It will get easier. But with the wedding coming up, I know it's going to take an emotional toll on her. She's very worried about who's going to walk her down the aisle.

From: Shelley Manning – January 12, 2014 – 11:12 AM
To: PBCupLover
Subject: Re: Reality Check

I'll do it. I can totally rock a tux.

From: PBCupLover – January 12, 2014 – 11:14 AM
To: Shelley Manning
Subject: Re: Reality Check

I'm sure you can. I'll make that suggestion. Certainly will bring a smile to her face.

From: Shelley Manning – January 12, 2014 – 11:16 AM
To: PBCupLover
Subject: Re: Reality Check

You do that. I'm so relieved to know she has you there. You continue to take care of her or else.

From: PBCupLover – January 12, 2014 – 11:18 AM
To: Shelley Manning
Subject: Re: Reality Check

Believe me, I will. Not only do I love her more than anything, I don't want to endure your wrath.

From: Shelley Manning – January 12, 2014 – 11:20 AM
To: PBCupLover
Subject: Re: Reality Check

Smart thinking on both counts. Let me know if you need anything. Talk with you soon.

CHAPTER 18: INTERNET FUN

From: Renee Greene – January 16, 2014 – 9:33 PM
To: Shelley Manning
Subject: My disgusting man

Ugh! Sorry! Skype just isn't a good idea when Ethan's around. I apologize for his unbelievably rude behavior. In his defense, he didn't know we were talking when he came in and...did that.

From: Shelley Manning – January 16, 2014 – 9:38 PM
To: Renee Greene
Subject: Re: My disgusting man

You mean farted, let out the anal exhale, dropped a booty bomb, broke wind, cut the cheese, exhumed the dinner corpse, gave a heinie hiccup, trouser coughed, and I've run out of ways to paraphrase.

From: Renee Greene – January 16, 2014 – 9:39 PM
To: Shelley Manning
Subject: Re: My disgusting man

Yes...that.

From: Shelley Manning – January 16, 2014 – 9:42 PM
To: Renee Greene
Subject: Re: My disgusting man

It was just a fart. Couples do that stuff in front of each other all the time. It's a sign of complete comfort with each other.

From: Renee Greene – January 16, 2014 – 9:43 PM
To: Shelley Manning
Subject: Re: My disgusting man

I've never farted in front of him.

From: Shelley Manning – January 16, 2014 – 9:43 PM
To: Renee Greene
Subject: Re: My disgusting man

Never?

From: Renee Greene – January 16, 2014 – 9:44 PM
To: Shelley Manning
Subject: Re: My disgusting man

Well once on accident after a particularly cruciferous meal.

From: Shelley Manning – January 16, 2014 – 9:45 PM
To: Renee Greene
Subject: Re: My disgusting man

Cruciferous?

From: Renee Greene – January 16, 2014 – 9:48 PM
To: Shelley Manning
Subject: Re: My disgusting man

Yeah, you know, broccoli, cauliflower and brussel sprouts or other veggies that are a bit... gassy.

From: Shelley Manning – January 16, 2014 – 9:50 PM
To: Renee Greene
Subject: Re: My disgusting man

Honestly, I don't know how he puts up with you.

From: Renee Greene – January 16, 2014 – 9:51 PM
To: Shelley Manning
Subject: Re: My disgusting man

What do you mean? I only let it slip once.

From: Shelley Manning – January 16, 2014 – 9:57 PM
To: Renee Greene
Subject: Re: My disgusting man

Sweetie, it's not that. It's that you use words like cruciferous and expect that we all know what it means. And then you use "gassy" but make it sound as if you are whispering it through the side of your mouth out of embarrassment. I might as well be talking to Ashley! We all do it. It's just air.

From: Renee Greene – January 16, 2014 – 10:00 PM
To: Shelley Manning
Subject: Re: My disgusting man

Well, that Ashley comment was just uncalled for. ;) You're right. It's just air...but stinky air coming from private places. You do it in front of Nick?

From: Shelley Manning – January 16, 2014 – 10:04 PM
To: Renee Greene
Subject: Re: My disgusting man

First of all, I don't have any private places when it comes to Nick. And second, my "air" doesn't stink. It's like roses and rainbows. Sometimes I even get a standing ovation and I don't mean that sexually.

From: Renee Greene – January 16, 2014 – 10:06 PM
To: Shelley Manning
Subject: Re: My disgusting man

Okay. Okay. This conversation has officially gone awry. Can we please change the subject?

From: Shelley Manning – January 16, 2014 – 10:08 PM
To: Renee Greene
Subject: Re: My disgusting man

Sure, I can talk about something I DO mean sexually if you would prefer.

From: Renee Greene – January 16, 2014 – 10:10 PM
To: Shelley Manning
Subject: Re: My disgusting man

Argh! How about the Middle East Peace Process?

From: Shelley Manning – January 16, 2014 – 10:13 PM
To: Renee Greene
Subject: Re: My disgusting man

I think a big orgy would solve all of the region's troubles. Love the one you're with, right?

From: Renee Greene – January 16, 2014 – 10:14 PM
To: Shelley Manning
Subject: Re: My disgusting man

Is there a sexual answer to all of the world's ills?

From: Shelley Manning – January 16, 2014 – 10:15 PM
To: Renee Greene
Subject: Re: My disgusting man

I don't know. Give me a try.

From: Renee Greene – January 16, 2014 – 10:16 PM
To: Shelley Manning
Subject: Re: My disgusting man

School bullying?

From: Shelley Manning – January 16, 2014 – 10:20 PM
To: Renee Greene
Subject: Re: My disgusting man

More sex for nerds! Kids who are getting laid regularly don't mind the occasional shove into the locker. It might actually turn them on. Next?

From: Renee Greene – January 16, 2014 – 10:22 PM
To: Shelley Manning
Subject: Re: My disgusting man

Obesity?

From: Shelley Manning – January 16, 2014 – 10:24 PM
To: Renee Greene
Subject: Re: My disgusting man

More cushion for pushin'!

From: Renee Greene – January 16, 2014 – 10:26 PM
To: Shelley Manning
Subject: Re: My disgusting man

Ew! That's gross. Okay, try this one...Proliferation of nuclear weapons?

From: Shelley Manning – January 16, 2014 – 10:37 PM
To: Renee Greene
Subject: Re: My disgusting man

Nuclear weapons were first used to bring an end to World War II and fear of a nuclear war spread. Young Americans returned home from war and there were almost 2.3 million marriages in 1946, an increase of more than six hundred thousand over the previous year. Many of these newlyweds had children within a year: a record 3.8 million babies were born in 1947. This was the first year of the baby boom, which lasted for most of the 1950s. Between 1948 and 1953 more babies were born than had been over the previous thirty years. Nukes lead to fucks.

From: Renee Greene – January 16, 2014 – 10:39 PM
To: Shelley Manning
Subject: Re: My disgusting man

Did you seriously just look that up? Not the last line, but the rest of it?

From: Shelley Manning – January 16, 2014 – 10:40 PM
To: Renee Greene
Subject: Re: My disgusting man

What makes you think that?

From: Renee Greene – January 16, 2014 – 10:41 PM
To: Shelley Manning
Subject: Re: My disgusting man

<tapping my foot disapprovingly on the floor...>

From: Shelley Manning – January 16, 2014 – 10:44 PM
To: Renee Greene
Subject: Re: My disgusting man

Yes, I did just look that up. But you never said Wikipedia was off limits. What's your next scourge on society that I can solve for you with my special and unique brand of magic?

From: Renee Greene – January 16, 2014 – 10:46 PM
To: Shelley Manning
Subject: Re: My disgusting man

I was going to say homelessness, but I already know you are going to say let's open up our homes and beds to everyone.

From: Shelley Manning – January 16, 2014 – 10:48 PM
To: Renee Greene
Subject: Re: My disgusting man

Indeed, that would have been my response. Glad to see I'm rubbing off on you.

From: Renee Greene – January 16, 2014 – 10:49 PM
To: Shelley Manning
Subject: Re: My disgusting man

You are insufferable, you know that?

From: Shelley Manning – January 16, 2014 – 10:52 PM
To: Renee Greene
Subject: Re: My disgusting man

I do and that is why you love me, miss me and stalk me. Gotta run, but will talk soon. Hang in there, Sweetie. Mwah! Mwah!

From: Shelley Manning – January 22, 2014 – 8:42 PM
To: Renee Greene
Subject: James Lipton Questionnaire

Hi, Sweetie. You sounded downright chipper yesterday talking about your own agency. I'm so glad you have something positive to focus on aside from how lucky you are to have me as a best friend. Oh, and your wedding to Ethan.

So Nick and I have become obsessed with Inside the Actor's Studio. Even though I hate celebrities, I can't seem to tear myself away from this series. My fav part is the James Lipton questions at the end. So much so, that I've put together my responses for when being as hot and fabulous as I am merits inclusion as a guest on the show.

Want to play along?

From: Renee Greene – January 22, 2014 – 8:48 PM
To: Shelley Manning
Subject: Re: James Lipton Questionnaire

I'm not surprised that Nick likes the show. He's totally star struck. He is constantly asking me about any celebrities I've worked with and when we saw that actress from The Good Wife, he was giddy. The questionnaire sounds fun. Send the questions over.

From: Shelley Manning – January 22, 2014 – 8:56 PM
To: Renee Greene
Subject: Re: James Lipton Questionnaire

He is pretty star struck. It's actually quite sexy. He likes to pretend that I'm a famous actress and he's a fan. But that's a story for another time. Okay, here are the James Lipton questions...

- What is your favorite word?
- What is your least favorite word?
- What turns you on?
- What turns you off?
- What sound or noise do you love?
- What sound or noise do you hate?
- What is your favorite curse word?
- What profession other than your own would like to attempt?
- What profession would you not like to do?
- If heaven exists, what would you like to hear God say when you arrive at the pearly gates?

From: Renee Greene – January 22, 2014 – 8:59 PM
To: Shelley Manning
Subject: Re: James Lipton Questionnaire

OMG! I am already reeling at the thought of your X-rated answers.

From: Shelley Manning – January 22, 2014 – 9:00 PM
To: Renee Greene
Subject: Re: James Lipton Questionnaire

Yeah, mine are pretty good.

From: Renee Greene – January 22, 2014 – 9:00 PM
To: Shelley Manning
Subject: Re: James Lipton Questionnaire

Are you going to share?

From: Shelley Manning – January 22, 2014 – 9:01 PM
To: Renee Greene
Subject: Re: James Lipton Questionnaire

You first.

Okay. Here goes...

- What is your favorite word? Thank you. Okay, it's two words but one phrase that I feel like no one says anymore. As you know, manners are very important to me.
- What is your least favorite word? It's a tie between "moist" and "panties" with extra "fingernails-down-the-blackboard-style chills" when the two words are used together. <shudder>
- What turns you on? Humor. That's probably why I'm head over heels in love with Jon Stewart...oh, and Ethan too. ;)
- What turns you off? Petty squabbles. The world has enough problems without arguing and fretting over inconsequential stuff.
- What sound or noise do you love? My sweet angel, Siobhan, in fits of giggles. And believe me, no one gets her laughing it up like Auntie Renee.
- What sound or noise do you hate? Airplanes taking off. Fatal accidents are more likely to occur during the climbing stage of flight and that sound of the engines revving up just fuh-reaks me out!
- What is your favorite curse word? Mother#@$%er! Enough said!
- What profession other than your own would like to attempt? Professional cake decorator. It looks so fun and yummy.
- What profession would you not like to do? Accountant. As you know, my checkbook rarely balances.
- If heaven exists, what would you like to hear God say when you arrive at the pearly gates? I know Jews don't believe in heaven, but we're happy to have you here, the cupcakes are calorie-free and your hair looks great.

From: Shelley Manning – January 22, 2014 – 9:25 PM
To: Renee Greene
Subject: Re: James Lipton Questionnaire

Moist panties? That was my answer for favorite word. Ha-larious! THANK YOU (I know you love hearing that) for the embellishments on the responses. Definitely puts things into more perspective for me. Time for my responses. Are you sitting down?

From: Renee Greene – January 22, 2014 – 9:29 PM
To: Shelley Manning
Subject: Re: James Lipton Questionnaire

I am sitting down. And I've got a cold drink of water on hand in case I need to douse the flames of the heat rising inside of my loins from your tawdry responses.

From: Shelley Manning – January 22, 2014 – 9:31 PM
To: Renee Greene
Subject: Re: James Lipton Questionnaire

LOL! You need to start writing cheesy romance novels. Perhaps that should be your new career.

From: Renee Greene – January 22, 2014 – 9:34 PM
To: Shelley Manning
Subject: Re: James Lipton Questionnaire

I will give it some thought if my own agency doesn't work out or I smother Skinny Skye out of sheer jealousy and end up in jail with lots of time on my blood-stained hands to write. For now, I need your answers, please.

From: Shelley Manning – January 22, 2014 – 9:45 PM
To: Renee Greene
Subject: Re: James Lipton Questionnaire

- What is your favorite word? Pleasure.
- What is your least favorite word? Intolerance.
- What turns you on? Experimentation.

- What turns you off? Monotony.
- What sound or noise do you love? Screams of ecstasy.
- What sound or noise do you hate? Morning alarm clock.
- What is your favorite curse word? Cocksucker!
- What profession other than your own would like to attempt? Sex phone operator   <just like yours, it also looks so fun and yummy>.
- What profession would you not like to do? Preschool teacher.
- If heaven exists, what would you like to hear God say when you arrive at the pearly gates? Yeah, right, like I'm going to Heaven. Ha-Larious! But, I suppose miracles do happen. If that's the case, I expect God to say, "Shake that heavenly ass on in."

From: Renee Greene – January 22, 2014 – 9:50 PM
To: Shelley Manning
Subject: Re: James Lipton Questionnaire

Somehow I doubt that God is using the phrase "heavenly ass" but otherwise, the answers are pretty spot on to what I had anticipated.

From: Shelley Manning – January 22, 2014 – 9:52 PM
To: Renee Greene
Subject: Re: James Lipton Questionnaire

Oh, no. Am I becoming too predictable? As we've just established, I think monotony is a turn off.

From: Renee Greene – January 22, 2014 – 9:54 PM
To: Shelley Manning
Subject: Re: James Lipton Questionnaire

You're not predictable. Your sexiness and sassiness are just anticipated because I know you so well.

From: Shelley Manning – January 22, 2014 – 9:56 PM
To: Renee Greene
Subject: Re: James Lipton Questionnaire

Works for me. Okay, I'm going to run. This heavenly ass is going to get some beauty rest, not that I need it.

From: Renee Greene – January 22, 2014 – 9:58 PM
To: Shelley Manning
Subject: Re: James Lipton Questionnaire

If you need beauty rest, I need to hibernate. Just kidding! Don't go all "pep talk" on me.

From: Shelley Manning – January 22, 2014 – 10:00 PM
To: Renee Greene
Subject: Re: James Lipton Questionnaire

Good one. And thank you for sparing me the pep talk. I'm definitely too tired for that tonight. Mwah! Mwah!

From: Shelley Manning – January 28, 2014 – 7:24 AM
To: Renee Greene
Subject: Happy birthday Sweetie

Wanted to be the first (well perhaps the second, since you literally wake up to Ethan) person to wish you a happy birthday, Sweetie. I hope you take some time to enjoy and celebrate yourself today. I'll call you later.

From: Renee Greene – January 28, 2014 – 8:12 AM
To: Shelley Manning
Subject: Re: Happy birthday Sweetie

Thanks, Shel. You are actually #3. My mom called a few minutes ago and of course I got a big kiss – and a lovely diamond tear drop necklace – from Ethan.

I have a TON of work I need to get done today in order to be up and running for Alistra on 2/1. Will call you tonight on our way to dinner. Thanks for thinking of me.

From: Mark Finlay – January 28, 2014 – 10:31 AM
To: Renee Greene
Subject: Happy Bday

Happy Bday, Renee. I know these past few weeks have been tough, but I hope you find a bit of happiness today.

From: Renee Greene – January 28, 2014 – 10:35 AM
To: Mark Finlay
Subject: Re: Happy Bday

Thanks, Mark. I appreciate you thinking of me.

From: Renee Greene – January 28, 2014 – 1:12 PM
To: PBCupLover
Subject: Need a pep talk

Hi, Babe. I tried you at work but you didn't answer. You're probably on a conference call – as usual. I could use a pep talk when you get a chance. Can you call me when you're free. Thanks!

From: PBCupLover – January 28, 2014 – 1:23 PM
To: Renee Greene
Subject: Re: Need a pep talk

I am on a conference call. What's wrong?

From: Renee Greene – January 28, 2014 – 1:31 PM
To: PBCupLover
Subject: Re: Need a pep talk

I'm just having a rough day. I sent Skye out to pick up some more printer ink so I could have some time alone. I was trying to figure out how to set up the account payable/receivable software and it wasn't working. I was growing increasingly frustrated. Then it made me think about calling my dad for help. He loved this kind of stuff. I've never met anyone else who would read books on C-DOS programming...for fun. And then it hit me like a thunderbolt – he's gone.

From: PBCupLover – January 28, 2014 – 1:38 PM
To: Renee Greene
Subject: Re: Need a pep talk

I can't imagine what you're going through. I haven't lost a parent. I hate to say this, but I think you're going to have a lot of days like this when you're going about doing your daily stuff and something will remind you of him. There's no getting around it. It just sucks.

From: Renee Greene – January 28, 2014 – 1:43 PM
To: PBCupLover
Subject: Re: Need a pep talk

It does suck! And once it hits me, the water works start. And you know once I start crying – a real good cry – it's hard for me to stop. I'm having a hard time typing right now because I'm in the throws of heaving sobs.

From: PBCupLover – January 28, 2014 – 1:50 PM
To: Renee Greene
Subject: Re: Need a pep talk

Calm down. Take a few deep breaths. I can't bring your dad back or help you overcome the sadness you're feeling right now. But I can set up your software for you and teach you how to use it. I am a CFO of a publicly-traded company, after all.

From: Renee Greene – January 28, 2014 – 1:52 PM
To: PBCupLover
Subject: Re: Need a pep talk

Okay. Okay. Deep breaths. Skye just walked in. I've got to get it together.

From: PBCupLover – January 28, 2014 – 1:59 PM
To: Renee Greene
Subject: Re: Need a pep talk

Babe, you're doing great. Wipe away the tears, take a few more deep breaths and put the software aside. I'll help you tonight after your bday dinner and we'll get it all figured out. I love you. Hang in there.

From: Ashley Gordon – January 28, 2014 – 7:29 PM
To: Renee Greene
Subject: Happy birthday

Sorry I wasn't able to connect with you by phone today. I left you a voicemail but your machine was making some weird beeps. I just wanted to make sure you know that I've been thinking about you today. Hope you're having a great birthday and congrats on Eureka!

From: Renee Greene – January 28, 2014 – 8:43 PM
To: Ashley Gordon
Subject: Re: Happy birthday

Thanks, Ash! I did get your voicemail. I'm having trouble with the machine and need to get a new one before I officially open for business in a few days from the new Eureka offices. Sorry I've been too busy to stay in touch, starting up the new business and all. And sorry we weren't able to celebrate together this year. We'll talk soon and make some plans.

From: Renee Greene – February 5, 2014 – 9:43 AM
To: Shelley Manning
Subject: Burn fat...fast!

I just read an article about the best 7 foods to burn fat. I've listed each below with my take on how to integrate them into my diet. Whadaya think?

- Oats – put 'em in a cookie with some chocolate and butterscotch chips.
- Eggs – need them for said cookies above.
- Apples – one word – Strudel!
- Garlic – garlic knots! So doughy and yummy.
- Green Tea – Bamboo makes that amazing green tea ice cream. After a big helping of mu shu chicken, vegetable fried rice and some eggrolls, it's nice to cool off the palate.
- Tomatoes – Make 'em green and fried and I'm in. Not only a good movie, but a tasty treat.
- Dark Chocolate – done.

From: Shelley Manning – February 5, 2014 – 10:02 AM
To: Renee Greene
Subject: Re: Burn fat...fast!

You already know what I'm going to say. And you should be thankful you didn't send this to Ashley too, because I'm quite certain we both know what she would say.

From: Renee Greene – February 5, 2014 – 10:05 AM
To: Shelley Manning
Subject: Re: Burn fat...fast!

Yeah, I know. I was just daydreaming. With only 5 months to the day away from my wedding, I know I can't be eating garlic knots and ice cream. I guess I was hoping you would take pity on me and give me permission to indulge.

From: Shelley Manning – February 5, 2014 – 10:11 AM
To: Renee Greene
Subject: Re: Burn fat...fast!

As supportive of a friend as I am, I cannot in good conscience allow you to eat fried green tomatoes and streudel in a fantasy-induced attempt to fit into your wedding gown.

From: Renee Greene – February 5, 2014 – 10:14 AM
To: Shelley Manning
Subject: Re: Burn fat...fast!

Nuts! Too bad those aren't on the fat-burning list. I could eat them straight from the jar.

From: Shelley Manning – February 5, 2014 – 10:17 AM
To: Renee Greene
Subject: Re: Burn fat...fast!

You're nuts! I give you permission to eat one ounce of dark chocolate after you complete a Curves workout. Go give those old biddies something to grumble about.

From: Renee Greene – February 5, 2014 – 10:20 AM
To: Shelley Manning
Subject: Re: Burn fat...fast!

Thanks, Shel. I appreciate you tossing me a bone.

From: Shelley Manning – February 5, 2014 – 10:22 AM
To: Renee Greene
Subject: Re: Burn fat...fast!

Just don't let that bone be the inside of a big steak. Lean meats only, Sweetie. Mwah! Mwah!

CHAPTER 19: FUNNY VALENTINE

From: Renee Greene – February 11, 2014 – 12:01 PM
To: Mark Finlay
Subject: Blue Party?

Hi there. Don't know if you have any plans for Valentine's Day this year. But Ethan mentioned our Blue Parties to his boss who LOVED the idea and is throwing a big Valentine's Day bash.

Although we explained that the party was for people who are single, Ethan and I have to go. I'm still feeling unbearably blue about my dad's passing, and quite frankly, I'm not really in a party mood these days. But again, my presence is mandated. Thought you might like to come and hang out with me.

From: Mark Finlay – February 11, 2014 – 12:59 PM
To: Renee Greene
Subject: Re: Blue Party?

Not sure I'm really in a party mood these days either. It's been a real crummy couple of months, hasn't it?

From: Renee Greene – February 11, 2014 – 1:06 PM
To: Mark Finlay
Subject: Re: Blue Party?

Yeah, it's been rough all around. But misery loves company, right? Come with me. There will be plenty of great food and booze. William may be young and impulsive, but he sure knows how to have a good time. Shelley won't be there, so there's no chance of a repeat of your embarrassing escapades from a few years past. Ethan and I will pick you up at 9:00?

From: Mark Finlay – February 11, 2014 – 1:08 PM
To: Renee Greene
Subject: Re: Blue Party?

You had to bring that up, didn't you?

From: Renee Greene – February 11, 2014 – 1:10 PM
To: Mark Finlay
Subject: Re: Blue Party?

Yes. Figured you could use a little laugh. Okay, so you're not laughing. Perhaps I figured I could use a little laugh. Say yes!

From: Mark Finlay – February 11, 2014 – 1:10 PM
To: Renee Greene
Subject: Re: Blue Party?

Okay. Yes.

From: Renee Greene – February 11, 2014 – 1:11 PM
To: Mark Finlay
Subject: Re: Blue Party?

Yippee!

From: Shelley Manning – February 13, 2014 – 9:01 AM
To: Renee Greene
Subject: Sweet Valentine's Day

I wanted to wish you a happy early Valentine's Day and give you permission to indulge that sweet tooth of yours for one day. I read that it's good to occasionally completely blow your diet because it shocks your body and causes you to burn everything off.
Don't know if it's true, but I'm using that as my excuse to indulge in whatever chocolately goodness Nick brings home. And if it happens to be melted all over his body, so much the better.

From: Renee Greene – February 13, 2014 – 9:06 AM
To: Shelley Manning
Subject: Re: Sweet Valentine's Day

I'm laughing and crying at the same time. Laughing so hard because you are hilarious. I'm sure whatever Nick brings home, you will find a way to turn it into something sexual. Actually, knowing Nick, it will probably be sexual to begin with. ;) I doubt you two will have trouble burning off all of those extra calories.

Crying because I had plans with my dad tomorrow. A while back, I bought us two tickets for a special walking tour of 6 bakeries and candy shops around Beverly Hills. They basically take you to each, telling you the history of various shops and then you get to enjoy tastings at each. I figured this would be a fun way for us to spend some time together. And honestly, did he really need another golf shirt?

From: Shelley Manning – February 13, 2014 – 9:11 AM
To: Renee Greene
Subject: Re: Sweet Valentine's Day

I'm sorry, Sweetie. Didn't mean to bring up a sore subject.

From: Renee Greene – February 13, 2014 – 9:16 AM
To: Shelley Manning
Subject: Re: Sweet Valentine's Day

I won't make a comment about you being sore the next day. Oh, did I say that out loud? ;) I appreciate knowing you are thinking about me. I decided not to go on the chocolate tour. It didn't seem right. Sadly, I need to put on a happy face anyway and a blue dress because Ethan's boss is hosting a Blue Party.

From: Shelley Manning – February 13, 2014 – 9:11 AM
To: Renee Greene
Subject: Re: Sweet Valentine's Day

Well, hang in there, Sweetie. I know things have been rough but you are loved – on Valentine's Day and always. Mwah! Mwah!

From: Shelley Manning – February 14, 2014 – 3:30 PM
To: Renee Greene
Subject: Fwd: Valentine's Day Cat Videos

Ha! Ha! Figured you could use a laugh. There are NO videos
attached to this email, but I figured you would get a kick out of
thinking that I missed dear old "cassidy" and had become interested
in cat videos.

From: Renee Greene – February 14, 2014 – 3:34 PM
To: Shelley Manning
Subject: Re: Fwd: Valentine's Day Cat Videos

OMG! I am cracking up. I saw the subject line and just about fell
out of my chair. If I had been drinking water, I would have taken a
sit-com spit take. That is just what I needed to brighten my day. Not
the cat videos, but you mocking the cat videos.

From: Shelley Manning – February 14, 2014 – 3:38 PM
To: Renee Greene
Subject: Re: Fwd: Valentine's Day Cat Videos

Are you saying you spit rather than swallow?

From: Renee Greene – February 14, 2014 – 3:42 PM
To: Shelley Manning
Subject: Re: Fwd: Valentine's Day Cat Videos

Holy cow! You did not just type that?!?

From: Shelley Manning – February 14, 2014 – 3:46 PM
To: Renee Greene
Subject: Re: Fwd: Valentine's Day Cat Videos

Oh, but I did. I figured you could really use a good laugh. I know
it's been a rough six weeks. How are you holding up – between the
sad of your dad and the stress of the new agency?

From: Renee Greene – February 14, 2014 – 3:52 PM
To: Shelley Manning
Subject: Re: Fwd: Valentine's Day Cat Videos

I cannot stop giggling like a school girl over how incredibly dirty you are! I've had my ups and downs. But honestly this new agency is giving me such a sense of purpose and so much to look forward to that it's hard not to feel hopeful. I'm hoping to take all of the lessons I learned from my Dad and put them not only toward this business but all of my relationships.

From: Shelley Manning – February 14, 2014 – 3:57 PM
To: Renee Greene
Subject: Re: Fwd: Valentine's Day Cat Videos

Wherever he is, I'm sure he's smiling and shooting under par. Let me know if you need anything, Sweetie. Mwah! Mwah!

From: Renee Greene – February 17, 2014 – 8:12 AM
To: Mark Finlay
Subject: Blue Party Fun?

Did you have fun at the party Friday night? I saw you talking with Marnie from Ethan's department. She's seems really cute and sweet. Ethan says she's really down to earth, has a fun, quirky sense of humor and can totally rock a spreadsheet. Is it too early for us to fix you up with someone?

From: Mark Finlay – February 17, 2014 – 9:32 AM
To: Renee Greene
Subject: Re: Blue Party Fun?

I don't know. What's the protocol here Miss Manners?

From: Renee Greene – February 17, 2014 – 9:39 AM
To: Mark Finlay
Subject: Re: Blue Party Fun?

Well, it's not like you're a widower for gosh sakes. You just had a bad break up. I think a four month recovery period (notice I didn't say mourning!) is respectable and appropriate. More importantly, do you feel ready to go on a date?

From: Mark Finlay – February 17, 2014 – 9:40 AM
To: Renee Greene
Subject: Re: Blue Party Fun?

I don't know.

From: Renee Greene – February 17, 2014 – 9:42 AM
To: Mark Finlay
Subject: Re: Blue Party Fun?

Why not go for it? You've got to get back out there sometime and she seems nice and normal.

From: Mark Finlay – February 17, 2014 – 9:44 AM
To: Renee Greene
Subject: Re: Blue Party Fun?

If she's so great, maybe I shouldn't go out with her. It never works out with the rebound girl.

From: Renee Greene – February 17, 2014 – 9:46 AM
To: Mark Finlay
Subject: Re: Blue Party Fun?

It's not like you have to marry the girl. Just go on a date with her. It's time for you to spend time someone nice and normal.

From: Mark Finlay – February 17, 2014 – 9:50 AM
To: Renee Greene
Subject: Re: Blue Party Fun?

Yeah, Cass wasn't nice or normal, was she? Marnie did seem pretty cool. But she's small. I mean really, really tiny – at least compared to me. How tall is she anyway?

From: Renee Greene – February 17, 2014 – 9:51 AM
To: Mark Finlay
Subject: Re: Blue Party Fun?

I will find out!

From: Renee Greene – February 17, 2014 – 9:51 AM
To: PBCupLover
Subject: Quick Q

How tall is Marnie in your office?

From: PBCupLover – February 17, 2014 – 9:52 AM
To: Renee Greene
Subject: Re: Quick Q

Why?

From: Renee Greene – February 17, 2014 – 9:52 AM
To: PBCupLover
Subject: Re: Quick Q

Just wondering.

From: PBCupLover – February 17, 2014 – 9:53 AM
To: Renee Greene
Subject: Re: Quick Q

I don't know. She's really short.

From: Renee Greene – February 17, 2014 – 9:53 AM
To: PBCupLover
Subject: Re: Quick Q

I know she's petite. But I want to know specifically how tall she is. Can you ask her?

From: PBCupLover – February 17, 2014 – 9:54 AM
To: Renee Greene
Subject: Re: Quick Q

You want me to ask her how tall she is?

From: Renee Greene – February 17, 2014 – 9:54 AM
To: PBCupLover
Subject: Re: Quick Q

Yes. Please.

From: PBCupLover – February 17, 2014 – 9:56 AM
To: Renee Greene
Subject: Re: Quick Q

I'm not asking her how tall she is. That's awkward. I don't really understand why you need to know.

From: Renee Greene – February 17, 2014 – 9:58 AM
To: PBCupLover
Subject: Re: Quick Q

I want to know because I want to fix her up with Mark and he wants to know.

From: PBCupLover – February 17, 2014 – 10:00 AM
To: Renee Greene
Subject: Re: Quick Q

Renee! Are you sure that's a wise idea? Maybe you should just let him move on when he's ready.

From: Renee Greene – February 17, 2014 – 10:02 AM
To: PBCupLover
Subject: Re: Quick Q

I already spoke with him and his hesitation is her height. I need to rule out the "she's too short for me" excuse. So please go ask her.

From: PBCupLover – February 17, 2014 – 10:04 AM
To: Renee Greene
Subject: Re: Quick Q

What do I say to her when she asks me why?

From: Renee Greene – February 17, 2014 – 10:05 AM
To: PBCupLover
Subject: Re: Quick Q

Why do you think she'll ask you why?

From: PBCupLover – February 17, 2014 – 10:06 AM
To: Renee Greene
Subject: Re: Quick Q

Wouldn't you?

From: Renee Greene – February 17, 2014 – 10:08 AM
To: PBCupLover
Subject: Re: Quick Q

Good point. Okay, tell her that I want to know and it's some sort of girl thing. You sounding clueless about girl things should satisfy her curiosity.

From: PBCupLover – February 17, 2014 – 10:09 AM
To: Renee Greene
Subject: Re: Quick Q

Not bad, actually. Okay. Be right back.

From: PBCupLover – February 17, 2014 – 10:12 AM
To: Renee Greene
Subject: Re: Quick Q

She said 5 feet. Can I get back to work now?

From: Renee Greene – February 17, 2014 – 10:13 AM
To: PBCupLover
Subject: Re: Quick Q

Yes, dear. Thank you. XO

From: Renee Greene – February 17, 2014 – 10:15 AM
To: Mark Finlay
Subject: Re: Blue Party Fun?

Ethan casually inquired (long story and I know how you hate that) and she said she was 5 feet tall. That's not that teeny. You're just really tall. Whaddaya say?

From: Renee Greene – February 17, 2014 – 11:16 AM
To: Mark Finlay
Subject: Re: Blue Party Fun?

Say yes!

From: Renee Greene – February 17, 2014 – 1:32 PM
To: Mark Finlay
Subject: Re: Blue Party Fun?

Say yes!

From: Renee Greene – February 18, 2014 – 9:02 AM
To: Mark Finlay
Subject: Re: Blue Party Fun?

Say yes!

From: Mark Finlay – February 18, 2014 – 10:06 AM
To: Renee Greene
Subject: Re: Blue Party Fun?

Alright. Alright already. Get me her number.

From: Renee Greene – February 18, 2014 – 10:07 AM
To: Mark Finlay
Subject: Re: Blue Party Fun?

Hurrah! I'll call you with it later.

CHAPTER 20: JAILBIRD

From: Renee Greene – February 22, 2014 – 12:08 PM
To: Shelley Manning
Subject: Unbelievable!

Ethan and I were planning to register today, however he just got a "get out of jail free card" on the shopping and the truly ironic reason why goes beyond unbelievable to truly astonishing. Ethan is down at central booking bailing his boss out of jail. His boss!

Now granted, his boss is 24 years old. But still, he runs an ecommerce company that just went public and made him a millionaire – many times over – in a heartbeat. And although he's brilliant, he's also stupid as shit. Right after the IPO last week, he went out and bought a Maserati (and paid cash!)

Because of the way his ownership in the company was structured, he got a ton of cash up-front. Sadly, Ethan can't sell his stock for 12 months. Just praying that the stock price holds up a bit over the next year so he (and by "he" I really mean "we") can cash in. But I digress.

William is an immature idiot who just crashed his Maserati into a brick wall because he was high on ecstasy. Ethan's spent the better part of the day trying to track down where is he and how to get him out of jail. Astonishing, no?

From: Shelley Manning – February 22, 2014 – 2:35 PM
To: Renee Greene
Subject: Re: Unbelievable!

Say what? Ethan's going to be a millionaire? I should have cuddled more. ;) Thought you could use a little humor, no?

Now to the matter at hand…say what? Why would he call Ethan to bail him out? Doesn't he have anyone else in his life – like his mommy and daddy – for that? He is only 24 after all.

From now on, he will be known as Billy the Kid. And what a fool for throwing it all away.

From: Renee Greene – February 22, 2014 – 2:50 PM
To: Shelley Manning
Subject: Re: Unbelievable!

Oh, he didn't call Ethan. Get this. Billy the Kid (LOVE IT, by the way!) was out with one of these ladies (possibly of the night) that seem to be clinging onto him these past few months as (1) it became apparent he was going to be filthy rich and (2) he's been hitting the night life scene. I guess after years of slaving away on programming, he feels like it's his turn to party it up.

He's always texting Ethan about some chick he's "hanging and banging" as he puts he. He's quite the immature misogynist. Friday night, he texted Ethan about this one particular fling. Ethan finally texted him this morning to find out how his weekend went. (I think Ethan is living vicariously through Billy the Kid.)

Rather than a return text, he gets a call from Billy the Kid's phone. It isn't him but this chick he was "hanging and banging" on Friday. Apparently, he and she were at a club, got high and then he crashed his car into a light pole on Sunset Blvd. She had his phone and didn't know who to call to help him.

Billy the Kid had been sitting in jail for nearly two days. He got arrested and she took his phone with her to the hospital to be treated for minor scrapes and such. Ethan has been on the phone with the Sherriff's department and LAPD for over an hour trying to figure out where Billy the Kid is, how much is bail is, etc. Craziness!

From: Shelley Manning – February 22, 2014 – 3:15 PM
To: Renee Greene
Subject: Re: Unbelievable!

Let me see if I understand this. This ho (using terms Billy the Kid likely used) has his cell phone and she's reading through unflattering texts about herself from Billy the Kid to Ethan and she had the decency to call Ethan back instead of tossing the phone in the trash?

She must be a ho with a heart of gold. I would definitely not be that forgiving. Then again, Billy the Kid has a TON of money and I'm sure she wouldn't mind a "finder's fee" for finding him a way out of jail.

From: Renee Greene – February 22, 2014 – 3:20 PM
To: Shelley Manning
Subject: Re: Unbelievable!

I know, really! I've seen a few of the texts. Needless to say, he paints a much less than flattering picture of women. I would have let the guy suffer.

From: Shelley Manning – February 22, 2014 – 3:24 PM
To: Renee Greene
Subject: Re: Unbelievable!

Really? You would have let him suffer? I think not! You are much too nice of a person – even if you were a ho – to do that. You would be like the *Pretty Woman* of whores.

From: Renee Greene – February 22, 2014 – 3:26 PM
To: Shelley Manning
Subject: Re: Unbelievable!

Awww. That's so sweet of you to say.

From: Shelley Manning – February 22, 2014 – 3:28 PM
To: Renee Greene
Subject: Re: Unbelievable!

This truly has to be one of our more odd conversations. So what happened next?

From: Renee Greene – February 22, 2014 – 3:36 PM
To: Shelley Manning
Subject: Re: Unbelievable!

Ethan finally found that he spent the weekend in a cell at central booking but was about to be transferred to county lock up. His bail is $50,000. Thankfully no one – aside from our ho with a heart of gold – was hurt or it would probably have been a lot more.

Ethan is at a bail bondsman office now. He has to put 10% down and the bondsman will cover the rest. I told him to put it on our credit card so at least we'll get the miles. ;) I'm trying to earn enough to fly first class on our honeymoon.

From: Shelley Manning – February 22, 2014 – 3:39 PM
To: Renee Greene
Subject: Re: Unbelievable!

HA-LARIOUS! Leave it to you to find a wedding-related silver lining to this fiasco. Keep me posted. I can't wait to hear more.

From: Renee Greene – February 22, 2014 – 3:40 PM
To: Shelley Manning
Subject: Re: Unbelievable!

I will!

From: Shelley Manning – February 23, 2014 – 2:12 PM
To: Renee Greene
Subject: Re: Unbelievable!

Well?

From: Renee Greene – February 23, 2014 – 2:20 PM
To: Shelley Manning
Subject: Re: Unbelievable!

OMG! So here's the scoop. Billy the Kid freaked out and got out of the car right after the crash but was too high to call anyone for help. He tossed his phone to Stella (if that's her real name) and told her to call his parents. She must have been too high, shell shocked or stupid to do so.

When the police arrived, it was pretty apparent he was on something and he got arrested. I asked Ethan why he didn't call someone from jail. (As we've established, I am an expert in the legal system due to my many hours of watching *Law & Order,* so I know he had to have been offered a phone call.)

That idiot doesn't know anyone's phone number. They're all programmed into his phone. He didn't know *how* to call anyone. So he sat in that jail cell and wondered how long it would take before anyone figured out he was missing.

From: Shelley Manning – February 23, 2014 – 2:24 PM
To: Renee Greene
Subject: Re: Unbelievable!

Of course his first call would be to Mommy and Daddy. Ha-larious. Just goes to show you, you need to memorize an emergency number. Kids today can be so lazy.

From: Renee Greene – February 23, 2014 – 2:26 PM
To: Shelley Manning
Subject: Re: Unbelievable!

Kids today? He's 24. You're 31. It's not like you're old enough to be his mother. Or are you?

From: Shelley Manning – February 23, 2014 – 2:28 PM
To: Renee Greene
Subject: Re: Unbelievable!

Are you suggesting I had sex at age 8?!? Sweetie, I may be advanced, but that's just wrong.

From: Renee Greene – February 23, 2014 – 2:29 PM
To: Shelley Manning
Subject: Re: Unbelievable!

Yeah, as I think about it now, pretty gross. Sorry.

From: Shelley Manning – February 23, 2014 – 2:32 PM
To: Renee Greene
Subject: Re: Unbelievable!

So is he just horrified and embarrassed? I'm sure its got to be hard going into the office the next day knowing everyone there is talking about you. I mean that's never bothered me, but I'm a rare breed.

From: Renee Greene – February 23, 2014 – 2:37 PM
To: Shelley Manning
Subject: Re: Unbelievable!

You are a rare breed indeed. I don't think anyone else, aside from Ethan, me, you and Stella (our ho) knows. Ethan sure as heck won't tell anyone. He wants to keep his job and, not that he's prone to blackmail, but I think having this info on your boss is a bit of job security.

From: Shelley Manning – February 23, 2014 – 2:41 PM
To: Renee Greene
Subject: Re: Unbelievable!

I'm prone to blackmail. Another reason I'm a rare breed. Damn! I would be so embarrassed if I were him, even if it's just being embarrassed around Ethan.

From: Renee Greene – February 23, 2014 – 2:43 PM
To: Shelley Manning
Subject: Re: Unbelievable!

Yes, you are a confident woman with a penchant for blackmail but I don't think even you would want to rock the proverbial boat on this one. Too much at stake.

From: Shelley Manning – February 23, 2014 – 2:45 PM
To: Renee Greene
Subject: Re: Unbelievable!

Yes, I forgot, our dear Ethan is on his way to millions. Damn! I really should have cuddled more.

From: Renee Greene – February 23, 2014 – 2:47 PM
To: Shelley Manning
Subject: Re: Unbelievable!

Not to "millions" but certainly to a nice nest egg for us. I'll be sure to keep you posted on our financial status as well as his bosses impending court proceedings.

From: Shelley Manning – February 23, 2014 – 2:49 PM
To: Renee Greene
Subject: Re: Unbelievable!

Sounds great. Gotta run. Talk with you later, Sweetie. Mwah! Mwah!

CHAPTER 21: WHAT HAPPENS...

From: Shelley Manning – February 24, 2014 – 9:43 AM
To: Renee Greene, PBCupLover, Mark Finlay, Ashley Gordon
Subject: What happens in Vegas could happen to us

Hi, everyone. I hate to admit it, but I miss you all. Yes, even you Finlay. What do you say we all meet for a fun weekend in Vegas? Nick and I were thinking the weekend of March 21.

From: Renee Greene – February 24, 2014 – 9:46 AM
To: PBCupLover
Subject: Fwd: What happens in Vegas could happen to us

I'm going through Shelley withdrawals. I could use an alcohol-fueled escape. Please tell me you are free that weekend?

From: PBCupLover – February 24, 2014 – 10:02 AM
To: Renee Greene
Subject: Re: Fwd: What happens in Vegas could happen to us

Alcohol-fueled escape? Is that to replace the cupcake-fueled escape I normally witness? J/K. Looks clear on my end. Consider it a go.

From: Renee Greene – February 24, 2014 – 10:06 AM
To: PBCupLover
Subject: Re: Fwd: What happens in Vegas could happen to us

That was a good one, my love! Be sure to tell Billy the Kid that (1) he cannot spring some work thing on you at the last minute because you are going to Vegas and (2) No! He can't come with us.

From: PBCupLover – February 24, 2014 – 10:07 AM
To: Renee Greene
Subject: Re: Fwd: What happens in Vegas could happen to us

Billy the Kid?

From: Renee Greene – February 24, 2014 – 10:08 AM
To: PBCupLover
Subject: Re: Fwd: What happens in Vegas could happen to us

That's Shelley's impossibly clever nickname for him.

From: PBCupLover – February 24, 2014 – 10:11 AM
To: Renee Greene
Subject: Re: Fwd: What happens in Vegas could happen to us

Why, of course it is. How silly of me. And you're right. He probably would invite himself along. But if he did, you know he'd pick up the tab for all of the drinks.

From: Renee Greene – February 24, 2014 – 10:15 AM
To: PBCupLover
Subject: Re: Fwd: What happens in Vegas could happen to us

Tempting, but I think I need a weekend of you away from work, him and his infantile behavior. And no emailing or texting him while we're there. He can live a few days without your clever and witty comments on his pathetic life.

From: PBCupLover – February 24, 2014 – 10:18 AM
To: Renee Greene
Subject: Re: Fwd: What happens in Vegas could happen to us

I think his lifestyle rivals most of what you would find in Vegas already. But you got it. Consider me all yours.

From: Renee Greene – February 24, 2014 – 10:21 AM
To: Shelley Manning, PBCupLover, Mark Finlay, Ashley Gordon
Subject: Re: What happens in Vegas could happen to us

Yes! Yes! Yes! Sounds like a ton of fun. Ethan and I are in.

From: Mark Finlay – February 24, 2014 – 11:02 AM
To: Shelley Manning, PBCupLover, Renee Greene, Ashley Gordon
Subject: Re: What happens in Vegas could happen to us

Sounds like a fun time. Count me in. I'll probably drive so let me know if anyone needs a ride from the airport.

From: Ashley Gordon – February 24, 2014 – 12:32 PM
To: Shelley Manning, PBCupLover, Renee Greene, Mark Finlay
Subject: Re: What happens in Vegas could happen to us

I can't imagine exposing Siobhan to the elements of Las Vegas – the smoke, the scantily clad bimbos, the booze, the gambling, etc. Let me see if I can get Greg's parents to watch her for the weekend so we can come. I'll let you know later today.

From: Shelley Manning – February 24, 2014 – 1:45 PM
To: Renee Greene
Subject: Fwd: Re: What happens in Vegas could happen to us

What is she talking about? The smoke, booze, gambling, etc. Those are the **best** parts of Vegas. And if there are going to be any scantily clad bimbos there, I better be one of them, right? But I suppose you don't want a baby around all of that. Good thing I'm all woman!

From: Renee Greene – February 24, 2014 – 1:49 PM
To: Shelley Manning
Subject: Re: Fwd: Re: What happens in Vegas could happen to us

You're "all" something alright. And I can't wait to see you (and see you do some things in Vegas that should stay there but certainly won't).

From: Shelley Manning – February 24, 2014 – 1:51 PM
To: Renee Greene
Subject: Re: Fwd: Re: What happens in Vegas could happen to us

Count on it, Sweetie. Mwah! Mwah!

From: Ashley Gordon – February 24, 2014 – 8:32 PM
To: Shelley Manning, PBCupLover, Renee Greene, Mark Finlay
Subject: Re: What happens in Vegas could happen to us

Greg's parents are able to watch Siobhan so count us in, too.

From: Shelley Manning – February 25, 2014 – 9:08 AM
To: Renee Greene, PBCupLover, Mark Finlay, Ashley Gordon
Subject: Re: What happens in Vegas could happen to us

Excellent. Some of Nick's friends are also flying in for the weekend, so there will be a big group of us for some Vegas fun. The weather is expected to be hot, so you might not want to wear skin, let alone clothes. ;) Be sure to pack a swimsuit.

We are staying at the Bellagio, but feel free to book wherever you want. Maybe we could all have dinner on Friday. Why don't I go ahead and make a reservation at Le Cirque at the Bellagio for 8:00 on Friday night? See you then.

From: Renee Greene – February 25, 2014 – 9:11 AM
To: Shelley Manning
Subject: Re: What happens in Vegas could happen to us

Yes! Yes! Yes! So excited. I really need this bit of escape. This is going to be fun, fun, fun!

From: Ashley Gordon – February 25, 2014 – 10:03 AM
To: Shelley Manning, PBCupLover, Renee Greene, Mark Finlay
Subject: Re: What happens in Vegas could happen to us

Le Cirque. That's French food, right?

From: Shelley Manning – February 25, 2014 – 10:05 AM
To: Ashley Gordon, PBCupLover, Renee Greene, Mark Finlay
Subject: Re: What happens in Vegas could happen to us

Yes, Ashley. It's French. They have a lovely menu and I'm confident you will find something you like.

From: Ashley Gordon – February 25, 2014 – 10:06 AM
To: Shelley Manning, PBCupLover, Renee Greene, Mark Finlay
Subject: Re: What happens in Vegas could happen to us

I always do my best to be flexible.

From: Shelley Manning – February 25, 2014 – 10:10 AM
To: Renee Greene
Subject: Fwd: Re: What happens in Vegas could happen to us

Flexible? She's killing me! I just hope for Greg's sake she's not so rigid in the sack. And I mean that both figuratively and literally.

From: Renee Greene – February 25, 2014 – 10:11 AM
To: Shelley Manning
Subject: Re: Fwd: Re: What happens in Vegas could happen to us

Now you're killing me…with laughter.

From: Shelley Manning – February 25, 2014 – 10:14 AM
To: Renee Greene
Subject: Re: Fwd: Re: What happens in Vegas could happen to us

Just doing my part to raise your spirits before we lift the spirits in multiple toasts in Vegas. Gotta run. Mwah! Mwah!

From: Shelley Manning – March 4, 2014 – 11:32 AM
To: Renee Greene
Subject: Shopping like your sister

Hey, there. I've decided to go "shopping" like your sister does. You know, sifting through your closet asking if you still wear something or whether she can have it. But you'll get off easy with me. I just want to borrow. What size is that little black dress with the pink satin bow? I want to borrow it in Vegas.

From: Renee Greene – March 4, 2014 – 11:34 AM
To: Shelley Manning
Subject: Re: Shopping like your sister

I don't know.

From: Shelley Manning – March 4, 2014 – 11:35 AM
To: Renee Greene
Subject: Re: Shopping like your sister

You don't know the size or you don't know if I can borrow it?

From: Renee Greene – March 4, 2014 – 11:36 AM
To: Shelley Manning
Subject: Re: Shopping like your sister

I don't know the size.

From: Shelley Manning – March 4, 2014 – 11:37 AM
To: Renee Greene
Subject: Re: Shopping like your sister

Are you at home? Can you run and check?

From: Renee Greene – March 4, 2014 – 11:37 AM
To: Shelley Manning
Subject: Re: Shopping like your sister

I don't know.

From: Shelley Manning – March 4, 2014 – 11:38 AM
To: Renee Greene
Subject: Re: Shopping like your sister

You don't know if you are at home?

From: Renee Greene – March 4, 2014 – 11:41 AM
To: Shelley Manning
Subject: Re: Shopping like your sister

I am at home. I just don't know the size. In a fit of paranoia, self loathing and frosting-induced psychosis, I cut all of the size tags out of all of my clothes. Don't judge!

From: Shelley Manning – March 4, 2014 – 11:42 AM
To: Renee Greene
Subject: Re: Shopping like your sister

Renee!

From: Renee Greene – March 4, 2014 – 11:42 AM
To: Shelley Manning
Subject: Re: Shopping like your sister

I know.

From: Shelley Manning – March 4, 2014 – 11:43 AM
To: Renee Greene
Subject: Re: Shopping like your sister

Well, at least you finally know *something*. Just bring it with you.
Gotta run. Mwah! Mwah!

CHAPTER 22: REVELATIONS

From: Ashley Gordon – March 9, 2014 – 2:59 PM
To: Renee Greene, Shelley Manning
Subject: From the mouths of babes

Siobhan just said her first word. It was mama. I've never cried so
hard from happiness in my life.

From: Renee Greene – March 9, 2014 – 3:06 PM
To: Ashley Gordon, Shelley Manning
Subject: Re: From the mouths of babes

WHAT? Her first words weren't Auntie Renee rocks! For shame,
my sweet angel. For shame! Otherwise, how exciting!

From: Shelley Manning – March 9, 2014 – 3:14 PM
To: Renee Greene, Ashley Gordon
Subject: Re: From the mouths of babes

Really? I would have thought her first words would have been
"Shelley's ass is sublime." Not only is it true, but I've been
whispering that to her over and over every time I see her. You would
think it would be part of her vernacular by now.

From: Ashley Gordon – March 9, 2014 – 3:20 PM
To: Renee Greene, Shelley Manning
Subject: Re: From the mouths of babes

I'm going to ignore that, Shelley. Just know I'll be keeping my eye
on you next time you're around her…if I let you around her again.
And Renee, as much as you are an amazing aunt, little Siobhan
clearly knows what's best for her. Despite all of Greg's "da-da" "da-
da"s, she said mama first. And it was the most amazing thing I've
ever heard. It really hit me. I'm her mommy.

From: Renee Greene – March 9, 2014 – 3:25 PM
To: Ashley Gordon, Shelley Manning
Subject: Re: From the mouths of babes

I know she said "mama" first and that's great. But now you've got to
teach Siobhan to say "dada" and call for dada when she needs or
wants something – especially in the middle of the night. As she gets
older and grows more vocal (and demanding, as kids do), you'll want
her calling for Daddy to do things for her, not Mommy. ;)

From: Ashley Gordon – March 9, 2014 – 3:31 PM
To: Renee Greene, Shelley Manning
Subject: Re: From the mouths of babes

I think I would have agreed with you yesterday. But for some
reason, I don't mind if she calls for me and asks me to do things for
her. That's what I *should* be doing. That's what I'm here for? All of
this time I've been looking for something to give me a greater
purpose when the greatest purpose I could have is being "mama."

From: Shelley Manning – March 9, 2014 – 3:34 PM
To: Renee Greene
Subject: Fwd: Re: From the mouths of babes

Oh, barf!

From: Renee Greene – March 9, 2014 – 3:37 PM
To: Shelley Manning
Subject: Re: Fwd: Re: From the mouths of babes

Knock it off. This is like a therapy breakthrough for her. You
haven't been around to see her spiral a bit out of control. She's been
really lost. I think this is a watershed moment for her.

From: Shelley Manning – March 9, 2014 – 3:40 PM
To: Renee Greene
Subject: Re: Fwd: Re: From the mouths of babes

Shouldn't she have had that watershed moment when she had the kid – not like more than a year later?

From: Renee Greene – March 9, 2014 – 3:44 PM
To: Shelley Manning
Subject: Re: Fwd: Re: From the mouths of babes

I'm just glad she's having it. It seems to have taken her a while to get the hang of this mommy thing, but I've really never heard her sound so happy and hopeful. So be nice! No, be more than nice. Be supportive. Genuinely supportive.

From: Shelley Manning – March 9, 2014 – 3:45 PM
To: Renee Greene
Subject: Re: Fwd: Re: From the mouths of babes

Fine! But only for Siobhan's sake.

From: Renee Greene – March 9, 2014 – 3:47 PM
To: Ashley Gordon, Shelley Manning
Subject: Re: From the mouths of babes

It's wonderful to see you feeling so hopeful and happy. I hope this is just the start of amazing things for you and your family.

From: Shelley Manning – March 9, 2014 – 3:48 PM
To: Renee Greene, Ashley Gordon
Subject: Re: From the mouths of babes

Ditto.

From: Renee Greene – March 9, 2014 – 3:48 PM
To: Shelley Manning
Subject: Fwd: Re: From the mouths of babes

Don't exert yourself too much there.

From: Shelley Manning – March 9, 2014 – 3:52 PM
To: Renee Greene
Subject: Re: Fwd: Re: From the mouths of babes

What? You said it so eloquently, there was really nothing for me to do but agree. Perhaps the problem isn't me being supportive enough, but you stealing all of the thunder.

From: Renee Greene – March 9, 2014 – 3:53 PM
To: Shelley Manning
Subject: Re: Fwd: Re: From the mouths of babes

Yeah, that's it.

From: Ashley Gordon – March 9, 2014 – 3:55 PM
To: Renee Greene, Shelley Manning
Subject: Re: From the mouths of babes

Thanks, ladies. I'm going to try and video chat with my folks so they can see her say it, too. I'll talk with you soon.

From: Renee Greene – March 16, 2014 – 2:30 PM
To: Ashley Gordon
Subject: Thrilled for you!

It was so great having lunch with you and my sweet angel, Siobhan, today. Not only do I always enjoy spending time with the two of you at Mel's, but it was wonderful to see you looking so happy. It's been a long time since I've seen that genuine, joyous smile on your face. I've missed it and am so glad that it's back.

From: Ashley Gordon – March 16, 2014 – 2:42 PM
To: Renee Greene
Subject: Re: Thrilled for you!

Thanks, Renee. Not only for saying those nice things but for being the kind of friend I've needed and don't always deserve. Knowing you've been here to stick by me, support me, encourage me, and put up with me has meant the world.

From: Renee Greene – March 16, 2014 – 2:44 PM
To: Ashley Gordon
Subject: Re: Thrilled for you!

Of course. We're friends for life. I'm just so happy to see you so happy.

From: Ashley Gordon – March 16, 2014 – 2:48 PM
To: Renee Greene
Subject: Re: Thrilled for you!

I'm almost off the meds. I weaned myself this past week, due to be completely off in two more. I'm feeling great. And I was glad to see you closer to your normal self, too.

From: Renee Greene – March 16, 2014 – 2:54 PM
To: Ashley Gordon
Subject: Re: Thrilled for you!

That's fantastic. I knew it would just be a matter of time before you were feeling good. And yes, I'm doing my best to focus on positive things like work and the wedding. Not that I'm trying to forget my dad or distract myself from thinking about him. I'm just doing what I know he would want me to do: be happy and enjoy life.

From: Ashley Gordon – March 16, 2014 – 2:56 PM
To: Renee Greene
Subject: Re: Thrilled for you!

I very much want to be the friend you need and merit.

From: Renee Greene – March 16, 2014 – 3:00 PM
To: Ashley Gordon
Subject: Re: Thrilled for you!

You are, Ashley. Like I said, friends for life. I've got to run. I have a few client things I've got to get done today. Again, I'm so happy you are doing well. We'll talk soon.

From: Shelley Manning – March 20, 2014 – 11:41 AM
To: Renee Greene, PBCupLover, Mark Finlay, Ashley Gordon
Subject: Viva Las Vegas!

We're all set to see you tomorrow night at Le Cirque at the Bellagio at 8:00. It's an upscale restaurant, so plan to dress accordingly. That means no flip flops, Finlay. And Ethan can't wear anything emblazoned with the Ohio State Buckeyes logo. I'm confident that Renee and Ashley will be appropriately dressed.

From: Mark Finlay – March 20, 2014 – 11:45 AM
To: Shelley Manning
Subject: Re: Viva Las Vegas!

Just because I am a computer programmer and live by the beach doesn't mean I don't know how to dress for the nightlife scene. I will find something black.

From: PBCupLover – March 20, 2014 – 11:48 AM
To: Shelley Manning
Subject: Re: Viva Las Vegas!

Damn! I had my Buckeye slippers and sweatshirt all packed and ready to go.

From: Renee Greene – March 20, 2014 – 11:49 AM
To: Shelley Manning
Subject: Fwd: Re: Viva Las Vegas!

YES! Thank you for that!

From: Shelley Manning – March 20, 2014 – 11:53 AM
To: Renee Greene
Subject: Re: Fwd: Re: Viva Las Vegas!

No problem. I've been around him enough to know that there is no dress code that he can't force his Buckeye gear into.

From: Renee Greene – March 20, 2014 – 11:57 AM
To: Shelley Manning
Subject: Re: Fwd: Re: Viva Las Vegas!

So true. Regarding me, you want me to dress "appropriately." Does this mean you know Ashley and I will be wearing something suitable for a nice restaurant or that we will be wearing something typically-suited to a night on the town in Vegas, which means something "inappropriate"?

From: Shelley Manning – March 20, 2014 – 12:02 PM
To: Renee Greene
Subject: Re: Fwd: Re: Viva Las Vegas!

Ha! I definitely mean that you will be wearing something suitable for a nice restaurant. I don't see you flaunting a leather bustier, sky high heels or other accoutrements you find when prowling the streets, drunk, at 3:00 am. I would PAY MONEY to see Ashley like that. Think we can slip her a mickey and watch her do unthinkable things in Vegas, which would later serve as fabulous blackmail fodder?

From: Renee Greene – March 20, 2014 – 12:06 PM
To: Shelley Manning
Subject: Re: Fwd: Re: Viva Las Vegas!

Accoutrements? Who are you?!? Hearing you bust out these fancy words just throws me for a loop. And while I too would pay money to see Ashley thrown for a loop, I don't want to get thrown in jail for drugging one of my best friends.

From: Shelley Manning – March 20, 2014 – 12:10 PM
To: Renee Greene
Subject: Re: Fwd: Re: Viva Las Vegas!

I hear what you're saying. We can just keep plying her with alcohol. Last time I saw her, she was a massive complainer about how Siobhan has cramped her – what she thinks passes for – style. Maybe she'll just cut loose on her own.

From: Renee Greene – March 20, 2014 – 12:15 PM
To: Shelley Manning
Subject: Re: Fwd: Re: Viva Las Vegas!

She's been so much better these past months. Something clicked and I think you're going to like the new Ashley. Well, maybe you won't like her, but I think you'll be able to tolerate her. ;)

Okay, I've got to go pack and oversee Ethan's packing. I need to ensure he puts in a nice outfit of *his* clothes. Did I tell you what happened last year?

From: Shelley Manning – March 20, 2014 – 12:19 PM
To: Renee Greene
Subject: Re: Fwd: Re: Viva Las Vegas!

I'd be surprised if you didn't tell me what happened last year, as it would seem implausible that something happens to you and I don't hear about it. But refresh my memory.

From: Renee Greene – March 20, 2014 – 12:21 PM
To: Shelley Manning
Subject: Re: Fwd: Re: Viva Las Vegas!

With an attitude like that, I'm just not going to tell you.

From: Shelley Manning – March 20, 2014 – 12:22 PM
To: Renee Greene
Subject: Re: Fwd: Re: Viva Las Vegas!

Oh c'mon. Don't be like that. Spill!

From: Renee Greene – March 20, 2014 – 12:27 PM
To: Shelley Manning
Subject: Re: Fwd: Re: Viva Las Vegas!

Last year, we went to a wedding in DC for one of his fraternity buddies. While packing, Ethan grabbed what he thought was his suit from the dry cleaning pile. Instead, he grabbed his suit jacket and my black pants. He didn't realize it until we were getting dressed a half hour before the ceremony. So he wore my pants.

From: Shelley Manning – March 20, 2014 – 12:30 PM
To: Renee Greene
Subject: Re: Fwd: Re: Viva Las Vegas!

Shockingly, I had not heard this story before. I suppose it's because you were too embarrassed to admit that Ethan fit into your pants.

From: Renee Greene – March 20, 2014 – 12:33 PM
To: Shelley Manning
Subject: Re: Fwd: Re: Viva Las Vegas!

UGH! You're right. That's probably why I never told anyone. Here I was sharing the story to shame him and in turn just shamed myself.

From: Shelley Manning – March 20, 2014 – 12:35 PM
To: Renee Greene
Subject: Re: Fwd: Re: Viva Las Vegas!

I won't tell a soul…except for Nick…and possibly Ethan when I see him dressed up. But no one else.

From: Renee Greene – March 20, 2014 – 12:36 PM
To: Shelley Manning
Subject: Re: Fwd: Re: Viva Las Vegas!

Don't say ANYTHING to Ethan. He would be mortified.

From: Shelley Manning – March 20, 2014 – 12:38 PM
To: Renee Greene
Subject: Re: Fwd: Re: Viva Las Vegas!

Well, that's exactly why I would say something to him. Don't you get me?

From: Renee Greene – March 20, 2014 – 12:39 PM
To: Shelley Manning
Subject: Re: Fwd: Re: Viva Las Vegas!

Shelley!

From: Shelley Manning – March 20, 2014 – 12:41 PM
To: Renee Greene
Subject: Re: Fwd: Re: Viva Las Vegas!

Don't worry. I won't say anything to him. But I have no secrets from Nick. He'll get a kick out of it. Yes, go help Ethan pack. See you tomorrow. Mwah! Mwah!

From: Ashley Gordon – March 20, 2014 – 4:32 PM
To: Shelley Manning, Renee Greene
Subject: Re: Viva Las Vegas!

Hey, ladies. Just got back from the pediatrician and Siobhan has
croup so I won't be able to make it to Vegas this weekend. Sorry for
the short notice. Hope you guys have fun without us.

From: Shelley Manning – March 20, 2014 – 4:45 PM
To: Ashley Gordon, Renee Greene
Subject: Re: Viva Las Vegas!

Croup? Crap! Poor little Siobhan! Hope she feels better soon.
Sorry you won't be joining us, Ashley. Take care, and we'll miss
you.

From: Renee Greene – March 20, 2014 – 5:02 PM
To: Shelley Manning, Ashley Gordon
Subject: Re: Viva Las Vegas!

What? My poor sweet angel.

From: Ashley Gordon – March 20, 2014 – 6:42 PM
To: Shelley Manning, Renee Greene
Subject: Re: Viva Las Vegas!

What about poor me who has to miss all of the fun. A trip to sin
city…with Shelley…really? It's like the mothership is calling her
home. As much as I never really enjoyed hearing about all of the
men she's been with, for old time's sake, it would have been fun to
see Shelley go crazy.

From: Renee Greene – March 20, 2014 – 7:03 PM
To: Shelley Manning, Ashley Gordon
Subject: Re: Viva Las Vegas!

Yes, poor you, too. I'm sorry you and Greg can't come. What a bummer! Well, I will be sure to take some hidden videos of Shelley and Nick and all of her debauchery and send them to you.

From: Renee Greene – March 21, 2014 – 9:32 PM
To: Ashley Gordon
Subject: OMG! OMG! OMG!

CALL ME! YOU WILL NOT BELIEVE THIS!

From: Ashley Gordon – March 22, 2014 – 1:31 AM
To: Renee Greene
Subject: Re: OMG! OMG! OMG!

I've been up all night with Siobhan. Poor little thing has been coughing nonstop. She's finally fallen asleep in my arms. What's going on?

From: Renee Greene – March 22, 2014 – 1:34 AM
To: Ashley Gordon
Subject: Re: OMG! OMG! OMG!

Shelley got married. Married! Shelley!

From: Ashley Gordon – March 22, 2014 – 1:38 AM
To: Renee Greene
Subject: Re: OMG! OMG! OMG!

Huh? Perhaps it is the lack of sleep but I'm having trouble processing this. And what are you doing awake?

From: Renee Greene – March 22, 2014 – 1:46 AM
To: Ashley Gordon
Subject: Re: OMG! OMG! OMG!

She and Nick planned their wedding for this weekend in Vegas. This weekend getaway was just a ruse to get us all there for their wedding. Agh! I can't believe it. And I'm awake because this is Vegas…for Shelley's wedding.

From: Ashley Gordon – March 22, 2014 – 1:48 AM
To: Renee Greene
Subject: Re: OMG! OMG! OMG!

Holy moly! Gimme details!

From: Renee Greene – March 22, 2014 – 1:49 AM
To: Ashley Gordon
Subject: Re: OMG! OMG! OMG!

We're all drunk and playing Keno in the hotel bar. Let me call you later.

From: Renee Greene – March 22, 2014 – 2:39 AM
To: Shelley Manning, Ashley Gordon
Subject: An inspired moment

OMG! You will NOT believe what I just did. So Ethan and I were in the hotel bar and decided we have had enough of the Vegas night life scene. It is 2:30 am so I feel we've given a respectable amount of time to some disrespectful activities. Anyhoo, I went to the ladies room and he went to close out our bar tab. (And seeing the tab, I'm sort of wishing Billy the Kid had come so he could pick up the bill!)

I saw him waiting at the bar talking to three hip dudes. I walked over to them – I still can't believe that I did this! – and started pointing to them one by one as I said, "eenie meenie miney moe" landing my pointing finger on Ethan. Then I said, "How would you like to come back to my hotel room with me?" Ethan looked at me, turned to these three super cool guys, then turned back to me and said, "Sure."

He wrapped his arm about my waist and we walked away. As we left, I turned back and blew the three guys a kiss. They were dumbfounded.

We laughed and laughed all of the way to our room. It was a moment straight from the Shelley Manning playbook. Okay, I have to go. Now that I've invited this "strange" man to my hotel room, I have to figure out what to do with him. Talk soon!

From: Shelley Manning – March 22, 2014 – 10:32 AM
To: Renee Greene, Ashley Gordon
Subject: Re: An inspired moment

You saucy minx! I prefer a variation called eat 'em, lick 'em, bite 'em, moan. But I think yours works, too.

From: Ashley Gordon – March 22, 2014 – 11:02 AM
To: Shelley Manning, Renee Greene
Subject: Re: An inspired moment

That really is a Shelley move. Or at least it was before she GOT MARRIED! Congratulations by the way. I'm so sorry I missed it. Fill me in on all of the details.

From: Shelley Manning – March 22, 2014 – 12:11 PM
To: Renee Greene, Ashley Gordon
Subject: Re: An inspired moment

I'll call you later, Ash.

From: Ashley Gordon – March 22, 2014 – 12:15 PM
To: Renee Greene
Subject: Fwd: Re: An inspired moment

Shelley is going to call me later. She never calls me. This really is huge.

From: Renee Greene – March 22, 2014 – 12:17 PM
To: Ashley Gordon
Subject: Fwd: Re: An inspired moment

I call you all of the time, so I know it's not that big of a deal. But I will try to call you later too. Or at least email you the details.

From: Renee Greene – March 23, 2014 – 12:31 PM
To: Ashley Gordon
Subject: Vegas wedding

Sorry for the delay in getting back to you. We're on the ride home and despite being exhausted and completely hung over (it is Vegas, after all), here's the scoop.

We all met at Le Cirque for what we thought was dinner. Once everyone arrived and we were all enjoying a cocktail, Nick said he had an announcement. He turned to Shelley, got down on one knee and asked her to marry him. I literally squealed out loud.

I was so excited to see her get engaged. She said yes and then a friend of Nick's walked over. Shelley said, "No time like the present" and then winked at me. They had planned this all along. The friend was ordained over the Internet and married them right on the spot and then we just partied and celebrated.

From: Ashley Gordon – March 23, 2014 – 12:45 PM
To: Renee Greene
Subject: Re: Vegas wedding

Did she wear white? Please tell me she did NOT wear white! Was there any "Elvis" presence there? Is she worried what her parents are going to say?

From: Renee Greene – March 24, 2014 – 1:11 PM
To: Ashley Gordon
Subject: Re: Vegas wedding

She did NOT wear white. She wore a really awesome, body hugging red dress with heels so high I thought she would topple over. And she did, after about 6 mojitos. But that's a story (and hilarious video!) for another time.

There was no Elvis presence per se although their ordained friend Andy did a little "thank you very much" impersonation when Nick's friend Charlie handed him the rings. We didn't really talk about what her parents would say. Although knowing Shelley, she's not worried what anyone – even Charlene and Frank – are going to say.

I, on the other hand, am worried what the flight attendants will say if I don't adhere to their third request to shut down my electronics in preparation for landing. Hope my sweet angel is feeling better. Let me call you later when we're home and I've had a much-needed nap.

From: Shelley Manning – March 24, 2014 – 1:15 PM
To: Renee Greene
Subject: Call me!

I just tried your cell but it's off. You must still be on the plane. Call me when you land.

From: Renee Greene – March 24, 2014 – 1:45 PM
To: Shelley Manning
Subject: Re: Call me!

Just tried you but *your* cell is off. You're probably on your way to Italy <cue jealousy>. Do you have in-flight wi-fi? What's up? I'm very intrigued and don't want to wait two weeks to find out what you want to tell me.

In the meantime, what I want to tell you is that I am so happy for you. I must say I was a bit surprised at first to see you getting married without telling me, letting me plan a bachelorette party or wedding shower, help you shop for a dress, etc.

But I understand that all of that stuff isn't really your thing. I just can't believe you are married. You are a Mrs.! No matter how or where it happened, it was a beautiful evening and the start to what I hope is a beautiful life for you and Nick.

From: Shelley Manning – March 24, 2014 – 1:54 PM
To: Renee Greene
Subject: Re: Call me!

Thanks, Sweetie. You're right. I'm not into all of that stuff, but I know you are. So don't worry. I'll be there right by your side for it all. I appreciate all of the warm sentiments about my life with Nick. I'm excited for what lays ahead.

From: Renee Greene – March 24, 2014 – 1:58 PM
To: Shelley Manning
Subject: Re: Call me!

Sorry to be the perpetual grammar hawk, but it's actually what "lies" ahead, not "lays" ahead.

From: Shelley Manning – March 24, 2014 – 2:00 PM
To: Renee Greene
Subject: Re: Call me!

Believe me, it's "lays" ahead as in "he's getting laid."

From: Renee Greene – March 24, 2014 – 2:03 PM
To: Shelley Manning
Subject: Re: Call me!

Well done, my friend. But what did you need to talk with me about? Certainly it was not the fact that you and your husband are going to consummate your marriage. That's a given.

From: Shelley Manning – March 24, 2014 – 2:05 PM
To: Renee Greene
Subject: Re: Call me!

The marriage has already been consummated. We took care of that in the bathroom at the restaurant.

From: Renee Greene – March 24, 2014 – 2:06 PM
To: Shelley Manning
Subject: Re: Call me!

Really?!? You don't think that's TMI?

From: Shelley Manning – March 24, 2014 – 2:09 PM
To: Renee Greene
Subject: Re: Call me!

Just because I'm married doesn't mean I've changed. But, like you most of the time, I digress. You will NOT believe who I bumped into at the airport.

From: Renee Greene – March 24, 2014 – 2:15 PM
To: Shelley Manning
Subject: Re: Call me!

Hmmm. Let's see. You are flying from Las Vegas to Italy. Andrea Bocelli?

From: Shelley Manning – March 24, 2014 – 2:17 PM
To: Renee Greene
Subject: Re: Call me!

That is actually an outstanding guess. Wrong. But well thought out and perfectly plausible. No, I bumped into Jason Kite.

From: Renee Greene – March 24, 2014 – 2:18 PM
To: Shelley Manning
Subject: Re: Call me!

What? How? Where? Huh?

From: Shelley Manning – March 24, 2014 – 2:19 PM
To: Renee Greene
Subject: Re: Call me!

Oh, how I wish I could see your face right now.

From: Renee Greene – March 24, 2014 – 2:20 PM
To: Shelley Manning
Subject: Re: Call me!

Don't keep me in suspense. Details, please.

From: Shelley Manning – March 24, 2014 – 2:24 PM
To: Renee Greene
Subject: Re: Call me!

Nick and I were hanging out in the first class lounge because, well, that's how we roll. Jason was there waiting on a flight to London. He recognized me, walked over and said hello. Given his penchant for gushing over celebrities, Nick was quite impressed that I was friends with a famous rock star. He asked how you were doing.

From: Renee Greene – March 24, 2014 – 2:31 PM
To: Shelley Manning
Subject: Re: Call me!

Of course he recognized you after the major display that you and his drummer put on a while back. And with touring rock stars, and the groupies that must follow them, that's saying a lot! So, Jason asked about me? What did he say? What did you say?

From: Shelley Manning – March 24, 2014 – 2:35 PM
To: Renee Greene
Subject: Re: Call me!

Of course he asked about you. He wanted to know how you were
doing, if you were seeing anyone, etc.

From: Renee Greene – March 24, 2014 – 2:37 PM
To: Shelley Manning
Subject: Re: Call me!

He asked if I was seeing someone? What did you say?

From: Shelley Manning – March 24, 2014 – 2:41 PM
To: Renee Greene
Subject: Re: Call me!

I told him you were engaged to Ethan, the man you were dating
when he tried to woo you back. And that you were getting married in
a few months.

From: Renee Greene – March 24, 2014 – 2:42 PM
To: Shelley Manning
Subject: Re: Call me!

What did he say?

From: Shelley Manning – March 24, 2014 – 2:42 PM
To: Renee Greene
Subject: Re: Call me!

He said he was happy for you and wished you well.

From: Renee Greene – March 24, 2014 – 2:43 PM
To: Shelley Manning
Subject: Re: Call me!

Whoa! How is he doing? Is he seeing anyone?

From: Shelley Manning – March 24, 2014 – 2:44 PM
To: Renee Greene
Subject: Re: Call me!

I didn't ask. Didn't seem to be my place.

From: Renee Greene – March 24, 2014 – 2:45 PM
To: Shelley Manning
Subject: Re: Call me!

Since when has that ever stopped you?

From: Shelley Manning – March 24, 2014 – 2:46 PM
To: Renee Greene
Subject: Re: Call me!

True. Maybe being an old married lady is mellowing me out.

From: Renee Greene – March 24, 2014 – 2:47 PM
To: Shelley Manning
Subject: Re: Call me!

Don't let that ever change you!

From: Shelley Manning – March 24, 2014 – 2:51 PM
To: Renee Greene
Subject: Re: Call me!

You're right. The restroom is free. Let me see if Nick wants to consummate our marriage again…at 30,000 feet. I'll call you when I'm back from our trip. Mwah! Mwah!

From: Mark Finlay – March 27, 2014 – 10:53 AM
To: Renee Greene
Subject: Shelley Withdrawals?

Hey, there. I know Shelley is on her honeymoon right now and you are probably going through withdrawals.
So I thought I would offer up my services. I'm happy to make inappropriate comments, mock people, come up with silly nicknames and eat cupcakes. I draw the line at a pedicure, but considering she lives in Seattle now, I'm not sure you two do that anyway.

From: Renee Greene – March 27, 2014 – 11:15 AM
To: Mark Finlay
Subject: Re: Shelley Withdrawals?

Well, aren't you just the best girlfriend a gal could have? Tee hee! Seriously, you are so sweet. It has been hard not to have her around. Plus I'm insanely jealous that she's in Italy right now. Sounds fab!

But honestly, ever since she moved to Seattle, I'm learning to handle more on my own. I'm not always successful at it, evidenced by some recent spats, bouts of friendship paranoia and excessive chocolate eating. But I'm working on it. A girl has to grow up sometime, right? But I so appreciate you checking in on me.

From: Mark Finlay – March 27, 2014 – 11:22 AM
To: Renee Greene
Subject: Re: Shelley Withdrawals?

That is indeed what friends are for. You've been so wonderful in my time of need that I just wanted to return the favor. Let me know if you need anything and let's make some plans soon.

From: Renee Greene – March 27, 2014 – 11:26 AM
To: Mark Finlay
Subject: Re: Shelley Withdrawals?

Sounds great. I'll give you a call next week and we'll set something up. Thanks again!

From: Renee Greene – April 1, 2014 – 9:41 AM
To: Ashley Gordon
Subject: Catholic Question

This is no April Fool's joke! I was trying on some wedding dresses with my mom yesterday. The saleswoman brought in this very puffy dress which looked terrible on me. Through the curtain I told her that maybe it was because I had a cupcake earlier that day. All of a sudden I felt like I was in a confessional! Is that what it's like?

From: Ashley Gordon – April 1, 2014 – 10:02 AM
To: Renee Greene
Subject: Re: Catholic Question

That's pretty funny. Yes, that is indeed what it's like. You say your sins aloud and then face the judgment. Don't mean to sound harsh, but why are you eating cupcakes months before your wedding?

From: Renee Greene – April 1, 2014 – 10:04 AM
To: Ashley Gordon
Subject: Re: Catholic Question

Stress eating for sure. There's another sin I can confess too. ;)

From: Renee Greene – April 6, 2014 – 9:00 AM
To: Shelley Manning
Subject: Benvenuti a casa!

(That's welcome home in Italian.) Hope you and Nick had the most incredible time in Italy on your (agh!) honeymoon. Can't wait to hear all about your adventures. Strike that! Can't wait to hear all about your G-rated, travel adventures. The X-rated, honeymoon adventures you can keep to yourself.

From: Shelley Manning – April 6, 2014 – 10:02 AM
To: Renee Greene
Subject: Re: Benvenuti a casa!

Really? You're not the least bit curious about my honeymoon escapades? The more I think about it, I don't think you could handle it.

From: Renee Greene – April 6, 2014 – 10:06 AM
To: Shelley Manning
Subject: Re: Benvenuti a casa!

Really? What if I pulled a Tom Cruise "I want the truth" (a la A Few Good Men) on you. Would you scream out, "You can't handle the truth"?

From: Shelley Manning – April 6, 2014 – 10:08 AM
To: Renee Greene
Subject: Re: Benvenuti a casa!

I would indeed! I could totally pull off that monologue.

From: Renee Greene – April 6, 2014 – 10:12 AM
To: Shelley Manning
Subject: Re: Benvenuti a casa!

I have no doubt you could pull it off. You're married. Married! I still can't believe you are married. And you planned it all within a month. Being in the midst of my own wedding planning (hurrah!), it's hard to believe you did it all so quickly. Shouldn't surprise me, though. You truly are amazing.

From: Shelley Manning – April 6, 2014 – 10:16 AM
To: Renee Greene
Subject: Re: Benvenuti a casa!

Why do in a year what I can just cram into a month, Sweetie? I'm just being efficient with my time.

From: Renee Greene – April 6, 2014 – 10:19 AM
To: Shelley Manning
Subject: Re: Benvenuti a casa!

I just feel badly that I wasn't able to throw you a shower or a bachelorette party. I always said I would do those things for you.

From: Shelley Manning – April 6, 2014 – 10:21 AM
To: Renee Greene
Subject: Re: Benvenuti a casa!

Bullshit! You never thought I would get married.

From: Renee Greene – April 6, 2014 – 10:23 AM
To: Shelley Manning
Subject: Re: Benvenuti a casa!

How dare you! ;) With comments like that, you're on thin ice.

From: Shelley Manning – April 6, 2014 – 10:27 AM
To: Renee Greene
Subject: Re: Benvenuti a casa!

Then let's skate! I am excited to share all of the trip details with you. But I've got to work before I can fly down for dress shopping next weekend. We'll have the day to catch up. Gotta run. Mwah! Mwah!

CHAPTER 23: PLAYING DRESS UP

From: Renee Greene – April 9, 2014 – 1:13 PM
To: Shelley Manning
Subject: This is the (work) life!

I'm listening to indie bands from LA right now for work. Can you believe it? I'm getting paid to listen to music. I'm heading out to a club this weekend to listen to one perform live…and I can bill my time for it. This is the (work) life, indeed! Counting down the days until you get here.

From: Shelley Manning – April 9, 2014 – 1:42 PM
To: Renee Greene
Subject: Re: This is the (work) life!

What client is this for? And how can I get in on this action?

From: Renee Greene – April 9, 2014 – 1:50 PM
To: Shelley Manning
Subject: Re: This is the (work) life!

It's a new hotel that will be opening in the hip Los Feliz/Silverlake district. They had hired an agency a year ago but are disappointed with what they are doing so they put out a new bid for the project. I beat out my old agency and a few others (insert pat on the back here) to conduct their grand opening in a few months and they want a cool indie band to headline the event.

It's right before the wedding but hard to turn down the work and opportunity to establish myself as an agency. And since I'm the agency, I need to be involved in selecting the band.

From: Shelley Manning – April 9, 2014 – 1:56 PM
To: Renee Greene
Subject: Re: This is the (work) life!

That's awesome. Hope those fuckers at the Carr Agency learned not to mess with you. Who are you considering?

From: Renee Greene – April 9, 2014 – 2:01 PM
To: Shelley Manning
Subject: Re: This is the (work) life!

We've narrowed it down to three: Luke's Crossing, The Velvet Biscuits and Blue Cloud Pie. I'm setting up a meeting between the client and each band for a few weeks from now. This is a dream assignment for me. I'm giddy. Giddy!

From: Shelley Manning – April 9, 2014 – 2:03 PM
To: Renee Greene
Subject: Re: This is the (work) life!

Float me some MP3's, will ya? I want to take a listen on my flight down.

From: Renee Greene – April 9, 2014 – 2:05 PM
To: Shelley Manning
Subject: Re: This is the (work) life!

Will do. Can't wait to see you and honeymoon photos on Saturday. Please leave the X-rated shots at home.

From: Shelley Manning – April 9, 2014 – 2:08 PM
To: Renee Greene
Subject: Re: This is the (work) life!

That will severely limit the number of photos you'll have access to. But you'll get the idea from what you see almost as well as from what you don't see. Mwah! Mwah!

From: Shelley Manning – April 12, 2014 – 7:52 PM
To: Renee Greene
Subject: Dress for success

Great fun hanging out with you today to look for bridesmaid dresses and have lunch with Ethan. Sorry I was only able to fly in for the afternoon, but that's the breaks when you take 2 weeks off to traipse across Italy. At least I have the flight to email you and continue gossiping. Speaking of gossip, so that was Billy the Kid, legendary jailbird? Seems harmless. Can't believe he's worth millions.

From: Renee Greene – April 12, 2014 – 8:09 PM
To: Shelley Manning
Subject: Re: Dress for success

Rethinking Nick?

From: Shelley Manning – April 12, 2014 – 8:11 PM
To: Renee Greene
Subject: Re: Dress for success

Hardly. It takes a lot more than some cash to impress me.

From: Renee Greene – April 12, 2014 – 8:13 PM
To: Shelley Manning
Subject: Re: Dress for success

Well, he was quite taken with you during your encounter, albeit brief.

From: Shelley Manning – April 12, 2014 – 8:14 PM
To: Renee Greene
Subject: Re: Dress for success

Of course he was. Aren't they all?

From: Renee Greene – April 12, 2014 – 8:15 PM
To: Shelley Manning
Subject: Re: Dress for success

I'm being serious.

From: Shelley Manning – April 12, 2014 – 8:15 PM
To: Renee Greene
Subject: Re: Dress for success

So am I!

From: Renee Greene – April 12, 2014 – 8:18 PM
To: Shelley Manning
Subject: Re: Dress for success

Stop it. I'm not joking. Ethan said he hasn't stopped talking about you all day. He wanted to know how serious you were with Nick.

From: Shelley Manning – April 12, 2014 – 8:23 PM
To: Renee Greene
Subject: Re: Dress for success

Nick and I are only married, so yeah, he's got a shot. HA! Well, of course he can't stop thinking about me. Was it my dazzling smile? Humor and wit? Rock hard ass? Do tell!

From: Renee Greene – April 12, 2014 – 8:26 PM
To: Shelley Manning
Subject: Re: Dress for success

I didn't get that level of detail but he's been texting Ethan all day and I'm confident it is about you. Should I peek at his phone? He's in the shower right now.

From: Shelley Manning – April 12, 2014 – 8:27 PM
To: Renee Greene
Subject: Re: Dress for success

Don't look at his phone. Nothing good can come from reading someone else's texts.

From: Renee Greene – April 12, 2014 – 8:27 PM
To: Shelley Manning
Subject: Re: Dress for success

But I'm so curious. Aren't you?

From: Shelley Manning – April 12, 2014 – 8:28 PM
To: Renee Greene
Subject: Re: Dress for success

Renee...

From: Renee Greene – April 12, 2014 – 8:28 PM
To: Shelley Manning
Subject: Re: Dress for success

I'm just going to take a harmless little peek...

From: Shelley Manning – April 12, 2014 – 8:28 PM
To: Renee Greene
Subject: Re: Dress for success

Renee! Do not do this!

From: Shelley Manning – April 12, 2014 – 8:30 PM
To: Renee Greene
Subject: Re: Dress for success

Well...

From: Renee Greene – April 12, 2014 – 8:30 PM
To: Shelley Manning
Subject: Re: Dress for success

You were right. I shouldn't have looked.

From: Shelley Manning – April 12, 2014 – 8:31 PM
To: Renee Greene
Subject: Re: Dress for success

Okay, now you have to tell me.

From: Renee Greene – April 12, 2014 – 8:31 PM
To: Shelley Manning
Subject: Re: Dress for success

I'm so angry right now I can barely type.

From: Shelley Manning – April 12, 2014 – 8:32 PM
To: Renee Greene
Subject: Re: Dress for success

Take a deep cleansing breath!

From: Renee Greene – April 12, 2014 – 8:32 PM
To: Shelley Manning
Subject: Re: Dress for success

Did you learn that from yoga?

From: Shelley Manning – April 12, 2014 – 8:33 PM
To: Renee Greene
Subject: Re: Dress for success

I did. Nice isn't it?

From: Renee Greene – April 12, 2014 – 8:34 PM
To: Shelley Manning
Subject: Re: Dress for success

It is. Thank you. Okay, BTK started off by objectifying you.

From: Shelley Manning – April 12, 2014 – 8:36 PM
To: Renee Greene
Subject: Re: Dress for success

I'm used to that. And honestly don't really mind. That can't be what's got you all riled up.

From: Renee Greene – April 12, 2014 – 8:39 PM
To: Shelley Manning
Subject: Re: Dress for success

Ethan replied, "Yeah she's pretty hot" to which BTK responded, "Pretty hot? You could never get a piece of ass like that!" Granted my ass is a bit bigger and flabbier than yours, but it's not like I'm an ogre or something.

From: Shelley Manning – April 12, 2014 – 8:42 PM
To: Renee Greene
Subject: Re: Dress for success

I can see where that would make you very upset. But Sweetie, I don't think BTK is making any kind of comment about your looks. Rather I think he's making a comment about Ethan's.

From: Renee Greene – April 12, 2014 – 8:46 PM
To: Shelley Manning
Subject: Re: Dress for success

Oh, that's not what's making my blood boil. Ethan wrote back, "I tapped that, dude." I TAPPED THAT, DUDE? I TAPPED THAT DUDE! Now Ethan just walked in with a towel around his waist and gave me a Joey-from-Friends "How you doin?" look. Are you f'ing kidding me?!?

From: Shelley Manning – April 12, 2014 – 8:53 PM
To: Renee Greene
Subject: Re: Dress for success

I hate to be one of those "I told you so" people - you know, like Ethan, but I told you so. Tsk! Tsk! Nothing good comes from reading other people's messages. In his defense, BTK is an immature womanizer who is clearly compensating for a brain that is bigger than his balls. He doesn't know any better.

Ethan does know better, but he's a guy and guys are competitive. When they get backed into a wall like that, they come out swinging. He's just trying to exert his manhood. If you really want my advice, tell him you are "doin' fine" and let him exert his manhood all over you right now.

From: Renee Greene – April 12, 2014 – 8:58 PM
To: Shelley Manning
Subject: Re: Dress for success

I can't even look at him right now. He just walked over and kissed my forehead. Now he's drinking a beer. I want to slug him.

From: Shelley Manning – April 12, 2014 – 9:00 PM
To: Renee Greene
Subject: Re: Dress for success

I am laughing out loud so hard that people on the plane are staring at me.

From: Renee Greene – April 12, 2014 – 9:01 PM
To: Shelley Manning
Subject: Re: Dress for success

This isn't funny!

From: Shelley Manning – April 12, 2014 – 9:04 PM
To: Renee Greene
Subject: Re: Dress for success

It is! You have two choices: (1) confess, have a huge fight with him about his behavior, personal boundaries, privacy expectations, etc. or (2) get over it and go let him tap THAT.

From: Renee Greene – April 12, 2014 – 9:06 PM
To: Shelley Manning
Subject: Re: Dress for success

Choice #3 - don't say anything yet secretly seethe and let it fester until one day it comes out in a huge ball of fists and anger.

From: Shelley Manning – April 12, 2014 – 9:07 PM
To: Renee Greene
Subject: Re: Dress for success

You're right. That is a third choice. My suggestion though is #2.

From: Renee Greene – April 12, 2014 – 9:08 PM
To: Shelley Manning
Subject: Re: Dress for success

Argh! You're probably right.

From: Shelley Manning – April 12, 2014 – 9:10 PM
To: Renee Greene
Subject: Re: Dress for success

Go! Go have angry sex. You'll love it. I'll call you in a day or two
and we'll figure out next steps with dresses. Mwah! Mwah!

CHAPTER 24: SURPRISES

From: Genie Fowler – April 14, 2014 – 7:31 AM
To: PBCupLover
Subject: Big Surprise!!!!

Hey there, stranger. Hope you are doing well. Sorry it's been a
while since we last spoke. Things have been super hectic around
here lately. And before I forget, I wanted to tell you that I bumped
into Misty Jean last week at the "going out of business" event at
Shakey's. She says hi. Hard to believe that place has closed down.
We had so many great memories there. Remember the night after
Claire Landry's homecoming party?

From: PBCupLover – April 14, 2014 – 9:02 AM
To: Genie Fowler
Subject: Re: Big Surprise!!!!

Hey, Eugenia. Great to hear from you. Wow! Shakey's closed
down. What a bummer. I think I ate my weight in pizza there junior
year. Of course I remember that night. We were pretty wild and
crazy back then, huh? So what is Misty doing these days?

From: Genie Fowler – April 14, 2014 – 9:11 AM
To: PBCupLover
Subject: Re: Big Surprise!!!!

We *were* pretty wild back then. Sad to think those days are over.
Wish I knew then how good I had it. Regarding Misty, she's living
in the suburbs near where we grew up and is working for her dad's
construction business. She thinks he's going to retire in about 10
years so he's grooming her to take over.

From: PBCupLover – April 14, 2014 – 9:15 AM
To: Genie Fowler
Subject: Re: Big Surprise!!!!

Construction, huh? Never would have thought that's where she'd end up. She was always kind of a girly girl.

From: Genie Fowler – April 14, 2014 – 9:17 AM
To: PBCupLover
Subject: Re: Big Surprise!!!!

She's still pretty girly but I think she likes the fact she's surrounded by big, burly, manly men.

From: PBCupLover – April 14, 2014 – 9:21 AM
To: Genie Fowler
Subject: Re: Big Surprise!!!!

Ha! I can see that. So that can't be the "Big Surprise!!!!" you mention. You used four exclamation points and you're usually not that liberal with them. So what's up?

From: Genie Fowler – April 14, 2014 – 9:29 AM
To: PBCupLover
Subject: Re: Big Surprise!!!!

I completely forgot. Yes, that's not the big surprise. The news is...(drumroll please!) I'm moving to LA. Can you believe it? I know you probably think I'm crazy, but I've decided that Columbus is just too midwest for me. I need to be where the action is.

I was thinking about New York, but figured LA would be better since I know someone there and I know you will help make sure I get settled in okay. I'm awaiting word on my job transfer request with Nordstrom and could start as early as a few weeks from now. So I just need to get out there and find an apartment. Do you think I could stay with you for a week or two until I get a place?

From: PBCupLover – April 14, 2014 – 9:35 AM
To: Genie Fowler
Subject: Re: Big Surprise!!!!

Well, that is a big surprise. A move across country is a big step. I think you'll like it out here and have no doubt that you'll make it an easy transition. Let me see how I can help. I'll be in touch soon.

From: PBCupLover – April 14, 2014 – 9:36 AM
To: Renee Greene
Subject: Fwd: Re: Big Surprise!!!!

Don't freak out, but…

From: Renee Greene – April 14, 2014 – 9:37 AM
To: Shelley Manning, Ashley Gordon
Subject: Fwd: Fwd: Big Surprise!!!!

I'm freaking out…

From: Shelley Manning – April 14, 2014 – 9:52 AM
To: Renee Greene, Ashley Gordon
Subject: Re: Fwd: Fwd: Big Surprise!!!!

Oh, hell no! You tell that conniving Fashionista that she is not welcome in your home. And you're not FREAKING OUT. You tell Ethan in no uncertain terms that there is NO FREAKING WAY Genie is staying with you. And your wedding is just a few months away!?!

From: Ashley Gordon – April 14, 2014 – 10:09 AM
To: Shelley Manning, Renee Greene
Subject: Re: Fwd: Fwd: Big Surprise!!!!

I beg to differ. You know that old expression, keep your friends close and your enemies closer. At least this way you can keep an eye on her for a few weeks and let her know that she can't shake the foundation of your relationship.

From: Shelley Manning – April 14, 2014 – 10:18 AM
To: Renee Greene, Ashley Gordon
Subject: Re: Fwd: Fwd: Big Surprise!!!!

A few weeks? We all know it could take a lot longer than a few weeks to find a good apartment in LA. It's hit or miss. Knowing her, she'll drag it out.

On one hand, you tell Ethan she can't stay. She's likely betting that will be your response. Ethan will protest, saying that he's just trying to help a friend and that you're being jealous/paranoid. You'll get into a huge fight and be cast as the bad guy.

On the other hand, you tell him she can stay with you and you're basically inviting the lioness into your den. She's brilliant!

From: Renee Greene – April 14, 2014 – 10:19 AM
To: Shelley Manning, Ashley Gordon
Subject: Re: Fwd: Fwd: Big Surprise!!!!

I'm screwed!

From: Shelley Manning – April 14, 2014 – 10:23 AM
To: Renee Greene, Ashley Gordon
Subject: Re: Fwd: Fwd: Big Surprise!!!!

She really is an evil genius. Too bad we don't like her. Under different circumstances, she would make a great addition to our little group.

From: Ashley Gordon – April 14, 2014 – 10:25 AM
To: Shelley Manning, Renee Greene
Subject: Re: Fwd: Fwd: Big Surprise!!!!

This is indeed a Catch 22. So what are you going to do?

From: Renee Greene – April 14, 2014 – 10:25 AM
To: Shelley Manning, Ashley Gordon
Subject: Re: Fwd: Fwd: Big Surprise!!!!

I don't know.

From: Shelley Manning – April 14, 2014 – 10:26 AM
To: Renee Greene, Ashley Gordon
Subject: Re: Fwd: Fwd: Big Surprise!!!!

Don't make any rash decisions. You need to think about this strategically.

From: Renee Greene – April 14, 2014 – 10:26 AM
To: Shelley Manning, Ashley Gordon
Subject: Re: Fwd: Fwd: Big Surprise!!!!

Strategically? What does that mean?

From: Shelley Manning – April 14, 2014 – 10:29 AM
To: Renee Greene, Ashley Gordon
Subject: Re: Fwd: Fwd: Big Surprise!!!!

We've got to figure out a way for him to see that Genie is manipulating the situation and she's really the villain in all of this.

From: Renee Greene – April 14, 2014 – 10:33 AM
To: Shelley Manning, Ashley Gordon
Subject: Re: Fwd: Fwd: Big Surprise!!!!

As much as I appreciate you putting your great and devilish mind to work on this problem, I honestly don't want to play games with Ethan. I'm just going to see how he feels about the situation and then let him make the decision.

From: Ashley Gordon – April 14, 2014 – 10:36 AM
To: Renee Greene, Shelley Manning
Subject: Re: Fwd: Fwd: Big Surprise!!!!

Oooh. That's good. Force him to make the choice and therefore deal with the fallout. Very smart.

From: Renee Greene – April 14, 2014 – 10:38 AM
To: Shelley Manning, Ashley Gordon
Subject: Re: Fwd: Fwd: Big Surprise!!!!

I'm not trying to be smart about this. I just want to deal with this in a mature way.

From: Shelley Manning – April 14, 2014 – 10:40 AM
To: Renee Greene, Ashley Gordon
Subject: Re: Fwd: Fwd: Big Surprise!!!!

Lucky for you, the "mature" way happens to be a "savvy" way, too. Good luck and keep us posted!

From: Renee Greene – April 14, 2014 – 10:45 AM
To: PBCupLover
Subject: Re: Fwd: Big Surprise!!!!

Should I freak out that you used to eat A LOT of pizza or that your ex-girlfriend wants to stay with us for a few weeks. ;) What are your thoughts?

From: PBCupLover – April 14, 2014 – 11:12 AM
To: Renee Greene
Subject: Re: Fwd: Big Surprise!!!!

Well, I would love to help her out. She is an old friend, after all. Nothing I wouldn't do for any one of the gang from back home. But I also could see where it would make you a bit uncomfortable.

Not that you have anything to worry about or be jealous about, but I know I wouldn't want one of your old boyfriends crashing on our couch. I'll let you decide.

From: Renee Greene – April 14, 2014 – 11:16 AM
To: PBCupLover
Subject: Re: Fwd: Big Surprise!!!!

You bring up some good points. But really, I think this needs to be your decision. I'm fine with whatever you decide.

From: PBCupLover – April 14, 2014 – 11:22 AM
To: Renee Greene
Subject: Re: Fwd: Big Surprise!!!!

Really? You don't have a strong opinion about this one way or another? Is that what Shelley and Ashley said to do? I assume you already talked with them about this. Are they bcc'd on these emails?

From: Renee Greene – April 14, 2014 – 11:28 AM
To: PBCupLover
Subject: Re: Fwd: Big Surprise!!!!

Yes, I did talk with Shelley and Ashley. And no, they are not copied on these emails. This is between you and me. And I decided – not them – that this decision needs to be yours. She's your friend.

From: PBCupLover – April 14, 2014 – 11:30 AM
To: Renee Greene
Subject: Re: Fwd: Big Surprise!!!!

Would you really be okay if she stayed with us for a week or two?

From: Renee Greene – April 14, 2014 – 11:31 AM
To: PBCupLover
Subject: Re: Fwd: Big Surprise!!!!

Babe, you do what you think is right.

From: PBCupLover – April 14, 2014 – 11:33 AM
To: Renee Greene
Subject: Re: Fwd: Big Surprise!!!!

So basically you're saying that I need to choose between my ex-girlfriend, who is still a dear friend, and my fiancé?

From: Renee Greene – April 14, 2014 – 11:37 AM
To: PBCupLover
Subject: Re: Fwd: Big Surprise!!!!

I'm not saying that at all. If you want to help out your old friend, then you should do that. And if you think it would be awkward for her to stay here, then you should tell her that. I am 100% behind whatever you decide.

From: PBCupLover – April 14, 2014 – 11:38 AM
To: Renee Greene
Subject: Re: Fwd: Big Surprise!!!!

Okay. We can talk about it more tonight.

From: Renee Greene – April 14, 2014 – 11:39 AM
To: PBCupLover
Subject: Re: Fwd: Big Surprise!!!!

No need to discuss any further. It's totally your call. XO

From: Shelley Manning – April 16, 2014 – 2:32 PM
To: Renee Greene, Ashley Gordon
Subject: Re: Fwd: Fwd: Big Surprise!!!!

So, what's going on with this?!?!

From: Renee Greene – April 16, 2014 – 2:54 PM
To: Shelley Manning, Ashley Gordon
Subject: Re: Fwd: Fwd: Big Surprise!!!!

As mentioned, I told him it was his decision and I was 100% behind whatever he decided. After a bit of back and forth, I made the mistake of saying that he should do what he thinks is right. It opened up the door for him to say that I was basically asking him to make a choice between me and her.

Thankfully, I stuck to the high ground and just stayed on message that it was his choice and I was okay with whatever he decided. All of that PR/media training we do for clients to "stay on message" certainly helped here. He's thinking about what to do and I'm just sitting silently (albeit anxiously) by waiting to see what he does.

From: Shelley Manning – April 16, 2014 – 3:00 PM
To: Renee Greene, Ashley Gordon
Subject: Re: Fwd: Fwd: Big Surprise!!!!

Oooh. That staying on message business can be tough but sounds like it was a good call. So curious to see what he does. What a dilemma for him.

From: Renee Greene – April 16, 2014 – 3:02 PM
To: Shelley Manning, Ashley Gordon
Subject: Re: Fwd: Fwd: Big Surprise!!!!

Don't feel too sorry for him. He's brought this on himself.

From: Shelley Manning – April 16, 2014 – 3:06 PM
To: Renee Greene, Ashley Gordon
Subject: Re: Fwd: Fwd: Big Surprise!!!!

So you think the choice should be simple? He should tell Fashionista that as much as he would like to help, she can't stay with him because it would be too weird for you and you are the most important person in his life.

From: Renee Greene – April 16, 2014 – 3:12 PM
To: Shelley Manning, Ashley Gordon
Subject: Re: Fwd: Fwd: Big Surprise!!!!

There is absolutely no way he would let my ex-boyfriend stay with us. And there's no evidence my ex-boyfriend is even remotely interested in getting back together with me.

But it's been well established – at least well established in my mind - that Genie is interested in stealing him back. So why the hell would it be okay for her to stay with us? (It's bad enough he had to invite her to our wedding!)

Even more so, I think he should tell her that LA isn't big enough for all of us and she should pursue her dream to hit the Big Apple or, better yet, stay in Columbus.

From: Ashley Gordon – April 16, 2014 – 3:15 PM
To: Renee Greene, Shelley Manning
Subject: Re: Fwd: Fwd: Big Surprise!!!!

No offense, Renee, but just because something is well-established in your mind, doesn't mean it's reality.

From: Shelley Manning – April 16, 2014 – 3:18 PM
To: Ashley Gordon, Renee Greene
Subject: Re: Fwd: Fwd: Big Surprise!!!!

And just because you say "no offense" Ashley, doesn't mean what's coming out of your mouth isn't going to piss a whole bunch of people off.

From: Renee Greene – April 16, 2014 – 3:20 PM
To: Shelley Manning, Ashley Gordon
Subject: Re: Fwd: Fwd: Big Surprise!!!!

Settle down, ladies. Let's keep our focus here. The enemy is Genie – not each other. I will let you know what Ethan decides.

From: Shelley Manning – April 16, 2014 – 3:21 PM
To: Renee Greene
Subject: Re: Fwd: Fwd: Big Surprise!!!!

She is such a pain in the ass!

From: Ashley Gordon – April 16, 2014 – 3:21 PM
To: Renee Greene
Subject: Re: Fwd: Fwd: Big Surprise!!!!

She can be so mean sometimes.

From: Renee Greene – April 16, 2014 – 3:22 PM
To: Shelley Manning
Subject: Re: Fwd: Fwd: Big Surprise!!!!

Never you mind her. I'll talk with you soon.

From: Renee Greene – April 16, 2014 – 3:22 PM
To: Ashley Gordon
Subject: Re: Fwd: Fwd: Big Surprise!!!!

Never you mind her. I'll talk with you soon.

From: Renee Greene – April 18, 2014 – 2:12 PM
To: Shelley Manning
Subject: Hate in my heart

I hate Skinny Skye. Do you know that waif eats a 1/4 gallon of ice cream every day? EVERY DAY! She's done this since she was a kid, which seems like last week. So she's spent more than a decade eating ice cream (DAILY!) and still looks Skinny.

From: Shelley Manning – April 18, 2014 – 2:16 PM
To: Renee Greene
Subject: Re: Hate in my heart

I Scream! You Scream! We all scream that we hate Skinny Skye!

From: Renee Greene – April 18, 2014 – 2:16 PM
To: Shelley Manning
Subject: Re: Hate in my heart

Exactly!

From: Shelley Manning – April 18, 2014 – 2:18 PM
To: Renee Greene
Subject: Re: Hate in my heart

Don't let her get you down. She may be skinny, but you're smart and successful. She's probably DYING to be like you.

From: Renee Greene – April 18, 2014 – 2:19 PM
To: Shelley Manning
Subject: Re: Hate in my heart

Somehow I doubt that, but I'll take it.

From: PBCupLover – April 21, 2014 – 10:12 AM
To: Genie Fowler
Subject: No Place Like Home

Eugenia: Hope you are on track to move out to LA because I have
some great news for you. I found you an awesome place to live. It's
a really nice one-bedroom apartment in Brentwood, which is a hip
part of west LA filled with young professionals. There are tons of
little shops and restaurants you can walk to and its centrally located
between downtown LA and the Santa Monica beach area. It will be
only a 10 minute drive to Nordstrom, too. By LA standards, that is
one hell of an easy commute.

One of my co-workers lives in the building and they just had a unit
open up. I went to look at it today and they agreed to hold it for two
days for you to mail them a first/last month's rent and deposit.

From: Genie Fowler – April 21, 2014 – 11:32 AM
To: PBCupLover
Subject: Re: No Place Like Home

Aren't you sweet? I certainly didn't mean for you to go to all of that
trouble on my behalf. I'm sure Renee, too, had a lot to do with
finding me a great place, so be sure to thank her for me.

But wouldn't you know it, but my plans have changed. Nordstrom
offered me a promotion so I would stay in Columbus. They made it
worth my while, so I guess I'm staying put...for now.

Thanks for being so concerned about me, as always. I think you've
really spoiled me for other men. ;) I'll see you soon at the wedding.

From: PBCupLover – April 21, 2014 – 11:36 AM
To: Genie Fowler
Subject: Re: No Place Like Home

Sorry to hear that you won't be making the move out west. But I'm
sure your promotion – and all that goes with it – will be great. Yes,
see you soon.

From: PBCupLover – April 21, 2014 – 11:38 AM
To: Renee Greene
Subject: Fwd: Re: No Place Like Home

See below. Looks like Genie got incentivized to stay in Columbus. Thanks for being so great about all of this. Just goes to show why I love you so much.

From: Renee Greene – April 21, 2014 – 11:40 AM
To: Shelley Manning, Ashley Gordon
Subject: Fwd: Fwd: Re: No Place Like Home

Can you believe this shit?

From: Shelley Manning – April 21, 2014 – 11:45 AM
To: Renee Greene, Ashley Gordon
Subject: Re: Fwd: Fwd: Re: No Place Like Home

Are you fucking kidding me? Was that her plan all along? Try to split the two of you up and only come out here if she had to? Was she playing an emotional high-stakes game of chicken with you?

From: Renee Greene – April 21, 2014 – 11:49 AM
To: Shelley Manning, Ashley Gordon
Subject: Re: Fwd: Fwd: Re: No Place Like Home

I love the line about how he's spoiled her for other men? More like she's just spoiled. Really? Is this appropriate to say to someone who is engaged?

From: Shelley Manning – April 21, 2014 – 11:52 AM
To: Renee Greene, Ashley Gordon
Subject: Re: Fwd: Fwd: Re: No Place Like Home

Ooh. The claws come out. All of this civility and handling things maturely has taken it's toll. I like it!

From: Renee Greene – April 21, 2014 – 11:56 AM
To: Shelley Manning, Ashley Gordon
Subject: Re: Fwd: Fwd: Re: No Place Like Home

Honestly, I've just been holding my breath for days on this and praying that she doesn't swoop in here and steal him away from me. I think a good cry will be cleansing.

From: Ashley Gordon – April 21, 2014 – 12:01 PM
To: Shelley Manning, Renee Greene
Subject: Re: Fwd: Fwd: Re: No Place Like Home

Oh, Renee. You have nothing to worry about. From what you've told me, she's obviously very beautiful and well put together. But Ethan loves you. Clearly he wouldn't have gone to the trouble of finding a solution that didn't involve having her stay with you if he wasn't fully committed to you.

From: Renee Greene – April 21, 2014 – 12:02 PM
To: Shelley Manning, Ashley Gordon
Subject: Re: Fwd: Fwd: Re: No Place Like Home

Thanks, Ashley.

From: Renee Greene – April 21, 2014 – 12:08 PM
To: Shelley Manning
Subject: Re: Fwd: Fwd: Re: No Place Like Home

So she's beautiful and well put together but he picked me. That's supposed to make me feel better? I'm off to cry and eat a spoonful or two of frosting. Not the whole can. I promise! Glad she's out of our lives for a while at least.

From: Shelley Manning – April 21, 2014 – 12:12 PM
To: Renee Greene
Subject: Re: Fwd: Fwd: Re: No Place Like Home

Glad Genie's out of your life for a while or Ashley? Ha! Just kidding. Not being around her all of the time, I've forgotten how backhanded Ashley's compliments can be. Trust me, Sweetie. You're the whole enchilada and that's why Ethan loves you.

From: Renee Greene – April 21, 2014 – 12:14 PM
To: Shelley Manning
Subject: Re: Fwd: Fwd: Re: No Place Like Home

And your pep talks are just one of the many reasons I love you.

From: Renee Greene – April 21, 2014 – 12:15 PM
To: PBCupLover
Subject: Re: No Place Like Home

Okay. Thanks for letting me know.

From: PBCupLover – April 21, 2014 – 12:21 PM
To: Renee Greene
Subject: Re: No Place Like Home

That's all. No other commentary on this, huh? That's why I love you…just the way you are.

From: Renee Greene – April 21, 2014 – 12:24 PM
To: PBCupLover
Subject: Re: No Place Like Home

Quoting Billy Joel now, are we? Did you expect me to have more to say about this "Uptown Girl"

From: PBCupLover – April 21, 2014 – 12:26 PM
To: Renee Greene
Subject: Re: No Place Like Home

Can we just "Leave a Tender Moment Alone" or do you really want to do this?

From: Renee Greene – April 21, 2014 – 12:28 PM
To: PBCupLover
Subject: Re: No Place Like Home

Ha! Ha! Too much "Pressure." See you home soon. XO

From: Shelley Manning – April 21, 2014 – 1:14 PM
To: Renee Greene
Subject: Re: Fwd: Fwd: Re: No Place Like Home

I do know how to make everything better.

From: Renee Greene – April 21, 2014 – 1:17 PM
To: Shelley Manning
Subject: Re: Fwd: Fwd: Re: No Place Like Home

You do indeed. Just emailed Ethan and we almost got into a Billy Joel-off. Told him it was too much "Pressure" right now. Ha!

From: Shelley Manning – April 21, 2014 – 1:21 PM
To: Renee Greene
Subject: Re: Fwd: Fwd: Re: No Place Like Home

Did you tell him to tell Genie to get in a "New York State of Mind" and "Say Goodbye to Hollywood?" Or did he decide not to "Tell Her About It?"

From: Renee Greene – April 21, 2014 – 1:25 PM
To: Shelley Manning
Subject: Re: Fwd: Fwd: Re: No Place Like Home

All this week I have been "Keeping the Faith." It's seemed like "The Longest Time" and as much as I wanted to eat some more frosting, "I'll Cry Instead."

From: Shelley Manning – April 21, 2014 – 1:28 PM
To: Renee Greene
Subject: Re: Fwd: Fwd: Re: No Place Like Home

Years ago he may have thought "She's Got a Way" but he is an "Innocent Man."

From: Renee Greene – April 21, 2014 – 1:32 PM
To: Shelley Manning
Subject: Re: Fwd: Fwd: Re: No Place Like Home

Well, as long as he doesn't think "She's Always a Woman" and "Sometimes a Fantasy," we'll be just fine. Otherwise, he'd be "Movin' Out."

From: Shelley Manning – April 21, 2014 – 1:35 PM
To: Renee Greene
Subject: Re: Fwd: Fwd: Re: No Place Like Home

I think if he made a different choice, he's be more than "Movin' Out." "You're Only Human," after all.

From: Renee Greene – April 21, 2014 – 1:36 PM
To: Shelley Manning
Subject: Re: Fwd: Fwd: Re: No Place Like Home

"You May Be Right."

From: Shelley Manning – April 21, 2014 – 1:36 PM
To: Renee Greene
Subject: Re: Fwd: Fwd: Re: No Place Like Home

"I May Be Crazy!"

From: Renee Greene – April 21, 2014 – 1:37 PM
To: Shelley Manning
Subject: Re: Fwd: Fwd: Re: No Place Like Home

No, you're "Shameless"

From: Shelley Manning – April 21, 2014 – 1:40 PM
To: Renee Greene
Subject: Re: Fwd: Fwd: Re: No Place Like Home

That's true. But as B.J. would say, "Only the Good Die Young."
Listen, Sweetie. As much as I would love to continue to let you
"Tell <me> About It," I've got to run. Call you later. Mwah! Mwah!

CHAPTER 25: FIESTA TIME

From: PBCupLover – April 23, 2014 – 9:08 AM
To: Renee Greene
Subject: Cabo Bound

We're heading to Cabo. You read correctly, Cabo! William just rented a villa in Cabo for me to have an accounting retreat with the finance team. You can come along and then we (and any friends we want to invite, too) can spend the weekend. We leave next Wednesday.

From: Renee Greene – April 23, 2014 – 9:13 AM
To: PBCupLover
Subject: Re: Cabo Bound

Next Wednesday? That doesn't leave me much time to get my body into bathing suit shape. But I'll gladly take a free vacation (well almost free; I do need airfare) to Mexico.

From: PBCupLover – April 23, 2014 – 9:16 AM
To: Renee Greene
Subject: Re: Cabo Bound

Oh, I forgot to mention. He's chartered a private jet for us to get down there.

From: Renee Greene – April 23, 2014 – 9:18 AM
To: PBCupLover
Subject: Re: Cabo Bound

Private jet? Are you kidding me? I could get used to being spoiled like this.

From: PBCupLover – April 23, 2014 – 9:24 AM
To: Renee Greene
Subject: Re: Cabo Bound

Me too! I'm going to invite a couple of my football buddies. Do you want to see if Mark, Shelley, Nick, Ashley and Greg want to go? Regarding Ashley and Greg, adults only. No offense to Siobhan, but I just don't think this is the kind of vacation where we want to have a kid around.

From: Renee Greene – April 23, 2014 – 9:29 AM
To: PBCupLover
Subject: Re: Cabo Bound

I'll email them all and see if they're up for it. I would guess that Ashley and Greg are a no but you never know. I'll keep you posted. Will there be enough room for everyone?

From: PBCupLover – April 23, 2014 – 9:32 AM
To: Renee Greene
Subject: Re: Cabo Bound

It's a 12 bedroom villa on the coast with a personal chef. I think we'll be able to accommodate everyone.

From: Renee Greene – April 23, 2014 – 9:34 AM
To: PBCupLover
Subject: Re: Cabo Bound

Get out! That sounds amazing. Well done, Billy the Kid.

From: PBCupLover – April 23, 2014 – 9:37 AM
To: Renee Greene
Subject: Re: Cabo Bound

Yeah, I think he's trying to make up for the whole "bailing me out of jail" incident. William won't be there and don't call him Billy the Kid if you want me to keep my job.

From: Renee Greene – April 23, 2014 – 9:37 AM
To: PBCupLover
Subject: Re: Cabo Bound

Got it!

From: Renee Greene – April 23, 2014 – 9:42 AM
To: Mark Finlay, Ashley Gordon, Shelley Manning
Subject: Pack your bikini!

You read that correctly, my friends. I'm Cabo Bound. But not just me. All of us! Ethan's boss rented a 12 bedroom villa (!) in Cabo for a finance retreat and Ethan can stay for the weekend and invite some friends to come enjoy.

You just need to get yourself down there on Friday. We'll give you a ride home on Sunday on the private jet. AGH! This is so cool. Do note, however, that some of Ethan's buddies will join us, as well as some of his finance team from work. But it should be great fun. Hope we can all hang out there.

From: Renee Greene – April 23, 2014 – 9:43 AM
To: Mark Finlay
Subject: Fwd: Pack your bikini!

Marnie's going to be there too, so I'm hopeful you can come. It will be great for us all to hang out together.

From: Ashley Gordon – April 23, 2014 – 10:02 AM
To: Renee Greene, Mark Finlay, Shelley Manning
Subject: Re: Pack your bikini!

It sounds so fantastic but we don't have anyone to watch Siobhan on such short notice. And I just don't feel safe bringing her to Mexico. And bikini?!? I don't think either of us should be wearing a bikini anytime soon. You could borrow one of my sarongs if you want.

From: Renee Greene – April 23, 2014 – 10:04 AM
To: PBCupLover
Subject: Fwd: Re: Pack your bikini!

Well, Ashley's out. Thank goodness. And not just because she spoke the cold hard truth that I shouldn't be wearing a bikini. Rather, I forgot to mention it was a grown-ups only weekend. That would have been an awkward conversation.

From: PBCupLover – April 23, 2014 – 10:06 AM
To: Renee Greene
Subject: Re: Fwd: Re: Pack your bikini!

I think you'd look hot in a bikini. Actually, you look pretty hot without anything on.

From: Renee Greene – April 23, 2014 – 10:08 AM
To: PBCupLover
Subject: Re: Fwd: Re: Pack your bikini!

<blush!> I shall reward you for those kind words tonight.

From: PBCupLover – April 23, 2014 – 10:08 AM
To: Renee Greene
Subject: Re: Fwd: Re: Pack your bikini!

Works for me!

From: Mark Finlay – April 23, 2014 – 10:32 AM
To: Renee Greene
Subject: Re: Fwd: Pack your bikini!

That should work – minus the bikini. I'm just not that comfortable in a two-piece suit. I'll look into flights now. Thank Ethan for me.

From: Renee Greene – April 23, 2014 – 10:33 AM
To: Mark Finlay
Subject: Re: Fwd: Pack your bikini!

Ha! Ha!

From: Renee Greene – April 23, 2014 – 10:34 AM
To: PBCupLover
Subject: Fwd: Re: Fwd: Pack your bikini!

Mark's in. I'll keep you posted.

From: PBCupLover – April 23, 2014 – 10:37 AM
To: Renee Greene
Subject: Re: Fwd: Re: Fwd: Pack your bikini!

Babe, as much as I love hearing from you, I also have work to do. Why don't you just fill me in tonight when I get home?

From: Renee Greene – April 23, 2014 – 10:40 AM
To: PBCupLover
Subject: Re: Fwd: Re: Fwd: Pack your bikini!

You mean you don't want a running commentary of my life throughout the day? And I would suggest being careful with your answer, since I previously offered to reward you for your kind words.

From: PBCupLover – April 23, 2014 – 10:44 AM
To: Renee Greene
Subject: Re: Fwd: Re: Fwd: Pack your bikini!

I love hearing about your day and your life. It's the bright and shining highlight in my otherwise dull day. After a long, hard day of work, I look forward to your brilliance and humor. Spreading it throughout the day just dilutes its magic.

From: Renee Greene – April 23, 2014 – 10:46 AM
To: PBCupLover
Subject: Re: Fwd: Re: Fwd: Pack your bikini!

Well played, Mr. Langer. Well played, indeed. I'll see you at home tonight…wearing a bikini or nothing at all.

From: PBCupLover – April 23, 2014 – 10:47 AM
To: Renee Greene
Subject: Re: Fwd: Re: Fwd: Pack your bikini!

:)

From: Shelley Manning – April 23, 2014 – 11:02 AM
To: Renee Greene
Subject: Re: Pack your bikini!

First of all, I'm glad Ashley's not going. I just might have to kick her ass for that bikini comment. I know you've been working out, Sweetie, and I'm sure you look hot. And sarong? SO WRONG!

Second, you know my motto. Unless I'm getting paid or getting laid, I'm not going anywhere. This freebie of a romantic getaway sounds like just the thing for me and Nick. It's been only a few weeks since our honeymoon and I could already use a vacation. We'll be there. I assume I need to arrange my own ride home to Seattle either from Cabo or Los Angeles, no?

From: Renee Greene – April 23, 2014 – 11:08 AM
To: Shelley Manning
Subject: Re: Pack your bikini!

So glad you have my back and the little bit of "back fat" I'm desperately trying to work off. But regarding your motto, I'm literally laughing out loud. Thrilled you guys can join in the for the fun.

Wasn't sure if you would be able to swing it considering you just got back from your honeymoon. And yes, we can give you a ride to LA on our private jet (listen to me, right?) but then you'll need to hitch a ride back to Seattle. It may be easier to just make a round trip – Seattle/Cabo.

From: Shelley Manning – April 23, 2014 – 11:11 AM
To: Renee Greene
Subject: Re: Pack your bikini!

I'll look into to it and let you know. But for now, save a space for the two of us.

From: Renee Greene – April 23, 2014 – 11:11 AM
To: Shelley Manning
Subject: Re: Pack your bikini!

Super!

From: Marnie Glass – April 24, 2014 – 9:02 AM
To: Renee Greene
Subject: Feeling lame

I hope you don't mind that Ethan gave me your email. Mark came over to hang out last night...again. But we just hung out and watched a movie – the 80's classic Breakfast Club. He didn't even try to kiss me...again. I'm beginning to think he's just not interested.

From: Renee Greene – April 24, 2014 – 9:05 AM
To: Marnie Glass
Subject: Re: Feeling lame

Don't despair. I can tell he likes you. I think he's just afraid to get hurt. It's going to happen this weekend. Just trust me.

From: Marnie Glass – April 24, 2014 – 9:07 AM
To: Renee Greene
Subject: Re: Feeling lame

I don't know, Renee. We've hung out three times and he just doesn't seem to feel that way about me.

From: Renee Greene – April 24, 2014 – 9:10 AM
To: Marnie Glass
Subject: Re: Feeling lame

He won't be able to resist you this weekend. We'll be in a totally romantic setting, drinking margaritas (not that he's going to need to be all liquored up to be with you, but it will certainly help relax him), wearing minimal clothing, etc.

From: Marnie Glass – April 24, 2014 – 9:13 AM
To: Renee Greene
Subject: Re: Feeling lame

Actually I was thinking the margaritas would help give him the courage to make a move. Or at the very least give *me* the courage to make a move on *him*.

From: Renee Greene – April 24, 2014 – 9:17 AM
To: Marnie Glass
Subject: Re: Feeling lame

Oh, it is on like Donkey Kong. (I put in an 80's reference, since I know you are fan of that era.) So, (and not to get all TMI on you, but…) time to pull out that matching bra and panty set, get a good waxing and shave your legs. Love (and lust) is in the air.

From: Marnie Glass – April 24, 2014 – 9:22 AM
To: Renee Greene
Subject: Re: Feeling lame

No! I should NOT do any of those things. In fact, I should come to Cabo with stubbly legs and wear big ol' granny panties. That's a sure way to guarantee he makes a move on me. At least that's they way it always happens in romantic comedies. You know, the girl is convinced she will be celibate forever and makes no effort to primp herself in anticipation of getting busy with someone. And of course that's exactly when it happens and they both have a good laugh about the enormous size of her underwear, etc.

From: Renee Greene – April 24, 2014 – 9:25 AM
To: Marnie Glass
Subject: Re: Feeling lame

That certainly does happen in the movies. But this is real life. So I say prep and primp away. It's going to happen. I'm sure of it.

From: Marnie Glass – April 24, 2014 – 9:27 AM
To: Renee Greene
Subject: Re: Feeling lame

Okay. I'm hoping so. I'll see you at the airport.

From: Mark Finlay – April 27, 2014 – 11:16 AM
To: Renee Greene
Subject: Re: Fwd: Pack your bikini!

I'm arriving on Friday around 10:00. I'll just get a cab from the airport to the villa. Or are you planning to send a limo for me?

From: Renee Greene – April 27, 2014 – 11:18 AM
To: Mark Finlay
Subject: Re: Fwd: Pack your bikini!

Limo? Getting a bit greedy, aren't we?

From: Mark Finlay – April 27, 2014 – 11:19 AM
To: Renee Greene
Subject: Re: Fwd: Pack your bikini!

Ha! Ha! I suppose so. I'll see you Friday.

From: Shelley Manning – April 28, 2014 – 9:42 AM
To: Renee Greene
Subject: Re: Pack your bikini!

Nick and I arrive at 1:30 on Friday and we've got a 3:00 flight back on Sunday. So you don't need to reserve a spot on the private jet for us. But feel free to send a limo to the airport to pick us up in Cabo.

From: Renee Greene – April 28, 2014 – 9:45 AM
To: Shelley Manning
Subject: Re: Pack your bikini!

A limo joke? Really? Mark pulled one of those on me yesterday.

From: Shelley Manning – April 28, 2014 – 9:48 AM
To: Renee Greene
Subject: Re: Pack your bikini!

I'm starting to share Finlay's sense of humor? Lord help me! As long as I don't share any of his other qualities, right? Is he still all hung up on cat-lovin' Cassidy?

From: Renee Greene – April 28, 2014 – 9:54 AM
To: Shelley Manning
Subject: Re: Pack your bikini!

It has been quite some time since we've been able to catch up on him, what with all your international travel and my wedding planning. Mark has a new love interest.

Her name is Marnie and she's on Ethan's finance team, so you'll get a chance to meet her this weekend. Between you and me, he hasn't even made a move on her yet, much to her dismay. But I think this weekend will provide the perfect romantic (and alcohol-fueled) setting to do so.

From: Shelley Manning – April 28, 2014 – 9:58 AM
To: Renee Greene
Subject: Re: Pack your bikini!

Shall I prepare myself to mock her (and him) incessantly? I've already got a nickname for them - Marklie.

From: Renee Greene – April 28, 2014 – 10:01 AM
To: Shelley Manning
Subject: Re: Pack your bikini!

No, she's fantastic. I think you'll really like her. She's got a fun sense of humor, a love of the 1980s (movies, TV shows, pop culture references, etc.) and has a dog, NOT a cat.

From: Shelley Manning – April 28, 2014 – 10:03 AM
To: Renee Greene
Subject: Re: Pack your bikini!

Okay, then I'll just be prepared to mock Finlay.

From: Renee Greene – April 28, 2014 – 10:04 AM
To: Shelley Manning
Subject: Re: Pack your bikini!

I wouldn't expect it any other way. See you Friday.

From: Shelley Manning – May 4, 2014 – 6:15 PM
To: Renee Greene, PBCupLover
Subject: Fun in the sun!

Thank you guys so much for a fantastic weekend. I told Nick that between first class travel to Italy and a weekend at a private villa in Mexico, I was finally getting the royal treatment that I deserve and that he had better keep it up. Thanks again for letting us tag along.

From: Renee Greene – May 4, 2014 – 6:19 PM
To: Shelley Manning
Subject: Re: Fun in the Sun!

I could get used to that kind of treatment, too. So glad you and Nick could come. You make such a cute married couple.

From: PBCupLover – May 4, 2014 – 6:22 PM
To: Shelley Manning
Subject: Re: Fun in the Sun!

Glad you guys were able to come for the weekend. It was fun and I enjoyed getting to know Nick better. I see a Buckeye's sweatshirt in his future!

From: Shelley Manning – May 4, 2014 – 6:24 PM
To: Renee Greene
Subject: Re: Fun in the Sun!

Cute couple? Clearly we need to work on our image a bit more.

From: Shelley Manning – May 4, 2014 – 6:28 PM
To: PBCupLover
Subject: Re: Fun in the Sun!

Don't go there, Ethan. He (and by he, I mean I) doesn't want or need anything with your alma mater logo on it. Although I'm living more than 1,000 miles away from your fiancé, I still have her ear and wield a lot of influence over her life. So if you ever want to get laid again, you'll back off.

From: Renee Greene – May 4, 2014 – 6:31 PM
To: Shelley Manning,
Subject: Re: Fun in the Sun!

Ha! I knew that would bug you. Seriously, you guys are so great together. I wish you lived closer because I know Ethan really clicked with Nick and we would have so much fun together. It's amazing how they bonded so much about college football over some Tecates and tequila.

From: PBCupLover – May 4, 2014 – 6:32 PM
To: Shelley Manning
Subject: Re: Fun in the Sun!

Well played, Shelley.

From: Shelley Manning – May 4, 2014 – 6:35 PM
To: PBCupLover
Subject: Re: Fun in the Sun!

I usually reserve these for Renee, but seeing as you two will be married soon, I'll toss you one. Mwah! Mwah!

From: Shelley Manning – May 4, 2014 – 6:36 PM
To: Renee Greene
Subject: Re: Fun in the Sun!

Yes, it was indeed fun to see them get along so well. However, we need to make sure they don't get along too well.

From: Renee Greene – May 4, 2014 – 6:37 PM
To: Shelley Manning
Subject: Re: Fun in the Sun!

Does Nick not know about you and Ethan?

From: Shelley Manning – May 4, 2014 – 6:41 PM
To: Renee Greene
Subject: Re: Fun in the Sun!

He knows about that. We have no secrets when it comes to our pasts. And believe me, mine pales in comparison to Nick's. The stories he could tell! No, I'm worried that Ethan is going to convince Nick that it's perfectly appropriate for a grown man – well out of college, mind you – to wear school paraphernalia.

From: Renee Greene – May 4, 2014 – 6:43 PM
To: Shelley Manning
Subject: Re: Fun in the Sun!

Ha! Ethan does love his Buckeyes.

From: Shelley Manning – May 4, 2014 – 6:45 PM
To: Renee Greene
Subject: Re: Fun in the Sun!

Yes, well, I think I nipped that one in the bud. We're about to land, Sweetie. Thanks again and we'll talk later in the week. Mwah! Mwah!

From: Renee Greene – May 4, 2014 – 8:02 PM
To: Ashley Gordon
Subject: Missed you

Hi there. We're home now and we completely missed you and Greg this weekend in Cabo. Don't want to make you jealous with details.

From: Ashley Gordon – May 4, 2014 – 9:54 PM
To: Renee Greene
Subject: Re: Missed you

But it was amazing, right? It's okay to tell me.

From: Renee Greene – May 4, 2014 – 10:05 PM
To: Ashley Gordon
Subject: Re: Missed you

It was! This place was INCREDIBLE! There were three huge and separate living spaces each outfitted with oversized, flat screen TVs and surround sound speakers. We didn't watch TV, but if we wanted to, it would have been like being in an IMAX theatre.

The outdoor living space (can't really call it a backyard) consisted of a huge swimming pool and Jacuzzi, enough plush lounge chairs to house a lazy army and a fire pit for relaxing to watch the sunset. The water was a Tiffany blue. So clear. I've never seen anything like it since being in Greece during my college backpacking trip.

The kitchen was bigger than our entire 2-bedroom apartment. Not that I had to spend any time in the kitchen. We had a personal chef that catered to our every whim 24/7. The chef could make anything you wanted - from fresh ceviche to chocolate soufflés. I say 24/7 because there were groups of people awake and partying at all times of the day and night. Some of Ethan's friends were night owls and stayed up into the wee hours with Nick and Shelley. Mark, Marnie and I enjoyed the fun in the sun right down a flight of stairs to our private strip of beach.

There were 12 bedrooms, each with a private bathroom that included a sunk-in tub. I'll never be able to stay at a Hyatt again!

From: Ashley Gordon – May 4, 2014 – 10:16 PM
To: Renee Greene
Subject: Re: Missed you

You don't want to make me jealous, but you are definitely making me jealous.
Want to know about my weekend? I was at a birthday party for a one year old at a children's gymnasium. Siobhan loved when Greg hung her upside down on the monkey bars until she vomited up all of the birthday cake he let her have (I keep telling him not to give her refined sugar!) and I had to clean it all up.

From: Renee Greene – May 4, 2014 – 10:22 PM
To: Ashley Gordon
Subject: Re: Missed you

Oy! Sorry to hear that. I would try to say something positive to make that seem less awful than it sounds, but I'm going to level with you here. That sucks! Ethan decided that this trip to Cabo for his team's "finance retreat" should be an annual event. We'll be sure to give you more notice next time so you can get Greg's parents or yours to watch Siobhan.

From: Ashley Gordon – May 4, 2014 – 10:26 PM
To: Renee Greene
Subject: Re: Missed you

Put us down for next year. That will give us both time to get fit to be seen in a swimsuit.

From: Renee Greene – May 4, 2014 – 10:30 PM
To: Ashley Gordon
Subject: Re: Missed you

You got it. Give my sweet angel a kiss for me - as long as you've managed to clean up all of the post-party puke. Yuck! Let's try to meet for lunch this week. I'll call you later.

From: Mark Finlay – May 5, 2014 – 8:25 AM
To: Renee Greene, PBCupLover
Subject: Thanks!

Hey, guys. Just wanted to say thank you again for letting me come along on this incredible weekend. That place was insane. I don't know how I will manage to stay at a Marriott ever again. I'm having a margarita right now thinking about it all and in honor of Cinco de Mayo.

From: Renee Greene – May 5, 2014 – 9:02 AM
To: Mark Finlay, PBCupLover
Subject: Re: Thanks!

Ha! I just made that same joke to Ashley last night but with a Hyatt instead of a Marriott. Too funny. Since we're chatting, anything else you might want to share about your enjoyment of the weekend?

From: PBCupLover – May 5, 2014 – 9:04 AM
To: Renee Greene
Subject: Fwd: Re: Thanks!

Butt out, Babe!

From: Renee Greene – May 5, 2014 – 9:06 AM
To: PBCupLover
Subject: Re: Fwd: Re: Thanks!

No way. I've got a vested interest in this relationship being a success.

From: PBCupLover – May 5, 2014 – 9:07 AM
To: Renee Greene
Subject: Re: Fwd: Re: Thanks!

Vested interest?

From: Renee Greene – May 5, 2014 – 9:12 AM
To: PBCupLover
Subject: Re: Fwd: Re: Thanks!

Yes! I like this girl. A lot. She is awesome and if Mark's going to move on with someone after the "cat"astrophe that was Cassidy, then I want it to be with Marnie. Plus, I'm the one who feels responsible for breaking Mark's heart. I know. I know. It wasn't my fault, it was Cassidy's. But still, I'm the one who found out and had to tell him. I want him to be happy and I want me to be happy about his happiness, too. If Mark wants me to butt out, he can tell me himself. So YOU butt out.

From: PBCupLover – May 5, 2014 – 9:14 AM
To: Renee Greene
Subject: Re: Fwd: Re: Thanks!

Me butt out? You talk to your fiancé like that?

From: Renee Greene – May 5, 2014 – 9:14 AM
To: PBCupLover
Subject: Re: Fwd: Re: Thanks!

You just did!

From: PBCupLover – May 5, 2014 – 9:15 AM
To: Renee Greene
Subject: Re: Fwd: Re: Thanks!

Touché! Okay, just tread lightly.

From: Renee Greene – May 5, 2014 – 9:15 AM
To: PBCupLover
Subject: Re: Fwd: Re: Thanks!

I will. Always do.

From: Mark Finlay – May 5, 2014 – 10:02 AM
To: Renee Greene, PBCupLover
Subject: Re: Thanks!

Marnie and I had a bet on how long it would take you to ask about that. Guess who won? Me. I said within a day and she said two days. I do know you well. We had a lot of fun together. She's really cool and I enjoyed hanging out with her.

From: Renee Greene – May 5, 2014 – 10:03 AM
To: Mark Finlay, PBCupLover
Subject: Re: Thanks!

Squee!

From: Mark Finlay – May 5, 2014 – 10:04 AM
To: Renee Greene, PBCupLover
Subject: Re: Thanks!

Okay, okay. That's enough. Thanks again for a fun weekend. I'll talk with you later.

From: PBCupLover – May 5, 2014 – 10:07 AM
To: Mark Finlay
Subject: Re: Thanks!

Great hanging with you, man. If Renee gets too nosey, just let me know and I'll see what I can do.

From: Mark Finlay – May 5, 2014 – 10:09 AM
To: PBCupLover
Subject: Re: Thanks!

I'm used to it. It's kind of nice knowing that she's looking out for me. Thanks.

From: Marnie Glass – May 6, 2014 – 9:53 AM
To: Renee Greene
Subject: Too soon?

Hi there. I have a favor to ask. A huge favor. Perhaps I'm level-jumping on our friendship. It's okay to tell me it's too soon. But I thought I would take a chance anyway. As you know, I am going to be in San Diego for the night with your fiancé (ha! that sounds inappropriate, right?) and I don't have anyone to watch my dog.

I would normally just board her, but she's been sick lately and I would feel better knowing that someone I trust is keeping an eye on her. My neighbor has been working the night shift at the hospital so she can't do it. Do you think you would mind swinging by my place on Thursday night/Friday morning to feed her/check in on her?

From: Renee Greene – May 6, 2014 – 10:01 AM
To: Marnie Glass
Subject: Re: Too soon?

Hey, Marnie. So is it too soon to be joking about getting busy with my man, or too soon to ask me to help with your dog? Ha! Honestly, it isn't too soon to ask me for a favor. I think you're great and I'm so glad you are a new friend and part of Ethan's team at work.

But you clearly do not know me well enough yet if you are asking me to help with your dog. I'm just not a pet person. If you asked me to bake a cake for you, I'd do it. Need a ride to or from the airport, I'm your girl. Heck, I'd probably even give you a kidney if you needed one. But I draw the line at canine.

From: Marnie Glass – May 6, 2014 – 10:08 AM
To: Renee Greene
Subject: Re: Too soon?

I had no idea you weren't an animal lover. You're so kind and compassionate, I just figured you were totally into them. No worries. I will find someone else for this. But if I need a kidney, I'll be sure to call.

From: Renee Greene – May 6, 2014 – 10:12 AM
To: Marnie Glass
Subject: Re: Too soon?

Have you thought about asking Mark? As I'm sure you know, he loves animals, especially his dog Finneus. I'm sure he would be happy to help care for your furry friend.

From: Marnie Glass – May 6, 2014 – 10:16 AM
To: Renee Greene
Subject: Re: Too soon?

I was going to ask him, but I didn't want to level jump on our relationship. I figured if I was being too bold, better to do it with you than with him.

From: Renee Greene – May 6, 2014 – 10:18 AM
To: Marnie Glass
Subject: Re: Too soon?

Good thinking. But seriously, I don't think he would mind at all.

From: Marnie Glass – May 6, 2014 – 10:19 AM
To: Renee Greene
Subject: Re: Too soon?

If you think I should…

From: Renee Greene – May 6, 2014 – 10:20 AM
To: Marnie Glass
Subject: Re: Too soon?

Yes!

From: Marnie Glass – May 6, 2014 – 10:20 AM
To: Renee Greene
Subject: Re: Too soon?

Okay. I'll tell him you suggested it. Is that okay?

From: Renee Greene – May 6, 2014 – 10:21 AM
To: Marnie Glass
Subject: Re: Too soon?

Yes! And have fun with Ethan. A finance symposium on institutional investors sounds sooooo fun.

From: Marnie Glass – May 6, 2014 – 10:23 AM
To: Renee Greene
Subject: Re: Too soon?

It sounds awful, doesn't it? Thank goodness for Happy Hour.

From: Marnie Glass – May 6, 2014 – 10:25 AM
To: Mark Finlay
Subject: Big favor

Hey, there. How's everything going? Are we still on for dinner on Saturday?

From: Mark Finlay – May 6, 2014 – 11:02 AM
To: Marnie Glass
Subject: Re: Big favor

Hey. Yes, dinner is still on for Saturday. Is having dinner with you considered a favor? If so, am I doing you one or are you doing me one?

From: Marnie Glass – May 6, 2014 – 11:08 AM
To: Mark Finlay
Subject: Re: Big favor

Oops. I meant to ask you a favor. If you're not cool with it, it's okay.
I had asked Renee but she's not available. She suggested I ask you.
I'm going to be in San Diego on Thursday night for work and my
dog, Ms. PacMan, has been really sick. Instead of boarding her, I
was hoping to find someone to feed her Thursday/Friday.

From: Mark Finlay – May 6, 2014 – 11:11 AM
To: Marnie Glass
Subject: Re: Big favor

You asked Renee to watch your dog? That's hilarious. She is NOT a
dog person – or pet person – for that matter.

From: Marnie Glass – May 6, 2014 – 11:14 AM
To: Mark Finlay
Subject: Re: Big favor

Yeah, I kind of figured that out based on her hilarious email
response. She thought you might be willing to do that favor for me.
If it's too much to ask, just say so. I don't want you to feel weird.

From: Mark Finlay – May 6, 2014 – 11:17 AM
To: Marnie Glass
Subject: Re: Big favor

I'd be happy to help with Ms. PacMan. Why don't I swing by your
office on Wednesday – take you to lunch – and you can give me the
details and a key?

From: Marnie Glass – May 6, 2014 – 11:18 AM
To: Mark Finlay
Subject: Re: Big favor

That would be great. Thanks.

From: Mark Finlay – May 6, 2014 – 11:18 AM
To: Marnie Glass
Subject: Re: Big favor

Okay. I'll see you then.

From: Marnie Glass – May 6, 2014 – 11:20 AM
To: Renee Greene
Subject: Re: Too soon?

Mark's going to watch Ms. PacMan for me. Thanks for giving me

the confidence to ask him.

From: Marnie Glass – May 6, 2014 – 11:21 AM
To: Renee Greene
Subject: Re: Too soon?

Squee!

CHAPTER 26: WORKPLACE FUN

From: Shelley Manning – May 7, 2014 – 10:01 AM
To: Renee Greene
Cc: Ashley Gordon
Subject: Save the date

Sweetie, save June 7 for your bachelorette party. We'll pick you up around 7. Don't plan on being home anytime specific (we are staying at a swanky boutique hotel that night) or having any early morning (or perhaps even early afternoon) plans the next day. That's all you get. Don't ask for more details.

From: Renee Greene – May 7, 2014 – 10:10 AM
To: Shelley Manning
Cc: Ashley Gordon
Subject: Re: Save the date

I beg of you, please, please, please do not make me wear a penis hat or bride sash. Other than that, I will reluctantly put myself in your hands.

From: Shelley Manning – May 7, 2014 – 10:13 AM
To: Renee Greene
Cc: Ashley Gordon
Subject: Re: Save the date

I can't make any promises. Just know you're going to have fun. While these will be memories for a lifetime, I'm not sure you'll remember anything. Can't wait!

From: Renee Greene – May 7, 2014 – 10:15 AM
To: Ashley Gordon
Subject: Re: Save the date

I'm a little scared. Anything you can tell me?

From: Ashley Gordon – May 7, 2014 – 11:21 AM
To: Renee Greene
Subject: Re: Save the date

I've been sworn to secrecy. As much as I would like to help you out, the penalty for revealing any details is too severe.

From: Renee Greene – May 10, 2014 – 8:02 PM
To: Shelley Manning
Subject: Small World Story Alert!

Small world story alert: My friend Stephanie, the one with the cute coffee shop in the valley, asked me if I could give her a hand today. One of her best employees had to take an emergency leave due to a burst appendix and she was short staffed. Although I've never worked as a waitress before, I figured I could handle the task for a day.

I'm doing my thing when I approach a new customer seated in my station. (Don't you love how I've got the lingo down?) It's the lead singer for Luke's Crossing - Luke Cross.

I got so flustered and started blabbering on and on about how I was just talking about wanting to work with him and his band and that this is just such a coincidence. He quickly excused himself to go to the restroom and never came back. I think I spooked him. I'm sure it will be awkward when I see him on Wednesday at our meeting.

From: Shelley Manning – May 10, 2014 – 9:32 PM
To: Renee Greene
Subject: Re: Small World Story Alert!

That is indeed a small world story. You must have really come across as quite the loon if he ran off and never returned. Ha-larious! Yes, can't wait to hear what transpires next week.

From: Renee Greene – May 10, 2014 – 9:38 PM
To: Shelley Manning
Subject: Re: Small World Story Alert!

Yeah, as I replay this all in my head, I really sounded like an idiot. When I told Ethan, he just shook his head and walked away.

From: Shelley Manning – May 10, 2014 – 9:41 PM
To: Renee Greene
Subject: Re: Small World Story Alert!

Keep me posted, Sweetie. Going now to get some beauty rest – not that I need it. Mwah! Mwah!

From: Renee Greene – May 14, 2014 – 12:32 PM
To: Shelley Manning
Subject: Re: Small World Story Alert!

We had our meeting with Luke's Crossing today. It was either a totally awkward conversation or happy reunion. Which do you think?

From: Shelley Manning – May 14, 2014 – 12:33 PM
To: Renee Greene
Subject: Re: Small World Story Alert!

Totally awkward conversation.

From: Renee Greene – May 14, 2014 – 12:34 PM
To: Shelley Manning
Subject: Re: Small World Story Alert!

Circle gets the square.

What happened?

From: Renee Greene – May 14, 2014 – 12:41 PM
To: Shelley Manning
Subject: Re: Small World Story Alert!

So Luke and his manager walk in. The client introduces himself and they start shaking hands. Luke walks over to me and this is what happened.

> Luke: Hi. Luke Cross.

> Me: I'm Renee Greene.

> Luke: Nice to meet you.

> Me: We've actually met before.

> Luke: We have? I don't remember meeting you before. Where did we meet?

> Me: Saturday.

> Luke: Saturday? I didn't have any meetings on Saturday. I didn't even leave the house on Saturday, well except to grab something at a local coffee shop.

> Me: Exactly.

> Luke: The only person I talked to was some crazy waitress who was going on and on about wanting to do a project with me. That chick was nuts. So I left.

> Me: Right.

> Luke: You're the crazy waitress?

> Me: Yep. Well sort of.

From: Shelley Manning – May 14, 2014 – 12:45 PM
To: Renee Greene
Subject: Re: Small World Story Alert!

I would say it's hard to believe this shit happens to you, but time and time again you've proven to me how easily these things indeed happen to you. So did he slip out of *this* meeting?

From: Renee Greene – May 14, 2014 – 12:47 PM
To: Shelley Manning
Subject: Re: Small World Story Alert!

No. Thankfully he let me explain that I was just helping out a friend and that I hope he doesn't hold that experience against me. Luke's manager seemed more concerned that Luke calling *me* "crazy" was going to impact us making a deal.

From: Shelley Manning – May 14, 2014 – 1:00 PM
To: Renee Greene
Subject: Re: Small World Story Alert!

And will it? Will being called crazy – to your face – unlike when we do it behind your back – be a deal breaker for you?

From: Renee Greene – May 14, 2014 – 1:02 PM
To: Shelley Manning
Subject: Re: Small World Story Alert!

You call me crazy behind my back? Who else does?

From: Shelley Manning – May 14, 2014 – 1:04 PM
To: Renee Greene
Subject: Re: Small World Story Alert!

All the time. And all of us do, especially Ethan.

From: Renee Greene – May 14, 2014 – 1:09 PM
To: Shelley Manning
Subject: Re: Small World Story Alert!

Hrmph! Well, it's neither a deal breaker with our friendship nor with this hotel opening deal. I'm not sure I can say the same for Ethan. I am his betrothed after all. He's supposed to be supporting me, not bad mouthing me behind my back.

From: Shelley Manning – May 14, 2014 – 1:13 PM
To: Renee Greene
Subject: Re: Small World Story Alert!

You should definitely call him out on that. And then let me be privy to how that conversation goes down. All of this is quite entertaining.

From: Renee Greene – May 14, 2014 – 1:14 PM
To: Shelley Manning
Subject: Re: Small World Story Alert!

Ha! Ha! I really am crazy, aren't I?

From: Shelley Manning – May 14, 2014 – 1:17 PM
To: Renee Greene
Subject: Re: Small World Story Alert!

Yes, Sweetie, but that's why we love you so much – including your betrothed. Talk with you later. See you in a few days for your bridal shower. Mwah! Mwah!

CHAPTER 27: GIVING THANKS

From: Renee Greene – May 18, 2014 – 9:09 AM
To: Shelley Manning, Ashley Gordon
Subject: THANK YOU! THANK YOU!

Thank you ladies SO much for throwing me such a lovely bridal shower. It was so elegant and the food was delicious. I also appreciate you not having any of those silly games, like see how well we know each other or bridal bingo. You are two of the best girlfriends a gal could have. I love you both!

From: Renee Greene – May 18, 2014 – 9:13 AM
To: Shelley Manning
Subject: Fess Up!

C'mon. Fess up. I know it was you. It HAD to be you. Who else would give me a black lace and silk body stocking and whip for my bridal shower. And signing the card "Cozette" was truly inspired.

From: Ashley Gordon – May 18, 2014 – 10:00 AM
To: Renee Greene, Shelley Manning
Subject: Re: THANK YOU! THANK YOU!

Our pleasure. Happy to return the favor. Can't wait to throw you a baby shower next. Is nine months from now too soon?

From: Renee Greene – May 18, 2014 – 10:03 AM
To: Shelley Manning, Ashley Gordon
Subject: Re: THANK YOU! THANK YOU!

I'm not sure we'll be having kids that quickly, but hope there are some sweet little angels in our future.

From: Shelley Manning – May 18, 2014 – 10:05 AM
To: Renee Greene
Subject: Re: THANK YOU! THANK YOU!

What?!? You don't think Ethan and you know each other well enough? The boy knows the name of your middle school for god's sake.

From: Shelley Manning – May 18, 2014 – 10:09 AM
To: Renee Greene
Subject: Re: Fess Up!

Sweetie, it wasn't me. I swear it wasn't. Believe me, if I had wanted to give you those things, I would have proudly signed my name. I'm afraid you'll have to look elsewhere.

From: Renee Greene – May 18, 2014 – 10:14 AM
To: Shelley Manning
Subject: Re: Fess Up!

Well, if it wasn't you then it must have been my Aunt Noreen. I always knew there was a dirty bird lurking in that frail little body of hers.

From: Shelley Manning – May 18, 2014 – 10:16 AM
To: Ashley Gordon
Subject: Fwd: Re: Fess Up!

Well? What do you have to say for yourself?

From: Ashley Gordon – May 18, 2014 – 11:59 AM
To: Shelley Manning
Subject: Re: Fwd: Re: Fess Up!

Whatever do you mean?

From: Shelley Manning – May 18, 2014 – 12:04 PM
To: Ashley Gordon
Subject: Re: Fwd: Re: Fess Up!

Drop the sweet and innocent act, Ash. I know it was you. It wasn't hard to track down the purchaser from the store receipt.

From: Ashley Gordon – May 18, 2014 – 12:08 PM
To: Shelley Manning
Subject: Re: Fwd: Re: Fess Up!

Don't tell Renee, okay? It's been sort of fun watching her try to figure out if it was her Aunt Noreen.

From: Shelley Manning – May 18, 2014 – 12:12 PM
To: Ashley Gordon
Subject: Re: Fwd: Re: Fess Up!

So it was you. HA! I was just bluffing. But, I KNEW it! Well done, young lady. Well done.

From: Ashley Gordon – May 18, 2014 – 12:14 PM
To: Shelley Manning
Subject: Re: Fwd: Re: Fess Up!

I thought you would like that.

From: Shelley Manning – May 18, 2014 – 12:16 PM
To: Ashley Gordon
Subject: Re: Fwd: Re: Fess Up!

Sorry now that I didn't have a bridal shower myself.

From: Ashley Gordon – May 18, 2014 – 12:17 PM
To: Shelley Manning
Subject: Re: Fwd: Re: Fess Up!

I figured you already had that stuff.

From: Shelley Manning – May 18, 2014 – 12:19 PM
To: Ashley Gordon
Subject: Re: Fwd: Re: Fess Up!

I do, but a girl always likes to get something new.

From: Ashley Gordon – May 18, 2014 – 12:20 PM
To: Shelley Manning
Subject: Re: Fwd: Re: Fess Up!

LOL!

From: Renee Greene – May 18, 2014 – 1:13 PM
To: Shelley Manning
Subject: Re: THANK YOU! THANK YOU!

He only knows where I went to middle school because it's one of the security question hints for our bank account. Otherwise, I think he couldn't care less.

From: Shelley Manning – May 18, 2014 – 2:39 PM
To: Renee Greene
Subject: Re: THANK YOU! THANK YOU!

LOL! Regardless of the reasons why or how, he does know you and despite it all, he loves you and wants to marry you.

From: Renee Greene – May 18, 2014 – 3:32 PM
To: Shelley Manning
Subject: Re: THANK YOU! THANK YOU!

I must have fooled him good. ;)

From: Renee Greene – May 24, 2014 – 7:28 PM
To: Shelley Manning
Subject: Rockin' a tux?

Ethan told me that you were wiling to walk me down the aisle and could totally rock a tux. I know you look hot in basic black among other things…or nothing at all, apparently…but I made a decision about this. I decided to have my mom walk me down the aisle and to carry a photo of my dad so he could be there with me. We'll have a seat empty at the front for him in spirit.

From: Shelley Manning – May 24, 2014 – 8:22 PM
To: Renee Greene
Subject: Re: Rockin' a tux?

I think that's wonderful, Sweetie. And while I do like the idea of me walking you down the aisle wearing nothing at all, I don't want to distract everyone's attention from the bride. That just wouldn't be cool.

From: Renee Greene – May 24, 2014 – 8:25 PM
To: Shelley Manning
Subject: Re: Rockin' a tux?

And that's exactly the reason we aren't going that direction.

From: Shelley Manning – May 24, 2014 – 8:22 PM
To: Renee Greene
Subject: Re: Rockin' a tux?

I figured. Mwah! Mwah!

From: Renee Greene – May 28, 2014 – 8:32 AM
To: PBCupLover
Subject: Tell me!

Tell me.

From: Renee Greene – May 28, 2014 – 10:14 AM
To: PBCupLover
Subject: Fwd: Tell me!

I know I said I didn't want to know. But I do. Tell me.

From: Renee Greene – May 28, 2014 – 11:45 AM
To: PBCupLover
Subject: Fwd: Fwd: Tell me!

C'mon. This is driving me crazy. You know my type-A personality can't hold out any longer. Tell me.

From: Renee Greene – May 28, 2014 – 12:02 PM
To: PBCupLover
Subject: Fwd: Fwd: Fwd: Tell me!

Please. Tell me, please.

From: PBCupLover – May 28, 2014 – 12:03 PM
To: Renee Greene
Subject: Re: Fwd: Fwd: Fwd: Tell me!

That's the magic word.

From: Renee Greene – May 28, 2014 – 12:04 PM
To: PBCupLover
Subject: Re: Fwd: Fwd: Fwd: Tell me!

You're kidding me, right? You've been waiting for me to say "please."

From: PBCupLover – May 28, 2014 – 12:05 PM
To: Renee Greene
Subject: Re: Fwd: Fwd: Fwd: Tell me!

Just be glad I didn't make you say, "pretty please with a cherry on top."

From: Renee Greene – May 28, 2014 – 12:07 PM
To: PBCupLover
Subject: Re: Fwd: Fwd: Fwd: Tell me!

You are so juvenile. Did you pull that crap with your sisters? No wonder they called you PITA.

From: PBCupLover – May 28, 2014 – 12:09 PM
To: Renee Greene
Subject: Re: Fwd: Fwd: Fwd: Tell me!

For someone who wants something from me, you're not being very nice.

From: Renee Greene – May 28, 2014 – 12:11 PM
To: PBCupLover
Subject: Re: Fwd: Fwd: Fwd: Tell me!

You're right. I apologize. And I say, "pretty, pretty please with a cherry on top." Now tell me!

From: PBCupLover – May 28, 2014 – 12:13 PM
To: Renee Greene
Subject: Re: Fwd: Fwd: Fwd: Tell me!

Okay. Drumroll please (or should I say "pretty pretty please with a cherry on top")…Australia. We are going to Australia.

From: Renee Greene – May 28, 2014 – 12:14 PM
To: PBCupLover
Subject: Re: Fwd: Fwd: Fwd: Tell me!

Squee! I have always wanted to go to Australia!

From: PBCupLover – May 28, 2014 – 12:15 PM
To: Renee Greene
Subject: Re: Fwd: Fwd: Fwd: Tell me!

I know. That's why I planned that for our honeymoon, silly.

From: Renee Greene – May 28, 2014 – 12:15 PM
To: PBCupLover
Subject: Re: Fwd: Fwd: Fwd: Tell me!

More. Tell me more.

From: PBCupLover – May 28, 2014 – 12:24 PM
To: Renee Greene
Subject: Re: Fwd: Fwd: Fwd: Tell me!

We fly to Sydney and will spend 2 days there. I figured we could walk around the city, visit the Opera House, etc. We then have a few days in Melbourne to do wine tastings at some local wineries. From there, we fly up to Cairns to visit the Great Barrier Reef. I have a tour set up for us to go snorkeling. (Don't worry. I've already purchased some sea sickness medicine for you.)

After two days, we take a small plane (don't freak out!) to a small resort called Lizard Island. It's a private island with only 40 suites. There's only one restaurant (5 stars!) on the island and no telephones or TVs. There is one highly-rated spa and you're set for a day of pampering. I've also arranged for us to get a boat ride to a small private stretch of beach where we will dine on a picnic lunch and a bottle of wine. Aside from that, we'll lounge, hike, relax, read and other things people typically do on their honeymoons. So?

From: Renee Greene – May 28, 2014 – 12:28 PM
To: PBCupLover
Subject: Re: Fwd: Fwd: Fwd: Tell me!

I'm absolutely speechless, which as you know is a big deal. I'm just stunned at how perfect this is.

From: PBCupLover – May 28, 2014 – 12:30 PM
To: Renee Greene
Subject: Re: Fwd: Fwd: Fwd: Tell me!

I thought you would be pleased. You're not sorry now that I told you…that it's not a surprise?

From: Renee Greene – May 28, 2014 – 12:32 PM
To: PBCupLover
Subject: Re: Fwd: Fwd: Fwd: Tell me!

Of course not. I'm surprised right now. You're fantastic. Thank you! And please don't ever stop surprising me.

From: PBCupLover – May 28, 2014 – 12:33 PM
To: Renee Greene
Subject: Re: Fwd: Fwd: Fwd: Tell me!

You mean "pretty pretty please with a cherry on top", right?

From: Renee Greene – May 28, 2014 – 12:34 PM
To: PBCupLover
Subject: Re: Fwd: Fwd: Fwd: Tell me!

Right. Love you. XO

From: Renee Greene – June 3, 2014 – 10:42 AM
To: Shelley Manning
Subject: One step forwards, two steps back?

So I got weighed and measured at Curves today as part of their regularl check ins. I've lost 7 pounds, 10 inches and a bunch of body fat. Wahoo! All of my new friends were so excited for me. I celebrated with a cupcake. One step forward, two steps back?

From: Shelley Manning – June 3, 2014 – 10:50 AM
To: Renee Greene
Subject: Re: One step forwards, two steps back?

Congrats on being such a loser. (Betcha never thought you'd hear me say that?) I'm so proud of you. I could tell that you had lost some weight the last time I saw you. But I know one of your "life lessons" is to not tell someone they've lost weight. You might have noticed that I kept telling you how great you looked.

From: Renee Greene – June 3, 2014 – 10:53 AM
To: Shelley Manning
Subject: Re: One step forwards, two steps back?

I did notice that, thank you. And I will take all of the compliments I can get.

From: Shelley Manning – June 3, 2014 – 10:57 AM
To: Renee Greene
Subject: Re: One step forwards, two steps back?

You're taking a compliment? When you lost the pounds, you must have also shed the <unwarranted, though it be> whiny insecurity that has seemed to saddle you down all your life. And who are these new friends of yours?

From: Renee Greene – June 3, 2014 – 11:03 AM
To: Shelley Manning
Subject: Re: One step forwards, two steps back?

The old ladies at Curves are quite the talkative bunch. I don't think they have much else going on, so they just gossip and chit chat during their workout. As much as I've tried to avoid eye contact and conversation, they've focused their cataract-corrected eyes on me. Now we're all pals.

From: Shelley Manning – June 3, 2014 – 11:06 AM
To: Renee Greene
Subject: Re: One step forwards, two steps back?

As you would say with a tinge of paranoia in your voice, "Don't go finding a new bestie." ;)

From: Renee Greene – June 3, 2014 – 11:10 AM
To: Shelley Manning
Subject: Re: One step forwards, two steps back?

Ha! Ha! Yes, Louise, the 75-year-old ringleader of our little group is quite the vixen. Her stories are legendary. And the nicknames she gives her men – Viagra Victor, Saggy-skin Stanley and Heart Condition Harry – are beyond compare.

From: Shelley Manning – June 3, 2014 – 11:12 AM
To: Renee Greene
Subject: Re: One step forwards, two steps back?

Good. I knew I didn't have to worry. Now, on to that celebratory cupcake…

From: Renee Greene – June 3, 2014 – 11:14 AM
To: Shelley Manning
Subject: Re: One step forwards, two steps back?

I thought you were going to let that slide…

From: Shelley Manning – June 3, 2014 – 11:17 AM
To: Renee Greene
Subject: Re: One step forwards, two steps back?

I can't in good conscience not chastise you a tiny bit for that. Shame! Shame! Seriously Sweetie, I think it's fine to indulge a little every once in a while. Charles Schulz once said, "All you need is love. But a little chocolate now and then doesn't hurt."

From: Renee Greene – June 3, 2014 – 11:19 AM
To: Shelley Manning
Subject: Re: One step forwards, two steps back?

Awww. Did you remember that from our trip to the Charles Schulz museum last year?

From: Shelley Manning – June 3, 2014 – 11:22 AM
To: Renee Greene
Subject: Re: One step forwards, two steps back?

No. I just Googled "inspirational food quotes" to come up with something to make you feel better.

From: Renee Greene – June 3, 2014 – 11:23 AM
To: Shelley Manning
Subject: Re: One step forwards, two steps back?

Find anything else that help me justify the lifestyle I want but my body can't sustain?

From: Shelley Manning – June 3, 2014 – 11:25 AM
To: Renee Greene
Subject: Re: One step forwards, two steps back?

Just keep doing what you're doing…eating healthy meals, exercising regularly, drinking one glass of wine a night…etc. You're gonna do great.

From: Renee Greene – June 3, 2014 – 11:26 AM
To: Shelley Manning
Subject: Re: One step forwards, two steps back?

One glass of wine, huh?

From: Shelley Manning – June 3, 2014 – 11:28 AM
To: Renee Greene
Subject: Re: One step forwards, two steps back?

Yes! I give you permission to have one glass of wine daily, which provides great health benefits.

From: Renee Greene – June 3, 2014 – 11:31 AM
To: Shelley Manning
Subject: Re: One step forwards, two steps back?

And what do the other glasses of wine a night provide? Increasing confidence and acceptance of my curvy figure? Tolerance of Ethan's dance moves? Witty and comedic comebacks to snarky comments?

From: Shelley Manning – June 3, 2014 – 11:33 AM
To: Renee Greene
Subject: Re: One step forwards, two steps back?

Ha-Larious! All of the above! Gotta run, Sweetie. I'll see you in a few days for your bachelorette party. Save some room for the mojitos!

CHAPTER 28: OH, WHAT A NIGHT

From: Renee Greene – June 7, 2014 – 4:32 PM
To: PBCupLover
Subject: Information vacuum

I know NOTHING about the bachelorette party that Shelley planned for me tonight. She has rebuffed every inquiry I've made and has put nothing in writing so there's nothing I can beg Ashley to send to me. She's threatened her with some sort of awful retribution if she even reveals anything to me. I've got to admit it. I'm a little scared. I also know NOTHING about the bachelor party that is being thrown in your honor this evening. That, too, has me a bit worried.

From: PBCupLover – June 7, 2014 – 4:39 PM
To: Renee Greene
Subject: Re: Information vacuum

FDR said, "The only thing we have to fear is fear itself." Although he hung out with Churchill who was quite the boozer, he never met Shelley. Seriously, I'm sure she's just doing this to throw you off a bit. I'm sure it will be fine. More than fine. I'm sure it will be fun. As for me, I don't know what the guys have planned for me either. And since I don't know what it is, I can't be held responsible for what they plan, right?

From: Renee Greene – June 7, 2014 – 4:43 PM
To: PBCupLover
Subject: Re: Information vacuum

Hmmm. Billy the Kid is throwing you a bachelor party and you don't want to be responsible for what might occur there?

From: PBCupLover – June 7, 2014 – 4:45 PM
To: Renee Greene
Subject: Re: Information vacuum

Well, when you put it that way, it does sound pretty bad, huh? By the same token, Shelley is planning your soiree.

From: Renee Greene – June 7, 2014 – 4:46 PM
To: PBCupLover
Subject: Re: Information vacuum

Booze, bimbos and strippers, oh my!

From: PBCupLover – June 7, 2014 – 4:47 PM
To: Renee Greene
Subject: Re: Information vacuum

Sounds about right. But seriously, you have nothing to worry about.

From: Renee Greene – June 7, 2014 – 4:49 PM
To: PBCupLover
Subject: Re: Information vacuum

I know. I trust you. And I trust myself. Let's make a pact to tell each other everything – no secrets. Okay?

From: PBCupLover – June 7, 2014 – 4:53 PM
To: Renee Greene
Subject: Re: Information vacuum

Works for me. I've got to get the last of this work done so I can go and enjoy myself tonight. Have fun and I'll look for an email later. Love you, Babe.

From: Renee Greene – June 7, 2014 – 7:35 PM
To: PBCupLover
Subject: Oh what a night!

Where are you? Shelley had a limo come by and it was filled with all of my friends including a few from college that flew in for the weekend. We're now at Flint's. She rented the whole place out. Having a blast. Hope you are too.

From: PBCupLover – June 7, 2014 – 8:02 PM
To: Renee Greene
Subject: Re: Oh what a night!

We're at Slab. Before you get your knickers in a twist, it's a new steak house in Beverly Hills. The only meat I'm planning to indulge in is a 16 oz bone-in ribeye wrapped in bacon. Mmmm.

From: Renee Greene – June 7, 2014 – 8:53 PM
To: PBCupLover
Subject: Re: Oh what a night!

First off, Shelley wants to know why you are eating bacon when you're Jewish.

Wish I could say the same. Shelley hired a male stripper to come to Flint's disguised as a waiter. I'm hiding in the bathroom right now because I am just so flustered. It was…awkward! He started off making small talk and congratulating me on my upcoming nuptials. Then he said he had a surprise for me.

The music turned on and apparently he was too. He started dancing and gyrating. I was so uncomfortable and so was everyone else there…except Shelley. He kept grinding up against my friends and they kept backing up or moving away.

Then he ripped off his velcro pants to show a gold g-string. He was waving his junk all around. Again, the only person that seemed to be enjoying it all was Shelley. When the music stopped, he took a bow and then I figured he would leave.

But he just stood there chatting with us while putting his velcro pants back on. He had to readjust them several times to make sure the two sides were aligned properly. I don't think I'll ever be able to hear that ripping sound again without shuddering. Oh no! Shelley's coming. Gotta go.

From: PBCupLover – June 7, 2014 – 10:25 PM
To: Renee Greene
Subject: Re: Oh what a night!

Tell Shelley, when it comes to food, I'm Jew"ish" not Jewish.

Next, what you're saying is that I should return the gold g-string and velcro pants I was planning on wearing to bed on our wedding night? Will do!

We're at a cigar bar right now enjoying some Cubans that William managed to smuggle into the country on his last trip to the Caribbean. Combine that with a 35 year old Scotch and I'm one happy man.

From: Renee Greene – June 7, 2014 – 11:12 PM
To: PBCupLover
Subject: Re: Oh what a night!

Oh, shoot. Here come the shots!

From: PBCupLover – June 8, 2014 – 1:02 AM
To: Renee Greene
Subject: Re: Oh what a night!

Just got to Bon Bons – a seedy strip club in Hollywood. A guy in the bathroom asked me if I had any cocaine. WTF!?!

From: Renee Greene – June 8, 2014 – 1:14 AM
To: PBCupLover
Subject: Re: Oh what a night!

Not too far away at the Rainbow Revolver, the gay dance bar in West Hollywood. I've never had so much fun in my life!!!

From: PBCupLover – June 8, 2014 – 1:39 AM
To: Renee Greene
Subject: Re: Oh what a night!

Don't judge me if I come home covered in glitter.

From: Renee Greene – June 8, 2014 – 2:04 AM
To: PBCupLover
Subject: Re: Oh what a night!

I so drink right now djl goin to bed I lovee yu. Slj;fa

From: PBCupLover – June 8, 2014 – 2:22 AM
To: Renee Greene
Subject: Re: Oh what a night!

Ath Kays Diner eating bacon. so much bacon. Mmmmmmm be home soon

---

From: Shelley Manning – June 8, 2014 – 9:13 AM
To: Renee Greene
Subject: Morning sunshine!

Your ringer is off. Good morning. Want to meet me for breakfast at Nina's Café at 10?

From: Renee Greene – June 8, 2014 – 11:01 AM
To: PBCupLover
Subject: Re: Oh what a night!

Why are you yelling at me?

From: PBCupLover – June 8, 2014 – 11:03 AM
To: Renee Greene
Subject: Re: Oh what a night!

I'm not yelling. I'm whispering. My mouth is so dry, I can barely talk.

From: Renee Greene – June 8, 2014 – 11:04 AM
To: PBCupLover
Subject: Re: Oh what a night!

Well it sounded like you were yelling. No talking!

From: PBCupLover – June 8, 2014 – 11:05 AM
To: Renee Greene
Subject: Re: Oh what a night!

That's because you are hung over.

From: Renee Greene – June 8, 2014 – 11:06 AM
To: PBCupLover
Subject: Re: Oh what a night!

You look like crap.

From: PBCupLover – June 8, 2014 – 11:07 AM
To: Renee Greene
Subject: Re: Oh what a night!

I feel like crap. You look beautiful. I'm so thirsty. Will you get me some water?

From: Renee Greene – June 8, 2014 – 11:08 AM
To: PBCupLover
Subject: Re: Oh what a night!

There's no way I look beautiful. I'm thirstier. Will you get me some water?

From: PBCupLover – June 8, 2014 – 11:09 AM
To: Renee Greene
Subject: Re: Oh what a night!

I can't move.

From: Renee Greene – June 8, 2014 – 11:10 AM
To: PBCupLover
Subject: Re: Oh what a night!

If you love me, you will get me some water.

From: Shelley Manning – June 8, 2014 – 11:13 AM
To: Renee Greene
Subject: Where are you?

Now I know you can't be ignoring me. After all, I just threw you the mother of all bachelorette parties. So I'm guessing you might be a bit hung over although I can't understand why. I matched you drink for drink and I feel fine.

In fact, I did a morning yoga routine on the beach at sunrise. My flight leaves in two hours, so I assume I won't get to see you before I head back. Call me when you're up and about.

From: Renee Greene – June 8, 2014 – 11:16 AM
To: PBCupLover
Subject: Re: Oh what a night!

STOP TALKING!

From: PBCupLover – June 8, 2014 – 11:18 AM
To: Renee Greene
Subject: Re: Oh what a night!

Sorry. I'm getting up to puke. After I do, I will get you some water.

From: PBCupLover – June 8, 2014 – 11:21 AM
To: Renee Greene
Subject: Re: Oh what a night!

You'll feel better if you throw up.

From: Renee Greene – June 8, 2014 – 11:41 AM
To: PBCupLover
Subject: Re: Oh what a night!

Never. You know I can't do that.

From: Renee Greene – June 8, 2014 – 11:43 AM
To: PBCupLover
Subject: Re: Oh what a night!

Thank you for the water. Going back to bed. I love you.

From: Renee Greene – June 8, 2014 – 4:12 PM
To: Shelley Manning
Subject: Re: Where are you?

UGH! I feel awful.

From: Shelley Manning – June 8, 2014 – 4:15 PM
To: Renee Greene
Subject: Re: Where are you?

Don't feel badly for dissing me this morning. I forgive you.

From: Renee Greene – June 8, 2014 – 4:19 PM
To: Shelley Manning
Subject: Re: Where are you?

No, I mean I feel awful from drinking too much. Why did you let me drink so much? What time did I get home? And why am I home? I thought I was staying at a hotel with you? Why aren't you sick?

From: Shelley Manning – June 8, 2014 – 4:25 PM
To: Renee Greene
Subject: Re: Where are you?

All good questions, Sweetie. 1. I couldn't stop you if I tried. 2. 2:00 am. 3. You insisted (and by insisted, I mean screamed at the top of your lungs) on going home and when I said I was going to stay with you, you insisted (and by insisted, I again mean screamed at the top of your lungs) that I leave. 4. I don't do hangovers.

From: Renee Greene – June 8, 2014 – 4:28 PM
To: Shelley Manning
Subject: Re: Where are you?

I don't remember everything but I do remember that I had fun. A lot of fun. Thank you. Just wish I felt better now.

From: Shelley Manning – June 8, 2014 – 4:32 PM
To: Renee Greene
Subject: Re: Where are you?

Want to know what will make you feel better?

From: Renee Greene – June 8, 2014 – 4:33 PM
To: Shelley Manning
Subject: Re: Where are you?

I thought you didn't do hangovers?

From: Shelley Manning – June 8, 2014 – 4:45 PM
To: Renee Greene
Subject: Re: Where are you?

I don't. But over the years I've been around enough drunkards to know what works.

From: Renee Greene – June 8, 2014 – 4:47 PM
To: Shelley Manning
Subject: Re: Where are you?

Don't tell me it's sex. PLEASE don't tell me it's sex.

From: Shelley Manning – June 8, 2014 – 4:50 PM
To: Renee Greene
Subject: Re: Where are you?

It's not sex. This is one instance where that is decidedly NOT the answer. 1/4 ounce Worcheshire sauce, 1/4 ounce Tabasco, 1/4 ounce pickle juice and one raw egg. Trust me. Do this and you WILL feel better.

From: Renee Greene – June 8, 2014 – 4:58 PM
To: Shelley Manning
Subject: Re: Where are you?

Uh, I don't know about this.

From: Shelley Manning – June 8, 2014 – 5:01 PM
To: Renee Greene
Subject: Re: Where are you?

Trust me. Have I ever steered you wrong? Before you answer, give that some real thought. I have NEVER steered you wrong and you know it.

From: Renee Greene – June 8, 2014 – 5:05 PM
To: Shelley Manning
Subject: Re: Where are you?

Okay. I will give it a try.

From: Shelley Manning – June 8, 2014 – 5:45 PM
To: Renee Greene
Subject: Re: Where are you?

So…feeling better?

From: Renee Greene – June 8, 2014 – 5:46 PM
To: Shelley Manning
Subject: Re: Where are you?

I threw up!

From: Shelley Manning – June 8, 2014 – 5:47 PM
To: Renee Greene
Subject: Re: Where are you?

And you feel better, don't you?

From: Shelley Manning – June 8, 2014 – 5:55 PM
To: Renee Greene
Subject: Re: Where are you?

Don't you? Don't make me come down there!

From: Renee Greene – June 8, 2014 – 5:59 PM
To: Shelley Manning
Subject: Re: Where are you?

Yes, I feel better.

From: Shelley Manning – June 8, 2014 – 6:01 PM
To: Renee Greene
Subject: Re: Where are you?

Like I said, I've never steered you wrong. Call me tomorrow when you are *really* feeling better. Mwah! Mwah!

CHAPTER 29: TRUTH OR CONSEQUENCES

From: Mark Finlay – June 12, 2014 – 3:30 PM
To: Marnie Glass
Subject: The truth shall set you free

You lied to me.

From: Marnie Glass – June 12, 2014 – 3:49 PM
To: Mark Finlay
Subject: Re: The truth shall set you free

What are you talking about?

From: Mark Finlay – June 12, 2014 – 3:54 PM
To: Marnie Glass
Subject: Re: The truth shall set you free

You are NOT 5 feet tall. I tried explaining to a friend how short (I mean petite, right?) you are and showed where you come up to my chest when we're standing next to each other. He said there is no way you are 5 feet tall.

From: Marnie Glass – June 12, 2014 – 3:57 PM
To: Mark Finlay
Subject: Re: The truth shall set you free

Oh. I'm ashamed to admit you are right. I'm 4'10. Are you angry with me? I can't tell if you're angry at me.

From: Mark Finlay – June 12, 2014 – 3:59 PM
To: Marnie Glass
Subject: Re: The truth shall set you free

You are not 4'10!

From: Marnie Glass – June 12, 2014 – 3:59 PM
To: Mark Finlay
Subject: Re: The truth shall set you free

I am!

From: Marnie Glass – June 12, 2014 – 4:03 PM
To: Mark Finlay
Subject: Re: The truth shall set you free

Oh no. I just used a measuring tape to measure myself. You're right. I'm 4'9. 4'9! Not only did I lie to you, I've been lying to myself for more than a decade.

From: Mark Finlay – June 12, 2014 – 4:04 PM
To: Marnie Glass
Subject: Re: The truth shall set you free

Anything else you want to confess?

From: Marnie Glass – June 12, 2014 – 4:09 PM
To: Mark Finlay
Subject: Re: The truth shall set you free

I don't like Star Trek. I ate two sprinkle donuts for breakfast. And I dye my hair because I'm going prematurely gray. That's everything. Now you know all of my darkest secrets. Still want to date me?

From: Mark Finlay – June 12, 2014 – 4:11 PM
To: Marnie Glass
Subject: Re: The truth shall set you free

Of course. I love you.

From: Marnie Glass – June 12, 2014 – 4:12 PM
To: Mark Finlay
Subject: Re: The truth shall set you free

You "love" me? You've never told me that before.

From: Mark Finlay – June 12, 2014 – 4:14 PM
To: Marnie Glass
Subject: Re: The truth shall set you free

I haven't? Well, I do.

From: Marnie Glass – June 12, 2014 – 4:19 PM
To: Mark Finlay
Subject: Re: The truth shall set you free

I know given everything you have gone through, that's big. And in case it wasn't obvious, I love you, too. And even if it was obvious, I want to say it. So I'll say it again. I love you. I've felt like that for a long while now but didn't want to freak you out or anything. So I guess THAT is my last confession. Now you truly know it all.

From: Mark Finlay – June 12, 2014 – 4:23 PM
To: Marnie Glass
Subject: Re: The truth shall set you free

And your response is one of the million things I love about you. Now get back to work. I hear Ethan is a tyrant for a boss.

From: Marnie Glass – June 12, 2014 – 4:24 PM
To: Mark Finlay
Subject: Re: The truth shall set you free

;)

From: Marnie Glass – June 16, 2014 – 2:11 PM
To: Renee Greene
Subject: Sunday Sundaes

Renee, Mark mentioned that diner Mel's is a favorite haunt for you and Ashley. I saw an article online that next Sunday they will be offering 35 cent sundaes to celebrate its 35th anniversary. And 35 lucky people will win free sundaes for a year. Wanted to pass that along so you two could check it out. Happy eating!

From: Renee Greene – June 16, 2014 – 2:19 PM
To: Marnie Glass
Subject: Re: Sunday Sundaes

Oh my gosh! That is amazing. We will definitely check it out. Thanks for thinking of us. Would you like to join us?

From: Marnie Glass – June 16, 2014 – 2:24 PM
To: Renee Greene
Subject: Re: Sunday Sundaes

That is such a nice offer. Thank you so much, but I think I'll pass. I know that place is special to you guys and I wouldn't want to impose. But I would love to grab a bite someplace else sometime.

From: Renee Greene – June 16, 2014 – 2:30 PM
To: Marnie Glass
Subject: Re: Sunday Sundaes

It wouldn't be an imposition. I just invited you. But I understand and appreciate your thoughtfulness. I would love to hang out. I know Mark is out of town this weekend visiting his brother. What about Saturday night?

From: Marnie Glass – June 16, 2014 – 2:32 PM
To: Renee Greene
Subject: Re: Sunday Sundaes

I can't on Saturday night. Maybe next Monday?

From: Renee Greene – June 16, 2014 – 2:34 PM
To: Marnie Glass
Subject: Re: Sunday Sundaes

Don't tell me that ogre of a boss of yours (Ha! Ha!) is making you work on a Saturday night.

From: Marnie Glass – June 16, 2014 – 2:40 PM
To: Renee Greene
Subject: Re: Sunday Sundaes

I'm going to tell Ethan you called him an ogre. I'm sure he'll love that. ;) No, I am having some of my best girlfriends over to watch a movie. We're not really big drinkers. We're kind of geeks. Not "Star Trek" type geeks, but just not into hanging out at bars all of the time. Once a month we take turns hosting an 80's movie. This Saturday it's my turn. We're watching Pretty in Pink. Do you want to come over?

From: Renee Greene – June 16, 2014 – 2:43 PM
To: Marnie Glass
Subject: Re: Sunday Sundaes

Someone really fun and cool just recently told me that she didn't want to impose on traditions among friends.

From: Marnie Glass – June 16, 2014 – 2:46 PM
To: Renee Greene
Subject: Re: Sunday Sundaes

And someone equally fun and cool told me it isn't an imposition when it's an invitation. Come! It will be fun.

From: Renee Greene – June 16, 2014 – 2:48 PM
To: Marnie Glass
Subject: Re: Sunday Sundaes

Okay. I'm in. Thanks. I'll bring my famous chocolate chip cookies.

From: Marnie Glass – June 16, 2014 – 2:50 PM
To: Renee Greene
Subject: Re: Sunday Sundaes

Yum! I'll give you a call later to give you directions to my place.

From: Renee Greene – June 16, 2014 – 2:53 PM
To: PBCupLover
Subject: Fwd: Re: Sunday Sundaes

See this email exchange. When I first saw the beginning I thought she might be pulling a "Cassidy" and trying to horn in on our Mel's lunches but she's so sweet and awesome. She was just being thoughtful. I really like this girl. I'm going to hang with her on Saturday night if that's okay.

From: PBCupLover – June 16, 2014 – 2:55 PM
To: Renee Greene
Subject: Re: Fwd: Re: Sunday Sundaes

So I'm an ogre?

From: Renee Greene – June 16, 2014 – 2:58 PM
To: PBCupLover
Subject: Re: Fwd: Re: Sunday Sundaes

Oops. Forgot that was in there. Ha! Well, of course I was just kidding. But seriously, that's your take away? It should be, "Good job, Babe, at setting Mark up with a really awesome girl."

From: PBCupLover – June 16, 2014 – 3:02 PM
To: Renee Greene
Subject: Re: Fwd: Re: Sunday Sundaes

Sorry, I was too busy eating a baby (and sticking a nose in where it doesn't belong, as we ogres tend to do) to comment you on sticking your nose in where it really doesn't belong. I'm glad you like this girl and even more glad that Mark likes her. I just hope it doesn't blow up in your face. I kind of like your nose.

From: Renee Greene – June 16, 2014 – 3:04 PM
To: PBCupLover
Subject: Re: Fwd: Re: Sunday Sundaes

Oh, don't worry about my nose. She's the one. I can just feel it.

From: Renee Greene – June 16, 2014 – 3:06 PM
To: Ashley Gordon, Shelley Manning
Subject: Fwd: Sunday Sundaes

See below from Marnie. Mel's is having a special promo on Sunday. Shelley, I know you probably can't fly down for the day, but Ashley, surely you can part with my sweet Angel for an hour or two and help me win free sundaes for a year.

From: Ashley Gordon – June 16, 2014 – 5:09 PM
To: Renee Greene, Shelley Manning
Subject: Re: Fwd: Sunday Sundaes

I'm there. I will pick you up at noon. Just because they are 35 cents, doesn't mean you need to eat more than one. And if you win, just promise me you won't start indulging in your free sundaes until after the wedding. You've been working so hard to look good in your dress.

From: Renee Greene – June 16, 2014 – 5:13 PM
To: Ashley Gordon, Shelley Manning
Subject: Re: Fwd: Sunday Sundaes

First I need to win and then I can work on resisting temptation until July 6. I'll be ready and waiting.

From: Shelley Manning – June 16, 2014 – 6:09 PM
To: Renee Greene
Subject: Fwd: Re: Fwd: Sunday Sundaes

I would need to eat a year's worth of ice cream just to put up with Ashley.

From: Renee Greene – June 16, 2014 – 6:13 PM
To: Shelley Manning
Subject: Re: Fwd: Re: Fwd: Sunday Sundaes

She's not that bad. You kind of get used to it. She speaks the truth. A cold, hard, ugly truth I don't always want to hear. But it's the truth and keeps me in check.

From: Shelley Manning – June 16, 2014 – 6:16 PM
To: Renee Greene
Subject: Re: Fwd: Re: Fwd: Sunday Sundaes

I'll give her a "hip check" if she doesn't lay off . Enjoy your sundaes, Sweetie. You've had a rough six months and deserve it. Mwah! Mwah!

From: Renee Greene – June 22, 2014 – 10:02 AM
To: Mark Finlay
Subject: Marnie rocks!

OMG Mark! I was at Marnie's last night. Have you been to her apartment? You see those amazing paintings? I mean I knew she was this analytical spreadsheet person by day, but I had no idea that she was this creative and funky artist at night. Amazing!

From: Mark Finlay – June 22, 2014 – 10:04 AM
To: Renee Greene
Subject: Re: Marnie rocks!

Yeah, I know. I'm dating her.

From: Renee Greene – June 22, 2014 – 10:06 AM
To: Mark Finlay
Subject: Re: Marnie rocks!

She's just so creative and cool and so fun to be around.

From: Mark Finlay – June 22, 2014 – 10:07 AM
To: Renee Greene
Subject: Re: Marnie rocks!

Yeah, I know. I'm dating her.

From: Renee Greene – June 22, 2014 – 10:09 AM
To: Mark Finlay
Subject: Re: Marnie rocks!

I mean, seriously. She's great. And so sweet too. She's like a hug in a box.

From: Mark Finlay – June 22, 2014 – 10:10 AM
To: Renee Greene
Subject: Re: Marnie rocks!

Yeah, I know. I'm dating her.

From: Renee Greene – June 22, 2014 – 10:11 AM
To: Mark Finlay
Subject: Re: Marnie rocks!

I just love her!

From: Mark Finlay – June 22, 2014 – 10:11 AM
To: Renee Greene
Subject: Re: Marnie rocks!

Me too.

From: Renee Greene – June 22, 2014 – 10:11 AM
To: Mark Finlay
Subject: Re: Marnie rocks!

Really?

From: Mark Finlay – June 22, 2014 – 10:12 AM
To: Renee Greene
Subject: Re: Marnie rocks!

Yeah, really.

From: Renee Greene – June 22, 2014 – 10:12 AM
To: Mark Finlay
Subject: Re: Marnie rocks!

Does she know that?

From: Mark Finlay – June 22, 2014 – 10:12 AM
To: Renee Greene
Subject: Re: Marnie rocks!

She does.

From: Renee Greene – June 22, 2014 – 10:13 AM
To: Mark Finlay
Subject: Re: Marnie rocks!

So you've said, "I love you" to her? Did she say it back?

From: Mark Finlay – June 22, 2014 – 10:13 AM
To: Renee Greene
Subject: Re: Marnie rocks!

Yes I've said it and yes she's said it back.

From: Renee Greene – June 22, 2014 – 10:14 AM
To: Mark Finlay
Subject: Re: Marnie rocks!

Oh, I have goosebumps. And to think this is all because of my meddling.

From: Mark Finlay – June 22, 2014 – 10:14 AM
To: Renee Greene
Subject: Re: Marnie rocks!

Really?

From: Renee Greene – June 22, 2014 – 10:15 AM
To: Mark Finlay
Subject: Re: Marnie rocks!

Couldn't resist. Tee hee! Talk soon, my friend.

From: Renee Greene – June 22, 2014 – 10:20 AM
To: Marnie Glass
Subject: You rock!

Thank you so much for having me over yesterday. I had so much fun. I had never seen "Pretty in Pink." Love that Ducky!

From: Marnie Glass – June 22, 2014 – 10:25 AM
To: Renee Greene
Subject: Re: You rock!

You rock, too! In fact, I'm "boulder"ed over by those amazing chocolate chip cookies you made. (Sorry for the bad pun. I just can't help myself.)

From: Renee Greene – June 22, 2014 – 10:27 AM
To: Marnie Glass
Subject: Re: You rock!

Are you kidding me? I love a good pun. You want some good rock/geology puns? I'll see if I can "dig" some up.

From: Marnie Glass – June 22, 2014 – 10:29 AM
To: Renee Greene
Subject: Re: You rock!

Yes, dig deep and you'll come up with something.

From: Renee Greene – June 22, 2014 – 10:31 AM
To: Marnie Glass
Subject: Re: You rock!

I'm not sure I'm going to be good under pressure.

From: Marnie Glass – June 22, 2014 – 10:31 AM
To: Renee Greene
Subject: Re: You rock!

That one was a gem.

From: Renee Greene – June 22, 2014 – 10:32 AM
To: Marnie Glass
Subject: Re: You rock!

If other pebble were reading this, they would be amazed.

From: Marnie Glass – June 22, 2014 – 10:33 AM
To: Renee Greene
Subject: Re: You rock!

That one wins by a landslide.

From: Renee Greene – June 22, 2014 – 10:35 AM
To: Marnie Glass
Subject: Re: You rock!

I feel like I'm between a rock and a hard place trying to come up with another one.

From: Marnie Glass – June 22, 2014 – 10:36 AM
To: Renee Greene
Subject: Re: You rock!

You've hit rock bottom?

From: Renee Greene – June 22, 2014 – 10:37 AM
To: Marnie Glass
Subject: Re: You rock!

That's not what I sediment.

From: Marnie Glass – June 22, 2014 – 10:38 AM
To: Renee Greene
Subject: Re: You rock!

Alright, enough. I feel like this conversation is eroding.

From: Renee Greene – June 22, 2014 – 10:40 AM
To: Marnie Glass
Subject: Re: You rock!

Okay. Last one. There's nothing "crater" than a good pun off.

From: Marnie Glass – June 22, 2014 – 10:43 AM
To: Renee Greene
Subject: Re: You rock!

I agree. I never take a good pun off for "granite." Seriously, it was really fun hanging out with you Saturday. My friends really liked you, too. In fact, they want to know if you want to become a permanent member of our 80's movie night fan club.

From: Renee Greene – June 22, 2014 – 10:45 AM
To: Marnie Glass
Subject: Re: You rock!

I would be honored. Thanks.

From: Ashley Gordon – June 25, 2014 – 11:06 AM
To: Renee Greene
Subject: Need help?

Hi there. I know you are really swamped between the wedding planning and your big hotel event next week. Just wanted to make sure you didn't need any help with anything.

From: Renee Greene – June 25, 2014 – 12:02 PM
To: Ashley Gordon
Subject: Re: Need help?

Well, aren't you just the sweetest? Thank you for thinking of me. Actually, everything seems to be under control. The wedding plans are on target, seating chart completed last night, appointment to test some hair-dos tomorrow (I knew you'd like that one!)

Event details seem on target, too. Skye (or Skinny Skye as Shelley calls her) is proving to be worth her weight in gold. Actually she's proving to be much more than her weight because she's so gosh darn skinny!

From: Ashley Gordon – June 25, 2014 – 12:14 PM
To: Renee Greene
Subject: Re: Need help?

Glad to hear you are checking out a few hair options. If you need an opinion, snap a few photos and I'll give my input. Just know I'm here if you need something.

From: Renee Greene – June 25, 2014 – 12:16 PM
To: Ashley Gordon
Subject: Re: Need help?

Thanks, Ash. I really appreciate it!

CHAPTER 30: EMERGENCY

From: Renee Greene – June 28, 2014 – 9:08 PM
To: Shelley Manning
Subject: EMERGENCY! (A "Renee" one)

Ohmygod, ohmygod, ohmygod. I need you? Where are you? This is an emergency, albeit a "Renee" emergency, not a real, life threatening one.

From: Shelley Manning – June 28, 2014 – 9:15 PM
To: Renee Greene
Subject: Re: EMERGENCY! (A "Renee" one)

I'm in the movies right now but my vibrating phone ('cuz who doesn't love an little extra vibrating. Am I right?) has alerted me that you've called three times. What's up?

From: Renee Greene – June 28, 2014 – 9:24 PM
To: Shelley Manning
Subject: Re: EMERGENCY! (A "Renee" one)

I'm at the grand opening of that hotel where Luke's Crossing is performing. I partnered with a friend who works at an entertainment PR firm and outsourced the celebrity outreach to them. They are also helping staff the event and interviews. I'm floating around the event making sure everyone is doing what they need to be doing.

I was about to walk over and check on Ethan who is here for moral support (and to fuel his celebrity curiosity). He's talking to...Jason Kite. Ohmygod, ohmygod, ohmygod. I'm hiding behind the stage curtain right now. What do I do?

From: Shelley Manning – June 28, 2014 – 9:25 PM
To: Renee Greene
Subject: Re: EMERGENCY! (A "Renee" one)

Ha-Larious!!! Worlds colliding!!!

From: Renee Greene – June 28, 2014 – 9:26 PM
To: Shelley Manning
Subject: Re: EMERGENCY! (A "Renee" one)

It's not funny. What should I do?

From: Shelley Manning – June 28, 2014 – 9:29 PM
To: Renee Greene
Subject: Re: EMERGENCY! (A "Renee" one)

Your best bet: go about your business and just leave those two to chat. What's the worst that could happen?

From: Renee Greene – June 28, 2014 – 9:29 PM
To: Shelley Manning
Subject: Re: EMERGENCY! (A "Renee" one)

Fist fight?

From: Shelley Manning – June 28, 2014 – 9:30 PM
To: Renee Greene
Subject: Re: EMERGENCY! (A "Renee" one)

Really? You think those two are going to come to blows over you?

From: Renee Greene – June 28, 2014 – 9:30 PM
To: Shelley Manning
Subject: Re: EMERGENCY! (A "Renee" one)

Why not?

From: Shelley Manning – June 28, 2014 – 9:35 PM
To: Renee Greene
Subject: Re: EMERGENCY! (A "Renee" one)

Renee! Of course you're worth fighting for, but there's already been a declared winner. You and Ethan are getting married in three weeks. He doesn't strike me as the jealous type. And last I heard (from you!), Jason had a baby with some British actress. So let the two of them chat it up and you just take care of business.

From: Renee Greene – June 28, 2014 – 9:38 PM
To: Shelley Manning
Subject: Re: EMERGENCY! (A "Renee" one)

You're probably right. But it would be kind of fun to see them come to blows over me. Tee hee!

From: Shelley Manning – June 28, 2014 – 9:39 PM
To: Renee Greene
Subject: Re: EMERGENCY! (A "Renee" one)

Probably?

From: Renee Greene – June 28, 2014 – 9:41 PM
To: Shelley Manning
Subject: Re: EMERGENCY! (A "Renee" one)

Okay, you're right. But I just can't stand here and hide. I'm going over.

From: Shelley Manning – June 28, 2014 – 9:43 PM
To: Renee Greene
Subject: Re: EMERGENCY! (A "Renee" one)

I was hoping that would be the case. I want the scoop and don't skimp on the details.

From: Renee Greene – June 29, 2014 – 2:33 AM
To: Shelley Manning
Subject: Re: EMERGENCY! (A "Renee" one)

I know you are dying to know the details of my worlds colliding.
And considering it's 2:30 a.m. and I just got home from my event, I
didn't think you'd want me to call.

Ethan went to bed because he was tired (it is 2:30 a.m., after all) and
because he's mad at me (we did just bump into the rock star who
wanted to steal me from him and I handled things less than well).

It started with me walking over where Jason's face lit up. He looked
completely surprised and happy to see me. He gave me a warm hug
and a kiss on the check. He said, "Renee! Wow! What a surprise.
It's great to see you."

Ethan immediately put his arm around me, gave me a big kiss on the
lips and said, "Hi, babe. Your event is going great. I'm so proud of
you." He says that I brushed him off a bit and looked more
interested in talking with Jason than with him. I know that's not the
case.
At least I think I know it. Jason looked very confused and Ethan
quickly said, "I forgot you know Renee. We're getting married next
month." Yeah, right? He "forgot" about Jason. He only brings it up
every time we argue about anything. Jason shook his hand and said,
"You're engaged to Renee? You're a lucky guy."

He then turned to me and just started talking about the event and how
fun it was. I asked him how he ended up at the event, etc. Ethan was
mad because he thought I was picking Jason over him. I tried to
explain that I was just catching up with an old friend. But at the end
of the day, he's the one I love and chose to go home with. Argh!

From: Shelley Manning – June 29, 2014 – 9:48 AM
To: Renee Greene
Subject: Re: EMERGENCY! (A "Renee" one)

First off, thank you for not calling me at 2:30 a.m. I know that must
have required quite a bit of restraint on your end. Second, really? I
didn't take Ethan for being the jealous type. It's now 7 hours since
your email was sent. Is he still upset?

From: Renee Greene – June 29, 2014 – 10:12 AM
To: Shelley Manning
Subject: Re: EMERGENCY! (A "Renee" one)

No, he's over it.

From: Shelley Manning – June 29, 2014 – 10:16 AM
To: Renee Greene
Subject: Re: EMERGENCY! (A "Renee" one)

So what *was* Jason doing at your event? Did he know you would be there? Is he angling to get you back? Don't hold back on me, Sweetie.

From: Renee Greene – June 29, 2014 – 10:23 AM
To: Shelley Manning
Subject: Re: EMERGENCY! (A "Renee" one)

Jason is a fan of Luke's Crossing and is considering asking them to be the opening act for Marsh 7's upcoming tour. So he came to check them out and chat them up. As far as me and Ethan, after I hit the "send" button, I contemplated calling you. (You're welcome for not giving in to that temptation.)

Then I started to have an imaginary conversation with you in my head. (I know that makes me sound a bit unhinged. But it was quite therapeutic and saved you from having to talk with me in your sleep.) Anyhoo, "we" had this very great conversation where you advised me on how to solve my problem. I took your advice and all is well.

From: Shelley Manning – June 29, 2014 – 10:24 AM
To: Renee Greene
Subject: Re: EMERGENCY! (A "Renee" one)

Blow job?

From: Renee Greene – June 29, 2014 – 10:25 AM
To: Shelley Manning
Subject: Re: EMERGENCY! (A "Renee" one)

I am literally laughing out loud right now. No. Not that. But something similar.

From: Shelley Manning – June 29, 2014 – 10:26 AM
To: Renee Greene
Subject: Re: EMERGENCY! (A "Renee" one)

Men. They are so easy.

From: Renee Greene – June 29, 2014 – 10:27 AM
To: Shelley Manning
Subject: Re: EMERGENCY! (A "Renee" one)

True. I would have required jewelry had the situation been reversed. (Did I ever show you the Tiffany bracelet he bought me for no particular reason…right after Genie almost moved here?)

From: Shelley Manning – June 29, 2014 – 10:29 AM
To: Renee Greene
Subject: Re: EMERGENCY! (A "Renee" one)

Ha-Larious! Glad it all worked out. And glad to know that I hold such sway over you, even when I'm not there. But as you would say, just don't go thinking you don't need me anymore.

From: Renee Greene – June 29, 2014 – 10:30 AM
To: Shelley Manning
Subject: Re: EMERGENCY! (A "Renee" one)

Never! Still need my bestie!

CHAPTER 31: WEDDED BLISS

From: Renee Greene – July 3, 2014 – 9:22 AM
To: Shelley Manning, Ashley Gordon, Mark Finlay
Subject: Thank you...now let's party

Two days until I tie the knot. AGH! I can hardly stand it. Thanks to each and every one of you for being so great during this time. You've helped with everything from setting up an RSVP spreadsheet and selecting hair combs to keeping me sane with your inappropriate humor. You all know which of you is which. ;)

Love you all to bits and can't wait until tomorrow when you can help me and Ethan celebrate our last night of independence....'cause it's the 4th of July. Get it?

From: Shelley Manning – July 3, 2014 – 10:30 AM
To: Renee Greene, Ashley Gordon, Mark Finlay
Subject: Re: Thank you...now let's party

We get it. And we're excited too, Sweetie. See you tomorrow. Mwah! Mwah!

From: Ashley Gordon – July 3, 2014 – 10:35 AM
To: Shelley Manning, Renee Greene, Mark Finlay
Subject: Re: Thank you...now let's party

Ditto from me. You're going to look great, especially with your hair in a classic bun. Good choice. We'll see you tomorrow night at the rehearsal.

From: Mark Finlay – July 3, 2014 – 11:02 AM
To: Shelley Manning, Renee Greene, Ashley Gordon
Subject: Re: Thank you...now let's party

Marnie and I will be a little early to help you with putting out flowers and candles at the restaurant. See you then.

From: Renee Greene – July 4, 2014 – 7:35 PM
To: Shelley Manning
Subject: Where are you?

Rehearsal dinner is about to start. Where are you?

From: Shelley Manning – July 4, 2014 – 7:40 PM
To: Renee Greene
Subject: Re: Where are you? .

Sorry. On our way. It is 4th of July after all. Can't deny me a bit of fireworks, can you?

From: Renee Greene – July 4, 2014 – 7:42 PM
To: Shelley Manning
Subject: Re: Where are you?

We were all just walking from the rehearsal room to the restaurant for dinner and you couldn't last without a quick detour to your room?

From: Shelley Manning – July 4, 2014 – 7:45 PM
To: Renee Greene
Subject: Re: Where are you?

Who said went to our room? I'm walking in the door now. Prepare for a "Mwah! Mwah!" in person.

From: Renee Greene – July 5, 2014 – 3:52 PM
To: PBCupLover
Subject: Easy out

You're not supposed to see me before the wedding, but I don't know of any rules about email. In fact, I'm fairly certain that the rule about not seeing the bride came out well before email did. But I digress. I just wanted to give you an out if you've changed your mind.

From: PBCupLover – July 5, 2014 – 3:53 PM
To: Renee Greene
Subject: Re: Easy out

Why would I change my mind?

From: Renee Greene – July 5, 2014 – 3:59 PM
To: PBCupLover
Subject: Re: Easy out

Oh, I don't know. Because I'm crazy and neurotic. I stick my nose in where it doesn't belong which sometimes results in trouble. I'm needy and overcommunicative. I clean the kitchen twice over – top to bottom – if raw chicken has made even a remote appearance. I'm always forgetting to turn off the lights. I drive too slowly. I can't make a long story short.

I could go on, because as I've just stated, I can't make a long story short. It's been a crazy year, with so many ups and downs, and I know I must make it hard for you to love me.

From: PBCupLover – July 5, 2014 – 4:06 PM
To: Renee Greene
Subject: Re: Easy out

That's true. You're all of those nutty and sometimes annoying things and more. But you're also kind-hearted, generous, warm, funny and loving. Who else would make me homemade chicken noodle soup when I get a sinus infection, let me warm up my cold feet on your bare legs in bed, surprise me by learning all of my favorite childhood recipes from my mom or let me invite three of my ex-girlfriends to our wedding? Quite frankly, I wonder what you're doing with a shmo like me.

From: Renee Greene – July 5, 2014 – 4:07 PM
To: PBCupLover
Subject: Re: Easy out

Awww. Are those the vows you wrote?

From: PBCupLover – July 5, 2014 – 4:11 PM
To: Renee Greene
Subject: Re: Easy out

No, but it's close. Babe, I love you…all of you. As Tom Cruise would say, "you complete me." I can't imagine my life without you. And luckily I don't have to. Can't wait to see you in less than an hour at the end of the rose-petal-covered, white runner you picked out. I may not look like I've been paying attention to this wedding stuff, but I have. I could only love you more if you would root for the Buckeyes.

From: Renee Greene – July 5, 2014 – 4:17 PM
To: PBCupLover
Subject: Re: Easy out

And I love you. You're witty and smart. You make me laugh - especially when you try to dance. (I mean, really?!?) You always make me feel like I'm the most important person in the room. And you believe in me even when I don't believe in myself. I always cry at weddings and now I'm crying a little bit ahead of schedule. I love you so much and can't imagine my life without you either.

From: PBCupLover – July 5, 2014 – 4:23 PM
To: Renee Greene
Subject: Re: Easy out

Back atcha, babe! Alright, my thumbs are getting tired of typing on my phone. I want to make sure they have enough energy for later when I walk around saying "What has two thumbs and is the happiest person here? This guy!" with my thumbs pointing back at me. Now I know what you're thinking. But don't "thumb your nose" at my awesome joke. That was a good one!

From: Renee Greene – July 5, 2014 – 4:24 PM
To: PBCupLover
Subject: Re: Easy out

<Thumbs down!> That was awful.

From: PBCupLover – July 5, 2014 – 4:25 PM
To: Renee Greene
Subject: Re: Easy out

Still want to marry me?

From: Renee Greene – July 5, 2014 – 4:27 PM
To: PBCupLover
Subject: Re: Easy out

Um...I do. I've seen the best and the worst of you, and I choose both. And you?

From: PBCupLover – July 5, 2014 – 4:29 PM
To: Renee Greene
Subject: Re: Easy out

I do. I love you not only for what you are, but for what I am when I'm with you. See you soon. I love you.

EPILOGUE

Hi, Renee. Just wanted to wish you and Ethan a happy one-year anniversary and to thank you again (!) for introducing me to Mark. He truly is the love of my life and I hope our marriage (3 months and going strong) is as happy as yours. Looking forward to meeting you and Ashley for lunch at Mel's next week. Bye for now!

Made in the USA
Charleston, SC
17 May 2014